ALL THAT GLITTERS

JOHN ANTHONY MILLER

Copyright (C) 2023 John Anthony Miller

Layout design and Copyright (C) 2023 by Next Chapter

Published 2023 by Next Chapter

Edited by Graham (Fading Street Services)

Cover art by Lordan June Pinote

This book is a work of fiction. Names, characters, places, and incidents are the product of the author's imagination or are used fictitiously. Any resemblance to actual events, locales, or persons, living or dead, is purely coincidental.

All rights reserved. No part of this book may be reproduced or transmitted in any form or by any means, electronic or mechanical, including photocopying, recording, or by any information storage and retrieval system, without the author's permission.

For Steffany, Danielle, and Christopher

ACKNOWLEDGMENT

Special thanks to the staff at Next Chapter

CHAPTER 1
PARIS, FRANCE - MAY, 1940

The Germans advanced quickly—faster than the world expected. First, they came through Holland and Belgium, luring Allied armies north from France. A second assault followed, south of the front, piercing defenses. The Germans raced for the sea, trapping the Allies between their armies, forcing a massive evacuation to England. The politicians who managed the masses, those who governed mankind, knew a different war now had to be fought. A battle birthed in secrets, deeds done in darkened alleys, risks taken that few could fathom, and most would never know existed.

Jacques Dufort parted the curtain at the front window of his Parisian apartment. A cobblestone street lay beyond, snaking out to the boulevard. Barely thirty, he had black hair and blue eyes that hid what lay behind them. He glanced at his watch, frowning. A black Renault then came down the street, stopping in front of his apartment.

A woman climbed out—not what he expected. Slender with brown eyes, blonde hair streaked with darker strands, she seemed too young, too feminine, to have mastered the skills he needed. She spoke to the driver, gestured that he wait, and crossed the pavement. A slight mist marred the city, an early rain bathing buildings in a crystal sheen. When she reached the door of the limestone townhouse, she tapped lightly with the brass knocker.

Emilie Dufort came from the parlor into the foyer. Slight, with waves of black hair difficult to tame, she had dark eyes and olive skin. Striking and unforgettable, she was better suited for films than the wife of a government official. She seemed surprised to find her husband at the window, ignoring the knock on the door.

"Shall I get that?" she asked with a curious glance.

Jacques looked away and shook his head. "No, it's for me," he said. "We'll be in my study. Please don't disturb us."

Emilie nodded and turned to leave. She wasn't to meet the visitor. Whoever came to call was part of the secret world her husband lived in—not accessible to her.

Jacques waited while the faint click of her heels grew dimmer. He opened the door. "May I help you?" he asked. He eyed the woman before him, a few faint freckles dotting her face.

"All that glitters is not gold," she said, mouthing a prearranged passcode.

He leaned from the doorway to glance up and down the street. "Are you Shakespeare?"

She smiled. "Camille."

"Come in," he said. "I'm Jacques Dufort. We'll use my study."

He led her into the foyer and then to the left. Open French doors spilled into a room lined with bookcases, a walnut desk in front of a twelve-paned window that faced a narrow alley, the curtains open.

"Please," Jacques offered, motioning to a leather chair.

Camille sat in front of the desk. Her gaze wandered the room.

He looked at her curiously, wondering what captured her attention. "You're admiring my study?"

"It's charming."

He smiled faintly. "Something interests you. What is it?"

"Many things," she said, her gaze now fixed on his. "The window, and the lock on top of the lower sash. The brass paperweight on your desk, a daunting weapon if needed. The umbrella stand in the foyer, holding two canes, one with a brass handle that could do much damage if swung at a foe. And I hear someone moving about—a wife or girlfriend. Maybe a child?" She paused, smiling politely. "It's important for me to know this. Should our meeting not go as planned."

Jacques's eyes widened and, for an instant, he felt a flicker of fear. He had misjudged her. "I'm impressed," he said softly.

Her expression remained unchanged. "No need. But don't underestimate me."

Jacques nodded respectfully. "I'm told you were recruited by French intelligence while a student at the Sorbonne. Stationed in Tournai before returning to Paris."

She nodded. "Two years in Tournai. I came back six months ago."

"Do you speak languages other than French?" he asked, already knowing the answer.

"Yes, two more."

He still had a nagging doubt. "Trained by Nicolas Chastain, a legend in French intelligence," he said in English.

"I've been fortunate," she replied in the same tongue.

"Your English is flawless."

"*Mein Deutsch auch,*" Camille countered. "My German, also."

He no longer wondered if she was too young or too fragile. "You're being sent to Belgium."

"My driver is waiting. I'll catch the first train."

"It'll be difficult, given the German advance," he said, glancing at his watch. "You don't have much time."

"No, I don't."

Jacques sat back in his chair. "Shall we begin?"

"Yes, of course."

He opened cabinet doors at the base of the bookshelf behind him. He withdrew a sturdy suitcase, carried it around the desk, and set it beside her. "Your radio. It weighs twelve kilograms. I'll show you how to use it."

She opened the lid and looked inside. "I know how to use it."

He was surprised by her confidence. "Make sure you're in a high location—an attic or church steeple."

She nodded. "Where's the crystal?"

He opened his hand, revealing a black device with short prongs on one end. "Start every message with all that glitters. That's the code."

She closed the radio and put the crystal in her skirt pocket. "Updates as needed?"

"As soon as possible after the mission. You'll then receive further instructions."

"I understand," she said, waiting for more.

He turned to the cabinet and withdrew a cloth bag. "Have you ever been to Antwerp?" he asked as he laid it on the desk.

"I have," she said, eyeing the satchel.

"Antwerp is the diamond capital of the world, as I'm sure you're aware. Most think of rings or necklaces when they think of diamonds."

"Industrial diamonds," she said quietly.

He nodded. "Yes, industrial diamonds."

"The passcode," she said. "All that glitters is not gold. It's about diamonds."

"It is," he admitted. "The war hinges on industrial

diamonds, especially those needed for advanced technologies like radar."

"Why haven't the diamonds been removed—taken to London or Paris?"

"Most have," he replied. "But we have a problem."

"A problem I am expected to solve."

He pursed his lips. "The best industrial diamonds in the world remain in ten safety deposit boxes at a trading house in Antwerp—Sternberg and Sons."

"Why are they still there?" she asked. "Especially if they're the best."

"Sternberg refuses to release them. We suspect he keeps them as insurance, to pay off the Nazis to protect his family should Antwerp be captured."

"Why be concerned with a small amount?" she asked. "If the rest has been removed."

"Sternberg's diamonds are superior, the best for radar technology. We can't let them fall into enemy hands."

"The Germans are almost there—not far from the city's outskirts."

"You need to get there first," he said, moving the satchel closer. "Two hand drills, with industrial diamond tips, to access the deposit boxes. Written instructions for entry by a back door, through a garden. Hidden on a wall behind a shrub, as the drawing shows, is an electric box. Wire number eight powers the alarm. A key to the door will be left on top of the box. A map of the building is enclosed, with instructions on how to get into the vault and different escape routes. Two items are missing."

She took the satchel and glanced through it. "The combination to the vault."

He nodded. "And the key to a secondary gate."

"How many diamonds do the boxes hold?"

He removed a canvass satchel from the cabinet, larger and sturdier than the first. "The diamonds will fit in this bag."

She moved the satchel closer. "Do I work alone?"

He handed her a paper with an address on it. "Your London contact is a man named Roger. Meet him tomorrow at ten p.m. He'll help you get the diamonds. Then take him to the docks—he has the address. He'll board a fishing trawler to London."

She paused, as if considering contingencies. "What if we can't get to the docks?"

He leaned forward. "Roger has to get to London. Only he knows where to take the diamonds."

"And if he can't get to London?" she asked, persisting.

Jacques frowned. "Bring the diamonds here—back to me."

"But only if all else fails."

He eyed her sternly. "You won't fail. Regardless of threats. The Germans cannot, under any circumstances, gain possession of these diamonds. Do I make myself clear?"

CHAPTER 2

Emilie Dufort was born in a small village near the Rhine River. She had come to Paris several years before to work in her uncle's store, All Things Napoleon. Specializing in military memorabilia: busts, books, sabers, guns, maps, clothing—it housed a huge collection devoted to the Napoleonic Wars. Located in the fifth arrondissement near the Sorbonne, her clientele included intellects from the university, collectors from all over Europe, and those who loved French history. Emilie had worked hard, saved her money and when her uncle passed, she inherited his shop. But she was much more than the owner of an antique store.

She had met Jacques Dufort through a planned introduction eighteen months before. He was a government official who supposedly worked in the transportation department although his role was never discussed. Even though she pretended she didn't, she knew exactly what he did. But she had learned early in their relationship not to ask questions, so she didn't. Married less than a year, not much escaped her, even though it seemed as if it did.

Jacques occasionally met acquaintances in his study. Most

came at night, speaking in hushed whispers she could never hear. His most frequent contact was a man named Guy Barbier, who Emilie never liked. She once interrupted their meeting and Barbier rudely asked her to leave. They had shared nothing but looks of disdain ever since. But Emilie suspected this meeting was different. Jacques had never met anyone so early in the morning, while he waited impatiently at the door for them to arrive. It must be critical. From the kitchen, she could faintly hear them, able to decipher a word or two.

Emilie glanced at the clock. She had to leave. It was almost time to open her store, and she wanted to first stop at the café around the corner. She would use the back door, so she didn't disturb Jacques and his mysterious guest. But she wanted the newspaper, which she had left in the parlor. As quietly as she could, she went to an Art Nouveau table by the sofa, the newspaper upon it. As she grabbed it and turned to go, she heard Jacques mention industrial diamonds and radar. She paused to listen.

She could hear them clearly: Camille, Antwerp, Sternberg & Sons, diamonds, a man named Roger, two satchels, London, the radio. It was her first detailed hint of her husband's clandestine operations. She shouldn't eavesdrop; it was too easy for her husband to catch her. But she couldn't resist. It was too important—something she needed to hear.

"Bring the diamonds to me as a last resort," Jacques said, his voice louder. He was coming closer.

"I understand," Camille replied. "But now I must go if I hope to catch the train."

"It might be the last one," Jacques said, "given how quickly the Germans advance."

Emilie leaned against the wall so she wouldn't be seen. The front door opened.

"I can't stress how important this is," Jacques said. "Or how dangerous."

Emilie hurried out the back door. She went through the alley to the intersection, eyeing dark clouds that had broken to show the sun. As she reached the corner, the black Renault that carried Camille turned onto the boulevard. Emilie looked away.

She went to a cafe on the Boulevard Saint-Germain and sat at her favorite outdoor table, close to a window box so she could smell the flowers. Military trucks drove by, and an occasional motorcycle, hurrying to reach their destination, as if the Germans would get there first. Pedestrians passed on the pavement, people living their lives as they knew they must. The café was crowded, tiny tables with patrons around them, many with newspapers. Sandbags hid nearby buildings, covering windows that would crack and shatter should bombs arrive.

Emilie sipped her coffee, scanning the *Paris-Soir*. Headlines screamed German victories: Holland conquered, Belgium falling, the enemy on Antwerp's doorstep. She thought of Camille, the woman who had met with her husband, and the limited time she had to get the diamonds—if she even reached Antwerp. Emilie was immersed in the article when interrupted.

"May I join you?" a man asked.

She looked up, shading her eyes with her hand. He stood by her table holding a cup of coffee, average height with brown hair and eyes, attractive and anxious, early forties at most. His suit was hand-tailored, his shirt silk. He seemed better off than most. Maybe not wealthy, but comfortable.

"I prefer to sit alone," she said. She looked away, wondering why he was there. Was it planned, or was he only interested in an attractive woman sitting alone?

"As do most," he replied. "I do offer my apologies. But we have something to discuss."

Emilie eyed him curiously—bold, but polite, a stranger wanting more. His accent wasn't quite right—French wasn't his primary language. English, maybe, but she couldn't say for sure.

"Holland falls, Belgium falters," he continued, pointing to her paper. "What does it mean for France?"

"I wonder the same," she said, glancing at the article.

He sat, uninvited but not caring. "Louie Bassett," he offered.

The corners of her lips curled in a smile. "You are persistent, M. Bassett."

"I have to be," he said. "My work demands it."

"It does?" she asked, not introducing herself. "What is your work, M. Bassett?"

He hesitated. "I'm in the information business."

She looked at him strangely. "A vague description."

"Yes, I suppose it is," he said. He leaned closer. "Intentionally, I might add."

Emilie smiled. She was beginning to like him, her unwanted visitor. "What can I do for you, M. Louie Bassett, who is in the information business and has come to my table uninvited? I suspect this isn't a chance meeting. Or do you often join women you don't know for coffee?"

He shifted in his seat. "No, not normally. Only women I've been instructed to contact."

With his simple reply, she knew his purpose. She feigned ignorance, casting a curious glance.

He leaned forward, as if sharing a secret. "But I'm sure you knew I would come. Or someone like me."

She tensed, her suspicions confirmed. Afraid of a trap, a clumsy attempt to convince her to cooperate before she was ready, she tried to disengage. "I thought I was special," she teased. "And that you found a woman you couldn't forget. Is that not the reason you are here, M. Louie Bassett?"

He smiled, nodding politely. "Yes, I suppose it is. You are special. But for reasons not obvious to most."

Emilie glanced at those around her, their thoughts consumed with a war coming closer. She turned to Louie. "Tell me what you want, M. Bassett."

"I have a message from your family."

She hesitated. "What might that message be?"

"It's time to play your part," he said softly.

She knew what he meant but pretended she didn't. "If my family wanted to send me a message, they would call me."

"Except the telephone lines are down from the fighting."

She knew he was right but didn't comment. "It's a strange message, delivered by a man I do not know."

"It's quite clear to me," Louie said. He averted her gaze to look at the tables closest, making sure no one could hear.

Emilie eyed him cautiously, unable to confirm what he claimed. "I have no information, M. Bassett, if that's what you want. Even if I did, I wouldn't share it."

He sat back in the chair, his gaze fixed on hers. "This can be easy, Mme. Dufort," he said, his smile fading. "Or it can be difficult."

Her eyes widened. She wasn't surprised he knew her name, only that he was so direct. "I don't like your tone."

"I know you don't," he continued. "I can't afford to be nice, to exchange pleasantries, to gradually get to know you. I don't have time. And quite frankly, neither do you."

Emilie folded her newspaper and prepared to depart. "Our conversation has ended."

He put his hand on her forearm. "It's important to stay a moment longer, Mme. Dufort."

"I prefer not to."

"You're in Paris for a reason. Just as I am."

She glared at his hand on her forearm. "I don't know what you're talking about."

His face firmed. "You know exactly what I'm talking about. No one in Paris knows who Emilie Dufort really is. No one except for me."

"Maybe no one cares," she said, standing to go.

"The time has come," Louie Bassett said, also standing. "As you knew it would."

She paused, eyeing him coldly. "I decide when the time has come, M. Bassett. Not you."

CHAPTER 3
ANTWERP, BELGIUM

The River Scheldt turned and twisted from northern France, through Belgium, to the North Sea. Eighty kilometers from the river's mouth, Antwerp straddled its banks, one of Europe's greatest ports and the diamond capital of the world. Over eighty percent of the world's diamonds came through Antwerp, and the merchants who traded them had done so for centuries.

Camille sat in a stolen 1936 Minerva, the green fender dented and scraped, a taillight missing. Parked a few blocks from the port, near warehouses and wharfs damaged by Nazi air raids—bricks, stone, shattered glass, and timber blocked some of the roads. A wisp of smoke spiraled skyward; an occasional explosion rocked the ground. It had been difficult getting to Antwerp, the Germans arriving just as she did.

She waited in darkness until just after ten p.m. A man approached, dressed in black, pausing to study the deserted street. Once satisfied it was safe, he approached the car, and opened the passenger door.

"All that glitters is not gold," he said in stilted English, poking his head in the car.

"Get in," she said, confused by the accent. She had expected an Englishman. Even though he pretended he was, he wasn't. "I'm Camille."

"Roger," he said. "We haven't much time. Just over an hour. I have to get into the vault."

"That's why I'm here," she said as they drove away.

"The Germans are close."

She left the river, clogged with wharfs and warehouses, and entered a residential neighborhood. She passed empty rowhomes, a few destroyed by errant bombs meant for the port. Debris clogged some streets, but destruction waned the farther they got from the river. Air raids had ebbed, the city soon to fall.

"Most of the Belgian army left," Roger said.

"They had no choice. The British and French have already gone."

Camille drove down cobblestone streets to the diamond district. A few residents still fled, hurrying down boulevards, but most who wanted to leave had already gone. She passed her destination, Sternberg & Sons, rounded the corner, drove another block, and parked beside a tree, the limbs sprawling over the road.

As they exited the car, she handed him an empty satchel. "For the diamonds," she said. She carried the cloth sack.

"What's in your bag?" he asked,

"A map of the building and tools to breach the deposit boxes."

She led him to the rear of Sternberg & Sons. It sat in a row of similar buildings, two or three stories high, scalloped rooflines and narrow six-pane windows. They entered a garden wrapped by buildings, a kaleidoscope of colors and scents, an oasis in a sea of stone. A winding walk led to the doorway, and she knelt when she reached it, a shrub next to the building. A metal box, hidden by branches, was attached to the wall. A key sat on the top. She grabbed it, put it in her pocket, and took wire cutters from her bag. She cut the lock on

All That Glitters

the box, and opened it. Finding wire number eight, she snipped it.

"The door alarm," she said simply. She fished the entry key from her pocket and opened the door. "If we get separated, find your way back to the car."

Roger glanced at his watch. "We have to hurry."

The Germans came closer, farther down the street, shouting. "They want what we want," she said. "The best industrial diamonds in the world."

"How were they missed?" he asked as they hurried through the building.

"The owner thought they would save his soul. But no souls are saved from the Germans."

She took the sketch from her bag and led him to a set of stairs. They descended one floor, the rattling of gunfire coming from nearby streets.

He looked at her nervously. "They fight just outside the door."

Camille took him down a second flight of steps. She studied the sketch, wondering who had drawn it, and pointed in the opposite direction. "Those stairs lead to the main lobby, the bank entrance."

"An escape path if we need it."

They hurried down the hallway and reached the vault, defined by a steel door with a combination lock.

Roger looked at her skeptically. "It seems impregnable."

She smiled faintly and put her satchel on the floor. She stood in front of the lock, listening, her fingers caressing the dial, eyes closed.

Gunfire erupted above them, closer than before, mixed with shouts in Flemish and German.

"We have to—"

"Hush!"

She turned the face of the dial, right, left, right, her delicate fingers feeling the tumblers. After a moment, and a failure or two, an audible click disturbed the silence. She turned the four-pronged handle and yanked the heavy door open.

"You did it!" he said.

"There's more." The opened vault exposed the next barrier, a flat steel door,

He pointed to the lock. "We don't have the key."

Camille referred to the sketch. She darted across the hallway and opened a narrow door, a utility closet filled with mops and brooms. Feeling inside the door frame, she found a strange key on a hook, twenty centimeters long with a triangular head. She took it to the vault, inserted it, and opened the steel door.

"How did you know where the key was hidden?" he asked.

"Another lock," she said, pointing to the vault.

A mesh gate blocked their path. She took a narrow wire from the bag, bending the end.

Shouts came from the street, close to the entrance. Gunfire followed, bullets spraying brick and cobblestone.

"Hurry," he hissed.

She inserted the wire into the lock, twisting and turning. Twenty seconds later, she frowned and withdrew it.

"They're almost here!" he said.

Camille bent the end of the wire and inserted it again, twisting left and then right. The tumbler clicked and she opened the gate,

"We're in!" he exclaimed but stopped abruptly.

"Over a hundred deposit boxes," she said. "We want sixty through sixty-nine."

Roger eyed her anxiously. "They'll be difficult to breach."

She took two drills with hand cranks from her satchel. She handed him one and touched the lock. "Drill here."

"But this will take hours," he said. "I have to hurry."

Camille pointed at the bit. "Industrial diamond. It'll take less than a minute."

They started drilling, moving from one box to the next, the drawers filled with small diamonds. As they breached the last two boxes, a crash erupted from the upstairs foyer.

"Germans!" he said. "They broke into the building."

"Hurry, we've only two more."

They finished drilling and flung open the lids. Roger dumped the diamonds into the satchel as she tossed the drills in her bag.

"Come on," she said, running from the vault. "Let's go."

Footsteps thundered down the stairs, coming toward them.

"We have to hide," he hissed.

She looked at the shadows quickly approaching. "In the closet," she said. "Hurry."

CHAPTER 4

Camille and Roger hid in the closet, barely breathing. Boot heels clicked on tiled floors, soldiers inspecting the vault. They summoned an officer, his voice loud but his words not clear enough to understand.

After they finished in the vault, the Germans left. They passed the utility closet and climbed the stairs, their footsteps fainter until they couldn't be heard at all.

"I have to get out," Roger hissed. "The boat won't wait."

"Where am I taking you?"

He withdrew a business card from his pocket, checking an address scribbled on the back. "Godefriduskaai 99, Pier #3."

Camille cracked open the door. The hallway was empty. She stepped out, no Germans nearby. "Come on!" she hissed, tugging on Roger's sleeve.

They ran toward the back stairwell. After only a dozen steps, heavy boots came down the front stairs.

Roger stopped, hesitant to continue.

"We can make it," Camille assured him, fearing he might surrender.

He followed her into the far stairwell, closing the door

behind them. They quietly ran up two flights of stairs, and exited near the garden door.

"We'll leave the same way we came in," she whispered.

As they approached the exit, shadows appeared on the hallway wall, coming closer.

"We're trapped," he hissed.

She glanced at the sketch. "This way," she whispered, pulling him in the opposite direction.

"Where are we going?"

"Second floor."

They retraced their steps and returned to the stairway. She eased the door open and urged him in.

"Halt!" a German called, rounding the corner as they closed the door.

Roger tugged on Camille's elbow. "We'll never make it!"

"Yes, we will," she said, urging him up the stairs. "Come on. Hurry."

They left the stairwell and ran to the end of the corridor.

"Where are we going?" he asked, gasping.

"In here," she said, opening a door.

The Germans ran from the stairway, heavy boots pounding the hallway floor. "Halt!" a soldier commanded.

Camille locked the door, slid a narrow table in front of it, and scanned the room. The office was small, a desk by the window, paintings on the walls—street scenes of Antwerp—a bookshelf behind the desk.

Hurry," she said. "To the window."

Roger hesitated, staring at the door. "They're right behind us!"

"We'll make it," she insisted, racing across the room. She opened the vertical windows, exposing a slender alley, an adjacent building a few feet away.

Roger looked at the ground two floors below. "What are you doing? We can't jump from here!"

"Open the door!" the Germans shouted, trying the knob.

"You go," Camille urged. "You're more important. Slide down the drainpipe."

He looked at her, eyes wide. "I can't," he said. "They'll kill you."

"Go!" she said. "Hurry!"

He started to climb out the window. Gunfire erupted, bullets destroying the lock and splintering the wood around it. A pattern of holes formed on the door, bullets burrowing into the wall across the room.

Camille dove behind the desk. She crouched low until the firing stopped. When she peeked out, Germans pushed the door, the table blocking them. She scrambled to her feet.

Roger lay on the floor, bloody holes across his chest. His eyes were open, staring at the ceiling.

The Germans barged through the door, tripping over the table.

Camille yanked the satchel from Roger's shoulder and climbed out the window. Bullets sprayed the jamb and molding, shattering the windows. Broken glass fell to the floor. She grasped the copper drainpipe that ran down the outside wall, put her feet against the brick, and shimmied to the ground. Staying close to the building, she darted down the alley.

A soldier appeared in the window, frantically searching below. He fired when he saw her, spraying bullets that ricocheted off the wall. Camille rounded the corner, slivers of stone flying past her. She sprinted down the street, more Germans at the corner of the main road.

"Halt," a soldier called, running toward her.

Camille kept going, staying in shadows, hiding behind trees and parked cars. She made her way to the Minerva, climbed in, and started the engine. The soldier chasing her fired, spraying bullets into the back of the vehicle. A bullet hit the dashboard, centimeters from her. She sped away, racing past an older couple watching from their stoop.

She turned left at the first intersection, drove two blocks, and made another left, speeding toward the river. She avoided debris and approached the docks, fires raging around her. When she reached Godefriduskaai 99, Pier #3, a fishing boat waited. She would use it to escape, taking Roger's place. But just as she was about to stop, German soldiers walked down the wharf. She drove to the next dock, where two men stood near a tugboat. She pulled over and rolled down the window.

"How do I get out of Antwerp?" she asked.

An older man with a grizzled beard leaned toward the window. "The Nazis hold the port. Nothing can get in or out."

His younger companion came closer. "Antwerp is almost surrounded."

"I have to get out," she said. "Should I go west?"

"The army went west, but the Germans followed."

"Go southwest," the companion suggested. "There's a sliver of the city open. Follow the west bank of the river and you'll stay ahead of the fighting."

"But hurry," the older man said. "You don't have much time."

"Thanks," she called as she drove away. She sped down winding streets away from the port, heading southwest. She had to get out of the city. The port was closed. She couldn't get to London.

She had to take the diamonds to Jacques Dufort in Paris.

CHAPTER 5

Major Josef Ziegler was tall and gaunt with dark eyes that saw what others often did not see. In his late forties, his hair was black with strands of grey, lines of life etching his face. His uniform was black, a red band with a Swastika around his left bicep. A member of the Gestapo, the German secret police, he had a unique assignment. A cache of high-quality industrial diamonds, the best in the world, were kept in the vault at Sternberg & Sons. Major Josef Ziegler was tasked with taking them. But he now had a problem.

Four German soldiers waited in the second-floor office when he entered. Bullet holes riddled the walls, barely missing landscapes hanging beside the window. He turned to his aide, Sergeant Ernst Bayer, a man who had served him in Austria and Poland—a man he trusted. "How do you access a bank overrun by the enemy, steal diamonds, and escape?"

Bayer shrugged. "It was well-planned, sir."

A soldier pointed to the floor. "The body was found just under the window, sir."

Ziegler crossed the room. He studied the bloodstained carpet and then looked out the shattered windows, eyeing the alley below. He turned to Bayer. "Do we know who he was?"

A soldier stepped forward. "No identification, sir."

"Did anyone see his accomplice?" Ziegler asked.

"It was a woman, sir. Young, with blonde hair."

Ziegler paused. "A man would be easier to find. Most are in the army. Few are in Antwerp."

"She may have fled the city, sir," Bayer said. "During the chaos."

"She didn't escape through the port, sir," another soldier said. "We captured it before the diamonds were stolen."

Ziegler evaluated possibilities, finding no solutions. "How did they get in the vault?"

"They knew the combination, sir," a soldier said.

Ziegler frowned. "Take me to the manager."

They went downstairs to the lobby, a spacious room with green plaster walls and broad white crown molding. Victorian couches welcomed waiting customers, paintings hung from the walls. With only a glance, Ziegler knew they were works of the masters—not reproductions. He also knew they wouldn't be there much longer. The Reich would take them.

They were met by an elderly man dressed in black, his long grey beard spilling onto his shirt. He had been waiting anxiously, knowing they wouldn't be pleased. "Good morning, Major," he said with frightened eyes. "I'm Jacob Sternberg, proprietor."

"Show me the vault," Ziegler directed.

"It's this way, sir," Sternberg said. He led them down two flights of stairs. "I had been holding the diamonds for your arrival. The British took the rest last week."

Ziegler didn't reply. He didn't care why the Jew held the diamonds. He only cared that they were gone.

A hall at the foot of the steps led to the vault. The thick door was open, as was an inner door with the key still in the lock, and a mesh grate. The vault was square, the walls lined with deposit boxes of different sizes. Ten of the drawers were open, empty trays on the floor.

Ziegler stepped in the vault, eyeing the boxes. "Why are only a few opened?"

Sternberg cringed. "Just those containing the diamonds were disturbed."

Ziegler surveyed the vault. "I'm told they were the finest industrial diamonds in the world."

"Industrial diamonds are our specialty," Sternberg explained. "They were the best of the best. That's why I kept them. As a gift for the Germans when you arrived."

Ziegler turned away. "Whoever stole them knew what they were doing."

"It seems so, sir," said Jacob Sternberg, his voice trembling.

"How did they get in the vault?"

"The first door was opened with the combination. They found the key to the second door, which was hanging in that utility closet," Sternberg said, pointing. "And they picked the lock on the gate."

Ziegler glared at Sternberg. "One of your employees must be the dead man's accomplice."

Sternberg shook his head. "No, sir. My employees would never do such a thing."

"Who knows the combination?"

"Only myself and a few others. Most employees don't have access."

"Give me their names."

Sternberg was hesitant to provide them—as if he knew he had nothing to trade for their safety.

Ziegler withdrew his pistol. He put the barrel against Sternberg's left temple. "Tell me who they are."

CHAPTER 6

Camille eluded the German noose that tightened around Antwerp, threading a needle through the German advance and Allied retreat. She sped southwest, avoiding Brussels. Her first objective was Tournai, where she had once been stationed. She had contacts there who could help her escape. If she got there before the Germans. But she had to get out of Belgium and into France, ahead of the advancing German army.

The bullets that sprayed her car had done some damage. Most pierced the trunk, burrowing into the back of the automobile. But one had hit the dashboard, passing through to the engine compartment, barely missing her. She eyed the petrol gauge—not enough to reach France. She would have to leave the highway, find a vehicle, and siphon petrol.

An hour from Tournai the engine began making a whirring noise. She wasn't sure what caused it, but suspected a German bullet did more damage than she had thought. When she saw a village with no sign of Allied or German soldiers, she left the highway and drove toward it. A church sat on the outskirts, the steeple staring at heaven.

Camille rode down a residential street, the houses undamaged, some people outside. The battle hadn't found them yet. But it would. She parked beside the church and waited. No vehicles were near, none from which she could siphon petrol, just a truck parked beside a house across the street. She got out of the car, opened the hood, and searched for whatever caused the strange noises. No damage was obvious.

She glanced at the houses, ensuring no one watched her. A man and woman a few doors down were loading crates onto a wagon, ready to flee. She studied them for a moment—she wanted to make sure it was safe to leave her car—and then opened the back door of her Minerva. The radio was stashed behind the driver's seat. The diamonds and bag with the drills lay beside it, a cloth bag with some clothes and personal belongings on top of them. She removed the radio, locked the door, made one last check to ensure no one was near, and approached the church.

The walkway was rimmed with flowers, splashing color onto an ordinary landscape. Farm fields stretched past the church, deserted, the wind kicking the dirt to dust. She hurried down the pavement, watching for any observers, and climbed stone steps. Arched doors marked the entrance, and she opened one to peek inside. The church seemed empty, she couldn't see anyone, but noises came from a room beside the altar—someone moving about. The stairs to the steeple were to her right. She quietly made her way toward them and started up the steps.

The stairs ended in a square room, open arches on each side, an iron bell centered in the open space. She unpacked her radio and laid the antenna wire against a windowsill. She inserted the crystal, ensured no one was coming up the stairs, and started to transmit. To ensure it was received, she sent the message twice, pausing in between. She watched the east, clouds of dust visible on the horizon.

She waited. As the dust clouds grew larger, she sent the

message a third time. A few seconds later, a reply came, requesting more information. She hesitated, watching the billowing dust—the retreating Allies or advancing Germans, she wasn't sure. Just as she was about to transmit a reply, she saw German motorcycles at the front of the dust cloud. She had no time to waste. She packed her radio and started down the stairs.

"What are you doing?" a male voice called from the altar.

She ran to the door. The pastor was coming down the aisle, an older man, tall and straight with gray hair. She ignored him.

"Stop!" he called.

She kept her head down so he couldn't see her face. As she flung open the door and sprinted out, he started running after her.

"What are you doing?" he called.

Camille dashed toward the car. The pastor exited the church and paused, looking in different directions, trying to find her. She tossed the radio on the seat and started the engine. The whirring noise was more pronounced.

"Stop!" he called, racing toward her.

She pulled away and turned at the first crossroad. The pastor kept coming, but slowed, watching her suspiciously, too far away to stop her. She turned again and went back on the highway to Tournai. A glance in the rearview mirror showed no one following, the dust cloud approaching on the horizon.

Camille drove as fast as she dared, the engine noise getting worse. When she was a half dozen kilometers from Tournai, the engine coughed and sputtered, the car slowed, and the engine died by a bridge that spanned a stream. She scanned the landscape, finding nothing but farm fields, a stone cottage not far away.

She had to hide the diamonds.

CHAPTER 7

Jacques Dufort paced the floor of his Parisian study. He had just received Camille's update from a member in his network. She had faced a difficult task, the Germans arriving in Antwerp on the same day that she did. Odds had been against her. But if anyone could do it, she could. But then her message came. He read it again.

ALL THAT GLITTERS. PACKAGE REMOVED. DID NOT REACH DESTINATION.

It was a cryptic message he had to decipher. It started with the prearranged passcode, so it was authentic. The diamonds had been removed from the Antwerp vault. But then something went drastically wrong. They either never got to the dock or, when they did, they couldn't get to London. Or worse, the diamonds had been taken from them, maybe by the Germans, but they had escaped. The message could have different meanings. A clarification had been requested; no reply had been received. Camille must have been rushed, facing capture or worse, and couldn't continue transmitting.

He tried to imagine what thwarted success. Was it the

Germans? A problem with the boat? An unexpected intrusion? He didn't know. He focused on what he did know, dissecting the message word by word. The diamonds had been stolen from the exchange—that was clear. Camille was safe—she had sent the message. But Roger hadn't reached the port. Or if he did, he couldn't get out of Antwerp. Jacques assumed Roger was with Camille. Maybe they were still in Antwerp. Or maybe they weren't.

He had to develop contingencies, offer help when she sent her next message. If she couldn't get to London, and her chances diminished with each day that passed, she would have to bring the diamonds to Paris. But with the Germans advancing across northern France, racing for the coast, she had little hope for success. She was likely trapped somewhere in Belgium. His thoughts were interrupted when Emilie came in with two glasses of merlot.

"I brought some wine," she said, handing him a glass. "You seem so focused—the wrinkles in your brow tell a tale I may not want to hear. I thought a distraction would help."

He smiled weakly. "Even wine won't ease the pain."

Her eyes widened. "What happened?"

He wouldn't share what she didn't need to know. It wasn't fair to her. He focused on the war. "Holland fell, Belgium follows. Antwerp and Brussels surrendered; Tournai is next."

She eyed him curiously. "Maybe there's a diplomatic solution, an armistice."

"I doubt it," he muttered. "Hitler steals Europe one country at a time. Why would he not take France?"

She eyed him uneasily. "Should we leave Paris?" she asked. "Some flee south. Maddie, the woman next door, has already gone."

"You have the store to manage," he reminded her. "Your life will continue as it is, despite who controls the country."

"But why would we stay if Paris is threatened?"

He leaned back in the chair. "I must remain, even if the Germans come. My duties demand it."

She hesitated. "I don't know why you would. Especially if you're in danger."

He laughed lightly. "I'm in danger every day."

Her face firmed. She wasn't amused. "You say you're in danger, but I don't know why."

"I misspoke," he said, not wanting to scare her. "No one in the transportation department is at risk."

She frowned. "Is it time, perhaps, to end this charade?"

His eyes widened, not sure of how much she knew. "I don't know what you mean."

"You won't tell me what it is that you do. But I doubt it has much to do with transportation."

"Why would you say that?"

She fixed her gaze on his. "You were in the military before I met you. And sometimes I think that you still are."

"Would it make a difference if I was?"

"I know it shouldn't concern me. But it does. I'm worried about you."

He sipped his wine. She deserved an explanation—she was his wife. But he couldn't reveal too much—for many reasons. "I am assigned to the transportation department, but I do very little work there, and only in regard to railroads. But I pretend to do much more."

She eyed him curiously. "You have an office in the transportation building."

"Yes, I do," he said. "And sometimes I perform a needed function." He paused, watching her expression. "But you're right. I actually work for the military."

She hesitated, her face marred by a hint of betrayal. "What do you do for the military, other than your duties with railroads."

He didn't want to reveal details. She couldn't be trusted with them—nobody could. "I collect information; sometimes I do more. Nothing dangerous."

"But you just said you're in danger every day."

"Haven't you been suspicious of what I do?" he asked, ignoring her question.

She shrugged. "I find the meetings in your study curious. If they were visits with friends, you wouldn't be so secretive. Maybe I haven't wanted to admit that something wasn't right. But you never offered any clues, so I know nothing."

"No matter what happens, I will continue to play the part of a civil servant," he said. "A role needed for a functioning government. But my primary responsibility is with the military."

"Even if the Germans come?"

He shrugged. "A war isn't always fought on the battlefield. A civil servant can win battles if he fights them correctly."

She was quiet, perhaps not understanding. "I suspect the danger is more than we know. My customers talk. They say horrible things."

"Citizens fuel fear with gossip and misinformation. But sometimes they know as much as the generals."

She sighed. "Is the war lost?"

"The next week will show what the world will become. If the German advance is halted, the war will be much like the last."

"And if it isn't?"

"It will be a dark day for France."

"Should we prepare for the worst?"

Jacques didn't reply. His thoughts wandered to a mission that could change the course of the war. And if it failed, priceless diamonds would fall into the wrong hands. He didn't have the luxury of running away. He had to find Camille.

And he had to do it quickly.

CHAPTER 8

Three German soldiers stood in the vault of Sternberg and Sons, eyeing Major Ziegler as he held his pistol to Jacob Sternberg's temple. Sternberg's eyes were wide, his body trembled. Sweat dotted his forehead. He raised his hands, not sure what he was expected to do, and started to sob.

Sergeant Ernst Bayer didn't want to watch. He had seen many terrified men, begging for their lives. He had no desire to see any more. Already sickened by a war that had just begun, he stepped farther into the vault, his back to the terrified Jacob Sternberg, and focused on the theft of the diamonds, avoiding the scene unfolding behind him.

He hadn't spent his entire life in the military. A foot soldier during the First World War, he had survived four years in trenches shared with rats, lice, and men more dead than alive, gaunt shadows who barely functioned, their minds damaged, their souls destroyed. After the war, he tried to lead a normal life, hiding the horrors he had witnessed, teaching history in a secondary school—an occupation he truly enjoyed. But he was recalled two years prior, before any fighting began. He had an ability much needed in the military. He had mastered several languages—French, Polish, and Italian. Now in his mid-forties,

All That Glitters

he was short and stocky, his hair laced with gray. But he had been fortunate, assigned as Major Ziegler's driver. It kept him from combat. He avoided the hell that most called war. He didn't have to relive his nightmares, images he wanted to forget but could not.

He examined the pilfered deposit boxes closely, brushing his finger across the drilled-out lock. The mechanism had been smoothly bored, a perfect hole replacing it. The thief had gained access easily. He wondered what type of drill pierces steel like paper. How long did it take to steal the diamonds with such an effective tool? Only minutes, he suspected.

He had listened while Ziegler questioned Jacob Sternberg, and the merchant explained how the vault doors were opened, pointing to a closet where a key had been kept. Not wanting to watch Ziegler threaten the old man, Bayer left the vault, eyeing the hallways to different stairways. He walked the corridors, turning a corner to a rear stairwell behind a closed door. But after finding nothing unusual, he returned to the vault, crossing the hall to the closet Sternberg had referenced.

Ziegler's demands and Sternberg's pleas were fainter, which was good. Bayer didn't want to listen. And he already knew the result—having witnessed the same scene before. He knew that a trembling, sobbing, groveling Jacob Sternberg would do anything to save his life and those of his family—no matter who he had to betray. Bayer didn't want to see it, hear it, or even know it occurred. Even though it did. Threats were tools the conqueror used, and they were usually effective.

Bayer opened the closet door. Shelves lined the upper third of the back wall, holding cleaning supplies and rags. Mops and brooms hung from holders beneath the shelves. He didn't see where the key was hung, as Sternberg had described. He stepped inside, examined the closet closely, and saw the hook beside the door jamb in the corner of the closet. He moved back into the hallway and was about to close the door when he saw something on the floor. He picked it up. It was a business card for a shop in Paris: *All Things Napoleon, 69 Boulevard St-Germain, Paris, France. Emilie Dufort, Proprietor.*

He turned the card over. Scribbled on the back was a name, Jacques Dufort, and an Antwerp address, Godefriduskaai 99, Pier #3.

CHAPTER 9
FOUR KILOMETERS NORTHWEST OF TOURNAI, BELGIUM

Lucien Bouchard knew the Germans were coming by the dust that rose from the road. Two weeks before it was a country lane. Now it was crammed with people hurrying nowhere. Parents led bewildered children; the old hobbled on canes. Bicycles kept to the side of the road, suitcases strapped to handlebars. Men pushed wheelbarrows, home to toddlers or overflowing with belongings—although an elderly woman rested in one, frail and frightened. An occasional motor car inched forward, taking its occupants as far as petrol allowed, some with a mattress strapped to the top, a shield from shrapnel, a bed when needed. The swollen tide flowed forward, fleeing death and destruction, searching for safety that didn't exist.

Tournai lay to the southeast, near the border with France. A commerce center since Roman times, sprinkled with Medieval cathedrals, much of it lay in ruins, pelted by German bombardments. Smoke spiraled from flickering flames, occasional explosions answered by gunfire. The fighting was ending. Allied soldiers scurried across farm fields.

The British and French had come first, thrusting into Belgium when the Germans invaded. Little more than a week before, it now seemed a lifetime. Tournai was a strategic location. The Allies occupied the city, a proven strategy in the last war. But the Germans weren't fighting the last war, they were fighting a new one. They swept through Belgium and northern France as the Allies fled in confusion.

Lucien Bouchard lived in a stone cottage, four rooms and a bath, fifty meters from the road. Perched beside a stream spanned by a stone bridge built fifty years before—it sat near a tiny village a few kilometers from France. At first, he wanted to run with the rest, but saw no reason why he should. The Germans wouldn't bother him. He was a farmer nursing a small plot of land. Other than some chickens, he had nothing they would want. He didn't fear them, he had no reason. The dreams most men have had already left him, no longer within his grasp. Tomorrow was insignificant, the same as yesterday, offering no promise, no light—only the darkness that came with the day before it. Most could see that in his eyes. He was sure the Germans would, too.

He sat by the window that faced the stream, watching the sun as it started to set, a half-empty bottle of whiskey beside him. He took a swig and felt the fire trickle down his throat. To the northwest, a remnant of the last war remained, a French troop truck damaged by artillery over twenty years before. It had rusted, its hood smashed, its tires rotted. Vines had grown around it, invading the interior through broken windows. For a moment, he marveled at man's determination to destroy each other. How many millions would die in the new war, forgotten like those in the last?

The Germans would come, filing down the dirt lane or crossing his farm to get to the highway. They would force the refugees from the road with tanks, trucks, and motorcycles. And once they passed, the long lines of refugees who had searched for safety and hadn't found it, would go back to their homes, finding some damaged, some not, but none quite the same as when they had left. All had been violated, losing more than freedom, and an aura of defeat drenched the countryside like a pelting rain from pregnant clouds.

He hadn't expected the knock on the door—he thought the Germans would kick it down. He turned, waiting for them to barge in, weapons drawn. Would they shoot him, assuming a broken man might find the courage to fight his last battle? Or would they eye him with disgust. But seconds passed and the door never opened. He put the top on the bottle, rose from the chair, and crossed the parlor, past the fireplace smudged with soot.

"What do you want?" he called.

"Dr. Bouchard, we need help!"

He hadn't expected the language—English—or the title, which no longer applied. He opened the door and squinted in the sunlight, the orange sun sinking in the horizon. A British sergeant stood on the stoop.

"I'm just a farmer," Lucien told him. "I can't help you." He started to close the door.

"You must," the sergeant insisted, blocking the door with his boot. "We've no one else to ask."

Lucien hesitated. "Shouldn't you retreat?"

"We're the last to leave. One of my men is wounded. A lady from the village said you're a doctor."

"I once was," he replied, the admission painful. "But no more."

"If you don't come, a good man will die," the soldier said. He lowered his rifle. Not enough to threaten Lucien, but enough to remind him that he should do as asked.

"I want to be left alone," Lucien muttered, eyeing the gun.

"Don't we all?" the sergeant asked. Defeat was drawn on his face—with a tired look of despair. His left sleeve was stained with blood, maybe his own, maybe not. He must wish he was elsewhere, as a million others did.

Lucien relented. "I'll just be a minute."

He still had his doctor's bag, although months might pass before he touched it. Why try to be what he never should have been? He went in the bedroom closet and retrieved it from the shelf where it stayed hidden among a stack of outdated medical journals.

"Hurry!" the soldier called from the doorway. "We don't have much time."

The sergeant led him to neighboring fields, humanity clogging the road. British and Belgian soldiers moved around them, leaving abandoned equipment—backpacks, guns, even a few vehicles, their tires flat or their petrol tanks empty. The soldiers hurried, knowing they would fight again if they escaped. But the refugees moved slower, running away but not knowing where. They used the road; the soldiers fanned across the fields. The road wound south, into France; the soldiers went west. Why west, Lucien wondered, when they could go south, into France? And then the answer came to him. The Germans were to the south. Just as they came from the north and east. The Allies had to go west, to the coast, if they hoped to escape. Belgium was lost, and each day that dawned would be harder than the last.

Just past his barn, an old stone building with red tile roof like his house, and close to the coop where he kept his chickens, three British soldiers scanned the terrain, rifles ready. They sought survival; dreams of conquest had long gone.

A fourth soldier lay on the ground. He was young, his eyes closed, his helmet beside him. A woman in a brown skirt and beige blouse knelt over him. Slender with brown eyes, her blonde hair was marked by brown strands that the sun hadn't found.

"He needs you, Dr. Bouchard," she said as he approached. A splatter of freckles dotted her cheeks, faded but still there.

He wondered how she knew his name, her face a mystery. "What's your name?"

"Camille."

"Camille who?"

"Just Camille."

"Shouldn't you flee with the others?" he asked. She must be from Tournai, a former patient.

"I've been running my whole life."

He wondered what she meant. Maybe we all spend our lives running from something, hoping it doesn't catch us. Or maybe we only think something is trying to catch us. Lucien didn't reply. He bent over the wounded soldier, shot in the left thigh above the knee. He was losing blood, his trousers wet, the green stained crimson. Lucien cut away his pants and cleaned the wound the best he could. He wrapped gauze around the soldier's thigh, tying it tightly to staunch the flow of blood. He made no effort to remove the bullet—it wasn't the time or place.

"Be careful moving him," Lucien said, looking up.

The sergeant scanned the terrain, fleeing soldiers growing smaller in the distance, and turned to Lucien. "Take good care of him."

"You can't leave him," Lucien protested.

"We have no choice," the sergeant said as he raced through the fields with his men.

"He needs a surgeon," Lucien called.

The sergeant turned and pointed east. "The Germans are coming."

CHAPTER 10

Emilie Dufort hadn't expected Jacques to admit he was in French intelligence and did little in the transportation department as he pretended. It was a stunning revelation—more than he had ever told her during their courtship and marriage. But why tell her now? Was it prompted by war? Or did he have another reason? As she opened her store the following morning and prepared for her customers, she decided to watch him more closely. Maybe he wasn't what she thought he was—maybe there was more.

All Things Napoleon did a brisk business during peace or war, always crowded with dedicated customers. With the Germans racing through France, some sought solace in history, reliving a time with France at its zenith, hoping those days would return. For Emilie, it offered opportunity—sellers of memorabilia far outnumbered buyers—as many parted with prized possessions, raising money with which to flee.

The book section attracted the most attention. Volumes about battles, generals and their strategies, and the mechanics of war sold well. Customers browsed through books, some resting on scattered chairs to preview a purchase. Toy soldier collections were also popular, the display dominating a large part of the store. The remaining space featured military medals, swords, uniforms, pistols—items found on the battlefield. Anything associated with the Napoleonic Wars had a home in Emilie's store.

Emilie stood behind the counter, close to the entrance, when a woman approached with a biography of the Empress Josephine. "I've been anxious to read this," she said, smiling.

"You'll enjoy it, I'm sure," Emilie replied as she rang the sale on the cash register, took the woman's money, and made change. "She was a remarkable woman in a remarkable time."

"I'll be back, I'm sure," the woman said. She took her purchase and went out the door.

A man behind her came forward with three military medals. "Hello, Mme. Dufort."

Emilie's eyes narrowed. "M. Bassett, I thought our discussion had ended."

"It's just begun, Mme. Dufort," he said as he put the medals on the counter. "I collect military memorabilia. Medals, mostly, French and British."

"No German, M. Basset?" she asked, eyeing him curiously. She wasn't surprised he had come to her store, or that he knew she owned it. She suspected he knew much about her, which only confirmed he was who he claimed.

"No German medals today," he replied politely. "Although I did see a Blücher biography that looked interesting."

"Our biographies sell very well, M. Basset. Regardless of nationality."

He nodded. "I am impressed with how well you run your business."

"It's my life," she said. "I love it. There is nothing else I would rather do."

"Except, perhaps, what your family has requested."

She frowned. "You're very persistent."

"I have no choice, Mme. Dufort. And you know why. You should have been expecting me."

Emilie leaned closer. "I was expecting someone," she admitted. "Especially given the state of the war. But I've yet to determine if that is you."

He chuckled, as if he enjoyed their game. "Maybe further discussion is warranted."

She shrugged. "Perhaps it is."

He glanced around the store, making sure no one was nearby. "Does your husband know you are not from France?"

She hesitated, ringing up the sale on the cash register. "My husband knows I'm from a town along the Rhine River. My family came to Paris for our wedding."

Bassett admired the medals, pretending to be distracted. "Does he know that the town you come from is on the *German* side of the Rhine River?"

"No, he does not," she said tersely.

"Your husband probably doesn't know that your family is active in the Nazi Party—your brother is a confidant of Hitler, your father a hero from the last war."

"No, M. Bassett, he does not. And he doesn't need to know. He thinks my family are farmers."

"I assume he doesn't know that you came to France with a purpose unrelated to managing a store."

"He knows the store means everything to me," she replied.

"Does he know that your initial meeting was not accidental?"

"I love my husband," she replied, not answering.

He paused to look at customers wandering the store. "You're German, not French. And you always will be."

"I've lived in Paris for several years," she said. "I blend in."

"Yes, you do," he admitted. "Your accent is barely detectable and passes for someone who lived along the border."

"What does your accent reveal, M. Bassett. French is not

your native language."

He ignored her. "No one knows why you are really in Paris. Do they, Mme. Dufort?"

"They don't need to know."

"It's time to do what's always been expected."

"I need to know who you are, M. Bassett, before I do anything. And until the phone lines are working again, and I can talk to my family, we have very little to say to each other."

He was quiet, reflective. "What if the people of Paris learned who you really are?"

"I don't think they would care."

"I suspect you're wrong," he said. "Most would find your family repulsive. It would destroy your reputation as an innocent shopkeeper who loves all things French—your precious store would cease to exist."

"People worry about their own lives, M. Bassett. Especially now. They don't care about mine."

He looked through the store, ensuring no one could hear. He leaned close. "You are in serious danger."

She eyed him curiously, wondering why the conversation had so abruptly shifted. She suspected he knew more than she did. "We're all in danger," she replied tentatively.

"No, Mme. Dufort. You face a very different danger. One you can't imagine. From those you would never suspect."

She hesitated. He seemed so certain. "Enlighten me, M. Bassett."

He took a paper from his pocket and handed it to her. "Observe this address," he suggested. "See who comes and goes. Evenings are best."

She looked at the address, only eight or nine blocks from her home. "Will this prove you are who you claim, M. Bassett?"

He picked up his medals and nodded politely. "It'll prove much more than that," he said. "I'm certain I'll see you again, Mme. Dufort."

CHAPTER 11

Jacob Sternberg closed his eyes, his entire body trembling. "It could have been anyone!" he cried, Ziegler's pistol against his temple. "Please, don't! I saved the diamonds for you—to protect my family and friends."

Ziegler snickered. "You're a fool."

"I swear," Sternberg said. "Please, Major."

"Was the vault open?"

"No, it couldn't have been."

"The dead man got in," Ziegler said. "He had an accomplice. Someone knew the combination."

"My employees would not do this," Sternberg insisted, beads of sweat on his forehead.

Ziegler ground the pistol against his skull. "Give me the names of everyone who knows the combination. If you don't, I will shoot you. And I'll find out anyway."

"No, don't!' Sternberg begged. "Please, I have a family."

"Then talk. How many have keys to the building and know the combination?"

"Five, including me," he stammered.

"Are any women?"

"Two women and two men."

Ziegler smiled as Sternberg shook beside him. "When did you last see them?"

"I saw two of them yesterday," Sternberg said, his breath in labored gasps. "The others left the city a few days ago."

"Is either of those you saw yesterday a woman?"

"Yes, Claudette Maes."

"What does she look like?"

"She's young, maybe thirty. Blonde hair."

"Our culprit, I'm sure," Ziegler said. "But I want all their names and addresses."

Sternberg closed his eyes, as if he couldn't cope. "I have them in my office."

Ziegler kept the barrel against Sternberg's temple. He turned as Bayer approached, coming from the utility closet.

"I may have found something, sir," Bayer said.

"What is it?" Ziegler asked, lowering his pistol as Sternberg sighed with relief.

"A business card from a Paris antique shop," Bayer replied. "But it has writing on the back."

Ziegler took the card and studied it. "What is Godefriduskaai 99, Pier #3?" he asked Sternberg.

"It's a road along the docks," Sternberg said, his face pale, as if he was about to vomit. "Pier #3 is one of the wharfs."

Ziegler put the card in his shirt pocket. "We're going to Herr Sternberg's office," he said to Bayer. "He has names and addresses for me."

Ziegler led Sternberg up the stairs, jabbing him with his pistol. They returned to the second floor and went to an office at the end of the hall, larger than where the dead body was found. Pleated leather chairs sat in front of a walnut desk, the walls adorned with framed scenes of Antwerp. A family photograph on the desk showed Sternberg, his wife and extended family: children, spouses, grandchildren.

"Stand in front of the desk," Ziegler directed.

Sternberg stopped, facing the desk.

Ziegler was just to his right, still pointing the gun. "Get me the names, addresses and phone numbers of those who know the combination, starting with the two still in Antwerp."

"May I open my desk drawer to get them?"

"Yes," Ziegler said as he picked up the photograph. "Is this your family?"

"Yes, Major."

"Do I need their addresses, too, or are you going to cooperate?"

"I will cooperate, Major, I swear."

Ziegler studied the merchant. "How do I know that you didn't steal the diamonds?"

"I swear I did not, sir. I arrived shortly before you did."

"Get me the information."

"Yes, Major," Sternberg said. He went behind his desk, sat in the leather chair, and opened the top drawer. He opened a notebook and wrote the information on a piece of paper.

Ziegler studied the family photograph. For a brief instant he thought of his own family, a wife, and two sons in the German army, both somewhere in Norway.

Sternberg handed him the paper.

Ziegler looked at five names and addresses. The locations meant nothing to him. "I want your children's addresses, too."

Sternberg collapsed in the chair, his breathing rapid, knowing Ziegler held his life in his hand. "Please, have mercy," he begged. "My address is the last listed. This has nothing to do with my children."

"Not yet," Ziegler muttered. "But it might."

"Any fault for the theft is mine," Sternberg said, his lips quivering.

Ziegler looked at the paper. "Where are these locations?"

"The employees live nearby. My home is a few kilometers outside of the city."

"Hopefully we won't have to go to your home," Ziegler said. "It will be very unpleasant if we do."

Sternberg glared at Ziegler, as if finding courage he didn't know he had. "I assure you, Major, that none of my employees were involved in the theft."

"I'll make that determination," Ziegler said. He studied Steinberg trembling. "I want you to come with me."

"But Major, I have no further information," Sternberg pleaded.

"Don't make me kill you, Herr Sternberg. It's far easier if you just do as I say."

"But Major—"

Ziegler pulled the trigger. The shot echoed through the room, the bullet narrowly missing Sternberg, embedding in the wall behind him.

"Ah!" Sternberg screamed, breaking down in tears.

Bayer hurried in the door. "Is everything all right, Major?"

"Yes, it is now," Ziegler replied. "Herr Sternberg has decided to accompany us to his employees' homes. I think one of them assisted the Allied spy in stealing the diamonds."

Sternberg was broken. He sunk in his seat, eyes clenched closed, weeping.

"Come along, Mr. Sternberg," Ziegler said. "I want to start with the woman."

Sternberg rose from the chair, took a hat from a rack, and put it on his head. He sniffled as his sobbing subsided and wiped his face with his handkerchief. "Aaron Peeters lives closest. Less than two blocks away."

Ziegler was intrigued. "Tell me about Mr. Peeters," he said as they walked from the office. "Perhaps he was involved, too."

"He's spent his whole life in diamonds," Sternberg said.

"How long has he worked here?"

"Fifty years?"

Ziegler was surprised. "How long have you owned the establishment?"

Sternberg shrugged. "It's been in my family for generations."

Ziegler considered the description of the dead man's accomplice. "I'm not interested in Mr. Peeters—at least not right now. Who's worked here the least?"

"Claudette Maes."

"Is she the woman you described—the blonde?"

"Yes, it is. She's been here almost six months."

Ziegler was convinced he'd found his culprit. He waved his gun at Sternberg. "Are you going to cooperate, Herr Sternberg?"

Sternberg's face was pale, his body still shaking. "Yes, sir, I swear I will cooperate."

"Can I put this gun away?"

He nodded. "I won't cause any trouble. I promise."

They went down the steps toward the entrance. Jacob Sternberg's expression showed his whole world collapsing.

Ziegler put his pistol in the holster. "You're very lucky, Herr Sternberg. I've decided not to hurt you. At least not yet."

CHAPTER 12

Camille heard the plane's engine, faint but coming closer. An aircraft poked through a fluffy cloud, French flags painted on the wings, smoke trailing behind it. The tail was riddled with holes, the top jagged and broken. It was losing altitude, whining as it dropped from the sky.

A burst of machine-gun fire came from behind it. A German plane dove from much higher, the body gray with black crosses on the wing and tail. The pilot fired rapidly, bullets running up and down the French aircraft.

Screaming refugees scattered—shouting, cursing, praying—darting in all directions. They hid behind trees and shrubs on the side of the road or lay in a gulley damp from rain. Scared parents covered wailing children, shouts and screams drowning the sound from the plane's engine. Wagons and motor cars were abandoned, horses kicking and neighing, their owners seeking safety on the side of the road. Bullets ran up and down the road, tufts of dirt springing skyward, burrowing into wagons, pinging as they hit fenders and hoods of automobiles.

The soldiers kept running, most far in the distance. The German pilot turned towards them, only a few hundred feet above the ground, spraying bullets through the fields. Soldiers dove to the ground, some meekly firing at a target they would never hit. After the plane passed, it arched up and circled, briefly hidden in a setting sun.

The French plane dropped lower, its engine spitting, until it passed the horizon. The ground shook seconds later, a flash of fire shooting skyward, black smoke launched behind it.

Camille watched the fight unfolding. Lucien stood beside her, as if walking into a dream—or maybe a nightmare. "Get down!" she hissed, yanking him to the ground. "You'll get yourself killed."

He kneeled. "Why didn't you go with them?" he asked, nodding toward the fleeing British.

"I'm staying with you."

He looked at her oddly. "Your life is in front of you. Mine is behind me."

Camille eyed the man beside her. "It depends which way you're facing."

Lucien studied her for a moment. "An interesting comment from an interesting woman. Not that I'm interested. Where are you from?"

"Nearby."

"Tournai, or the village?"

She pointed toward Tournai. "I live near the church," she said, even though she didn't. But it's where her home had been until she went back to Paris. "Do you see the steeple, peeking from behind the smoke?"

"Yes."

"Have you ever been in that church?"

"No, I haven't. God left me years ago."

"Maybe it was you who left God."

"It's the same."

"No, it isn't."

"Why do you care?" he asked.

She refused to show pity for a broken man. "Because I knew you when you were a man."

"What am I now?"

"A shadow."

He didn't reply, his expression not changing. "You're young."

"Not much younger than you," she said, scanning the landscape, searching for Germans.

"Ten years, maybe more," he said, then shrugged. "Or maybe not. I'm not an old man, only tired and broken like old men sometimes are."

"Tired and broken men can be repaired, they can start life where they think it ended."

The wounded soldier groaned and shifted on the soil. His eyes fluttered but stayed closed. Blood had begun to stain his bandage, the wound in his thigh still weeping.

"I hope he doesn't lose his leg," Lucien muttered.

"Can you give him something for the pain?"

"Whiskey," he replied.

"No medicine?"

Lucien hesitated. "I have some medicine. I used it once. But no more. I have no need."

"You're a doctor," she said. "You should have something."

"I was a doctor," he clarified. He stood and peeked around the chicken coop.

"Are they coming?"

"Not yet," he said. "But they will soon."

"We have to bring him inside," Camille said. "Before they get here."

The German plane circled, coming toward them. The refugees remained on the ground, screaming, hands over their heads. The bullets strafed the fields where the soldiers were running.

CHAPTER 13

Emilie Dufort didn't understand Louie Bassett's warning. What danger could she be facing? She wasn't involved in the war effort—at least not yet. But he wouldn't elaborate, leaving abruptly and teasing her for more. She wasn't sure if a person posed the threat or her German heritage and family's Nazi sympathies. But she was determined to find out.

After dinner that evening, as she finished washing the dishes, Jacques came into the kitchen. "I have to meet one of my contacts," he said, offering no more.

"Where are you going?" she asked, trying to seem casual. His clandestine meetings had increased greatly since the Germans attacked. Formerly infrequent, he had claimed he had been meeting friends. Now he could no longer do so—perhaps what drove his recent confession.

"Much is happening," he said with a shrug. "I must stay ahead of it, prepare for the worst."

She frowned. "I was hoping we could spend the evening together."

"I go because I must," he said, watching her reaction. "Not because I want to."

She fixed her gaze on his, but he looked away. He left

almost every evening, sometimes missing dinner, rarely offering an explanation. But maybe there was no explanation. Maybe he did what he could to save France.

"I know war rages," she said, "and you have much to do. But must you go every night?"

"I meet with people when they are available," he said, trying to explain. "Not when it's best for me."

"Who are these people?" she asked. Louie Bassett's warning made her doubt everything—even if Jacques told the truth. "If I knew more, I wouldn't worry. The worse the war gets, the more concerned I am for you."

He put his hands on her shoulders, pulled her close, and kissed her lips. "No one knows what I do or who I meet," he said. "That's how it must be."

"Do what you must," she muttered, stepping aside. Could Jacques be the danger Bassett had warned about? If nothing else, she was now suspicious. It was time she learned more—for a variety of reasons.

"I won't be long," he promised as he stepped out, closing the door behind him.

She waited a moment, gazing around an empty room. Did his meeting have to do with the war? Or was it something else? Why spend so much time in secret locations with faceless people? Did his duties demand it? Or did they not? But then she felt guilty. Maybe it was her secret, a German woman pretending to be French, that forced all to be viewed through a cloudy lens. Was she assuming everyone pretended to be what they weren't only because she did?

Emilie removed the paper from her pocket, the address from Louie Bassett. He was a stranger trying to convince her to do what her family wanted—an agreement she made when she first came to Paris. He seemed authentic, but she doubted he was French. And he didn't seem German—his accent wasn't right. But he must somehow be linked to Germany. How else would he know about her and her family? She looked at the address: 8 Rue Serpente, eight or nine blocks from her apartment.

She put the paper back in her pocket and went out the front door, locking it behind her. The streets were dark, no lights, house shades drawn, minimizing targets for Luftwaffe bombs—should they ever come. Few people walked the street, but more walked the boulevard.

Jacques was far ahead. He moved quickly, hunched over, hands in his pockets. He had reached the corner, headed in the direction she would take if she went to the address Louie Bassett had given her. She hurried after him, staying close to buildings, knowing he might turn to see if anyone followed. She had to be more careful than he was if she wanted her presence to remain unknown.

He stopped at the next corner, turning abruptly. Emilie ducked in the recessed entrance to a hat store, hiding behind merchandise on display. She waited, her heart racing, knowing she shouldn't do what she did. Or maybe she was only afraid of what she might find. But it would look horrible if she was caught. She waited a moment more and stepped out.

Jacques continued on his way, farther down the block. He was in a hurry, nothing distracting him, although not many strolled the pavement.

Emilie couldn't keep up. If she hurried to get closer, he would see her. As she approached the corner, a taxi pulled up to the curb and discharged a passenger. As the man paid his fare, she climbed in.

"Where are you going, Madame?" the driver asked.

"Eight Rue Serpente."

The driver hesitated. "That's only five or six blocks. You can walk and save yourself money."

"I'm late for an engagement," she explained. "I have no choice."

"I understand," the driver said. He pulled away from the curb and rounded the corner.

Emilie wasn't sure why she decided to visit the address offered by Louie Bassett. But she was certain that's where Jacques was going. Was it instinct? A sneaking suspicion? The taxi went on a parallel street, a block from Jacques, and would approach the address from the opposite direction.

When the taxi reached Rue Serpente, she watched the addresses as they passed the buildings—twenty, eighteen, sixteen. "Can you please stop here?"

The driver pulled to the curb and turned, looking at her quizzically. "But your destination is only ten meters away?"

She smiled weakly. "I know, but I want to see who else arrives. Could you wait for a moment?"

The driver shrugged. "Yes, of course."

A few minutes later, Jacques Dufort rounded the corner. He went to number eight, a two-story apartment building, paying no attention to the taxi. He rapped loudly on the entrance to the second-floor flat.

Emilie rolled down the window, hoping to overhear. A moment later, the door opened. An attractive woman stepped out, tall with brown hair that fell to her shoulders, wearing a crisp green dress that looked recently purchased.

"I've been waiting," the woman said. She gave him a quick hug.

Jacques shrugged. "I couldn't get away."

"Did anyone see you?" she asked.

"No, it's safe."

CHAPTER 14

Sergeant Bayer drove to the home of Claudette Maes, a three-story apartment building constructed a hundred years before. Two soldiers on a motorcycle with a sidecar followed them. The street was lined with trees, only a few parked cars—many refugees had yet to return. A woman pushed a baby carriage down the pavement, hurrying away as they approached, as an older man watched them curiously from his stoop, enjoying his pipe.

Bayer parked the car and opened the door for Ziegler and Sternberg. As the motorcycle approached, Ziegler called to one of the soldiers. "Go around back and guard the fire escape."

As the soldier went behind the building, Sternberg led them up the walkway. "She lives on the second floor."

"Let's hope she's our culprit, Herr Sternberg," Ziegler said. "The sooner the diamonds are recovered, the easier it will be for you."

Sternberg didn't reply, his hand trembling as he reached for the door. They paused at the entrance while the soldier checked the hallway. A central staircase led to upper floors, the wooden stairs worn in the center from thousands of shoes that had walked upon them.

The soldier came back down the corridor. "Nothing unusual, sir."

"Take us to her apartment," Ziegler said to Sternberg.

The soldier climbed the stairs first, his machine gun at the ready. A landing on the second floor opened into a hallway, apartment doors on both sides. The soldier scanned the corridor and nodded to Ziegler.

Sternberg turned to the right, went to the second door, and knocked. "Claudette," he called. "It's Jacob."

A moment passed with no reply. "Knock again," Ziegler ordered.

Sternberg knocked harder. "Claudette, please, it's very important."

Ziegler was impatient. "Missen Maes, this is Major Ziegler of the Gestapo. Please don't waste my time."

It was quiet, the door still closed. "I don't think she's home," Sternberg said nervously.

Ziegler motioned to the soldier. "Break it down."

The soldier kicked the door, his boot centered just below the handle, near the jamb. The wood split and the door swung open. He lowered his machine gun and entered the flat.

The room was dark, the curtains closed. The soldier stood with gun ready, moving in a circle. They all followed, stepping into a parlor, a kitchen to the left, a bedroom and bath to the right. A cat darted across the floor.

"Come here, kitty," Ziegler said. He picked up the cat and held it, gently petting him. "I have a fondness for animals, Herr Sternberg," he said, turning to the diamond dealer. "But I despise people."

Sternberg's eyes widened, as if suspecting his fate was predetermined.

"Describe Maes," Ziegler said. His gaze wandered the room while he held the cat.

Sternberg shrugged. "She's average, nothing distinct about

her. Blonde hair, dark eyes, maybe thirty. She's loyal, accomplished, very good with diamonds and our clients."

"Missen Maes," Ziegler called. "You had best come out. I can make it very difficult for you."

The flat was quiet. Ziegler turned on the light. "When is the last time you saw her?"

"Yesterday," Sternberg said. "She left the bank when I did."

They could see most of the apartment—all except the bedroom and bath.

"I'll check the kitchen," Bayer said, pistol drawn.

Ziegler motioned for the soldier to check the bedroom. He stayed a step behind him. The bed was made, the room nicely kept. A closet was off to one side, the door closed. Ziegler pointed toward it.

The soldier stepped forward. He glanced behind a bureau, then stopped at the closet. Standing off to the side, he opened the door, pointing his gun inside.

Clothes hung on the rod, boxes were stacked on the floor, a shelf above. No space for anyone to hide. The soldier turned away and stood beside the bed. He looked at Ziegler and pointed downward. He knelt, sticking his gun under the bed.

A second later, he stood. "No one."

Ziegler pointed to the bath.

The soldier stepped from the bedroom and quietly entered. The door was open, a closed shower curtain across from it. Beside the sink, a glass, toothbrush, and bar of soap sat under a mirrored medicine cabinet. He crept toward the shower. Pushing his machine gun forward, he whisked the curtain to the side. No one was there.

Ziegler left the bath and walked into the kitchen. "Check the fire escape," he said to Bayer.

The sergeant went to a window at the rear of the kitchen and moved the drapes aside. Sunlight streamed in. He lifted the lower sash and stuck his head out, looking in all directions.

"Nothing," he said.

CHAPTER 15

Camille waited for the plane to return. No one moved, muffled cries and curses coming from the road. After a few minutes, the refugees rose from the ground, screaming and sobbing. None were shot, although bullets came close. The pilot wanted to terrorize them, and he did. They again clogged the road, running to nowhere, assuming anywhere else would be safe. The line stretched south as far as Camille could see, but behind her, the end was less than fifty meters away. No more would flee. At least not today.

"Can you help me get him inside?" she asked Lucien. "We can't leave him lying here."

"We'll have to lift him," he replied, scanning the horizon.

"Do you have a wheelbarrow?"

He nodded. "Yes, wait here," he said and went behind the chicken coop. He returned with a wooden wheelbarrow, weathered, the red paint faded, the wheel wobbly. He put it next to the Englishman. "Can you lift his legs?"

She struggled, protecting his wound, the bandage slowly staining. Lucien lifted his torso into the wheelbarrow, steadied it, and then helped her.

"We have to hurry," he said. He pushed the wheelbarrow forward, the soldier's limbs dangling over the edge.

Camille stood beside him, keeping the wheelbarrow steady. They pushed it across the lawn, moving as fast as they could. On any other day, they would attract the attention of all who saw them. But now no one cared. The refugees thought only of themselves. They had to. No one else would save them.

They shoved the wheelbarrow across uneven ground. Billowing clouds of dust formed in the east, floating across fields. "They're coming," she said quietly.

They wheeled the Englishman around shrubs that split the farm from the house. When they reached the cottage, Lucien opened the door and pushed the wheelbarrow across the threshold. "There's a spare room," he said, winded, nodding toward a closed door on the right.

She opened the door. The room was furnished sparsely, a worn green sofa, two half-filled bookcases flanking a closet, a picture on the wall of a mother and child. She paused to look at it, then went to a window with open white curtains. "Look," she said, pointing east.

Vehicles approached. A staff car led, still far away, followed by troop trucks with gray canvas backs. Motorcycles rode between them, with sidecars and machine guns that brought death from any direction. The Germans came from Tournai. The city had fallen. Or maybe they had gone around it. But they were on their way to the main road, moving west.

"Put him on the couch," she said. "We have to hurry."

He pushed the wheelbarrow next to the sofa. "Grab his legs," he said. "Gently."

She lifted his feet as Lucien grasped him under the arms. The soldier groaned as they swung him on to the sofa.

"Take the wheelbarrow outside," she said. "Quickly. Use the back door so they won't see you." She looked at the tracks on the floor. "Clean the dirt, too. Hurry."

He looked at her curiously, the calm woman in control of a situation that was out of control. But he did what she said. As she watched the Germans from the window, he pushed the wheelbarrow through the kitchen and out the back door. He returned a moment later with a rag from the kitchen cupboard.

Camille came to the threshold. "They're close."

The German vehicles came down the road, infantry walking through the fields. They could come in the house, or they might assume it was safe—that no Allied soldiers hid within. Except one did—an unconscious Englishman sprawled on a worn couch.

She went back to the doorway as Lucien wiped the dirt from the floor and returned the rag to the kitchen. The British soldier grunted, his eyes fluttering open. He started to thrash about, as if trying to escape but not knowing from what.

"Please be still," Lucien said in stilted English as he came back in the room.

The soldier stopped moving. His frightened eyes scanned the room. "Who are you?"

"We won't hurt you," Lucien said, not answering.

"We'll help you," Camille added. "You've been shot in the leg and lost a lot of blood. You were unconscious."

"Where are the others?"

"They're gone," Lucien said.

"Germans are coming," Camille warned. She looked out and drew the curtains. "They're just up the road."

Lucien glanced around the cottage, as if not sure what to do. "We have nowhere to hide you. You must be very quiet."

"I'll wait with him," Camille said. "Just until they pass."

"I hear their engines," Lucien said quietly, the rumbling increasing.

Camille peeked from the window. "Soldiers cross the fields. They're almost here."

"I'll go in the parlor," Lucien said. "They may come to the door. Please, be still."

Lucien went in the parlor, closing the door. Camille looked out the window. The refugees had passed, the end of the line beyond the edge of the farm, near the bridge that crossed the stream. They moved to the side of the road, making way for their new masters.

The first vehicle approached. Soldiers on foot came closer. They walked around the house, poking through shrubs, searching for an enemy that wasn't there.

The front door burst open.

CHAPTER 16

Jacques Dufort entered the second-floor apartment at #8 Rue Serpente and followed Sophie Silvain up the stairs. Not yet thirty, married to an army officer stationed in Tunisia, she was an integral part of his network, an expert in logistics. With contacts that spanned the continent, she had obtained the information Camille needed to steal the diamonds from Sternberg and Sons—the building layout, escape paths, keys required, and the security circuit. She had worked with Jacques since the war began. They trusted each other, knowing difficult days lay ahead for both France and the world.

"Sit down," she said. "I'll get us a glass of wine."

Jacques waited in the parlor. He went to the window, pulled the curtain aside and looked out, watching a taxi pull away from the curb and drive down the street. A few pedestrians wandered the pavement, an occasional automobile passed. He scanned nearby buildings, ensuring no one watched Sophie's apartment. He could take no chances. And neither could she.

"Is it safe?" she asked as she came back with two glasses of chardonnay.

"I don't see anyone," he muttered, taking one last look.

She sat on the sofa, putting the glasses on a coffee table. "I haven't received any more messages from Camille. Even though I expected an update."

He sat beside her and picked up a glass. "I need to find out where she is. Guy Barbier is getting impatient. The diamonds are too valuable to the war effort."

"Do you know if Roger is still with her?"

He shrugged. "I know as much as you," he said. "Does your Antwerp contact have any updates?"

Sophie shook her head. "She hasn't contacted me since the Germans came. But I expect a message from her as soon as she can send one."

Jacques pursed his lips. "It's harder to get information every day, especially in regions controlled by the Germans. Is it the woman who works at Sternberg and Sons?"

Sophie nodded. "Claudette Maes, a valuable resource. But don't reveal her name to anyone—not even Barbier."

"I never would," he said, always amazed at Sophie's reach. "Maybe she can tell us about Camille."

"She'll know more than we do. I only hope Camille is safe. Especially with the Germans after the diamonds, too. She took a lot of risks."

"She did," Jacques agreed. "But we all do." He sat back and sighed. "I hesitate to contact her. It's too dangerous. But I have to know what happened."

Sophie sipped her wine. "It's better we wait. She'll send a message when she can." She paused and gave him an anxious glance. "Assuming she can contact us."

Jacques wanted to consider all possibilities—even those he hoped hadn't occurred. "Do you think something happened to her?"

"I don't know," she said. "But we should be prepared for anything."

He knew she was right. "What are your thoughts?"

"She could have been captured by the Germans."

"I hope not," he said, frowning. "I assumed she was safe. She managed to send a message. But they must be looking for her. They want the diamonds as badly as we do."

"Maybe she's hiding, and that's why she can't contact us."

"Don't underestimate her," he said. "She's clever. When she came to my apartment, she noticed everything: a locked window, a brass-handled cane, faint footsteps in another room."

Sophie paused, assessing a woman she did not know. "Are you certain she wouldn't betray us—kill Roger and steal the diamonds?"

Jacques hesitated. It was a scenario he couldn't envision. "Anything's possible. But it's unlikely. She has an unblemished record. And she's highly regarded."

"Everyone has a price," Sophie said softly.

"Yes, I suppose," he muttered. "But not her."

"What were her contingency plans, assuming something went wrong?"

"I told her if she couldn't get Roger to the port, or anything else went wrong, she should bring the diamonds back to Paris—but only as a last resort."

"Something did go wrong," Sophie said. "We know that from her message."

Jacques nodded. "They probably couldn't get to the port."

"We should assume Camille has the diamonds and she's trying to get them to you. She's somewhere between Antwerp and Paris."

"Not an easy task," he mumbled. "The war wages across northern France. She can't get to Paris."

Sophie was quiet for a moment. "Unless she's not even trying. She may sell the diamonds to the highest bidder."

Jacques shook his head. "I doubt it," he said. "We don't know what she did. And we won't until she contacts us again."

"Did you provide a route, should the port be closed, or identify where she could hide?"

Jacques frowned, seeing a weakness in a plan he thought was well developed. "No, I didn't. I should have asked you to do everything. You're the expert."

"It's too late now," she said. She paused, pensive. "If we assume she avoided the fighting, we can narrow down her location."

"We don't even know if she got out of Antwerp."

"That wouldn't be good," Sophie said. "Antwerp fell the day she was there."

"Now all of Belgium has fallen."

Sophie hesitated. "Do you know anything about her—other than her name is Camille?"

"She was recruited at the Sorbonne, trained by the best—Nicolas Chastain. She speaks three languages, has been in Paris for less than six months, and was assigned to Tournai for two years before that."

"Tournai?" she asked.

He paused, wondering why he hadn't thought of the obvious explanation. "Yes, Tournai."

"That's where she is," Sophie said. "She knows the city and has contacts there."

"It does makes sense," he admitted, annoyed that Sophie was always a step ahead of him.

"But Tournai has fallen to the Germans," Sophie said. "She's trapped."

Jacques bit his fingernail. "We have to find her. The diamonds are too critical. We can't let anyone else get them."

CHAPTER 17

Major Ziegler sat on the couch in Claudette Maes' apartment, fussing over her purring cat. Bayer and Sternberg were in chairs across from him, neither speaking. The soldier stood in the kitchen, looking out the back window.

They had only been there a few minutes when a woman walked in the door. About thirty with blonde hair and brown eyes, she carried a bag in her arm, a loaf of bread sticking out of the top. "What is going on?" she asked, eyes wide.

"Come in," Ziegler commanded.

She looked at Sternberg. "Jacob, what are you doing in my apartment?" She eyed the broken door jamb. "What did you do?"

"Claudette, someone stole the diamonds," Sternberg said as he got out of the chair, trying to explain. "The industrial diamonds in the vault."

Maes came closer, her face pale. "I didn't do anything. I swear."

"Sit down," Ziegler said, distracted. "What a lovely cat you have Missen Maes. I've enjoyed getting to know him."

Maes sat down, glancing at her bedroom, the opened door to her closet, and then looked at him strangely. "Thank you.

All That Glitters

He's a good pet." She put her groceries on the floor beside her, hands shaking, and glanced at the splintered jamb on her door. She seemed to understand her life was in danger.

Ziegler smiled, petting the cat that sat on his lap, its eyes drifting closed. "Where is your key to the diamond exchange?"

"It is here," Maes said, holding up her key ring. "I used it yesterday."

"After you stole the diamonds," Ziegler said. He turned to the soldier. "Arrest this woman."

"No, wait!" Maes protested. Tears welled in her eyes; fear flickered across her face. "I didn't take the diamonds."

"You were the last to leave the exchange," Ziegler said. "You said yourself that you used your key."

"I did," Maes said, pleading. "But I used it to enter. I was the first to arrive yesterday morning. I unlocked the door."

Ziegler studied the woman closely, searching for any sign she didn't speak the truth. He glanced at Bayer, who gave him a slight shrug. "If I find out you're lying, I will kill you."

She gasped. "I'm not lying, I swear."

"She's a good woman," Sternberg interjected. "She wouldn't lie, and she didn't steal the diamonds."

Ziegler glared at Sternberg, who took a step back. "You have worked at the exchange six months," he continued. "With so little experience, a diamond theft would be tempting."

"I've only worked for Jacob for six months, but I came from one of the other exchanges."

"Why did you leave?" Ziegler asked. "Because it was easier to steal diamonds from Herr Sternberg?"

"No, of course not. I left because the business changed hands. I've known Jacob for many years."

"It's true," Sternberg said timidly. "I've known Claudette since she was a child."

"And you trust her?"

"Yes, implicitly," Sternberg said. "I trust all my employees."

Ziegler studied the pair. It seemed they were telling the truth. They were both afraid, wide-eyed, trembling, sweating—aware that they were in serious trouble. He glanced at Bayer, nodding subtly.

"I have no reason to steal the diamonds," Maes said, her gaze again shifting to her bedroom. "I make a good living."

"No husband?" Ziegler asked abruptly.

"He's gone," she said. "With the army."

"Where is your husband stationed?" Bayer asked, as if to confirm she spoke the truth.

She turned to face him, wiping a tear trailing down her cheek. "I don't know where he is," she said. "He had been at one of the forts outside the city. But I haven't heard from him since they fell."

"Claudette would never steal the diamonds," Sternberg insisted. "And neither would I. Please, I beg you to believe us."

Ziegler paused, studying two pale faces before him. He decided that neither was guilty of the theft. But he couldn't let them know that. At least not yet.

"I swear, sir, I did not do anything wrong," Maes pleaded.

"Who left the exchange after you did?" Ziegler asked.

She glanced at Sternberg. "We left together. All of us. Except…"

"Except who?"

"Mr. Peeters," Maes said.

"He's the older man I told you about," Sternberg added.

"And who else?" Ziegler demanded.

"No one," Maes replied. "He was alone."

CHAPTER 18

"Halt!" the German commanded as he burst through Lucien's door, his machine gun drawn and ready.

Lucien raised his hands, heart racing, eyes wide. He tried to pretend he wasn't afraid, but his body trembled. He thought he would welcome death, the escape he had wanted for eighteen months, or at least not fear it. But as soon as it stared at him, he realized he wasn't as brave as he thought he was.

Two soldiers crossed the threshold while the third kept his gun ready. Lucien was surprised by their youth, boys trying to be men. But he realized boys could kill, too. Especially if trained to do so. One soldier walked to the back of the cottage and checked the kitchen. He stood at the threshold, rifle poised, scanning the room. He went to the bedroom, walking through the open door. Bureau drawers opened and slammed shut, followed by closet doors. He came out a few seconds later, glanced in the bathroom, and started toward the spare room.

The door opened just as he reached it. Camille stepped out. "*Die Engländer sind weg,*" she said, pointing to the west. "The English are gone."

The soldier's eyes widened, but he seemed to relax when

she spoke German. He glanced at the soldiers by the door, as if no longer threatened by what he might find.

Camille stayed in the entrance. The door was ajar, but closed enough so they couldn't see in. She blocked their way, studying them as they studied her.

The leader walked forward, his boots thumping the floor. He stood in front of Camille, so close they almost touched. "*Wann sind die Soldaten gegangen?*" he asked. "When did the soldiers leave?"

"*Zwanzig minuten,*" she said, not moving. "Twenty minutes."

The German backed away, but slowly lowered his rifle until the barrel pointed at her breast. "*Gehen,*" he directed. "Move."

She stepped aside, but slowly, her gaze locked on his, showing no fear.

The German went through the doorway, took another step, and paused, listening. A few seconds later, he took another step. His finger stayed on the trigger, ready to fire.

"What do you want?" Lucien asked trying to distract him.

The second soldier swung his rifle, the butt hitting Lucien on the side of his head. His vision clouded and he fell to the floor, the room spinning in a kaleidoscope of faces and colors. He almost fainted, the pain overwhelming. He touched his head, a warm sticky fluid oozing through his fingers.

"*Tu uns nicht weh,*" Camille said, moving toward him. "Don't hurt us."

The second soldier stood in her way, poking his rifle.

She stopped, turning to watch the soldier who entered the spare room, sensing he was the leader. "*Bitte lass uns in Ruhe,*" she said. "Please leave us alone."

The soldier stepped farther into the room. He scanned the walls, the furniture, along the floor. Then he turned, nodding to the others. They abruptly crossed the parlor and left, leaving the front door open.

Lucien struggled to his knees, holding his head, the pain sharp.

"Are you all right?' Camille asked, rushing to his side.

He blinked, trying to clear his vision. "I think so," he mumbled, the room still spinning. He rose, his legs wobbly, but managed to stand. He took a minute to steady himself, staggered to the door, and looked out.

The Germans who came in the house had mingled with their comrades. Most of the column had passed, but the remainder would stop for the night. Not for long, though. The Allies were trapped, either in a pocket near Tournai or all across Belgium, he couldn't say for sure.

"Where is he?" Lucien asked softly, his head pounding, eyes trained on the enemy.

"I hid him," Camille replied.

He was trying to think clearly, but it was difficult. He wondered who this woman was, who appeared from nowhere and stood defiant in the enemy's face. "Where?"

"I'll tell you when they leave."

"They won't be gone until morning," he said. He looked far up the road, the refugees in the distance, split by the Germans on the road.

"Wait until they move away from the house."

"Where did you learn to speak German?" It was one of a dozen questions he wanted to ask.

"Where did you learn to speak English?" she asked in perfect English, much better than his.

He glanced down the road, at first not replying. "They're stopping," he said. "They'll camp in the field overnight. They stole eggs from my chickens."

She went to the window and peered out. "They're away from the house, closer to the stream."

He closed the door, some of the molding splintered where the German had kicked it in. His head throbbed, matching his pulse. He took a few more steps, felt dizzy and plopped in an armchair.

Camille came over and lightly touched his head. "It's bruised badly. Swollen, but the bleeding stopped."

Lucien looked at her, seeing so much more than a local woman who had spent her life in the Belgian towns along the French border. He wasn't sure who she was, or where she came from, but she was different—in a dangerous way. And he didn't know why. First, he had to worry about the Englishman.

"Where is he?" he demanded, still unable to think clearly.

CHAPTER 19

Emilie glanced back at the apartment building as the taxi pulled away. Jacques seemed to know the woman well. The hug may have been a greeting—it seemed innocent. But it could have been more. Their conversation was cryptic—intelligence contacts ensuring they weren't watched. Or lovers, leery of discovery?

She assumed the worst. She had no reason not to. Even though she had a role to play in Paris, and Jacques was part of it, she did care about him. She never dreamed he would fall in love with another woman. He was married to his work—or at least he seemed to be—and she understood that. They lived in dangerous times. She had willingly taken second place since the day they had exchanged their wedding vows.

Now she wondered how long the affair had gone on, assuming it was an affair. She had no hints, no suspicions, although Jacques had become distant. But he was overwhelmed with the war. Everyone was. His meetings had increased, but he could be plotting strategy—based on his latest revelations. He usually met with Guy Barbier, a scary man who made her uncomfortable. But now it seemed he had a secret lover, an explanation for where he spent most evenings—if her assumptions were correct.

As the taxi rounded the corner, she leaned forward. "You can stop here."

The driver eyed her in the rearview mirror. "Is anything wrong, Madame? You seem upset."

"I'm all right," she said, even though she wasn't.

"Your eyes are misty," he continued, occasionally glancing in the mirror. "Did you see something you didn't expect to see?"

She closed her eyes for a moment, more for the driver's benefit. When she first came to Paris, she was part of a grander plan. Betrayal was part of the equation. But she hadn't expected to be the one betrayed—regardless of the reason. Unless there was a plausible explanation, and the woman was merely a contact in the murky world of intelligence.

"Let me take you home," the driver offered. "I am turning off the meter. There will be no more cost to you."

Emilie hesitated, but then gave him her address.

"Was it the man?" the driver pried as he drove to her apartment.

"It wasn't what I expected," she confessed.

He shrugged. "Maybe it isn't what you think. An old friend, perhaps."

She smiled weakly. "Yes, I suppose it could be. Or a work associate."

The driver hesitated, his lips taut. "It's always better to know the truth, is it not?"

A few minutes later, the taxi came to a stop. "Thank you so much," Emilie said. "For everything."

She paid the driver his partial fare, got out of the taxi, and went to the front door, not sure what to do. She had to be cautious—more than ever before. Jacques may not be the man she thought he was. But that would make it easier to betray him—as she had always known she must. Except now he might betray her first. Maybe it was a game they played, each pretending to be what they weren't, prepared to turn on the other. It was much more complicated than she had assumed. And as much as she didn't want to admit it, her life was about to change. She just wasn't sure how.

Louie Bassett had insisted she was in danger, but had offered no explanation. Maybe his warning referred to what she had just witnessed. Had she been given the address to open her eyes, so she saw what she never would have expected to see? Or was it a different danger, one that remained a mystery?

She entered the apartment, locking the door behind her. She paused in the foyer, looking in Jacques's study. It was the only room that might have answers to her questions. She knew his routine. He wouldn't be home for at least two hours. After a moment's hesitation, she went in his study, where she rarely ventured, not unless he was in it. She sat behind his desk and eyed his domain.

She opened the top drawer and looked through it. Pens, notepads, pencils, paper clips, an address book—typical of any office. She skimmed through the address book, not recognizing the names. She opened the drawers on the right. Filled with files, military papers depicting plans that might never be realized, different contingencies for war, efforts to continue regardless of battle conditions—all what she would expect from a man who was part of military intelligence. A quick glance at the documents proved her husband was far more involved in clandestine operations than she had ever imagined. The remaining drawers contained similar information but related to railroads—what she would find in his government office. After a quick review, she saw nothing to indicate who the woman was at #8 Rue Serpente.

She came out from behind the desk and scanned the office. Bookshelves were scattered along three walls, most filled with leather volumes, paintings of Napoleonic battles dressing the open space, all from her antique shop. She looked at some of the ornaments resting on the shelves, a miniature of Napoleon on his horse, a bust of Davout, one of the emperor's greatest generals. As she scanned the items, she noticed a thick leather volume, lying on its side on a shelf behind his desk. She didn't recognize it, even though the title *Napoleon's Battlefields*, was a volume that would have come from her shop.

She took the book from the shelf. It was surprisingly light. When she opened it, she found the text had been hollowed out. The open space contained folded documents marked secret, identity papers, forged and almost completed—missing only photographs with a few empty lines. But most surprising, were several stacks of currency in large denominations.

It was a lot of money, more than Jacques could ever earn in a lifetime.

CHAPTER 20

Ziegler got in the back of the staff car with Jacob Sternberg, Bayer driving. "Take us to Aaron Peeters' home."

"Turn right," Sternberg said, "and two blocks down, turn left."

Peeters' apartment was not far from Claudette Maes. It was a charming street, flower beds by the curb and in window boxes. But in the distance, two houses lay in ruins, victims of German air raids, bombs likely meant for the port.

As they got out of the car, Ziegler turned toward the main road. "This seems familiar."

"The exchange is only a block away," Sternberg said, pointing. "The thieves got in through a back entrance in the garden."

Ziegler looked up the street, trying to visualize the route the blonde woman had taken. He turned to Sternberg. "Let's see what Mr. Peeters has to say."

"I assure you he had nothing to do with the missing diamonds," Sternberg said, drawn and pale. "He knows I planned to give them to the Germans."

"We would have taken them anyway," Ziegler said curtly. "With no special treatment."

"Is this Herr Peeters' address?" Bayer asked as they approached the building.

"Yes," Sternberg said, looking like his world was ending. "He's on the first floor,"

The building was a few centuries old but well maintained, with a sweeping arch that led to the entrance. They entered, finding a tiled vestibule, and Sternberg took them to an apartment that faced the road.

"Mr. Peeters," Sternberg called as he knocked on the door.

It was opened a moment later by an elderly woman, slender, her white hair showing streaks of gray. "Mr. Sternberg," she said, her eyes wide when she saw the soldiers.

"Move," a soldier directed, pushing her out of the way.

"Aaron," the woman called, frightened. "Jacob Sternberg is here with German soldiers."

An older man came from a bedroom, slightly stooped, wearing a white shirt and red tie with a brown sleeveless sweater. Thick glasses with black rims were perched on his nose, his hair short and white.

"What's wrong?" he asked, confused.

"Aaron, the exchange has been robbed," Sternberg explained. "The industrial diamonds we had saved for the Germans were stolen."

"That's terrible," Peeters groaned, as if he understood the consequences. "When did this happen?"

"During the night," Sternberg replied. "When the Germans took the city."

Peeters blinked several times. "I know nothing about this."

"Were you the last to leave the exchange?" Sternberg asked.

The old man thought for a moment, but then nodded. "Yes, I was."

"Was the vault closed?" Ziegler asked, not introducing himself.

"It was," Peeters replied. "I check it every night before I go."

"Why are you here?" Mrs. Peeters asked, her voice trembling. "My husband has done nothing wrong."

Ziegler ignored her and fixed his gaze on her husband. "Did you lock the doors?"

"Yes, of course," Peeters said. "Why would I not lock the doors? I always do."

"Nothing unusual happened?" Ziegler asked.

Peeters thought for a moment and slowly shook his head. "No, not that I can recall. I locked the doors and walked home."

"Did you come straight home?" Ziegler asked.

"No, he stopped to get me hamantash," Mrs. Peeters said. "At the bakery on the corner."

"Cookies," Sternberg clarified to the Germans' confused looks.

Ziegler studied the older couple, trembling with pale faces. They knew nothing. He changed tactics. "You live close to the exchange," he said, his focus now on information.

"Yes, we do," Peeters nodded.

"Did you notice anything unusual that night, around eleven?" Ziegler asked.

Peeters glanced at his wife. "We were frightened. German soldiers were coming."

"Many of our neighbors had already left," Mrs. Peeters said. "We're one of the few who stayed."

Ziegler watched them closely, searching for signs of deception. "Did you see anyone suspicious, a civilian, maybe someone who didn't belong."

Peeters thought for a moment. "No, not that I remember."

"The young lady," Mrs. Peeters reminded him.

"What young lady?" Ziegler asked,

"Yes, we did see a young woman," Peeters said, as if he had just remembered. "We went out on the front stoop because of all the shouting, and she was running down the street."

"What did she look like?" Ziegler asked.

"She was young, blonde," Peeters said. "She got in a car."

"The soldiers fired at her when she drove away," Mrs. Peeters added.

Ziegler glanced at Bayer standing by the door. "Did she have anything with her?"

"Yes, a canvass bag and a smaller satchel," Mrs. Peeters said.

Ziegler turned to Sternberg. "Perhaps an Allied spy does exist. That would be very good for you."

Sternberg sighed audibly and glanced at Mr. and Mrs. Peeters. "No one at the bank would steal diamonds. I would bet my life on it."

Ziegler looked at Bayer and chuckled. "You are betting your life on it, Herr Sternberg. You just don't realize it."

Sternberg briefly closed his eyes, as if trying to will the nightmare away.

"What type of car did she drive?" Ziegler asked.

"It was green, I think," Peeters said. "A dark green."

Ziegler rolled his eyes. "What model car?" he asked loudly.

"It was a Minerva, I'm sure of that," Peeters stammered. "A few years old, maybe a '35 or '36."

"Did you see the license plate?" Ziegler asked.

Peeters slowly shook his head. "No, I didn't. But it was damaged, the automobile."

"How was it damaged?" Ziegler asked. "By bullets?"

"The back fender on the passenger's side was dented and scraped, and the back taillight was missing. And whatever damage the bullets did."

CHAPTER 21

Camille hesitated, not sure if she should share where she hid the Englishman, even if it was his house. Not with Germans just outside. She glanced at the half-empty bottle of whiskey, went to the window, and looked out, and then walked to the kitchen and did the same. She made sure the back door was locked. Not that it mattered.

"Check from my bedroom windows," Lucien said as she eyed the partially closed door.

She went in and looked out the windows. "No more Germans are coming. But a handful wait near the stream."

"They're camping for the night."

She paused. "They may come back at any time."

His eyes narrowed. "Where's the Englishman?"

"Come," she said.

She led him into the spare room, just past the threshold. They stood in the doorway, the empty couch to their right.

He glanced at the photograph on the wall for a moment, and then looked away, pain on his face. He sighed, studying the room. It took him a moment to notice.

"The two bookcases had flanked a closet door," she

explained. "I hid the Englishman in the closet, and slid the bookcases together."

"Brilliant," he said, moving his hand to rub the welt on his head. "I'm impressed."

"It's all I could think to do."

"It worked," he said, glancing at her curiously. "At least for now."

She slid the first bookcase far enough to expose the closet door. She opened it and the Englishman slumped on the floor. "Are you all right?" she asked, kneeling over him.

"Yes," he mumbled, barely conscious. "A bit thirsty."

"What's your name?" Lucien asked.

"Henry Green."

"We'll take good care of you, Henry," Camille promised. "Where are you from?"

"St. Albans," he said. "Just outside of London."

"London is a fabulous city," she said.

"Yes, it is ma'am."

Lucien studied her for a moment. "Have you ever been to London?"

She ignored him. "Lie down on the floor, Henry. But if the Germans come back, we have to rush you back in the closet."

Lucien went in the kitchen and got a glass of water. When he returned, he put the glass to Henry's lips and helped him drink.

"Are you in pain?" Camille asked.

Henry nodded. "I can't stand much more."

Lucien looked at his flush face. "The bullet has to come out," he said softly.

Camille glanced at Lucien. She suspected Henry Green would get worse with each hour that passed. "You can't do it with the Germans so close."

"We may have no choice."

Henry's eyes fluttered closed. He was losing strength.

"He's just a boy," Camille whispered. "Maybe twenty, not much more."

What are we going to do with him?"

"We have to hide him in the closet overnight."

He looked at her, perplexed. "Why are you here? Don't you have to go home?"

"How?" she asked tartly. "Should I run across fields filled with Germans?"

"Do you have a husband?" he asked bluntly.

"Is he going to die?" she asked, pointing at Henry.

Lucien touched his forehead. "We have to get him to a doctor."

"You're a doctor."

He frowned. "I was a doctor."

"You're still a doctor."

"I can't help him," he snapped.

She left the room and circled the house, checking all the windows. "The Germans will leave in the morning."

Lucien studied the bandaged leg, blood staining the gauze. "I can't be responsible for him—and I shouldn't have to be." He paused, glaring at her. "I can't be responsible for you, either."

"You're not even responsible for yourself," she muttered. "Will he last until morning?"

"I think so."

"They'll leave at dawn. They're moving quickly."

"The Allies retreat," he said. "The Germans trapped them."

"It's worse than you know," she said, and looked at Henry Green. "Can you give him something for the pain?"

Lucien opened his medical bag, removed a glass syringe, and drew medication into it. He stuck it into Henry's leg. "This should help him."

"I'll stay with him," she offered. "If the Germans come, I'll get him in the closet."

"We'll take turns," he offered. "We can't take chances. The Germans will kill us both if they find him."

They went in the parlor, looking from the window. The last of the Germans had stopped down the road and were setting camp for the night. Many more sprawled across distant fields, hundreds of them.

"In the morning they'll be gone," Camille said. "And the chase will continue. An occupation force will stay in Tournai."

He sat in the chair by the window, holding his throbbing head, a knot by his right temple. He picked up the bottle of whiskey, removed the cap and took a swig.

"To calm your nerves?" she asked. "Or ease the pain?"

Lucien didn't reply. He took another drink, and the tremor in his hands eased.

He took another swig. And then another.

CHAPTER 22

Emilie sat at an outdoor table in her favorite café on Boulevard Saint-Germain. She sipped her coffee, listening intently to Louie Bassett. She had told him about following Jacques, and what she had found in his study.

"Are you now convinced I am who I claim?' he asked.

She hesitated. "I'm more convinced than I was. I'll feel better when telephone lines are restored, and I can talk to my family."

"They will tell you that I'm your designated contact. It should come as no surprise. You knew this day was coming."

Her face firmed. "I did know this day would come. But I didn't know you would be part of it."

He eyed the patrons, his gaze shifting to passing pedestrians and traffic on the street. "Are you ready to cooperate?" he asked.

"I would prefer to speak to my family first."

He cocked his head. "Even with what you now know about your husband?"

At first, she didn't reply, reliving the image of Jacques hugging another woman. It could have been innocent. But not when combined with what she found in his study. "I was surprised he had a lover."

"It was something you needed to see."

Emilie tried to put the pieces together. "I never expected Jacques to betray me. But between the woman, identity papers, and money, it made me realize the possibility exists."

Louie frowned, eyeing a waiter with a hint of suspicion. "Sometimes we refuse to believe what we see."

"Perhaps I should have listened when you first approached me," she muttered, beginning to doubt herself.

"What was more persuasive, the mistress or the hidden documents?"

She sipped her coffee, eyeing those nearby. "The mistress and forged identity papers are personal—the physical descriptions match them perfectly. It's likely an affair. He leaves me, and they run away together. But the documents are political, and I suspect very valuable to the German war effort."

"What about the money?"

"It shocked me most," she said. "There's only one explanation. Jacques is selling secrets."

"I suspect he is. Regardless of his role in French intelligence, he would never have such huge sums of cash."

She nodded, forced to agree. "But he's so patriotic. It doesn't make any sense."

"He plays a role, just as you do. Part of the danger you face."

She still didn't understand what he meant. "I do have questions."

"As anyone would," he replied. "Some I can answer, some I cannot."

She paused, pensive. "Who has fake identity papers—for themselves and their mistress—unless they're involved in a sinister plot? Where did the money come from, especially large sums in different currencies? Did he accumulate it over time, or is it to aid his escape? What's in the sealed envelopes stamped secret?"

"Now you understand why we need to know all that he

does. And we need to know before he flees. This is why I approached you. Timing is important."

She glanced at a bus stopping across the street, students getting off to attend classes at the Sorbonne. "I knew someone would come. I just didn't know when."

"You are German," he reminded her. "And you were prepared to prove it. You've known since you met him that you might be forced to betray him. Now is the time."

She sipped her coffee, not sure how to proceed.

He watched her curiously. "You have doubts?"

She shrugged. "It's difficult to believe. I suspected nothing. I thought it would be hard to betray him—if the time ever came for me to do so. And all the while he planned to betray me."

"Now that you know, it makes it easier."

She didn't reply, eyeing a store across the street, a shop that sold radios. It was doing a brisk business.

"What else is your husband involved in?" he asked, leaning closer.

"I know a little," she admitted with some hesitation. "Something I overheard."

"I suspect you know more than you realize," he said, coaxing her.

Emilie knew it was time. She fixed her gaze on Louie and began. "A woman named Camille came to see him. She's French intelligence, stationed in Paris, but was in Tournai."

He leaned closer. "She's a contact?"

Emilie shook her head. "No, it was different. They didn't know each other. Jacques was expecting someone else, someone older, more experienced."

He eyed those nearby, ensuring no one listened. "We know Jacques is working on something critical, but we don't know what it is. What else did you hear?"

"He gave her an assignment in Antwerp."

Louie arched his eyebrows. "Diamonds?"

She nodded. "Something for radar. A cache of rare industrial diamonds."

Louie sat back in the chair. "The English were tasked with getting all diamonds out of Antwerp, not French intelligence. But some were left behind, the best of the best."

"It seems this woman Camille has unique talents, although I'm not sure what they are. She was supposed to meet a man named Roger—I think he was from London—get him into the vault, steal the diamonds, and take him to the port."

"How do you know Roger was from London?"

Emilie hesitated, recalling what she overheard. "I don't," she admitted. "I only heard Jacques say that he was taking the diamonds to London."

Louie eyed Emilie closely. "We have to find those diamonds, no matter what the cost."

"Will they impact the war?"

"Absolutely," he said. "They're critical, which is why everyone wants them."

"Do you think Camille has them?"

"Somebody does," he replied. "And she seems most likely. You need to get all the information you possibly can. The entire war hinges on your efforts."

Emilie sighed. "I suppose I have to betray Jacques before he betrays me."

CHAPTER 23

When they left Aaron Peeters' apartment, Major Ziegler released the two soldiers who had supported him. As they drove away on their motorcycle, he turned to Jacob Sternberg. "Would the diamonds fit in the trunk of a car?" he asked.

"They would fit in a satchel or a small duffel bag," Sternberg replied. "They're valuable for their quality, not the quantity."

"But Peeters said the woman carried two satchels," Ziegler said.

"Maybe her drill was in the smaller bag, sir," Bayer suggested. "And whatever else she needed to breach the vault."

Ziegler paused by the car. "Could Peeters have forgotten to close the vault?"

"No, he's very conscientious," Sternberg said.

"How about the blonde woman?" Ziegler asked. "Do you know who she was, maybe a competitor or former employee?"

"No, I don't," Sternberg replied. "Aaron would have recognized her if she was anyone we knew."

Ziegler pondered his next move. After a moment, he turned to Bayer. "We need to find that car."

"There are thousands of Minervas in Belgium, sir," Bayer said. "And probably hundreds just in Antwerp."

"But we're not looking for a Minerva. We're looking for a green Minerva, four years old, with the passenger side fender dented and scratched, missing a taillight."

"With the back riddled by bullets," Bayer added.

Ziegler turned to Sternberg. "I'm done with you, Herr Sternberg. You can go. You're very fortunate. I've decided not to hurt you."

They climbed in the car, leaving a stunned Jacob Sternberg standing on the pavement, wide-eyed and trembling.

Bayer started the engine and pulled away from the curb. "We can check government offices," he suggested, referring to the green Minerva.

Ziegler looked out the window as they drove back to headquarters, a hotel the Germans had commandeered along the river. "We have to hurry. She gets farther away each hour that passes."

"We can also contact the police," Bayer said. "Maybe there's a record of the car accident that caused the fender damage."

"But that might take days," Ziegler mumbled. "We only have hours."

"If you were the thief, what would you do, sir?" Bayer asked.

Ziegler thought for a moment. "We controlled most of the city when the robbery occurred. Escape would have been difficult."

"She could have taken advantage of the chaos."

"Or she might have remained in Antwerp, thinking we might search elsewhere."

"But someone is waiting for the diamonds," Bayer countered. "Either the Allies or a secret buyer. She had to flee to deliver them."

Ziegler was quiet for a moment. "Yes, the most likely

scenario, I agree. If she's a thief, she makes delivery to get paid. If she's a spy, someone waits for the diamonds."

"Maybe the business card I found will lead us in the right direction," Bayer said.

Ziegler removed it from his pocket. "All Things Napoleon," he said, reading the card. He flipped it over. "Jacques Dufort. And an address for the port."

"She couldn't have escaped by boat. We had already captured the port."

"Yes, perhaps," Ziegler mused. "Maybe this is unrelated trash, dropped by a janitor."

Bayer shrugged. "We may never know."

"I'll keep the card," he mumbled. "We'll find out who this Jacques Dufort is as soon as the phone lines are operating. Maybe he is the thief's contact."

"The port address suggests a delivery location," Bayer offered. "Maybe she didn't have to flee to make delivery. Someone may have waited right here in Antwerp."

Ziegler was quiet. His chances of catching the woman were dwindling. "We'll stop at the port on our way back to headquarters. Just to ask a few questions. But the car, and her vague description, are the only clues we have."

"Do you think this woman knew anyone at the exchange?"

"Not unless it's one of the employees who had already fled the city," Ziegler said. "Those we questioned weren't lying."

Bayer nodded. "They were terrified. None seemed like accomplices to a spy or thief—not the typical profile."

"The woman acted strangely, though," Ziegler mumbled. "Claudette Maes. She kept glancing toward her bedroom. We probably should have searched her apartment."

"Do you think she was hiding something?"

Ziegler sighed. "I'm not sure. Something wasn't right."

"We can always go back and question her."

"Yes, I suppose," Ziegler said, gazing out the window.

"Especially if she acted suspiciously. Something may have been hidden in her bedroom."

"We'll return if we don't find the car," Ziegler said. "And I won't be as kind the next time. Maybe I'll take her cat and see what she'll do to get him back."

Bayer chuckled. "That will make her talk, I'm sure."

Ziegler paused, thinking of the employees at the exchange. "Sternberg thought he could use the diamonds to buy protection."

"He lives in a world that no longer exists."

"But he's learning quickly," Ziegler said and then considered the crime scene. "This woman and the dead man still had to get into the vault somehow."

"Maybe they picked the lock," Bayer suggested. "Especially if they're common thieves."

"For now, that remains a mystery."

"How will we find her, sir?"

"I'll issue a radio bulletin for the woman and the car," Ziegler said. "I suspect she went south if she fled. There was a slender corridor she could have slithered through."

"She may have hidden among refugees, too. But even if she did escape and made it to Paris, she won't be safe for long. The city will fall within the week."

"You and I know that," Ziegler said, "and so does the German army. But those who oppose us do not. They think we're fighting the last war, about to construct miles of trenches. They don't realize that we don't intend to lose this time."

CHAPTER 24

"Can you climb out of the whiskey bottle?" Camille asked the following morning.

Lucien lifted his chin from his chest and blinked, his eyes offended by the light. "I must have dozed off," he muttered, rubbing his eyes. He sat in the same chair by the window where he had been the night before.

She handed him a cup of coffee. "Drink it black."

"I always do," he mumbled as he took the mug. He rubbed his hand across his face, rough from the shadow of a beard. He touched the knot on his head and winced.

She stood beside him, looking out the window, waiting for him to fully awaken, the ache in his head to subside.

"Are the Germans gone?" he asked, his voice raspy.

"Most of them."

He sat up straight, as if suddenly remembering their dilemma, and sipped the coffee. "What do you mean most of them?"

"Those in the fields and along the road left at dawn."

"There's more?"

"A half dozen are camped on the other side of the chicken

coop. Past where we found the British soldier, near the rusted troop truck from the last war."

He took another sip. "They didn't leave?"

"Not yet."

"What are they doing here?" he asked. "Waiting for someone?"

"Or searching for someone."

He looked at her, head cocked. "I don't understand. Who could they be looking for?"

Camille was about to reply but didn't. "He's still alive," she said, referring to the Englishman. "But he's very weak."

Lucien took another swig of coffee and stood, closing his eyes tightly.

"Your head must be pounding."

He nodded. "Not as bad as it was."

She watched him, more ghost than man. "You have to take the bullet out."

He rubbed his face with his hands. "I can't do it."

"He'll die if you don't."

"He may die if I do. The last time I tried to be a doctor, I lost two people I loved."

"An accident killed them," she argued. "And you couldn't save them. Nobody could. It doesn't make you less of a doctor. Or less of a man."

He blinked, as if he didn't expect the confrontation. "You know what happened?"

"Yes, I know what happened. You lost your wife and daughter. I feel for you, I really do. I wouldn't be able to cope either if our roles were reversed. But you can save the Englishman if you remove the bullet."

He sighed, wrestling with the past, as well as the present. "I don't think I can do it."

"At least you'll try," she said. "Or is that something you

forgot how to do? Why don't you drink some more whiskey? Maybe you'll find your courage."

Lucien ignored her. He drank the rest of his coffee and went into the kitchen. He drank a glass of water, and then another, and poured one more cup of coffee.

"He's still in there," she reminded him, pointing to the spare room. "And he's getting worse."

He closed his eyes for a moment, as if trying to will the problem away. "Have any Germans come near the house?"

"Not yet," Camille said. "But that doesn't mean they won't."

He went to the window, gazing at the chicken coop. "They're sitting around a campfire. It doesn't look like they're leaving."

"Henry Green is dying. We have to do something."

He took a long swallow of coffee, and then another, as if mentally preparing for a fight he didn't think he could win.

She watched him closely—his battle with the bottle that coffee couldn't cure. "Are you going to remove the bullet?" she asked, her hands on her hips. "Or should I?"

He closed his eyes and took a deep breath. "I'm no longer a doctor."

"You'll always be a doctor."

"Doctors don't kill people."

"No, they don't. God does."

He grimaced, the wound still fresh, the slice still deep. "I know you're trying to help. But you can't make me into something I'm not."

"Just be Dr. Lucien Bouchard."

"I'll fail you like I failed everyone else who ever trusted me," he mumbled. He sipped more coffee and stared at the Germans. "They don't look like they're searching for anyone."

"Go ask them if it's that important for you to know. Maybe they can give you another reason to pretend that Henry Green isn't dying."

He looked in her eyes, his gaze meeting hers. "It's not that easy."

"You're only avoiding what has to be done," she said. "I know it and so do you. Just as you've avoided each day that dawned for the last eighteen months."

Lucien closed his eyes and rubbed them with his fingers, like a blind man wishing for sight.

"Are you going to let him die?"

He was quiet. After a moment passed, he raised the cup to his lips and drained the contents. He put the cup in the sink and washed his hands very thoroughly, scrubbing them with soap and water. And then, with a deep breath, he walked to the spare room, but paused at the door, as if knowing what waited on the other side.

"Do you need your courage?" she asked, pointing at the whiskey bottle, almost empty.

He looked at the bottle and then at her. "Watch the Germans," he said. "Tell me if they move, even an inch."

He went into the spare room and shut the door behind him.

CHAPTER 25

Jacques Dufort leaned back on the park bench. It was a secluded location, twisting off the main path, used by birdwatchers and those who sought solitude. No one was nearby. He checked his watch, waiting for his contact.

A few minutes later, a slight figure approached, glancing over his shoulder as he came down the lane. Guy Barbier was more mystery than man, more fiction than fact. He was older, late fifties, with a harsh face and hawkish nose. Even with his diminutive stature, he instilled fear in whoever he chose—usually those who crossed him, but not always. Some claimed he was an integral part of the vast French intelligence apparatus. Others swore he was a swindler. But most were somewhere in between, suspecting he bought and sold secrets to those who were willing to pay. No one really knew for sure. And that's how Guy Barbier wanted it.

"Another day passes," Barbier said as he sat down.

Jacques cringed. He had failed—at least temporarily. "I know you expected delivery."

"We all did," Barbier said. "The diamonds are important. What happened?"

"We had a problem. But I'll get it fixed."

Barbier took a pack of cigarettes from his pocket, lit one, and blew the smoke away from Jacques. "This is our most critical task, Jacques. I gave it to you because you're the best."

"I'll get them, Guy, I promise."

Barbier eyed a bird for a moment, watching it on a tree branch. He took another drag of his cigarette. "Tell me what's going on."

Jacques hesitated, not sure how to explain. "Camille did get the diamonds."

"Then why aren't they in London?"

Jacques hated to make excuses, but he had no choice. "The Germans took Antwerp the day she got there."

"I know that, Jacques," Barbier said. "And so does the rest of the world."

"But it became more than a robbery after they arrived," Jacques said, trying not to whine. "They had to steal the diamonds *and* fight off the Germans."

Barbier sighed but seemed to agree. "Do you need help?"

Jacques hesitated. "No, not yet. I have Sophie."

"She'll think of something. She has contacts everywhere."

"We're working on a few different plans, some alternatives we can give to Camille the next time she contacts us."

"Do you know where she is now?"

"We think she's trapped in Belgium. She sent a message—said she has the diamonds but couldn't deliver them."

Barbier frowned. "The port must have already been captured. Is Roger with her?"

Jacques shrugged. "I don't know. The message was only a few short phrases, as if she was rushed."

"She probably was. But why not mention Roger?"

"I don't know," Jacques said. "I think it was just a quick update to tell us she has the diamonds but got no farther."

Barbier frowned. "We need to find out. Roger is a valuable asset."

"I will," Jacques replied. "As soon as Camille contacts us again."

"Maybe someone in Sophie's network can help."

"Sophie does have a contact in Antwerp, but she hasn't transmitted, either."

"Probably surrounded by Germans," Barbier muttered. "She hasn't had the chance."

"Camille's contingency plan was to bring the diamonds to Paris," Jacques said. "If we assume the port was captured, and the Germans already occupied northern France when she got there, she's likely hiding somewhere in Belgium, maybe Tournai."

"She probably is," Barbier agreed. "That was her last assignment."

"Once she contacts us again, and we get more details, we can help her."

"How much time do you need?"

Jacques shrugged. "I know it's important, Guy. But we can't do much until we hear from Camille."

Barbier nodded, as if he understood, and rose to go. "A few more days, Jacques. But no more. The diamonds are too valuable."

CHAPTER 26

Major Ziegler sat in the back of the staff car, watching Bayer talk to a group of men at Godefriduskaai 99, Pier #3. A fishing trawler, its paint faded and chipped, was docked on one side of the wharf, a tugboat on the other. After a ten-minute discussion, the men went back to their boats and Bayer returned.

"I have more information," he said as he climbed in the car. "Both boats were in Antwerp the evening we took the port."

"Did they have any passengers?" Ziegler asked.

"No, neither was at this location," Bayer replied. "The tugboat was docked at the next pier, the fishing trawler on the other side of the river."

"Did those in the tugboat see anything unusual?"

"Yes, they did. A woman approached near midnight and asked if the port was closed."

Ziegler leaned forward. "Was it the blonde in the green Minerva?"

"They didn't get a good look at her," Bayer replied. "But they told her that we controlled the port, and no one could get out. She then raced away."

"Was it a green Minerva?"

"They said it was a Minerva, dark, but not sure if it was green."

Ziegler frowned. "Did they know where she went?"

"She was trying to get out of Antwerp, but they told her it was likely too late."

"It was her," Ziegler said. "And she still could be here. If we find the car, we find her."

They spent the rest of the day gathering information on green Minervas from the police department and government agencies. Bayer took the list, not sorted in any way, and gave it to Ziegler.

"We'll start with those cars identified with damage," Ziegler said, scanning the report and giving it back to Bayer. "It's all we can do."

An hour later, they stood beside a green Minerva with a dent in the passenger's side door. It was parked on a side street facing the River Scheldt. "Who does it belong to?" Ziegler asked.

Bayer shuffled through the papers. "An elderly woman who works at a clothing store. She's a widow. Her husband died a few years ago."

Ziegler shook his head. "Enough," he said. "We can go. She has nothing to do with it. No bullet holes, either."

"The bullets may have missed," Bayer offered.

"This is the second car we've checked," Ziegler said, frowning. "And I'm sure there are more. But we're no closer to the diamonds than when we arrived."

Bayer thumbed through the report. "The local police assembled this. It isn't organized very well. Maybe we can eliminate some and investigate others."

"How many more are on the list?"

"Probably a hundred, twenty with known damage" Bayer said. "But it's for all of Belgium."

Ziegler was quiet, imagining what he would do if he had

stolen some of the rarest diamonds in the world. He would flee. By boat would be easiest, maybe to England or Sweden. But the port had been captured. The woman had to escape by land—or hide in Antwerp.

"The thief is probably long gone by now, sir," Bayer mumbled.

Ziegler was struck with another thought. "Maybe she wasn't from Antwerp and arrived only to get the diamonds. Are any stolen cars on the list?"

Bayer scanned the paperwork. "Yes, there are two."

"Where were they stolen from?"

"One in Brussels, the other in Antwerp."

"Has either been found?"

Bayer shrugged. "Refugees left cars all over Belgium when they ran out of petrol. But the police did have a report that one of the stolen cars has been found."

Ziegler was confused. "With so many abandoned automobiles, how did the police find this one?"

Bayer smiled. "The car belonged to the police chief's sister."

Ziegler's eyes narrowed. "Where did she live?"

"Near the zoo, not far from the diamond exchange."

"And it's green with a dented fender and broken taillight?"

"Yes, according to the reports."

Ziegler's interest was piqued. "Where was the car found?"

"Near the French border. Just west of Tournai."

Ziegler's eyes widened. "The business card you found on the floor. If we assume Paris was her destination, maybe that's as far as she got before she ran out of petrol. That's our thief."

CHAPTER 27

It took Lucien over an hour to remove the bullet, not including the time it took to keep his hands from shaking before he started. But somehow, he had managed to do it. The next day or two would be critical. Lucien wiped his hands with a rag and paused at the door. He took a deep breath, hoping he didn't look as bad as he felt, and went into the parlor.

Camille stood by the window, watching the Germans in the field. "How is he?"

"Weak," he said, not feeling very strong himself.

"Will he survive?" she asked, eyebrows arched.

He shrugged. "I don't know," he admitted, completely drained. "He's sleeping. I did the best I could."

A hint of compassion flickered across her face. "That's all anyone could ask."

"He's young," he said. "He doesn't deserve to die."

"Then pray that he lives."

Lucien nodded, wishing he could have done more, had a steadier hand, found the bullet easier, did less damage to the muscle, cleaned the wound better, made the stitches tighter— or any one of a dozen other tasks that would improve Henry

Green's chances of survival. "We should have found him a doctor."

"I did," Camille said.

"No," he said, closing his eyes and shaking his head. "You found me."

"You sheltered him and kept him alive," she said, her gaze still fixed on his. "Most would say that's brave."

"He deserved better," he mumbled, glancing at the whiskey bottle.

She saw him, her gaze following his. "One swig," she said. "But that is all. I need you sharp."

He nodded, not knowing why he needed her permission, but somehow understanding. He grabbed the bottle and took off the cap, took a long swallow, letting it burn all the way to his stomach. It felt good. He put the cap back on and set the bottle on the table.

She didn't say anything, only peered out the window. "The Germans are leaving."

He went and looked out. The soldiers stood in the field behind the chicken coop, close to the old French troop truck. They gathered their belongings. "I hope no more come."

"You did good," she said softly, lightly touching his arm.

"Thank you," he replied, wondering how he found the courage to remove a bullet from an Englishman's thigh. "But I can't pretend I'm a doctor again."

"But you are a doctor."

"No, I'm not," he said. "You weren't there when—"

"Take a shower," she said, interrupting him. "It will make you feel better."

"I don't want to feel better," he said, his stomach queasy.

"Then drink more whiskey. That makes everything go away, doesn't it?"

He sighed. "Why are you trying to make me something I'm not—and never will be."

"Sometimes we can't choose who we are or what we want to be. Like now."

"I don't need to be fixed. It's better if I stay broken. Then I won't harm anyone else."

"I'm not trying to fix you. I'm trying to save Henry Green. I need to do it through you."

Lucien looked at her strangely. She seemed so worldly and wise, yet somehow, she knew him, a doctor in the Belgian countryside who should have chosen to do something else with his life. "Where were you going when you stopped here?"

She studied him, as if wondering whether she could tell the truth. "Paris," she said. "But I couldn't get there. Now I have to stay until it's safe to leave."

He was confused. She was shrouded in mystery—and he had no clues. "Tell me what you're doing. And why you have to get to Paris."

"A German is coming," she hissed. "I'll get Henry into the closet."

A soldier walked toward the house. Lucien looked in the spare room, watching Camille ease the Englishman into the closet and slide the bookshelf in front of the door.

The knock came a moment later—more time than he expected. He made sure Camille was ready and walked closer to the door.

"Yes," he called as he crossed the parlor.

"*Öffne die Tür,*" a voice called. "Open the door."

"*Nur eine Minute,*" Camille called, coming from the spare room.

"What are you doing?" he hissed.

"Saving our lives," she whispered as she opened the door.

The soldier looked surprised, seeing an attractive woman who spoke German. "*Wasser?*" he asked, pointing into the kitchen.

"There's a pump outside," Lucien said. "Over by the barn."

The soldier looked at him quizzically.

"*Es gibt eine Pumpe bei der Scheune,*" Camille said. "There's a pump by the barn."

"*Danke,*" the German said nodding. "*Sie sind Deutsch?*"

"*Nein, aber meine großmutter war aus der Sch*weiz," Camille said. "No, but my grandmother was from Switzerland."

The soldier nodded and turned to go.

She closed the door. "They'll go once they fill their canteens."

"Where did you learn to speak German so perfectly?" he asked.

Noises came from the spare room, Henry stirring.

"Watch the Germans," Lucien said. "I'll check on him."

He went into the spare room, moved the bookshelf and opened the door.

"I'm feeling better," Henry muttered. "Weak, but better."

Camille came to the doorway. "Do you want anything, Henry?"

"Not just yet," he said. "I'm still groggy, a bit nauseous."

"You must be ready to hide quickly," Camille said.

Henry nodded. "I understand."

She went back in the parlor, over to the window to watch the Germans.

"Your wife is a wonderful woman," Henry said to Lucien. "I would have died if she hadn't told the sergeant about you."

Lucien looked in the parlor, where he could see Camille. Should he explain that she wasn't his wife, that he didn't even know who she was, that he had only met her a day before, a stranger who told him she had to get to Paris? Henry Green didn't need to know. Just as he didn't need to know that once, in what seemed so long ago, Lucien had a wife and a child.

"Do you have a bicycle?" Camille asked, appearing in the doorway again.

"Just outside the back door, leaning against the house."

"Your husband hides the bicycle?" Henry asked, grinning.

Lucien glanced at Camille and shrugged.

"He's full of secrets," she said with a disarming smile.

"Where are you going?' Lucien asked.

"I have to go into Tournai. As soon as the Germans go."

He hesitated. He was afraid she wouldn't come back. But he wasn't sure why.

"You need a gun," Henry said. "To be safe. Germans are everywhere."

"What good is a gun?" Lucien asked. "Thousands of Germans and a lone woman."

"Yes, exactly," Henry said. "A lone woman. Germans are capable of anything. They could—"

"You'll have to hide in the closet while I'm gone," Camille said, interrupting him. "Just in case more Germans come."

Henry smiled. "I'm starting to like it in there."

Lucien went into the parlor and motioned for Camille to follow. They stood at the window, watching the Germans walk down the road.

"I won't be long," she said.

He searched her face but saw nothing. "Are you sure you're coming back?"

"Yes," she replied, hiding a slight smile.

"Why would you want to?"

"I have reasons."

"Do you want a gun?" he asked, worried she wouldn't be safe.

She turned to look at him. "Do you have one?"

"Yes, a pistol," he said. "In my bedroom there is a safe in the closet, built into the wall. It has a combination lock."

She tilted her head. "I don't care where you keep it," she said. "Go get it."

He hesitated, not wanting to admit the truth. Not that it mattered. "I forgot the combination."

Camille sighed. "Maybe it's at the bottom of the whiskey bottle."

He was about to retort, but he didn't. She never said anything that wasn't true. He lived his life in a bottle. And he didn't want to come out. Life was too hard; it hurt too much. "Maybe," he admitted. "Or maybe I forgot it on purpose, the gun too tempting."

A sense of sadness flickered in her eyes. A moment later she went into his bedroom.

"You're wasting your time," he called. "I can't remember."

It was quiet, a few moments passing. He waited, wondering what she was doing. He looked at Henry, and then out the window to the Germans, disappearing down the road.

Camille emerged from the bedroom holding the pistol. "You don't have many bullets."

"How did you get that?" he asked in amazement.

"I'll only be an hour. Two at the most."

"Camille, how did you get that?" he asked again.

"Stay out of the bottle while I'm gone," she said, face taut. "Or should I take it with me?"

He looked at the bottle on the table, so tempting, knowing there was more in the kitchen cabinet. He wouldn't give it up. He had no reason to. And he couldn't, even if he wanted. Enemy or friend, he wasn't sure.

"Don't touch it," she said firmly as she walked out the back door, closing it behind her.

A moment later, Lucien watched her ride the bicycle down the road, a small suitcase on the handlebars. But he didn't know where she got it.

CHAPTER 28

"I received two messages," Sophie Silvain told Jacques as she opened the door to her apartment. "One from Camille, the other from Claudette Maes, my Antwerp contact."

"What did Camille say," Jacques asked, as they hurried up the steps. "Barbier is getting anxious."

"She's at a farmhouse near the French border."

Jacques pictured the geography, wondering where she might be. "Where did she transmit from?"

"A church steeple near Tournai."

Jacques sat on the sofa. "It's good she made contact, but we have to find a way to get her to Paris. Did she tell you what happened?"

"She had little time," Sophie said. "The Germans were close."

"Is Roger with her?"

Sophie sighed, a pained expression crossing her face. "Roger was killed at the diamond exchange. The Germans held the port, so she fled by car. She's trapped by the fighting, at least for now."

Jacques frowned. "Roger was a good man. I hate to lose him."

"I was able to confirm what happened through Claudette Maes—the Germans shot him."

"I suppose we have no reason to doubt Camille then."

Sophie looked at him curiously. "Did you ever?"

He shrugged. "No, not really. But I wanted to consider all possibilities."

"It gets worse," she said. "Claudette Maes said the Gestapo came to her apartment, looking for Roger's accomplice. They had a description of Camille. At first, they thought it was Claudette."

"Did she convince them she was innocent?"

"Yes, for now. But she's frightened. She said not to expect any messages until she's sure they no longer suspect her."

"They didn't arrest her, did they?"

"No, she convinced them she wasn't involved. But her transmitter was hidden in her bedroom closet while the Gestapo sat in her parlor. She was terrified they'd search her apartment."

Jacques frowned. "Too much risk for her. They could be back."

"She knows that. She hid her radio at her mother's house. But she'll be silent for a while, four to six weeks at least."

Jacques shook his head, the situation getting worse. "Did she say anything else?"

"The Gestapo is chasing Camille, a Major Ziegler. He's close, has a description of her car—a green Minerva with some damage to a rear fender." She hesitated, her face firm. "With bullet holes in the back."

Jacques' eyes widened. "Is Camille hurt?"

"She didn't mention any injuries in her message."

"Did you warn her about the Gestapo?"

"I couldn't," Sophie said. "Camille's message came first."

Jacques sighed. "It's worse than I thought," he said. "Claudette compromised, Roger dead, Camille in hiding with the Gestapo chasing her."

"At least she has the diamonds. And she's safe."

"But we don't know if she's safe. We have to warn her. Before it's too late."

"If she's in Tournai, she may have eluded the Gestapo."

"Not if she has the same car. They'll find her. She should keep moving."

"She can't get through the fighting. She's trapped in Tournai."

Jacques's face firmed. "We have to find a way to get those diamonds."

"France will fall in weeks if not sooner," Sophie said. "Camille may be waiting for the surrender before she moves south."

Jacques was quiet, trying to imagine what Camille was planning. "I'm sure she has contacts in Tournai. She was stationed there for two years. They can help her."

"So can we," Sophie said. "I told her that."

Jacques thought of the woman who had come to his apartment, easy to underestimate. "If anyone can get the diamonds to Paris, it's Camille."

"But she may not know the Gestapo are so close."

He hesitated, starting to feel desperate. "Those diamonds impact the entire war effort. We have to get them. And we have to do it quickly. We're running out of time."

CHAPTER 29

The green Minerva was parked off the road on the edge of a farm field. The rear fender was dented, scratches ran along the side, and the taillight was broken. It matched the description provided by Aaron Peeters, the elderly diamond exchange employee, with one important addition: the rear was riddled with bullet holes.

The German staff car pulled up behind it and Ziegler and Bayer got out. They walked around the car, trying to open the doors. They were locked.

"Should I break the window, sir?" Bayer asked.

Ziegler nodded. "We have no choice."

Bayer smashed the rear passenger window, unlocked the door, and looked through the car, including the boot. He was meticulous, combing underneath the seats, removing the spare tire from the well. After ten minutes, he finished.

"Nothing, sir."

"I didn't think so," Ziegler mumbled. "She's too smart."

"Why do you think she left it?" Bayer asked.

"Either she ran out of petrol or something malfunctioned."

"One of the bullets may have done damage."

Ziegler scanned the surrounding countryside. Farm fields

stretched into the distance; slender streams fed the River Scheldt that flowed northeast to the sea. A village was perched at the end of the highway, barely visible, a church steeple poking the clouds. Tournai, home to the Notre Dame Cathedral, its five towers dwarfing neighboring buildings, sat on the southeast horizon.

Bayer pointed across farm fields. A handful of Germans were marching down a rural road. "Troops moving south."

"Into France, which will fall in days," Ziegler said. "England will follow."

They were quiet for a moment, studying crops in the fields, birds above, chirping at the intrusion. It was quiet, obscenely so, given that war ravaged the country. But the fighting had come and gone through this part of Belgium. It now served as a crossroad for German troops moving south and west.

"Where could she have gone?" Ziegler asked, eyeing the southern horizon.

"Someone could have given her a ride, maybe an accomplice," Bayer offered.

"It's a strange location to meet if she did have an accomplice," Ziegler muttered, eyeing the stream. "Unless she left by boat."

Bayer scanned the terrain. "I see nothing but farms. Maybe she went to the village or city beyond."

"She would have carried the diamonds," Ziegler said.

"And whatever baggage she had. She couldn't have gone too far."

Ziegler hesitated. "Sternberg said the diamonds would fit in a satchel. If she had one suitcase, or even a duffel bag, she could manage."

"If she had an accomplice who came by boat or car, it'll be difficult for us to find her."

"We're closer, but still far away."

"Fighting rages to the south," Bayer said.

Ziegler nodded. "Assuming she left Antwerp when the diamonds were stolen, even this area saw heavy fighting—the Allies retreating, our armies advancing."

"She's fortunate she got this far."

"Let's see if the nearby houses are occupied. Maybe they saw her."

"We can start with the farmhouse across the road, sir."

They left the staff car where it was, crossed the street and went down a winding drive to a stone farmhouse. Livestock wandered a pen to their left, goats and a cow, a chicken coop behind it. A barn in the back was in disrepair, wooden shingles cracked and rotting.

"It looks deserted," Bayer observed.

"Maybe the owners fled when the fighting began."

Bayer knocked on the door, but there was no reply. He knocked louder, and then tried the doorknob. It was locked.

"Break it down," Ziegler ordered.

Bayer kicked the door. The jamb splintered and the door swung open. He entered, his machine gun over his shoulder, and checked the interior. "It's empty," he announced a moment later.

Ziegler followed. It was a cramped cottage, family photographs on the wall, a young couple with two small children—a boy and a girl. It was clean and functional, home to hard-working people who earned a living but not much more.

They went into each room, the furniture just as the family had left it. In the kitchen, glasses sat on the counter next to a basket filled with apples, some cucumbers lying by the sink.

"They left in a hurry," Bayer said. "And they haven't been gone long. The fruit is still fresh."

"Why leave it?" Ziegler asked. "Unless they expect to return."

"Maybe they're not refugees," Bayer said. "Maybe they went to Tournai, or they're with relatives nearby."

"Perhaps," Ziegler muttered. "There's nowhere else for them to go."

"Do you want anything here?"

Ziegler shook his head. "Innocent people in the war's path. Nothing more. Let's go. We have a half dozen farmhouses and the village to check."

"The road in the distance that winds south has an isolated cottage or two, not much more."

They left the house, making sure the door could close with the splintered jamb, and went to the staff car. Ziegler paused, studying the terrain.

"What is it, Major?"

Ziegler looked at the livestock and listened to the chickens cackling. "Feed the animals before we go."

CHAPTER 30

Lucien watched Germans coming down the road. Troop trucks formed a line in the distance, on the crossroad that led to the highway. They were moving to the west, chasing remnants of the Allied army. Other trucks rumbled south, into France.

When they were gone, only specks on the horizon, he made some chicken broth for Henry, and brought it into the spare room. "This will make you feel better."

"I'm starting to get an appetite," Henry said as he took the cup. He leaned against the wall and took a sip. "This is good."

"The Germans left," Lucien said. "But I want to make sure no more are coming."

He went into the parlor and looked out the window that faced the stream. He wondered why Camille stayed at the window, studying the Germans so intently. With the drapes opened they could easily be seen from most of the cottage. Unless she watched something else. Or maybe she was afraid that one would stray from the remainder and approach without being seen. If they found the Englishman, the Nazis would kill them all, and she was a young woman with her whole life to live. Henry Green was barely a man. His life was before him, too. He would father children and carry his family's name through another generation. But Lucien had nothing left in his life. Every decision he ever made had been wrong, and he had paid dearly for it.

After a few minutes passed, he heard vehicles. He peeked out the front window and saw troop trucks coming from Tournai, moving toward the highway where they could go faster. After they passed, more Germans came on foot, marching to the next battle.

Lucien had to hide the Englishman. After looking out the window and making sure no Germans approached, he hurried into the spare room.

"Henry, you have to get back in the closet," he said. "Germans are just outside."

"Of course," the Englishman said. He eased into the closet with Lucien's help.

"Be still," Lucien said as he closed the door and slid the bookcase in front of the closet.

He went into the parlor and looked out the window. There were many Germans now. But they moved quickly; they were not stopping. Belgium was not their destination. It was only a means of getting there.

The bottle of whiskey sat on the table, almost empty, only a half dozen swigs remaining. It was silly to let it sit there. He peeked out the window. The Germans continued down the road, over the bridge that spanned the stream. He picked up the bottle and removed the cap, taking a long sip, feeling it burn down his throat to his stomach.

Lucien wondered if Camille would return. He would not if he were in her place. Why should she? Why get involved with a broken man and an Englishman with a gunshot wound in his leg, surrounded by a sea of Germans. She said she had gone to Tournai. Maybe the Germans bypassed the city, waiting while it withered and died.

He took another swig, a long, slow swallow. It made him feel better. It always did. It dulled yesterday, tempered today, and made tomorrow not seem as painful. He took another swig, and then finished what was left in the bottle.

When he took the empty bottle into the kitchen, he noticed the Germans were gone. The last of the vehicles had passed, the dust still visible far down the road, some on foot following. No more French planes, or British soldiers, or even Belgian soldiers. Only Germans. But now they too had gone.

He opened the kitchen cabinet and got another bottle, the last one he had. He opened it and took a swig, feeling much stronger, his senses starting to dull. He went into the parlor and put the bottle on the table.

Lucien opened the front door and looked out. Far to the east he could see more vehicles, coming quickly. But other than that, the fields were deserted. Even the refugees had gone, filled with fear but in a different location. He went inside and closed the door.

He sat in the chair by the window, removed the cap from the bottle, and took another sip. The Englishman slept, still in pain, but the bullet removed. Lucien was amazed he had been able to do it, especially without killing him. But he had gotten through it. He doubted he could ever do it again.

He was drowsy, tired by the lingering hours of afternoon and all the excitement that had come and gone. He felt his eyelids closing. He dreamed, but he wasn't sure of what, only an insistent tapping he couldn't explain. It got louder and louder, until he started to waken.

The door burst open, and a German soldier barged in, a machine gun pointing into the room. "*Hast du mich nicht klopfen hören?*" he shouted. "Didn't you hear me knocking?"

Lucien blinked and sat up, his hands in the air. He wasn't sure what the German said, but he could guess. "I'm sorry," he said. "I was sleeping."

"*Bist du allein?*" the German asked, eyeing the whiskey. "Are you alone?"

Lucien looked at him, his mind not clear, unable to understand. "It's just me," he said.

A muffled cry came from the spare bedroom.

CHAPTER 31

Emilie Dufort waited at a café around the corner from All Things Napoleon. She sat at an indoor table, near the back, partially hidden by a half wall that led to a side entrance. She sipped her coffee, plotting what she would do next. So much had happened in so short a time—some expected, some not.

It was time to choose sides. She had been prepared, knowing the day would come, but still not ready when it arrived. She had hoped to spend the war as an innocent Parisian shopkeeper in a store she loved. But her family, and those they associated with, demanded more. It seemed that Louie Bassett was the vehicle to drive her to that destination. He sought her help, but she wasn't yet sure if it was limited to exposing her husband's web of deceit or if he wanted more. And although she didn't know what to do, she suspected the decision would be made for her.

Louie Bassett arrived a few minutes later. He ordered coffee at the counter and studied each patron he passed on the way to Emilie's table. "Good morning," he said.

"How are you today?" she asked, wondering what he might want.

"I'm well," he said as he sat beside her. He glanced around the café, making sure no one watched or listened. He leaned closer. "I have something for you."

She was leery. "What is it?"

"It's a camera."

She hesitated. "I don't know if I can use it."

"Why not?" he asked, eyebrows arched.

"Eavesdropping on a conversation or looking through Jacques' study doesn't seem as sinister as photographing what I find."

He was quiet, sipping his coffee. "But I need proof. I suspect your husband knows much more than military secrets. He was never assigned the theft of the Antwerp diamonds. He did that on his own, probably for some unknown buyer."

"Are you certain he's stealing them?"

Louie nodded. "With a few trusted associates."

"The woman?"

"Yes, she's definitely involved. Maybe others, too."

Emilie was quiet for a moment, reflecting on a marriage she thought had been good. "I suppose the time has come for me to betray him."

"Hasn't he betrayed you?" Louie asked. "In more ways than one?"

She sighed, her questions still unanswered. "You claim I'm in danger. But you never told me why."

"You're German," he whispered. "With family at high levels of the Nazi Party. If your husband becomes compromised, and we're fairly certain he is, and he's caught, he might offer you in trade to secure his freedom?"

Emilie looked at him curiously. He wasn't making sense. "Jacques doesn't know I'm German."

"He's an intelligence operative," Louie scoffed. "Believe me, he knows."

It was something she hadn't considered. Jacques must know

where she came from. It was easy enough to find. Louie was right. She was in a precarious position. "Why should I keep helping you?" she asked tentatively. "I could make it worse. Especially if he suspects something."

"Because it must be done," he replied firmly.

She paused. "I don't know what else I can do."

"For now, photograph documents. If the Germans come, you can do more. You can spy for them."

Her eyes widened. "I struggle to do what you ask now. I can't betray neighbors and friends."

He hesitated. "Start with photographs." He looked at those nearby and, when satisfied they weren't watching, he handed her the camera.

"It's tiny," she said, holding it in her hand below the table.

"Eight by eleven millimeters, a Minox Riga."

"German?" she asked.

He nodded. "They're the best."

"What will I do if someone asks why I have a German camera?"

He shrugged. "It's two years old. Something you bought before the war."

"It's risky. Don't you have a French camera?"

"Not as good as this."

She studied those nearby and eased the camera into her pocketbook, under a cosmetic case. Jacques would never look in her purse.

"When can you photograph the documents hidden in his study?" Louie asked.

"I'll try to do it tonight."

"Take a photo of the money, too. And the fake identity papers."

"If they're still there," she said. "He may have given it all to his lover, or one of the contacts who come to see him."

Louie sipped his coffee, watching a policeman direct traffic on the street. "If you can get close enough, listen to his conversations. Whether it's on the telephone or with a visitor."

Emilie sighed. "It's not that easy. Even when Camille came, I only overheard fragments."

"But even a fragment can be valuable. Especially if it's about Camille. We have to get the diamonds before anyone else."

CHAPTER 32

Major Ziegler leaned on the hood of his staff car, eyeing the small Belgian village. Sergeant Bayer was asking residents about the woman who stole the diamonds and the abandoned green Minerva. He spoke French, it was easier for him. People weren't as intimidated when he approached, they spoke more freely. It was different when an officer like Ziegler loomed over the interrogation—the fear showed in their eyes, their faces paled, their voices quivered.

On their way to the village, they had questioned residents of two farmhouses. The farmers knew nothing, saw no one, offered little. But they lived simply, farming their land, raising their families. They had no reason to suspect a diamond thief might be among them. A third farmhouse had been empty. It was closest to the abandoned car and the residents would have likely seen something. Perhaps another visit if no other clues were found.

Ziegler watched as Bayer asked questions. Most shook their heads in response. It was difficult. Many young blonde women lived in Belgium. The description fit thousands and, unless linked to the car or unusual behavior, his efforts were futile. But Ziegler knew they were close. The green Minerva was driven by the thief—he was sure of it. And he suspected she hadn't gotten far.

A dozen German soldiers passed through the village, some pausing to visit shops or stores. Troops constantly moved, supporting battles and occupation of conquered territories. Some of the town was still empty, stores closed and boarded up, prepared for bombing that never came. The fighting had eluded the village. Once dormant, it now began to awaken. Those who had fled were returning, as in much of Belgium— except for the coast where the fighting continued. The battle had advanced faster than the refugees, overtaking them, and now they were behind the front lines. It was safer to return to their homes, even though a different master reigned and life would not be the same as when they had left.

Ziegler liked the village. It reminded him of his childhood. He admired the old buildings, some begging for paint, with crooked rooflines and smudged windows. A collection of shops and stores centered around a town square, where people sat on benches and children played. He left the staff car and wandered down the pavement, glancing at goods in windows, pausing to buy chocolate, amused when passing pedestrians avoided eye contact.

He went to a café, the outdoor tables facing the square. He sat down and ordered a coffee. The owner served him but avoided conversation. Ziegler was not surprised. He sipped his coffee, watching residents as they passed on the pavement or lingered in the park. Two boys played soccer, and he smiled as he watched, thinking of his sons when they were young. He wondered where they were, both in the army, somewhere in Norway. At least they were away from the fighting, their lives not in jeopardy each day that dawned, like so many other young men throughout Europe.

An older woman passed with a dog on a leash, a brown shepherd with a lovely coat, highlighted by patches of black fur.

The dog was young, no longer a puppy but not much older, and inquisitive, looking at all he saw with more than passing interest. The woman turned away when she saw Ziegler. She faced the park to avoid him and continued down the pavement.

He wasn't deterred. "That's a handsome dog," he said, rising from the table.

The woman stopped, fright in her eyes. She couldn't understand German and feared she had done something wrong.

"May I pet him?" Ziegler asked, smiling to put her at ease. He motioned with his hand to define his request.

She nodded, still afraid, expecting the worst.

Ziegler reached out. The dog playfully responded, wiggling his back end, pleased to have a new friend. He knelt, petting the puppy's face and head. "He's a good boy."

The woman forced a smile, her expression not as anxious.

The dog licked Ziegler's hand. "He likes me," he said, laughing. He fussed with the dog for a several minutes, exhibiting a behavior few ever saw—the real man and not the mask. "Thank you," he said, nodding to the woman as he rose. "He's a wonderful dog. I enjoyed getting to know him."

She smiled curiously and continued on her way. The only positive experience she would ever have with the Gestapo had quickly come and gone.

Ziegler returned to his seat. He sipped his coffee, scanning the town. His thoughts returned to the blonde woman and where she may have gone. Maybe she was in the village, watching him from a second-floor window, wondering what his intentions were. Or maybe she had gone, destination unknown. Two rural roads led into the village, the main highway brushing beside it, passing on the outskirts. If his assumption was correct, and the deserted Minerva belonged to her, she couldn't have gone far, carrying a satchel and luggage—especially with combat raging.

He took a map from his pocket and laid it on the table. A

road parallel to the highway, where the Minerva had been abandoned, looked promising. A few kilometers away, closer as it neared the village, it wound south into France. The stream cut through the road and the highway; two arch bridges built of stone spanned the distance. Again, he wondered if she had a boat hidden under the bridge, waiting for her arrival. She could have left the car on the side of the road, loaded her satchels, and traveled south via streams and canals, at least for a few kilometers.

 He assumed she was going to Paris. But how would she get there?

CHAPTER 33

"*Was war das für ein Geräusch?*" the soldier asked. He lowered his machine gun, eyes wide. "What was that noise?"

Lucien shrugged, his heart racing. "I didn't hear anything," he said, even though he did. He rose from the chair, lowered his hands, and took a step toward the soldier.

The German turned, pointing his gun, fear on his face. Lucien stopped. The German shook his head, a signal for him not to move. The soldier eased toward the spare room. He took a step, paused, and took another.

"I swear I'm alone," Lucien said loudly—a bit too loud.

The German eyed him sternly, demanding silence.

Lucien kept his arms raised. He couldn't let the German in the spare room. But he didn't know how to stop him.

The soldier took another step. He paused, only a few feet from the door, listening. It was quiet. He took another step.

"*Was ist los?*" said a female voice from the kitchen. "What's the matter?"

Lucien was startled. So was the German. They turned toward the kitchen. Camille stood, head cocked, with an innocent smile.

"Who are you?" the soldier asked in German.

"His wife," she said, still speaking German. "I just came in."

The German looked at her. He was confused by the noise, not expecting the language she spoke. He paused by the spare room.

"She was out on her bicycle," Lucien said. He was surprised Camille came back. Why would she? "Our friends live nearby. She wanted to make sure they were safe. She made the noise you heard."

The German didn't understand. He seemed to grasp a few words, maybe enough to guess what was said. He relaxed, but just a little. But he didn't lower the rifle.

Camille stepped forward. "You heard a noise?"

The German didn't reply. He glanced in the spare room, finding it empty, and watched Camille approach. He pointed the machine gun at her, signaling her to stop.

She ignored him and walked into the parlor, not afraid. "Sorry to trouble you."

The German eyed her suspiciously. He stepped back towards the entrance, but faced them, his machine gun still ready.

Camille went to the table and picked up the bottle of whiskey. She handed it to the German. "Please, take this."

The German studied the bottle in her outstretched hand. There was an awkward pause while neither spoke. He lowered his weapon and took the whiskey. "*Danke*," he said.

Camille nodded and smiled.

The German walked out. Camille closed the door behind him.

"You gave him my whiskey," Lucien protested.

"No, I gave him your soul," she muttered.

"It was my last bottle."

"Better for you than him."

He glared at her, wondering why she had returned. "I didn't think you would come back?"

"Check on the Englishman," she said curtly. "I'll watch the Germans."

"How many are there?" he asked, moving to the window.

"Most have already passed, few are stopping."

"What will we do with the Englishman?"

"Make sure he's all right," she said. "And then I'll tell you."

CHAPTER 34

Jacques Dufort opened the door of his Parisian apartment and glanced out at a dark street. No lights could be seen, window shades drawn; no vehicles were on the road. Paris was at war, bracing for an attack that could arrive in minutes.

"Come in," he said to his visitor. "I had to see you. Sophie got two radio messages, one from a contact in Antwerp, the other from Camille."

Guy Barbier was dressed in black pants and jacket, a white shirt with no tie. He came in the foyer, glanced in the parlor, and went straight in Jacques's study. A frequent visitor, but usually during the day when Emilie was at her store, he sat in front of the desk, a dim floor lamp lit, curtains pulled closed.

"Is Emilie home?" Barbier asked.

Jacques nodded. "She's in the bedroom. She won't bother us."

Barbier frowned. "You need to be careful," he said, and then paused. "For a lot of different reasons."

"I know," he said. "It's all part of the plan."

"Just make sure it is," Barbier said cryptically.

Jacques sat behind his desk and took some documents from a drawer. He wasn't interested in discussing Emilie. She and

Barbier had a mutual disdain for each other. He didn't know why, and he really didn't care. "I have some papers for you."

Barbier took the documents and scanned the first few. "Good, just in time," he said. He rolled them up and stuck them in the inner pocket of his jacket.

Jacques hesitated. "Much has happened since we last talked."

Barbier gave him a guarded glance. "It doesn't seem good."

Jacques sighed, not sure where to begin. "No, it isn't."

"Roger?"

Jacques fixed his gaze on Barbier's. "He's dead."

Barbier frowned. "I was afraid of that. Do you know what happened?"

"The Germans killed him at the exchange. Camille escaped with the diamonds. As far as we know, she wasn't injured."

Barbier shook his head. "He'll be missed," he mumbled. "One of our best. Are you sure he's dead? Camille escaped. She may not know for sure."

Jacques nodded. "Sophie's contact in Antwerp confirmed it."

Barbier sighed and sat back in the chair. His gaze wandered the room, eyeing some of the collectables that came from Emilie's shop. "Did her contact know anything else?"

"Yes, she did," Jacques replied, his face grim. "The Gestapo are after Camille. They have her description, and they know the car she was driving."

Barbier frowned. "That's not good. They could be close. Did you warn her?"

"Not yet," Jacques replied. "I couldn't. We got the information after she had already messaged."

Barbier slowly shook his head. "I don't like this at all. It adds risk and uncertainty that we're not prepared for. Camille is in serious trouble, and she doesn't know it. And we have no way of telling her."

"I can't message her," Jacques said. "Not unless she's waiting for it. We could expose her."

"Where is she?"

"She's hiding on a farm near Tournai."

"Does she have the diamonds with her, or did she hide them?"

"She didn't say. But if she hid them, they're in a good place."

Barbier paused, his face firm. "We can't let anyone get those diamonds. Did you ask if she needs help?"

"Not yet," Jacques replied. "Sophie has contacts finding ways to help her get to Paris. But don't underestimate Camille. If anyone can do it, it's her."

"Except she has a huge problem."

Jacques nodded. "The front line is between us and Tournai."

"But getting closer to us every day," Barbier mumbled. "What does she intend to do?"

"I'm not sure. I suspect she'll hide in Belgium until she can get through. No one thought the Germans would advance so quickly, including her."

"But they did," Barbier said. "She has to get the diamonds to us. The sooner the better. We can't risk having them fall into the wrong hands."

"We don't know her situation, either," Jacques said. "She could be in serious danger, worse every day, or she could be safe, waiting for the opportunity to come south."

Barbier paused, glancing at a Napoleon bust on a shelf, and then fixing his gaze on Jacques. "She won't have to wait long. The government is evacuating Paris in a few days. It's the beginning of the end for France."

CHAPTER 35

Sergeant Bayer questioned residents in the village, stopping those that came through the town square. He glanced back at the café, Ziegler playing with a passing dog, then sipping his espresso. In the years since he had been assigned to the major, he still didn't feel like he knew him. He could be a vicious man—shown by his treatment of Jacob Sternberg. But he was sometimes compassionate, feeding livestock on an abandoned farm, ensuring a broken door was closed. He was an enigma, a man who detested humans but loved animals. Bayer could never guess which man would surface next—the cruel Gestapo major or the country gentleman, kind and compassionate, considerate of others.

Bayer got little information from those that walked through town. He entered a pharmacy, finding an older man with round spectacles behind the counter. He watched Bayer closely, a frightened look on his face. But his lips were firm, as if he tried to be brave.

"Have you seen a young blonde woman, a stranger, carrying a satchel or duffel bag, along with some other luggage?" Bayer asked.

The pharmacist shrugged meekly. "There are many blonde

women who passed through town. Most fleeing for somewhere else."

Bayer realized it wasn't much of a description—especially with all the refugees. But it was all he had. "Did you see any women that you know, maybe someone who lives nearby?"

The pharmacist shrugged. "I wasn't really watching," he admitted. "I've been worried about my own family and my employees."

Bayer nodded and turned to go. Why would people notice a stranger with baggage in a sea of refugees? Especially when they had loved ones to protect. But when his hand was on the doorknob, the pharmacist spoke.

"Wait, just a minute, sir," he said.

Bayer turned to face him, smiling faintly to put the man at ease. "What is it?"

"I did see a blonde woman on a bicycle. I've seen her before, but not lately."

"When was the last time you saw her if she was someone you've seen before?"

The pharmacist shrugged. "Before today it's been six months, maybe more. I think she used to live nearby. But maybe not now."

"Was she carrying a satchel?"

He shook his head slowly. "No, not a satchel. She had a rugged suitcase on her handlebars, not very big."

Bayer was quiet, wondering if it was relevant. "Where did she go?"

The pharmacist pointed across the town square. "She took her suitcase into the church."

Bayer nodded, dismissing the observation. "Thank you," he said, and again turned to go.

"Sergeant," the pharmacist continued. "I saw her up in the steeple." He pointed to the church spire. "All the way at the top."

Bayer raised his eyebrows. "What was she doing in the church steeple?" he asked, although he suspected he already knew.

The pharmacist shrugged and chuckled nervously. "I don't know. I wondered myself."

"How long ago was this?"

"Maybe an hour, two at the most."

Bayer looked at the church. "Thank you, sir. I appreciate your help."

He walked across the square, walkways wandering through scattered beds of flowers, shrubs, and trees. A young couple sat on a bench, whispering among themselves. Their eyes widened as he approached.

"Do you live in this town?" he asked.

The man glanced at the woman, as if wondering what to say. "Yes, we do."

"Did you flee with the refugees?"

"For a bit," the man replied. "We made it about twenty miles. But the Germans went past us, so we came back home."

"Have you seen a blonde woman carrying a satchel?"

The woman shrugged. "So many refugees have come through."

Bayer nodded. "How about a blonde woman who once lived here, maybe someone you haven't seen for a while?"

They were quiet. Bayer couldn't tell if they were hiding something. Or maybe they were just frightened. A blonde woman wasn't much of a description. But that's all he knew to ask.

"I'm sorry," the man said, shaking his head.

Bayer turned to the church. "Did you see a blonde woman on a bicycle stop at the church an hour ago? She would have been carrying a rugged suitcase, not very large. I'm told she went up in the steeple, the arched window by the bell."

The woman's eyes widened, but she quickly averted her gaze from Bayer to her partner. "No, I didn't."

The man shrugged. "Not that I remember," he replied. "But as I said, many refugees are now returning. We may not have noticed her."

Bayer studied them a moment more, fear housed in their eyes. "Thank you," he said, walking away. He took no pleasure in scaring innocent people.

Even when they failed to tell the truth.

CHAPTER 36

Camille watched from the window as the last of the Germans filtered past. They moved quickly, down the dirt lane that had been deserted a month before, soon to be deserted again. She went out the front door and stood in the yard, looking in both directions. More Germans were coming down the road, but farther away. She went back in the house and into the spare room.

"He's not doing as well as I had hoped," Lucien said as she entered.

Henry Green was sprawled on the floor. He had been asleep in the closet, crouched up against the door.

"What's wrong?" Camille asked, looking at the Englishman. She went to the window, watching the enemy approach. "He was fine when I left."

"He's warm, a fever. Maybe infection."

"Be careful," she warned, still at the window. "More Germans."

"Where are they?"

"Coming down the road."

"Are they stopping?"

She looked closer. "No, but some are walking across your farm."

"Keep watching."

"What will you do with him?"

Lucien looked at Henry sprawled on his floor. "He needs a doctor," he said. "Someone who can help him."

"You're a doctor. You can help him."

"No, I can't," he said and stood, gazing around the room. He went to the doorway, looking at the other rooms.

"The whiskey bottle has no answers."

He frowned. "You gave the German my last bottle."

"You don't need it."

"No, I don't need it. But I want it."

She ignored him and glanced at Henry. "Will he live?"

"I don't know. He needs medicine."

"I thought you had some," she said.

He shook his head. "I do, but not what he needs."

"Can you get it?"

He shrugged. "I don't know how."

"At a pharmacy."

"Not now," he said. "The world is collapsing."

She watched him for a moment, feeling pity for a destroyed man. "If you could only be what you once were."

"I'll never be what I once was," he said. "It's better for the world that way."

"When you forgive yourself, life will begin again. But not before."

"Water," Henry gasped, his eyes fluttering open.

"Just a minute," Lucien said, as he hurried to the kitchen.

"You'll be all right," Camille assured him, her eyes trained on the Germans outside the window. "A few more days."

"I feel weaker," he whispered. "Like I might not have a few more days."

"I have water for you," Lucien said, coming back into the room.

He knelt beside the Englishman, lifted his head, and helped him drink.

"I'm burning up," Henry whispered.

"I brought a moist cloth," Lucien said. He folded it and laid it on his forehead.

"We have to hide you again," Camille said. "The road is filling with Germans. They're slowing down."

"All right," Henry said, trying to rise.

"Let me help you," Lucien offered.

He eased Henry into the closet, made sure he was comfortable, and laid the moist cloth on his head. "You have to be quiet," he said. "Just until the Germans are gone."

Henry nodded, his eyes drifting closed.

Lucien glanced at Camille, cringing. He closed the closet door and slid the bookcase in front of it.

"I'll stay here," Camille said. "Maybe you should watch from the other window."

Lucien wasn't listening. "Let me check my medical bag," he said. "I think I have something that might help. Not the best, but better than nothing."

The bag was on the floor beside the sofa. Lucien rummaged through it, not finding what he wanted. He started to empty the bag. At the bottom, he found a glass vial. He withdrew it, eyed the label, and returned the rest of the contents to the bag.

"These pills will help him," he said.

"Germans are everywhere," she warned.

"I need to give him this," Lucien said, starting to move the bookcase.

"No, not now," she said. "They're just outside the window."

Lucien sighed, frustrated. They couldn't hide him forever. "I thought you had a plan, something we could do with the Englishman."

"I do," she assured him.

"What is it?" he asked. "Because it's no longer a question of whether the Germans will find him—it's a question of when. Assuming he lives."

She eyed him closely, her thoughts elsewhere. "The truck beside the barn, does it run?"

Lucien shrugged. "It did the last I tried it."

"Does it have petrol?"

"Some."

She held a finger to her lips to signal silence. She went to the window, scanning the terrain. "As soon as the Germans are gone."

CHAPTER 37

Emilie glanced at the clock when the front door opened. It was almost seven p.m. Jacques was later than usual. It became harder each day to maintain the charade—a devoted couple facing a world war. Not when they were each someone else. Jacques planned to trade her life for his safety. But she spied on him, as directed by her German family through Louie Bassett. It was an evil deed she had known might be requested, even though she had hoped it never would be. It was part of the price she paid for inheriting All Things Napoleon. And her store was her life—she wouldn't give it up for anything.

She had been surprised by Jacques' hidden cash and forged documents. She never thought he would betray her, even as she prepared to betray him. But such were the ways of war. Although she was plagued by a question: why did he ever marry her? It couldn't have been to use her to bargain with the enemy. There had to be another reason. Unless he had loved her but no longer did. She sighed, preparing to play the actress she wasn't.

She went in the foyer to greet him. "You're late," she said, and kissed him lightly on the lips. "I have dinner ready."

"I had to go to the office," he said as he walked into his

All That Glitters

study. He took papers from his briefcase. He laid them on his desk and put his briefcase on the floor. "The government is leaving Paris. I had to remove my most important documents. The Germans will be here soon. I can't risk having them find anything."

Emilie knew the papers were critical. She stood at the study entrance, not glancing at the Napoleon book where he hid his secrets. But she suspected that's where his papers would go. Somehow, she had to find a way to photograph them.

"We have a day or two before they get here," he continued. "Then we must be very cautious, me more than you. You have your shop to run."

"More residents leave every day," she said, subtly offering a suggestion, wondering how he would reply.

"You have nothing to fear. You're a woman with a business, trying to make a living. They won't bother you."

She hesitated. He hadn't denied he was leaving. "I worry more for you than me," she said softly.

"I have a role to fill," he said simply.

She urged him on, knowing his escape was already planned. "But why risk your life?" she asked. "What could be so critical?"

"I'm waiting for a package," he replied. "After it arrives, I'll receive different instructions. But until then, I remain in Paris."

She suspected it was the diamonds, but feigned ignorance. "But aren't you in danger if you stay, especially if the Germans learn who you are?"

"I'm in danger every day, no matter where I go," he said. "You are not, and you never will be." He stood, picking up the papers that had been on his desk.

Emilie tried not to stare at them. He wasn't putting them in a desk drawer. He would hide them in the Napoleon book, where all his sinister communications went.

He watched her curiously. "Is dinner ready?"

"Yes, of course," she said. "It's only garlic soup with some bread. It's harder to get food."

"It'll get worse," he warned.

She went into the kitchen and heated up the soup, poured glasses of red wine, and set a plate on the table with large chunks of dark bread, butter beside it.

Jacques came in a few minutes later. He sat down, sipped his wine, and buttered a hunk of bread.

"Can you tell me what's happening with the war?" she asked. "I only know what I read in the papers. Tell me the truth. I need to know."

He dipped his bread in the soup and chewed on it. "Assume it's worse than what you read. That's all I can say."

"But I'm your wife," she said testily. "You can trust me."

Jacques studied her for a moment, as if deciding whether to say anything more. "I'll tell you when the time is right. But for now, the less you know the better. It's for your own protection."

She rolled her eyes. She suspected he was lying. "At least tell me what I should do to prepare. I have the store to think about."

He sat back in the chair. "The Germans will come," he said. "In a few days, maybe less."

Emilie's face firmed. She hid her anger. It was hard to pretend she didn't know Jacques planned to flee. "Should I leave regardless, even if you remain?"

"No, the Germans won't bother you," he insisted. "We both know that. If you flee, you'll only have to come back. Stay and manage your store. The Germans will become your best customers."

She was quiet, eating her dinner, drinking her wine. If it was so important for him to stay, why did he have fake identity papers?

CHAPTER 38

Major Ziegler sat at the café and sipped his coffee, admiring the village and reminiscing of days long passed. Small towns thrived wherever they were, and they always would, bonded by people who worked hard and believed in their community. He was convinced this hamlet would return to what it once was, as soon as all the refugees came home. The German army had moved on, ready to fight the next battle. But the occupation force would remain, imposing fees and taxes, rules, and regulations, squeezing the local economy so they could take what wasn't theirs.

When he saw Bayer's stocky frame crossing the square, he ordered another coffee. "Sit, Sergeant," he called as he approached. "I've ordered you an espresso."

Bayer sat at the oval table. He rearranged his chair to better see the square. "I had interesting conversations with the residents."

Their discussion was interrupted by the owner, who brought a coffee to his table. Ziegler handed him a few coins.

The owner took them, was about to speak, but decided not to. He went back in the café.

A rare smile turned Ziegler's lips. "He was about to say that he doesn't take German money. But then he realized he has no choice."

Bayer nodded, anxious to tell what he had learned. "I have relevant information."

"I was raised in a village in Bavaria much like this," Ziegler said, ignoring him. "The town square and the buildings around it—the church, the pharmacy, the seamstress. My father owned a market—he still does—and I worked there when I was young. It was a good childhood, one I enjoyed very much."

"Sir, I think I may have found something," Bayer said, gently interrupting.

"Good memories of more innocent times," Ziegler continued, gazing out on the village square. "Those two boys playing soccer remind me of my sons. Years ago, of course. They were inseparable. Still are. They're a little more than a year apart. Brothers and close friends."

"Major, if I may."

Ziegler looked at him curiously. "What is it, Sergeant?"

"The pharmacist told me he saw a blonde woman who seemed familiar—he thinks she lives nearby or once did. She rode a bicycle, but had a rigid case strapped to the handlebars."

"I don't think the diamonds would fit in a small case," Ziegler said. "Not according to Sternberg."

"Wait, sir, there's more. The pharmacist said she went into the church."

Ziegler shrugged. "A local peasant who came to worship," he said. "Not that uncommon."

"But he saw her up in the steeple, in the arched window by the church bell."

Ziegler glanced up at the top of the church. He turned to Bayer, eyes wide. "A radio transmitter."

"My thoughts, also, sir."

"How long ago was this?"

"About an hour, maybe more."

"Did he see where she went?"

"No, sir."

"It's her," Ziegler said. "It has to be."

"She would have no reason to be in the steeple, except to use a radio."

Ziegler grabbed the map still lying on the table. "She has to be nearby."

"She's probably not from this village," Bayer said. "Or she wouldn't have needed the bicycle. She would have walked. Unless the radio was too heavy."

"And she wouldn't be in Tournai, or she would have used one of those churches."

"She must be hiding on one of these farms, or in a nearby town," Bayer suggested.

Ziegler studied the map and then looked at the roads coming in and out of the square. "We need to think like a thief. And determine if she'll hide or flee."

"Assuming the green Minerva was her car," Bayer said, "and the business card is her contact, she's trying to get to Paris."

"But she was trapped by our army cutting across northern France. From where we found the car, to where our army swept through, gives her a twenty-mile-wide swath at most."

Bayer sipped his coffee. "But she must know that now. If Paris is her destination, she'll likely hide somewhere until France surrenders."

"It won't be long. Days at most."

"We don't have much time to find her."

"No, we don't," Ziegler said. "If we look at the roads leaving town, and those near where the car was found, her best approach is the highway."

"Which she'll avoid," Bayer said. "It doesn't run directly south."

"These two roads go to the east, too far out of her way."

Bayer pointed to the map. "This road goes to Tournai."

"A possibility, but not likely since she came here to use the radio," Ziegler muttered. "This road goes into France."

"A secondary route for our troops. Even though it's only a country road."

"But look," Ziegler said, pointing to the map. "This is where the car was, and this is the country road that goes into France. They're not far apart, just across a few fields. Assuming she's trying to get to Paris."

"Once France surrenders and the occupation begins, Paris may not be the sanctuary she thinks it is."

Ziegler was quiet, considering what they had learned. "I don't think it matters," he said. "I suspect she has to get the diamonds to Paris, no matter who controls the city."

CHAPTER 39

Lucien watched the road, empty except for a German staff car in the distance. He went into the spare room.

"We have to get him out of this uniform," Camille said. "Do you have clothes for him?"

Lucien looked at Henry Green, hoping he would live, hoping that he had somehow done the right thing, even though his past had been marked by failures. "He's bigger than me. But he may be able to squeeze into a pair of my pants and a shirt."

"It doesn't have to be perfect. But hurry, we don't have much time."

Lucien wondered why she was in such a hurry, but he didn't question her. He went into his bedroom, rifled through his closet, and removed a pair of brown trousers that he knew were loose on him. He had lost weight, more than he was willing to admit. But he never ate anymore. He only drank. But now he had nothing to drink.

"No Germans are coming," Camille called from the spare room. "At least not now."

Lucien took a beige shirt off the hanger and grabbed a pair of old shoes from the floor. He went to the bureau, got a pair of socks, opened different drawers to see if there was anything else the Englishman might need, and returned to the spare room.

"I think these might fit," he said.

Camille was at the window, watching. "Wait a few more minutes," she said. "Just to be sure that those who passed are gone."

Lucien laid the clothes on the couch and went into the kitchen. He needed a drink badly. His hands were starting to shake. He tried not to think about it. But it was hard not to. He poured a glass of water, drank it, washed the glass, and refilled it, and went back to the spare room.

"I want to give him medicine," he said. "The pills I had in my bag. They might help."

He opened the closet door. The Englishman was propped up against the wall, sleeping but agitated, mumbling and shifting. Lucien shook him gently. "Are you all right?" he asked softly.

Henry's eyes stayed closed. Lucien shook him again. They fluttered open, and he wet his lips with his tongue. "Water?" he gasped.

Lucien raised the glass to his lips. "I have a pill for you to take."

Henry swallowed the pill and took more water. His eyes drifted closed.

Lucien removed the wet cloth from Henry's forehead and wiped his face.

"Where are the keys to the truck?" Camille asked.

Lucien looked up at her, not sure what she was going to do. "They're hanging by the back door."

She went into the kitchen, found the keys, and reappeared at the door. "Change his clothes and get him to the front door. I'll pull the truck around."

Lucien didn't reply but wondered why she rushed. Henry had been there for days. Lucien felt his forehead. It did seem cooler. Maybe he was starting to improve. The medicine would help. He shook him gently and Henry opened his eyes.

"What is it?" he muttered.

"You have to help me," Lucien said. "We're going to change your clothes and take you away."

"Where are we going?"

"Let's change your clothes first."

Lucien undid Henry's boots, slipped them off, and managed to get what remained of his torn trousers removed. "Are you feeling a little better?"

"Yes, a bit. Very tired."

"You need rest. It will be good for you. Now lift up, so I can slide these trousers on you."

Henry managed to lift his rump enough for Lucien to slide his pants on. They were a little short, and he couldn't button them at the waist, but he zipped them up as high as he could and held them on with a belt, hooked on the last hole. Lucien slipped shoes over his feet, forcing them on, and tied them the best he could.

"Good," Lucien said. "Now let's get your shirt."

"I do feel better than yesterday," Henry said. "Not as much pain."

"You'll feel better in a day or two," Lucien said, although he wasn't sure. "Let's see if you can stand."

"I'm not sure I can."

"I'll help you," Lucien said as he helped him rise. They staggered forward, moving slowly. It took a few minutes, but they made it out of the spare room and into the parlor.

"I need to rest a minute," Henry gasped.

The door opened and Camille came in. "Are you ready?"

"Almost," Lucien said, looking at her curiously. "But I don't understand the rush."

She didn't reply. She walked past him, looking in the spare room. "We have to hide his clothes," she said. "I'll put them in the closet for now." She shoved everything in the closet, along with some bloody bandages, and slid the bookcase in front of the door. "Come on."

"Just a minute more," Lucien said.

"No," Camille said firmly. "We must go. More Germans will come. We have to leave now."

CHAPTER 40

Emilie Dufort lay on her back, eyes wide open. She resisted falling asleep, fighting the urge to rest after a busy day. She looked at the clock on the nightstand. It was past midnight.

Jacques snored lightly beside her. He had been asleep for over an hour. She had waited, making sure he didn't stir. But now it was safe.

She slowly slid to the edge of the bed and paused. When he didn't move, she gently rose, sitting on the edge of the mattress. Just as she was about to leave, the snoring stopped. She froze. As she started to ease herself back down, he shuffled, muttered an incoherent word or two, and again started snoring.

She waited, her heart racing. She didn't move for several minutes. But neither did Jacques. As gently as she could, she got out of bed. She took one step and paused, listening closely. The rhythm of his snoring remained unchanged. She tiptoed to the doorway, wearing only a nightgown. She stopped when she entered the hallway. Jacques still slept.

She crept down the corridor. She hesitated every few feet, listening. Jacques snored, but so lightly she could barely hear him. She had to act quickly. She crossed the parlor and stepped in the foyer. When she heard no noise from the bedroom, no signs that Jacques was awake and climbing out of bed, she reached in her pocketbook. She rummaged through it and removed the camera Louie had given her. She waited a moment more, making sure Jacques didn't stir.

Once satisfied it was safe, she hurried into his study. She went to the fake Napoleon book, opened it, and looked inside. The currency and forged identity papers were gone—likely taken to #8 Rue Serpente. The papers marked secret had also vanished, maybe given to the sinister Guy Barbier. In their place, were loose pages, those removed from Jacque's briefcase when he arrived home. She took them from the book and sat quietly behind his desk. She turned on a desk lamp, cringing as the switch made an audible click. She started photographing the pages, one at a time, almost twenty in total. Her pulse raced, her breathing rapid. Moving as fast as she could, she briefly scanned the documents: maps, government edicts, information on troop movements.

"Emilie," Jacques called from the bedroom. "Are you all right?"

She jumped. Three pages remained. "Yes," she called, snapping photographs. "I couldn't sleep."

"What are you doing?"

"I was restless and didn't want to wake you."

She heard footsteps. He had climbed out of bed. She hurriedly took the last photo and turned off the light.

Jacques crossed the bedroom and came into the hall. "Where are you?" he called.

She gathered the papers and hurried to the bookshelf. She stuffed them in the fake Napoleon book and tiptoed out of the study.

Jacques was coming through the parlor as she reached the foyer. She held the camera in her hand. She would never make it to her pocketbook.

"Now I can't sleep," he grumbled. "I thought I would get a glass of milk." He looked at her strangely, standing in the foyer, her hands behind her back. "What are you doing?"

She leaned against the wall, lightly dropping the camera into a potted plant. "Nothing," she said. "I was just looking outside."

"Anything going on?" he asked, coming closer.

She moved from the pot, distracting him. She turned to the window. "No, not really."

"What did you expect to find?" he asked, chuckling. "We're in a blackout. You can barely see the building across the street."

"I was afraid," she lied. "I had a dream the Germans attacked. It was so vivid I woke, thinking it was real. And then I couldn't sleep."

He came close and hugged her. "Don't worry, we'll get through it."

She wrapped her arms around him, holding him tightly. She glanced over his shoulder at the plant. The camera peeked from behind one of the leaves. "Go get your milk," she said, gently pushing him away. "I'm going back to bed."

He kissed her lightly. "I'll be right in," he said, turning toward the kitchen.

She went in the parlor but waited. When she heard the cabinet open, she hurried to the plant. She got the camera and buried it at the bottom of her pocketbook, covering it with her cosmetic case. Her heart racing, she hurried to the bedroom.

CHAPTER 41

Ziegler stood at the curb while Bayer opened the back door of the staff car. He scanned the village square and studied those who studied him, all averting their eyes when his gaze met theirs. There weren't many, six or seven and a few German soldiers. But the residents seemed to realize that their lives had changed forever and there was nothing they could do about it. He glanced up at the church steeple, where a mysterious blonde woman may have transmitted a radio message only an hour before. They were getting closer.

"Which direction?" Bayer asked, as he started the engine.

"Take the dirt road that leads to the French border."

Bayer left the town square, drove a few blocks down cobblestone streets, and then out to the dirt road. "Troops were here when we first arrived. I could see them from the highway."

"Most are in France now," Ziegler remarked. "Only the occupation forces remain."

They approached the first farm, a long winding driveway off to their left. "Should we stop at each house?" Bayer asked.

Ziegler looked down the dirt road stretching into the distance, and all the small farms that straddled it. "Let's drive to the French border, maybe a bit beyond," he said. "We'll see what we find. But look for a bicycle. If you see one, we'll stop at the farmhouse and ask for the woman."

"Yes, sir," Bayer said. "She doesn't know we're closing in. She might be careless, leaving the bicycle out rather than hiding it in a barn."

"I'm trying to determine how large of an area she may be trapped in, between German forces in Belgium and the battle in France. I doubt she went east, where our troops are strongest. When she left Antwerp, battles raged to the west, we had defeated Holland to the north. She could only go south."

"Once defined, we can come back and question farmers if needed," Bayer said. "Her whereabouts may be obvious."

Ziegler was quiet for a moment. "I don't think we can underestimate this woman. She's managed to elude us and the German army. Not an easy feat."

"She had the diamonds and a radio to carry, too."

Ziegler didn't reply. He watched the passing landscape, crops in the field, livestock behind stockade fences, pigs, cattle, and goats. When they passed a coop that sat near the road, chickens cackled.

"The pharmacist said she looked familiar," Bayer said. "She might live in the area, maybe one of these farmhouses."

"But it doesn't fit," Ziegler mused. "A farmer would hardly have the skills to steal the most precious industrial diamonds in the world. If she's from the area, I wouldn't think she lived on a farm. She would live in Tournai."

"But why go to the village with the radio?"

Ziegler thought for a moment. "We have a large force in Tournai, but just a few soldiers passing through the village. She may have thought it was safer. She's cautious and clever. She did get into the vault."

"Maybe not, sir," Bayer countered. "She might be a courier. The dead man could have cracked the safe."

"But she still managed to escape. Regardless of her role, she's cunning."

"If what we know so far proves true, we've almost got her," Bayer said. "We found her abandoned car, the business card she lost in Antwerp, and we know she was in the church steeple with a radio transmitter."

Ziegler pursed his lips. "Whether we're right or not, it's all we have. We have to pursue it." He looked up ahead, small farmhouses along the road, all a good distance apart. "Stop by that stream. It runs north, out to the highway."

Bayer pulled the staff car over to the side of the road. They got out and Ziegler removed a pair of field glasses. He stood by the car, peering at the landscape beyond, and turned to examine the village. He put the glasses down and studied the farm that bordered the stream, a simple cottage, barn, chicken coop, not different than the other Belgian farms reaching into the horizon.

"An old French troop truck," Bayer said, pointing past the chicken coop, toward the barn.

"A relic from the last war," Ziegler muttered as he handed the glasses to Bayer. "The French will fare far worse in this one."

Bayer looked along the stream, following it back to the highway. "I can see her car, stranded on the side of the road."

"She may have come this way," Ziegler said, eyeing the stream as it meandered through the countryside. "Or she could have taken the highway to Tournai and hid somewhere close to the village."

Bayer handed the glasses back to Ziegler. "This farmhouse is nearest her car."

Ziegler paused, studying Lucien Bouchard's quaint cottage.

CHAPTER 42

Camille drove Lucien's pickup truck down the dirt road that rolled through the fields. Some farms were still abandoned, but others were occupied, refugees returning or residents who had never left. Henry sat in the middle of the bench seat, Lucien beside the window. It was quiet, a calm afternoon. If the landscape hadn't been littered with abandoned military equipment, it would seem like the battle had never been fought. But it was, and no one would ever forget.

"Are you all right?" Lucien asked.

Henry nodded. "Better, but still weak."

Lucien felt his forehead. It was still warm, but cooler than it had been. "You'll feel stronger each day."

"Where are you taking me?" Henry asked.

Camille hesitated, studying the landscape. "The less you know, the better."

Lucien watched her, always alert, prepared for the unexpected. She knew danger—how to react and stay calm when most would panic. But he wasn't sure why. How did a young woman from a Belgian city on the French border know how to open his safe without the combination, show no fear when confronted by the enemy, speak French, English, and German flawlessly? Now she helped a man she didn't know, risking her life to save his. She was a mystery, a riddle to unravel. If he was interested. And he wasn't sure that he was. But there was much he could learn from her. If he had any desire to learn.

They continued, traveling southeast. The lane merged with a cobblestone road. Farms disappeared, houses closer together, and a moment later they entered Tournai. It was a city of brick buildings and red tile roofs. Some had suffered minor damage during the fighting, others were nothing but heaps of debris. A bridge over the River Scheldt, the waterway that meandered northward through Belgium to Antwerp, had been destroyed, but others remained intact. The Notre Dame Cathedral and the belfry, among the oldest in Belgium, were undamaged. But the block before it was decimated.

Camille drove toward the center of town. They surveyed the damage—debris, shattered glass, and downed trees clogging some roads. No one spoke. They only observed. The German presence was intimidating—soldiers on street corners, sitting at outdoor cafes, walking the streets. But it seemed the city was starting to awaken, having emptied for the initial assaults. With the fighting ended and the battle lost, refugees had again become residents. Some shops were opened, others still abandoned. But the clientele was different. They were German. Most Belgians stayed in their homes, afraid to face a world that had changed so drastically in so short a time.

Camille eased the truck to a stop on the corner of a square. A handful of Germans sat at an outdoor café across the street, the building beside it a crumpled heap of broken bricks.

"What are you doing?" Lucien asked.

"You have to get out," she said.

Lucien was confused. "Why would I do that?"

"The less you see, the better. The less you know, the longer you live."

His eyes widened "Why did I even come?"

"I watch over you. No one else can."

Lucien pursed his lips. "You don't have to watch over me."

"Someone does," she insisted. "No one is better suited than me."

Lucien studied the street, the damaged buildings, piles of debris. A few Belgians walked the pavement, the café had only German customers. "What am I supposed to do?"

"I won't be long. Walk around or go in the stores. I'll be back in ten or fifteen minutes."

Lucien knew they had no time to argue. Not that he wanted to. Who had the strength? He turned to Henry Green and grasped his hand. "Good bye, my friend. Best of luck."

"I don't know how to thank you," Henry said. "You saved my life."

"I did nothing," Lucien said.

Henry squeezed his hand tightly and then let go. Lucien got out and stood on the corner, watching as the truck pulled away. Camille turned left, drove for two blocks, and turned left again, away from the city center.

Lucien studied the café. The Germans sipped their coffee and glanced at the residents walking by, trying to live their lives. The locals didn't look scared; their fear had come and gone. But they were empty shells with nothing inside, like mannequins in store windows. They looked like he felt.

Lucien waited a few minutes, watching people. He noticed a German officer at the café staring at him. He realized he looked suspicious, a man standing on the corner, eyeing those around him.

A small grocery store was behind him. The windows were cracked from the bombings but still intact. Lucien went inside and strolled up and down the aisles. Many shelves were bare, goods stolen by the enemy and not yet replenished. A clerk brought crates from a back room and started stocking shelves. When Lucien reached the rear of the store, he saw bottles of whiskey on the top shelf. He stared at them for a moment. He hesitated, aware he had reached a crossroad. Should he walk away and never touch another bottle? A strong man could do it easily. But he wasn't a strong man.

He reached for a flask, a slender bottle he could easily hide. He held it in his hand, looked at it for a moment. He almost returned it to the shelf. But after a moment, he took it the counter and paid for it. He went outside and waited on the corner. After making sure no one watched, he turned to face the wall, removed the cap, and took a long swallow, waiting for Camille to return.

CHAPTER 43

Emilie was behind the counter at All Things Napoleon when Louie Bassett came through the door. She glanced nervously around the shop. Three or four customers wandered the aisles, one of her employees ready to assist if needed. He was an older man named Denis. He had worked at the store for many years, having been employed by her uncle.

Bassett wandered the store. He eyed a sword display and then looked through the toy soldier collection. While he did, he watched the customers, gradually making his way to the counter. He picked up a military magazine that featured an article comparing Wellington to Napoleon.

"Good morning, Emilie," Louie said as he laid the magazine on the counter. "Do you have anything for me?"

"I do," she said, reaching under the counter.

"Wait," he hissed.

Denis, her employee, approached. He nodded to Bassett and addressed Emilie. "The gentleman in the blue shirt is interested in purchasing the entire toy soldier collection from the Egyptian campaign. Should we offer a discount, due to the volume?"

"Yes, of course," Emilie said. "Fifteen percent."

"I'll start with ten percent," Denis said with a wink. "And we'll see if he's interested." He nodded to Bassett and returned to his customer.

"Do you trust him?" Louie asked.

Emilie looked at him strangely. "Implicitly. He loves the store as much as I do. He's worked here many years."

Louie leaned closer. "Loyalties may change with the prospects of France. Be careful."

Emilie eyed him curiously. "Denis is the last person I would ever doubt," she said. But then she hesitated. "Although a few weeks ago, I would have never doubted Jacques."

"Just remember that," Louie said. "Be suspicious of everyone."

She nodded, eyeing Denis as he walked away. She could trust no one, regardless of how long she knew them or how loyal they had been to her or her family. Survival came first—for her and them.

Louie waited until no one was nearby. He leaned closer. "What do you have?"

Emilie eyed those in the store and reached under the counter. She took her pocketbook from a shelf and withdrew the tiny roll of film.

"Did you find money and fake identity papers?"

She shook her head. "No, it was gone, even the papers marked as secret. These were all different."

He cocked his head. "What happened to what was there?"

She shrugged. "I don't know. Jacques' lover probably has the money and identity papers. I suspect a man who visits frequently has the top-secret documents. Maybe he'll get these, too."

"Try to find out. What did you discover last night?"

"Maps, troop strengths and positions, government orders—all military information."

"Any dates?"

She nodded. "All issued yesterday."

"Good," he whispered. "This is just what I wanted. It helps prove the case against Jacques."

"He almost caught me. He came downstairs in the middle of the night."

Louie' eyes widened. "You have to be more careful. We can't risk the operation."

"I know," she said. "I'm just not..."

"Not what?"

"A very good spy."

"You have to learn quickly," he said sternly. "The consequences are severe. Be careful and take no chances."

"I understand," she said. She reached across the counter, about to hand him the film, when the door opened.

Jacques Dufort walked in.

CHAPTER 44

Major Ziegler stood by his staff car and eyed Lucien Bouchard's farm. He scanned the outbuildings, the old French troop truck, and rows of crops in the fields—corn, wheat, and potatoes poking through the soil.

"I don't see any vehicles," Bayer said, scanning the property. "It may be abandoned."

"Yes, maybe," Ziegler muttered. He looked down the stream to the highway in the distance, the Minerva on the side of the road.

"Should we check?" Bayer asked. "It's the closest house to the car."

Ziegler shifted his gaze to the farmhouse. "It's also the most obvious. Not the best place to hide. I think this woman is too smart for that."

"Yes, I suppose you're right, sir," Bayer agreed.

Ziegler put the field glasses back in the case. "Let's drive into France. Maybe she's traveling by bicycle and only stopped in the village to send a message."

It took only a minute to reach the French border, but the scenery didn't change. Farms sprawled before them, high buildings from nearby cities poking the horizon, church steeples and an occasional roofline, shimmering in the haze like a watercolor painting.

Ziegler turned and looked through the rear window at the farms they had passed, the streams that meandered through them, and the highway off in the distance.

"She was close," Bayer said. "Almost in France."

"Her car must have malfunctioned," Ziegler said. "Unless the fighting kept her from going farther."

The dirt road joined another, a bit wider, and a sedan passed, traveling in the opposite direction. A few miles farther they came to the outskirts of a city, long brick buildings housing factories, some damaged by bombs, roofs and walls collapsed.

Ziegler took the map from his pocket. "What is this city?"

"Roubaix, sir," Bayer said. "I believe it's known for its textiles."

At one of the bombed buildings, men cleaned up the debris and made repairs. Two Germans observed them, but it wasn't clear what their purpose was.

"I don't think she came here," Ziegler said.

"Why not?"

"It's one of those towns that exists because it always has. People live here because their ancestors did. Not a place where a skilled thief or spy would live. And it's too far from the village where the pharmacist claimed he saw her."

Bayer nodded. "Why go all the way to the village if she was here? Many buildings are high enough for her radio transmission."

Ziegler thought for a moment, afraid the trail was getting cold. "The city of Tournai offers more to the thief. Even a place to sell the diamonds."

"The highway where she abandoned her car led to Tournai," Bayer said. "Maybe she wasn't going to France. Maybe her contact is in Tournai."

"It's much easier to hide there than a small village or a farm."

"And Tournai has a train station, should she have a different destination."

"If she did want to get to Paris," Ziegler mused. "And maybe she does, given the business card. But what does she do with a satchel filled with diamonds?"

"Maybe she puts them in different suitcases."

"Which only attracts attention," Ziegler said. "Sternberg said they would fit in a satchel or duffel bag. Would she dare travel with them? She could be stopped and searched at any moment."

Bayer glanced in the rearview mirror. "Maybe she's not moving all the diamonds at once," he suggested. "What if she took a handful at a time, sewn in the lining of her dress or her hat and they were passed from one contact to the other."

Ziegler frowned. "The worst scenario for us, and the easiest for her."

"Which makes me wonder if that's her intention."

Ziegler considered the possibility. "She would need a network. I'm not sure one exists."

"We don't know that, sir. They could have developed one over the last year. Ever since the war in Poland."

"Yes, you're right," Ziegler muttered. "I suppose the question becomes, could such an operation be managed from a farm, or is it best suited for the city?"

"I think it depends on the network. It would be easier from a city, where she can hide in basements or attics, a secluded apartment on a narrow alley, and use different methods of transportation."

"I agree," Ziegler mumbled. "Or she could have hidden the diamonds and intends to get them later."

"Maybe the answer is in Tournai."

"If not, we'll come back to these farms."

Bayer looked at the passing landscape. "They lead a simple life. They may not know anything."

"Someone does," Ziegler said. "We just have to find them."

CHAPTER 45

Camille said goodbye to Mme. Abadie, an elderly woman who owned a dress shop. She stepped outside, lace, quilts, and dresses displayed in the front window. In a nearby alley, Lucien's truck was parked by the corner. Henry Green was safe. At least for now.

She got in the truck and drove away. She had been gone twenty minutes, maybe longer, when she parked close to the corner where Lucien waited. He stood a few meters away, leaning against a building. She nodded to him and glanced at two German soldiers who passed, eyeing an attractive woman.

Lucien opened the door and climbed in. "Did it go as planned?"

"As well as it could."

"Is Henry safe?"

She looked in the side mirror and eased out onto the street. "Yes, he's safe."

"I hope he makes it out."

"The Germans imposed a curfew," she said, not really replying. "But as residents return, they're permitted to open their businesses."

"They need the local economy. It makes the occupation easier, less resistance."

Camille braked to let an elderly woman carrying a loaf of freshly baked bread cross the street. "Belgium, Holland, and northern France are under occupation, run by German military personnel who direct civil authorities."

"Just like the last war."

She glanced at him as she turned on the road that led out of the city. "No, not like the last war. France will fall in days. It'll be much worse than the last war."

Lucien started to speak but stopped, as if he knew she wouldn't tell him. "Is that a guess, or is it based on information you have?"

"You don't need to know."

"Where did you take the Englishman?" he asked.

"To a friend."

"Your husband?"

"I don't have a husband."

Lucien hesitated. "To your lover?"

Camille hid a smile. Lucien seemed jealous, but she wasn't sure why. "To a friend," she said. "I don't have a lover."

"How do you know such a man?" he asked. "Someone who can shelter an Englishman when the Germans are everywhere."

"I didn't say it was a man."

Lucien paused. "How do you know these people?"

"Germans are everywhere," she replied, not answering. "We need to be careful."

Lucien looked at her, puzzled. "Will they get him back to England?"

"I don't know," she said. "And I don't want to know."

"Then how do you know he'll be safe?"

She turned to look at him, briefly taking her eyes off the road. "I don't."

He was confused. "Then why did you take him there?"

"Think of it this way," she said. "It's a link in a chain."

"The place where you took him?" he asked, confused.

"Yes," she replied. "I know the chain is strong, reliable, and it will not break. But I don't know where the next link is."

He didn't reply, and for a moment they didn't speak. "You're not going to answer any questions, are you?"

"I know it isn't easy," she said, glancing at the bump in his pocket. "And that you're trying."

He sighed. "What are you talking about?"

Camille was quiet, watching the road. "You know what I'm talking about."

"No, I don't."

She slowed down and turned to face him. "The flask in your pocket."

His eyes widened, as if he wondered how she knew. "I'm doing the best I can," he said softly.

"It's progress," she said. "I can see but you cannot."

"I don't want to see. I have no reason to."

"Two bottles to one bottle to a flask," she said. "Soon there will be nothing at all."

"I'm not so sure."

"But you're trying."

He hesitated. "I am trying," he admitted.

"Why are you trying?" she asked. "Do you know?"

He paused, at first unable to answer the question. But his eyes then widened, as if he was starting to understand. "For you?"

"No, not for me," she said. "For you."

They reached the farm and she drove the truck behind the cottage. But instead of parking it beside the barn, where it had been, she backed in on the other side of the barn, closer to the chicken coop, the rusted relic of a WWI French troop truck twenty meters behind it.

"I don't park the truck here," he said.

"You do now."

He looked at her, puzzled. "Why?"

"We may have to leave quickly."

"I'm not leaving," he said. "I have no need."

They got out of the truck and walked toward the cottage. Just as they reached the back door, she stopped.

"What's the matter?" he asked.

"Hurry," she said. "Get inside."

"What's wrong?"

She went into the spare room and slid the bookshelf away from the closet door. She got the Englishman's clothes, and the bloodied bandages, picked them all up in a pile and hurried into the kitchen.

"What are you doing?" he asked.

"Watch for Germans. I'll be back in a minute."

"I don't understand," he said, shrugging. "Where are you going?"

She hurried out the back door.

CHAPTER 46

Emilie was giving the film to Louie Bassett, her hand in midair, when Jacques entered. She hid her astonishment—he rarely came to see her. And his timing couldn't have been worse.

"Darling, what are you doing here?" she asked, snapping her hand back, clenching the film.

Bassett's face firmed. He turned to the doorway and glanced at Jacques. Then he slid the magazine along the counter. First a prop, it was now a purchase.

"I was passing by and thought I would stop in," he said, not smiling.

Emilie could tell something was wrong, but she didn't know what it was. Her gaze met Bassett's, pleading for caution. She put the film in her skirt pocket.

Bassett handed her a few bills and picked up the magazine. "I'm sure I'll enjoy this," he said, playing the role of customer.

She smiled. "Many of our customers do. It sells out every month." She opened the register and counted his change.

Jacques came closer, so close to Bassett they almost touched. He watched Emilie closely.

"Thank you," she said cheerily as Bassett turned to go. "Please come again." Her heart was racing, wondering what had happened. What had she done to arouse Jacques' suspicion?

Bassett nodded. "Excuse me," he said to Jacques. He stepped past him and went to the door.

Jacques took his place at the counter, his eyes narrowed. "Who was that?"

"What do you mean?"

"Who was that man?"

She pretended not to understand, glancing at the door as Bassett left. "Him?"

"Yes, who is he?"

She shrugged. "Only a customer. He collects military medals."

"What were you handing him, just as I came in?"

She fought to maintain her composure, thinking of how to hide the film. "I don't know what you mean," she said with a confused expression. "I gave him change. At first, I made a mistake, and then I corrected it."

"But I saw him pay you," he said sternly. "How were you making change when he hadn't given you the money yet?"

She had to think quickly. She looked at him quizzically. "Oh, he said he had a large bill, and I made change as he got his money. But it turned out that he didn't. I opened the drawer and corrected it."

Jacques seemed to relax. He glanced around the store, noticing all the customers. "Business is good," he said. "You would never know the country is collapsing."

Emilie sighed with relief. Jacques believed her. He must not have seen the film. "You seem cross today."

He shook his head, still studying the store. "Denis is busy," he said, referring to her employee.

"He's in the process of a large sale. Toy soldiers from the Egyptian campaign."

"It sounds fascinating," he said, with no enthusiasm.

She eyed him uneasily, still wondering why he was there. She had to find out. "Would you like to go and get a croissant."

He shook his head. "No, I just came in to say hello."

She smiled. "That's nice," she replied, although she sensed there was more.

Jacques paused, and then looked at her directly. "Were you in my study last night?"

Her heart raced, but she feigned ignorance. "No, I don't think so," she said, shaking her head. "Unless I was cleaning. Why?"

"I found one of my papers on my desk this morning. I never leave anything on my desk." His glare was penetrating, assessing her reaction, searching her soul.

Her heart raced; her hands trembled. "I don't remember seeing it. But I wouldn't have noticed anyway."

He looked away. "Maybe I missed it when I put other papers away."

"Yes, perhaps," she said. "But what does it matter? No one came to the house."

"No, I suppose not," he muttered. He glanced at his watch. "I have to meet someone."

She knitted her eyebrows. "Anything serious?"

He leaned toward her. "Very soon, Paris will be declared an open city, to prevent it from being destroyed. A German occupation will follow."

Her eyes widened, afraid of the unknown. "What should we do?"

"Nothing," he replied. "At least not now." He took her hand and squeezed it. "I have to go. Please, do not go in my study unless I'm there. Too many important papers."

She smiled, playing dumb. "I'm sure there is. But I wouldn't know what I was looking at."

He studied her a moment more. Doubt flickered in his eyes and then faded. "Yes, of course," he said, his gaze trained on hers. He turned and left.

CHAPTER 47

Sergeant Bayer drove across the border, back into Belgium, and minutes later they entered Tournai. Ziegler admired the city as it sprawled before them—brick buildings and tile roofs, anchored by the belfry tower and the cathedral. It seemed a nice town to visit, even holiday for a few days if times were different. But soldiers now patrolled the streets, machine guns at the ready. No one resisted. The residents went about their business, trying to pretend it was the same as before the Germans came. Even though they knew it never would be.

The German occupation force had commandeered a hotel near the town center to house officers and aides. Around the corner, next to a Belgian bank, the Gestapo had confiscated the law offices of a Jewish attorney. Ziegler was given a cramped space in the rear of the building while he recovered the diamonds—and for whatever other duties he might be assigned while in Tournai.

"Sergeant, find someone to monitor radio communications," Ziegler said as they entered. "I'm sure the woman will transmit again."

Bayer went to another part of the building while Ziegler walked in his office. He sat behind the desk, filing cabinets along the wall behind him. He took out his map, unfolded it, and studied Tournai—the town center and railroad terminal. It was a brick and concrete building with arches and pillars, close to a hundred years old. No trains operated for civilians, at least not yet. The Germans had taken control of the railroads, using them exclusively to move troops and supplies.

He located the village on the map, a collection of streets with a town square, a few kilometers from Tournai. He then studied the farms that spread around it, rolling across the border into France. He marked the highway where they had found the Minerva with a pen, and made a note by the village where the woman was seen in the church steeple. They weren't that far apart. Tournai was just a few kilometers beyond. If he assumed she was headed south, based on the Parisian business card found in Antwerp, and only strayed slightly east or west, it wasn't that large of an area in which she was pinched—from the battlefields of northern France to where her car was found.

"Major," Bayer said as he tapped on the door jamb, poking his head in the office.

"Come in," Ziegler said, still scanning the map.

"I instructed a sergeant in the communications room to monitor radio broadcasts. He'll check different frequencies to intercept any messages."

"Well done, Bayer," Ziegler said, looking up from the map. "Let's hope she transmits soon."

"Did you find anything on the map that we should investigate?"

"Not really," Ziegler muttered. "I'm trying to define the area in which she's trapped."

Bayer looked at the map. "It may not be as large as we thought," he said, studying some of the markings Ziegler had made.

"No, it isn't," Ziegler agreed. "And if she's traveling by bicycle, several people probably saw her."

"Where do you think we should check next?"

"Let's start with the farmhouse by the stream, closest to where the car was left."

Bayer paused, thinking. "Is that the farm with the deserted French army truck behind the barn?"

"Yes, it was a direct line from the highway."

Bayer shrugged. "It seemed deserted. But I suppose the owner could have been out, running errands or selling produce."

Ziegler's gaze returned to the map. "If the owner does still live there, he may have seen her abandon the car."

"If just a single soul saw her, we can condense the search area. As soon as we know which direction she took."

Ziegler sat back in the chair. "We're very close. I can sense it."

Bayer nodded. "She may not be as cautious now. She thinks she escaped."

Ziegler eyed Bayer with an arrogant smile. "Which will make her arrest so much more satisfying."

CHAPTER 48

Lucien stayed at the window, watching for Germans. He eyed the clock, waiting for Camille to return. A few minutes passed, and then a few more. What could she be doing with the Englishman's clothes?

The kitchen door opened, and she came in. "Where were you?" he asked.

"I had to do something with Henry's clothes," she said. "We can't keep them in here."

"If we hid Henry, we can hide his uniform," he scoffed.

She was quiet, watching him. "The Germans who come next won't be as easy to fool."

"Why would more Germans come? Belgium surrendered. The fighting is in France."

"The forces that occupy Belgium are assisted by the Gestapo. They're ruthless, far more dangerous than those who passed through to chase an enemy that had already run away."

Lucien realized she was right. They couldn't underestimate the enemy. Not if they hoped to stay alive. "Where did you put his clothes?"

"It's better that you don't know."

He frowned. "Why do you know everything while I know nothing?"

"I want to protect you?"

"Protect me from what?"

"Any harm."

"Harm?" he asked. "I don't fear harm. But I fear a woman who speaks several languages, is not afraid of the enemy, knows how to hide a wounded British soldier in the midst of thousands of Germans, and opens my safe without knowing the combination. Is that what you are trying to protect me from?"

"You speak nonsense."

"Who are you?" he asked. "Tell me, Camille with no last name, Camille who has no home, Camille who has no husband or lover, no friends except for links in a chain."

She didn't reply and a soft silence consumed the room. After a moment, she spoke. "I was your patient once," she said quietly. "A woman who watched a good man wither away until he almost died."

"Maybe he wanted to die."

"Maybe he only thought he did."

A knock on the front door interrupted them. Camille nodded to Lucien, as if she had expected visitors. "Answer the door. I'll go in the kitchen."

He went to the front door and opened it. Two Germans stood on the doorstep, wearing black uniforms of the Gestapo, a major and a sergeant. Now he knew what Camille meant. She must have seen them when they returned from Tournai.

"We would like to ask you a few questions," the sergeant said in French, the accent stilted but understandable.

Lucien was alarmed but tried not to show it. "Yes, of course," he said, thinking of the Englishman. "The soldiers passed through days ago."

"We're not looking for soldiers," the sergeant continued.

"We're looking for the owner of the green Minerva abandoned on the highway."

Lucien shrugged. "I know nothing about a car left on the highway."

"Who is it, Lucien?" Camille asked in French as she walked in from the kitchen.

"Wer ist sie," the major asked the sergeant in German. "Who is she?"

The sergeant repeated the question in French.

Lucien looked at Camille and shrugged. He had no intention of replying. He knew it was better for her to address them.

"Ich bin seine Frau," Camille said, replying in German. "I am his wife."

"You speak German?" the major asked in his native tongue, his face showing surprise.

"Yes, I do," she replied, still speaking German. "What do you want with this car?"

The major knitted his eyebrows. "Where did you learn to speak German?"

"I spent much of my childhood in Germany," she said. "My grandmother had a farm near the Dutch border."

The expression on the Germans' faces softened, but didn't relax completely.

"I am Major Ziegler, and this is Sergeant Bayer," the major said. "We have questions to ask you."

Camille shrugged, showing no fear. "Ask."

"Is that your car on the highway?" Sergeant Bayer asked.

"I don't know what car you're talking about," Camille said.

Lucien watched everyone's expression, including Camille's. He knew a little German, and tried to piece together the conversation. But he realized Camille had told the last soldier that her grandmother was from Switzerland; this time she was from the Dutch border. He wondered why the Germans were so interested in her and not him.

"Have you ever been to Antwerp?" Ziegler asked.

"Yes, I have," she said. "But it was many years ago."

"How long have you lived here?" Bayer asked.

"Almost two years," Camille replied.

"Where before that?" Bayer asked.

"In Tournai," she replied.

Lucien noticed that Bayer had raised his machine gun slightly, as if he suspected they were more than innocent peasants. Had the Englishman been caught? Had he told the Germans who helped him?

"Many soldiers came through here," Lucien said in French. "They took our food and water."

Ziegler glanced at him, paid little attention, and turned to Camille. "We're going to search the house."

Camille shrugged. "We have nothing to hide."

She stood beside Lucien, clinging to his arm and keeping close, like a wife would.

Bayer stood at the door, his weapon slightly raised, not pointed at them but making it clear it could be. Ziegler walked into the spare room.

Lucien peeked in the room as Ziegler went through the closet, removed the cushions from the couch, looked for loose floorboards. After a few minutes he went in the bedroom, and they could hear the closet door open. It was quiet for a moment—maybe he checked the opened safe. A bureau drawer then opened and closed followed by silence.

He came out a few moments later and went through a few kitchen cabinets, not all. The search seemed half-hearted, as if he didn't expect to find anything. He then walked back into the parlor.

"Did you see a blonde woman crossing the fields several days ago?" he asked. "She would have arrived in the car abandoned on the highway."

Lucien looked at Camille, knowing she had suddenly appeared, but he tried not to show it. "No, we saw no one."

"We lead a simple life," Camille added.

"Do you have a bicycle?" Ziegler asked.

Camille chuckled. "Everyone has a bicycle. We use little petrol. It's saved for the tractor."

Ziegler kept his gaze fixed on hers, suspicion crawling across his gaunt face. She didn't flinch, and neither did he. After a moment, he turned to Bayer and motioned to leave.

"We're going to search the barn and chicken coop," Bayer said in French.

Lucien shrugged. "Only chickens and my equipment to manage the farm."

They started to leave, but Ziegler leaned back in the house. "If you see a blonde woman, a stranger, you must notify us immediately. Our Tournai headquarters is where the Jewish lawyer used to have his practice, by the bank. This woman is very dangerous."

Lucien resisted the urge to look at Camille. "Yes, of course," he stammered.

"Are we in danger?" Camille asked, feigning fear.

Ziegler glared at her for a moment before he replied. "I haven't yet decided."

CHAPTER 49

The people of Paris awakened to the faint smell of smoke, a sooty haze drifting over rooftops. Most thought the battle had come closer and some fled, using whatever transportation they could find—wagons, bicycles, automobiles.

Jacques sipped his coffee, his thoughts elsewhere. The smoke was a signal. It announced that the French army had gone, leaving Paris undefended. In days, or even hours, the Germans would come. He had much to do. He had to prepare.

"Where is the smoke coming from?" Emilie asked, looking out the back door.

"The French are burning petrol supplies, so the Germans don't get it."

Emilie looked at him anxiously and sat at the kitchen table. "When will the Germans arrive?"

He drank down the rest of his coffee and rose from the table. He didn't want to explain it. "Paris is an open city. The French army is gone. It will last hours, maybe a day, two at the most, and then the Germans will come."

She watched him curiously, as if wondering why he was rushing off. "Where are you going?" she asked, her voice crisp.

She was annoyed. still eating a buttered croissant with her coffee.

He bent over and kissed her on the top of the head. "I have to meet someone," he said. "It's important."

He went out the front door, his nose crinkled from the smoke. It was worse on the Right Bank, the other side of the Seine. The oil depot was north of Paris. He hurried down the sidewalk, watching those around him. Some loaded belongings in automobiles, others hurried to catch trains or busses before they stopped running. Chaos had gripped the city. Many who remained prepared to flee, afraid to face the enemy. He hurried nine blocks to Sophie's apartment and knocked at the street entrance.

She answered a moment later, pinching her nose with her fingers. "Ugh," she said.

"They're burning petrol supplies," he said simply as he entered. "The Germans will be here soon."

"No message from Camille," she said as she led him upstairs and into her apartment. "And Claudette Maes, my Antwerp contact, is still silent, terrified by the Gestapo's visit."

Jacques Dufort paced the floor. "What was the name of the Gestapo major who's hunting Camille?"

"Ziegler," Sophie replied.

He pursed his lips. "Have we been able to warn her? He may be close."

Sophie shook her head. "I don't dare try to contact her."

Jacques sighed. "No, we can't do that. But there must be some way we can help her. She's in danger, whether she knows it or not."

"She's still hiding," Sophie said. "We can do nothing but wait."

Jacques sat on the couch and ran his hand through his black hair. "I suppose we have no choice. We can't go looking for her."

"I started preparing routes from Tournai to Paris, using my contacts along the way and as many different modes of transportation as possible—just to confuse the Gestapo. I can give her the information when she contacts us."

"Assuming she does contact us," he said. "The longer we go with no message, the more worried I become."

Sophie hesitated. She was smart, prepared for any situation. "I think we should assess every possibility—whether we want to or not."

Jacques studied her for a moment, but then nodded reluctantly. "Logic versus emotion."

Sophie smiled. "I don't like to be surprised."

Jacques sat back on the sofa. "First scenario. Camille has the diamonds. The Gestapo is chasing her and she's hiding near Tournai. She can't go any farther because of the fighting."

"Second scenario," Sophie said. "Camille has been captured. She either hid the diamonds or the Germans have them."

Jacques cringed. "I don't like that scenario."

"How about this one?" she asked. "Camille is a double agent. She's not on her way to Paris. The Germans have the diamonds."

Jacques shook his head. "We talked about this before. She's not a double agent and she's not a thief. If she claims to be trapped near Tournai, then I believe her."

Sophie shrugged. "All right. That's fine. But we need to be aware that we could be betrayed. We can't verify what she's saying."

"Except for what Claudette Maes told us."

"Agreed. But Tournai is far from Antwerp. Claudette can't help us now. Even if she was transmitting."

Jacques rubbed his chin. "Why wouldn't Camille message again, even if just a brief update?"

"Maybe she can't," Sophie said. "She could be surrounded by Germans."

"But she said she was hiding at a farm near Tournai."

"Germans could be camped in the fields," Sophie offered. "Or even nearby. She could have a dozen reasons for not using the radio."

Jacques sighed. "I suppose," he mumbled. "She'll message when she can."

"That's all we can hope for. I'll try some of my contacts near Tournai. Maybe we can make sure she's safe."

"Do you think she hid the diamonds somewhere?"

"We have no way of knowing," Sophie said.

Jacques glanced at the radio. "We can give her another day or so. But then we have to act. The diamonds are too critical to let them fall into German hands."

CHAPTER 50

"Did you believe them, sir?" Bayer asked Ziegler as they left Lucien Bouchard's house and walked toward the barn.

"I don't know," Ziegler muttered, considering the brief encounter. "If they live here, and she is the thief, she probably wouldn't abandon her car a farm field away."

"And if she did, she would have gone to get it by now."

Ziegler nodded. His instincts told him something wasn't right. But he had known from the moment he saw the vault breached in Antwerp that he could make no assumptions—it was too easy to be fooled. He stopped, studying the barn and outbuildings. "One vehicle," he said pointing to the truck.

"Suitable for a farmer."

"A bicycle leaning against the back of the house."

"Which she admitted she had," Bayer said with a shrug. "Everyone has a bicycle. It's the primary mode of transportation. Especially now with the petrol shortage."

They went in the barn, waiting while their eyes became accustomed to the dim lighting. A tractor was parked by the front door, rust blemishing the red paint, the tread on the tires worn. Stalls for animals lined the left wall, all empty, but once home to cows or goats. Doorways led to an empty yard, enclosed with a split-rail fence. Storage bins for hay and other grains were also empty, with scattered remnants of what was once stored there. The right wall was lined with farm utensils —hoes and shovels, an old saddle for a horse that no longer existed or had been given away. A half dozen wooden crates lay scattered near the tractor.

"It doesn't look like they farm much," Bayer noted. "No livestock, anyway."

Ziegler walked from one end of the building to the other. "Someone used this barn, but it isn't the present owners."

"There are chickens in the coop and crops planted," Bayer said as they walked back out of the building.

They went toward the chicken coop, pausing at the truck. Ziegler circled it, looking at the tires, the scratched paint. "They use the truck, seem to use the tractor, but have no livestock."

"Must live simply," Bayer commented.

They went to the chicken coop, listened to the chickens cackling, and then moved around to the other side.

"Someone camped here," Ziegler said, pointing to ashes from a campfire, some scattered debris.

Bayer picked up an empty can with German labeling. "Our troops," he said. "Probably resting before going into France."

Ziegler walked to the edge of the building and studied the grass. He knelt, looking closer.

"What is it?" Bayer asked.

"Blood," Ziegler replied. "And a British helmet."

"From the initial fighting, most likely."

"Yes, I suppose," Ziegler mumbled. He looked across the farm field, the rusted relic of a French troop truck captured by weeds and vines growing around it. "Just like the last war."

Bayer pointed north. "It's almost a straight line to where the car was abandoned. Only a kilometer away."

Ziegler looked at the stream, twenty meters to the west. It

trickled north to the highway where the car had been left. "She still could have left by boat. Maybe it wasn't her on the bicycle in the village."

Bayer looked at the stream and then towards the highway. "She leaves the car, loads the diamonds into the boat, and heads south into France."

Ziegler sighed. "If she was trying to get to Paris. But she couldn't have gone far, not with all the fighting."

"Which brings us back to this twenty-mile swath of land," Bayer said. "She has to be trapped here somewhere."

Ziegler nodded. "If we consider the timeline from when the diamonds were taken, where the car was found, and the advance of our troops, she couldn't have gotten much farther than where we now stand."

"But what did she do with the diamonds?"

Ziegler looked at the cottage, the simple farmhouse with the blonde woman and her husband. "A mystery we need to solve."

"What do we do next?"

Ziegler pointed to another farmhouse down the road, less than a kilometer away. "Let's talk to that farmer."

"Maybe he saw the woman cross the fields. Or she could have gone in the other direction."

Ziegler looked back at Lucien Bouchard's cottage. He paused a moment, but then turned to go. "We'll see what we can learn about this supposedly simple farmer with the whiskey flask on the table and the blonde wife who may or may not fit the description of the woman who stole the diamonds."

"Do you think it's her?"

Ziegler shrugged. "Leaving the car so close to the farm makes no sense. Not for someone as cunning as she is."

"What do you suspect them of doing?"

Ziegler again glanced at the cottage and then looked at Bayer. "Not being who they say they are."

CHAPTER 51

Lucien watched Camille looking out the window, but not at the Germans. She moved from window to window, scanning the entire farm.

"What are you doing?" he asked, her behavior perplexing.

"I'm making sure no Germans are coming."

"Weren't those two enough?" he asked. "They were Gestapo."

"They'll be back," she said simply.

She returned to the window nearest him, studying the barn and outbuildings. She looked toward the stream and the abandoned French troop truck.

"Isn't it odd that they're looking for a blonde woman who arrived on my farm on the same day that you did?"

"They checked where the soldiers camped and where we found Henry," she said, not replying.

"But didn't they keep looking across the field to an abandoned car on the highway?"

"Do you have more petrol?" she asked, still ignoring him.

Lucien paused. She was planning something, but he didn't know what. "Why do you need petrol?"

"When we went to Tournai the petrol tank in your truck was half full. Do you have more?"

"Yes, I have two ten-liter cans in the barn," he said.

"How about the tractor? Is there petrol in the tank?"

"Yes, but I'm not sure how much. I don't know why it matters."

She kept scanning the landscape. "We may need it."

"What are you looking at?"

"In the barn there are some wooden crates. Are they empty?"

"What are you talking about?" he asked, confused by all of her questions. He studied her expression, calm but calculating.

"I need solid wood or metal boxes to put in the back of the truck."

"For what?"

"What's in the crates?"

Lucien shrugged. "I don't know," he said, louder. "I have to look."

"Come, we have to hurry," she said. "The Germans will be back. Throw some clothes in a bag and put them in the truck. Take your medical bag and whatever supplies you have, too."

"Hold on a minute," he said, totally confused. "What's going on?"

She walked into the spare room, returning a moment later. "Take this," she said, handing him the framed photo of the woman and little girl that had hung on the wall.

He hesitated, as if he finally understood. "It is you they're after, isn't it? What did you do?"

Her gaze met his. "We don't have time to talk. We have to go. Quickly. If they don't come back today, they'll be back tomorrow."

He crossed his arms. "I'm not going anywhere until I know what's going on."

She grabbed his whiskey flask. "You can't know what's going on because I can't trust a drunk."

"Tell me."

She handed him the flask. "Dump the whiskey and promise me you'll drink no more."

He looked at the flask, which held his strength and courage, dulling the dawn when it brought memories he couldn't avoid. "I can't promise that," he admitted softly. "I'm not that strong."

"Then I can't tell you."

He hesitated, searching her eyes for clues but finding none. "Then I'm not going with you."

She came closer, standing in front of him. She took his face in her hands, lightly caressing his cheeks. "You have no choice, Lucien," she whispered. "If they come back, and I'm gone and you're still here, they will kill you. It will be a horrible death, I promise you."

He kept his gaze fixed on hers, fought the urge to sob, to admit he was a broken man that couldn't be fixed. His face firm, he took the flask and poured the whiskey down the sink.

"Now tell me all that you know," he said softly.

CHAPTER 52

Emilie Dufort strolled down a residential street. Limestone townhouses lined one side; an old cemetery sprawled along the other. She glanced at the graveyard, crooked tombstones poking through the soil, mausoleums scattered about the grounds, some housing entire families, the newly dead and long deceased. Halfway down the block, tucked among a string of similar properties, she found her destination. She approached the entrance, using the brass knocker to announce her presence.

A moment later, Louie Bassett opened the door. He glanced up and down the street, ensuring no one suspicious lurked nearby. "Come in," he said, leading her into a tiled foyer.

"The soot is starting to dissipate," she said as she entered. A grand stairway stood at the far end of the foyer, a corridor behind it, arched entryways on each side.

"The petrol has burned all day," he said, leading her to the right. "Let's go in my study."

She followed him into a room with muted green walls and wide white moldings. A walnut desk sat in front of double windows with triangular mullions, a Chantelle sofa and chairs in the center, by a fireplace. When Emilie had first met Louie

Bassett, she thought he pretended to be wealthy. Now she felt differently—he was wealthy.

"You have a beautiful home," she said, admiring the room.

"Yes, it's very nice," Louie said, offering a quick glance. He pointed to an Art Deco radio, the announcer's voice faint in the background. "Paris is an open city."

"To save it from destruction."

He nodded. "If the French army honors the terms. But they have no choice. Why let the most beautiful city in the world be destroyed?"

"When will the Germans arrive?" she asked. "Jacques said in a day or two."

"If not sooner."

She sat on a chair by the fireplace. "What do we do? Will we hide in the shadows when the Germans come, waiting for the right moment to step forward? I worry about my store, and the customers who are so loyal to me."

He paused, as if his thoughts wandered in different directions. "For now, we do nothing. You go to your shop every day, as if nothing changed except the nationality of your customers."

"Will the occupation be peaceful?"

"As long as everyone obeys. The French were defeated. The victor sets the rules."

"Half the city has fled."

"And many will return," he said. "They left jobs and businesses that can still operate, just like All Things Napoleon."

She reached into the pocket of her dress. "The film," she said, handing it to him.

"Was Jacques suspicious?"

She nodded. "He saw me hand you something, but I said I made the wrong change."

"Did that satisfy him?"

"Only after I lied and gave him a detailed explanation," she said. "But he was already suspicious. I left one of the papers I photographed lying on his desk. That's why he came to the store."

His eyes widened. "Emilie, you can't afford to make mistakes. Jacques is a dangerous man."

She studied the stranger managing the clandestine efforts against her husband, a foreigner whose accent hadn't been determined, early forties, nondescript, brown hair and eyes. Sometimes she wondered if she had been tricked. There had been no message from her family, the phone lines still disabled. Maybe Jacques wasn't the villain. Maybe Louie Bassett was.

"You don't seem convinced," he said, watching her closely.

"I'm not," she said. "You claim Jacques poses a threat. But other than a potential affair, currency, and faked identification papers, I've seen nothing. Maybe the forged papers are for me, not the other woman."

Louie frowned. "I doubt it. And so do you. Especially since you told me that the physical description matches her, not you."

"But Jacques doesn't behave any differently—other than meeting more contacts at night. He still goes to the building where he has always worked, pretending to be a transportation official. Yet I don't know who you work for. Why don't you tell me?""

He didn't answer. "Jacques still works for military intelligence. Even though he's been compromised. He wants the same thing we do."

"The diamonds?"

Louie nodded. "Yes, but a question remains. Does he want the diamonds for the Allies? Or does he sell them to the highest bidder?"

"Is that what the woman does, sells what he steals?"

He shrugged. "I don't know. But it wouldn't surprise me."

"Why am I in danger?"

"You're his insurance policy, regardless of his intentions."

Emilie was quiet, starting to understand. "The disposable wife from the border. He'll claim I have ties to Germany."

"We don't know what he will do. But he'll get more dangerous each day he doesn't have the diamonds. He's supposed to deliver them to someone, whether friend or foe we've yet to determine. I suspect his buyer is losing his patience."

Emilie sat back, trying to make sense of what was and what could be.

"Until he gets those diamonds," Louie emphasized, "he'll take bigger risks, behave more strangely."

She nodded, her heart torn, starting to see a future without her husband, regardless of the ways of war. "I've heard nothing about Camille."

"She's the missing link," Louie said. "If we find her, or anyone connected to her, we'll know what Jacques has planned. The money and forged identity papers suggest that you're not part of it. He's been planning it all for some time. You're just a pawn in his chess match. But we don't know when the game was started."

She frowned, forced to agree. He said what she had been thinking, his words serving as confirmation.

"Do you have anything new?"

She shook her head. "I'm convinced he gives the papers to one of his contacts, a man who comes to see him."

Louie cocked his head. "Who is this man?"

"Guy Barbier."

His eyes widened. "I know Guy Barbier. He's the most dangerous man in Paris."

CHAPTER 53

Ziegler and Bayer went to a farmhouse a kilometer down the road from Lucien Bouchard, but found it deserted. The residents had fled, probably weeks before at the first sign of fighting. Maybe they lived through the First World War and didn't want to repeat it.

"Should we visit any more farms?" Bayer asked, turning back toward Tournai.

Ziegler glanced at his watch. "I have to go back to headquarters. I'm expecting a cable from Antwerp. Maybe after I receive it, we'll come back."

They continued along the dirt road and entered Tournai a few minutes later. Bayer took a back way, avoiding the main boulevards, and they cruised a few side streets, eyeing the houses without really knowing what they were looking for.

"She could be hiding in any one of these apartments," Bayer said, as he turned down one narrow lane and onto another.

"Or tucked away in someone's attic," Ziegler added, eyeing passing pedestrians. "But we do have a slight advantage. She doesn't know we're close."

"And at some point, she'll get careless and make a mistake," Bayer said. "We just need to be ready when she does."

Ziegler studied the shops and cafes. Tournai was no different than dozens of other cities he had passed through in Poland, Austria, Germany, and Denmark. Only language and architecture defined the country. Except somewhere in the buildings of Tournai, a woman might be hiding with a satchel of industrial diamonds that could alter the course of the war.

Bayer parked on a narrow lane beside Gestapo headquarters, and they went to their cramped office in the rear of the building. Ziegler sat behind the desk, pondering their next move, Bayer just across from him.

"What would you do if you had stolen the diamonds, Sergeant?" Ziegler asked.

Bayer shrugged. "I'm not sure, sir," he said. "Her plans were interrupted, whatever they may have been. We know we have the right car. The description matches and the bullet holes confirm it."

"We also have those in the village."

Bayer nodded. "Two witnesses, one willing, the other reluctant, who saw a mysterious woman carry a rigid suitcase to the top of a church steeple."

"The only explanation is a radio communication," Ziegler muttered. "If she transmits again, we'll find her."

"Do you think she has an accomplice?" Bayer asked. "Even if it's only to help her hide."

Ziegler thought for a moment. "It may not be an accomplice. Someone could hide her, unaware of who she is."

They were interrupted by a tap on the door jamb, and a soldier appeared at the entrance. "The cable from Antwerp you've been expecting, sir."

"Thank you," Ziegler said. He took the message and the soldier left.

"It's either about the diamonds or the dead man at the exchange," Bayer said.

Ziegler opened the envelope and scanned the cable. "The corpse," he said.

"Do they know who he was?"

"Yes, it seems so. Authorities believe he was a man named Roger Daubert, from Paris."

"The business card," Bayer said. "He must have dropped it."

Ziegler nodded. "He may have been brought in to breach the vault. And as you once mentioned, she may be the courier, delivering the diamonds to an unknown destination."

"It is plausible, sir. Although it seems like she's trying to get to France. She's only a couple kilometers away."

"Yes, it does," Ziegler mumbled, his thoughts drifting.

"Did authorities in Antwerp have any more information?"

Ziegler scanned the message. "It's not known if this Roger Daubert is military intelligence or a common thief."

"If we learn what he is, we'll know what she is. And a common thief might be the best explanation."

"Except she's managed to elude us," Ziegler muttered. "She's not acting like a caged animal, as you would expect a thief to behave."

Bayer sighed. "She has to be close—her car, the church steeple. She's likely right here in Tournai."

Ziegler sighed and stood. "Before we start canvassing the city, let's check a few more of the farms. Maybe someone saw her abandon the car. They might know where she went."

CHAPTER 54

Camille eyed Lucien closely, the whiskey dumped down the drain. She had to force him to choose, to realize his life was worth living. She even hinted she might be part of it, or she would at least prop him up until he was strong enough to stand alone.

He took the flask and put it in his pocket.

"What are you doing?" she asked. "You don't need that. It's empty."

"But it isn't empty," he said softly. "It's filled with what little courage I have. I want to keep it with me. At least for a while."

She looked at him, head cocked. "I don't understand."

"It's a reminder," he explained. "A crutch. A memory of when I was strong enough to dump good whiskey down the drain."

"If it helps you, keep it. But I'll help you, too."

He smiled. "Thank you," he said. "I suspected you would. Now tell me what I need to know."

She studied him a moment more, convinced of his sincerity. "Pack some clothes first," she said. "And then I'll tell you."

He hesitated, staring at her curiously, as if sensing something was different but not knowing when it changed.

She kissed him lightly on the lips. "I'm proud of you. I know it isn't easy."

He wasn't expecting the kiss. But he didn't refuse it. "Why would you care so much about me?"

She sighed, knowing they didn't have much time. She lifted her blouse, showing a scar just under her ribcage. "Because you cared about me."

He looked at the scar, his gaze shifting to her face. "I'm sorry," he said, shrugging.

"It's all right. You don't remember me. You helped a lot of people. But I will never forget you."

He was starting to understand. "I saved your life?"

She nodded. "And many others."

He didn't move, processing emotions dormant for so long. "Thank you," he whispered. He leaned forward and kissed her again.

She let his lips linger on hers for a moment, but then pulled away. "Come on," she urged. "We have to hurry."

"I'll go pack," he said, and started for the bedroom. "I'll just be a minute."

She moved from window to window, studying the terrain, looking for Germans. She recognized the risk that Lucien did not. The Gestapo only had to talk to a nearby farmer, or someone in Tournai that remembered Lucien, to learn that he lived alone, that there was no blonde wife. The Gestapo would come back quickly.

"I'm ready," Lucien said a moment later, emerging from the bedroom with a duffel bag. "But I'm not leaving until you tell me something, even a little. It doesn't have to be everything."

She hesitated, wondering how much to reveal. She studied him for a moment, ensuring he could be trusted—without the bottle—and began. "The Gestapo are looking for industrial diamonds, the best in the world. But so are the Allies. They're needed for radar technology. The diamonds were stolen from an Antwerp bank, minutes before the Germans got them."

He kept his gaze fixed on hers. A vague understanding crossed his face. "You stole them."

She nodded.

"It's your car abandoned on the highway."

"Yes," she admitted. "Although it was stolen in Antwerp. The engine died."

"And that's how you ended up on my farm the day the Englishman was shot."

She glanced out the window. "Come on, we have to go."

"Wait," he said, even though he followed her. "Where are the diamonds?"

She locked the front door and led him out the back, locking it behind her. "I hid them in the old troop truck."

As they stepped outside, he looked at the relic from the last war, vines growing through the windows. "That's brilliant," he said, eyes wide. "Now I know why you were always looking out the window."

"I was watching the Germans," she said. "But for more than one reason."

"You had to make sure they didn't check the old truck."

She smiled. "Come on. The sooner we're gone, the better."

"Where are we going?"

"We'll hide at a safe house in Tournai for a few days."

He paused. "Is that where you rode your bicycle, and where you took Henry?"

"You only need to do as I tell you and stop drinking," she said, not answering the question as she led him across the yard.

CHAPTER 55

The Parisian warehouse was reached through an alley barely wide enough for wagons and trucks. Broad double doors marked the vehicle entrance, enclosed by gates of wire mesh, dented and scratched from years of use. A few feet away, a steel personnel entry had no windows, the paint scuffed, a dent near the bottom of the door. The brick building had narrow windows along the top, offering privacy but allowing light to filter in. The front, which faced a street that intersected the Boulevard St. Germain, was home to a rare coin dealer—open by appointment only. Normally dark, the interior was barely visible through dirty display windows.

Jacques Dufort came early, not long after dawn. The Germans would soon swarm the city, parading down boulevards to intimidate those who hadn't fled. When he reached the personnel door, he scanned the alley to make sure no one watched, and used a special knock to announce his presence: one tap, pause, three taps, pause, two taps. A moment later the door opened.

Guy Barbier let him in. The warehouse was full, stocked with crates, bins, and metal containers—contents unknown. Empty only a month before, the goods had been acquired quietly, stolen when needed, in preparation for upcoming days. Crates reached the roof in some locations, only the aisles free. A dimly lit office sat to the right.

"Fully loaded and ready when needed," Barbier said, pointing to the bins and crates. "Everything we need."

They passed a wooden box. The lid was askew, revealing rifles packed inside. "We don't intend to fight in the streets, do we?" Jacques asked.

Barbier shook his head. "No," he replied, but then hesitated. "At least not yet."

They entered the office, a cluttered room filled with dust. A worn desk with a crooked chair consumed most of the space, a straight-backed wooden chair near the door. Metal shelves lined the walls, crowded with oil cans, folders, and cardboard boxes. Papers and a half-empty pack of cigarettes shared the desk with a stained coffee cup and dirty ash tray.

"The Germans will be here shortly," Jacques said as he sat in front of the desk. "Later today or tomorrow."

Barbier grabbed two mugs and filled them with coffee. He handed a cup to Jacques. "Enjoy it," he said. "It's the real stuff. Not the chicory garbage you've been drinking."

Jacques sipped the coffee, hot and fresh, the aroma intoxicating. "I didn't realize how much I missed it."

"It could be a long time before you have more."

Jacques sat back in the chair, dwelling on what was to come. "What can we expect?" he asked. "Based on other conquered countries."

"The Germans will be pleasant for the first few days," Barbier replied. "Then restrictions will start, a little at a time so people don't realize they're losing their freedom. But before long, six months at most, everyone will realize that they're slave labor, existing only to serve the Reich."

Jacques was quiet for a moment. Each day would get harder until the war turned. It could take weeks, months, years—or even decades. But the fight had to go on. He looked at the stocked warehouse. "You seem prepared. You have a little of everything, even coffee."

Barbier leaned back in his chair. "We need more. But we have enough radios and rifles to start the networks. Soon we'll be able to help people get out—those most at risk."

"To Switzerland?" Jacques asked.

Barbier nodded. "And Spain, too. Eventually to England, maybe through some of the fishing villages along the coast."

Jacques was quiet for a moment. "I was raised not far from the Spanish border. My parents sell supplies to the wineries." He looked at Barbier and smiled. "If this war ever ends, maybe I will, too."

Barbier chuckled. "I'm not so sure about that. You like the excitement too much. I think you'll always be in intelligence."

Jacques shrugged. "Maybe you're right," he muttered. He sipped his coffee and glanced at the crates in the warehouse. "Isn't it risky to keep supplies here?"

"It's only temporary. Some will go to locations in Paris. We'll move the rest to the networks when they're ready."

Jacques considered the preparations and participants needed for a successful operation. "We'll have to watch who we recruit."

Barbier nodded. "We can't make mistakes. People will die if we do."

Jacques didn't reply. Traitors were everywhere. Even where no one expected.

"Any updates from Camille?" Barbier asked. "London can really use those diamonds."

"No messages," Jacques said. "I assume she's still in Tournai, trying to get to Paris. Sophie laid out escape routes, using what contacts are still in place."

"Not much of a network left in northern France."

"No, it's in shambles," Jacques said. "But Sophie will do what she can—if Camille needs help."

"It'll be easier now that Paris has fallen. Fighting in the north will end. Pockets of resistance, not much more."

"And with Paris captured, France will surrender," Jacques said. "A week at most. She'll be able to move through the country."

Barbier sipped his coffee. "Should we contact her, regardless of the risk? Tell her to bring the diamonds as fast as she can? We can't let anyone else get them."

Jacques shrugged. "We might make it worse. What if she's surrounded by Germans?"

Barbier was quiet for a moment, as if considering alternatives. "It may get harder when the fighting ends, not easier. The Germans will watch us more closely."

"I hadn't thought of that," Jacques admitted. "We'll warn her when she sends her next message. She should only need a few more days."

Barbier leaned across the desk. "But that's just it, Jacques. We may not have a few more days."

CHAPTER 56

Ziegler and Bayer drove out of Tournai, down the dirt road that crossed the stream and went into France. They stopped at the farmhouse closest to the city, still several kilometers from the border, and got out of the car.

"It looks deserted," Ziegler said as they walked up to the entrance.

Bayer knocked on the door. They waited a moment. When no one answered, he knocked harder.

Ziegler walked to the side of the house, scanned the property, and continued around the back. The barn doors were closed, no livestock was visible. He saw no vehicles, although a tractor was likely in the barn.

When he returned, Bayer was still on the porch. "Should I break down the door?"

Ziegler shook his head. "No," he replied. "If they're not here now, they weren't here for the fighting."

"Let's check the next farmhouse," Bayer suggested. "We can always come back."

They got in the car and drove away.

"The road curves," Ziegler observed. "This next farmhouse

has a better view of the abandoned car even though its farther away."

A moment later they pulled into a narrow drive that led to an older farmhouse, a rail fence rimming the property. A dozen cows wandered the pasture. As they stopped the car, a man dressed in blue overalls, dirt smudges on the knees, exited the house. He stood on the porch, his arms folded across his chest, and waited for them.

"Good afternoon," Bayer said to the man in French.

The farmer nodded. "How can I help you?"

Bayer continued in French. "We're looking for a young woman, blonde, who abandoned her car on the highway, probably a week or so ago."

The farmer shrugged. "I didn't see anyone."

"She would have crossed the fields, carrying satchels or bags."

He shook his head. "Sorry."

Ziegler didn't speak French, but he could tell by the man's posture that he didn't want to cooperate. He decided to prompt him.

"Is he not answering your questions, Sergeant?" he demanded in German, not knowing whether the man spoke the language or not.

Bayer knew Ziegler wanted to intimidate the farmer. "No, Major, he is. It's all right."

The farmer unfolded his arms and held up his hands. "Please, I don't want any trouble. I have a family."

"He wants no trouble," Bayer said to Ziegler in German.

Ziegler nodded and pretended to relax, amused that a simple sentence, and the tone in which he delivered it, had so frightened the man. "Ask him about the farmer with the French troop truck in his field."

Bayer nodded. "Do you know the farmer who lives by the stream?"

"The doctor?" the farmer asked.

"Doctor?" Bayer asked.

"Yes, he was a doctor in Tournai."

"And now he's a farmer?"

The man shrugged. "I don't know him well. I just know he used to be a doctor."

"How long has he lived there?" Bayer asked.

"About eighteen months."

Bayer turned to Ziegler and related what the farmer had said.

"Interesting," Ziegler muttered. "Ask why he's no longer a doctor?"

The front door of the cottage opened, and a child walked out, a girl, six or seven years old, with blonde hair and big brown eyes. She stared at the Germans curiously, as if she found new playmates.

"Chloe, go back inside," the farmer said, looking at the Germans, eyes wide.

"I want to stay with you, papa."

"Let us talk to your father," Bayer said, offering a smile.

"Chloe," the father scolded. "Listen to me."

The child stood there, studying Ziegler closely.

The major, a man known for ruthlessly destroying his enemies, managed a weak smile. He reached inside his pocket and withdrew the piece of candy he had bought in the village. He handed it to the girl. "Chocolate," he said in German.

"Chloe, go inside," the father said.

Ziegler held up his hand and turned to Bayer. "Tell him it's all right."

Bayer complied. The farmer nodded, fear still etched on his face.

The girl opened the wrapper and took a bite of the chocolate. "Hmm, it's so good papa."

Ziegler chuckled. "I thought you would like that."

The farmer eyed Ziegler uneasily, as if suspecting a trick.

Ziegler met his gaze, not flinching. "Ask him about the doctor."

"Why did the doctor become a farmer?" Bayer asked in French.

"His wife and daughter were in an automobile accident. They were hurt very badly. He tried to save them but couldn't. They both died."

"But a doctor can't be God," Bayer said. "Why not continue helping others?"

The farmer shrugged, either unable to answer the question, or unwilling to volunteer information.

Bayer watched him for a moment and, when no more was offered, he continued. "I'm sure it was a terrible tragedy," he said. "I can certainly understand. But what could have been so horrible that he no longer practices medicine?"

The farmer studied the two Germans for a moment and then replied. "He was driving the automobile."

Bayer cringed. He relayed the information to Ziegler, who showed a hint of compassion.

"Ask him about the blonde," Ziegler said.

"If he was so devastated that he gave up being a doctor, why did he marry again so soon—the blonde woman?"

The farmer looked at them strangely. "He's not married. He lives alone."

CHAPTER 57

Lucien followed Camille out to the truck, nervously watching farm fields for approaching Germans. He now recognized the danger and, even though he still didn't know who she was, he realized she had special skills. If anyone could escape the enemy, she could.

She tossed the satchel with her belongings in the front seat. "Put your bags in here."

Lucien did as requested, wondering what was next. It wasn't the time to ask. He would do what he was told.

"Let's go in the barn," she said.

"For the petrol?"

"No, we can't take the petrol," she said. "It'll look suspicious. Maybe if we had gone before the Gestapo came. But not now."

She bent over the wooden crates stacked by the door and took the lid off the largest. It was filled with junk—machinery parts, nuts, and bolts. She opened two more and found the same.

Lucien watched her, curious. "What do we need those for?"

She stood up and stepped to the door, glancing down the road. "I have to empty three crates, put two satchels and a suitcase in the bottom, and then cover them with parts."

"Show me which ones, and I'll empty them."

"These three," she said, pointing. "I'll get everything from the troop truck."

He did as she requested. After he removed material from two of the crates, he paused and peered out of the barn. She was at the French truck. She had climbed inside the vehicle.

"What are you doing?" he called.

"Come help me," she said.

He emptied the third crate and ran to the truck. When he got there, she was climbing out through the window. Two satchels and a suitcase were lying on the ground. "I have to get these on the truck but hidden inside the crates."

He picked up the suitcase, straining to lift it. "What is this? It must weigh fifteen kilos."

"A radio," she said. "Be careful with it."

She lifted a larger satchel, and then grabbed the cloth sack.

"What's in the sack?" he asked.

"Two hand drills and some papers. I can't risk having them found."

"Do we need them?"

She shrugged. "We may. But probably not."

"What's in the large satchel?"

"Come in the barn," she said, not replying.

They went inside. She laid one of the satchels in the base of the crate, and put some of the original parts back in. "Put this in the truck. We have to hurry."

He still had many questions. But the time would come to ask them, so he kept quiet. He helped her lay the satchel in the bottom of another crate and cover it with junk—old tools, pipe fittings, machine parts. They did the same for the radio, enclosed in its case, and loaded them on the truck, along with the remaining three crates that they never emptied—six in total.

She looked at her watch and then to the adjacent farmhouses that ran down the road. She paused, peering at a farm that was farthest away, around a bend.

"What are you looking at?" he asked, watching her curiously.

"Get in the truck, we have to go."

"Is it safe to go to Tournai?" he asked. "Germans were everywhere the last time we went."

"Come on," she replied, not answering his question. "We have to hurry. Before they come back."

CHAPTER 58

The German army didn't flood Paris. It trickled in from different directions. At first, only a few motorcycles drove down the streets. But the rest soon followed, marching down broad boulevards. The streets lined with timid residents; tears streamed down some faces. By late morning, the swastika hung from the Arc de Triomphe, the Hotel Crillon and many other landmarks in the most beautiful city in the world, announcing to all who now ruled Paris.

Many residents kept their shutters closed. But as morning yielded to afternoon, and the conqueror committed no crimes, engaged in no atrocities, shutters began to open, and people peeked from windows. Some stepped onto pavements, while others were brave enough to leave the twisting lanes of Paris to watch the Germans parade down the wide avenues that made the city so beautiful. Cafés opened near noon. Some proprietors offered free drinks to the soldiers, knowing they now lived in a world far different from when they woke that morning.

Emilie Dufort was alone in her apartment. Jacques had left just after dawn, before the first Germans had begun to trickle in. He said he had to meet a contact to begin the subversive war he was about to fight. He wouldn't discuss it, just as he wouldn't discuss whatever war he had fought before it, clouded in the murky world of espionage. She wondered if he was instead wrapped in the arms of his girlfriend or plotting in a darkened room with the mysterious Guy Barbier.

She waited anxiously, her drapes pulled closed like her neighbors, expecting the enemy to break down her door. But when the morning passed quietly and afternoon arrived, she ventured from the house to the café on the Boulevard Saint-Germain. The tables were empty except for an older man who sat in a corner, an unread newspaper folded before him. She sat a few tables away, under the shade of a plane tree, and stared at the nearly empty avenue.

The waiter had just served her when a German staff car came down the boulevard, two motorcycles in front and rear. She suspected someone of rank rode in the car, but realized if it was really an important official, a much larger presence would protect him, especially on the first day that the enemy controlled the city.

Emilie stared at the car as it stopped. The driver got out and opened the rear passenger door. An officer emerged, tall and thin and straight, and he stood at the curb, studying the establishment, the two patrons, and the waiter, who all stared back wide-eyed and afraid.

Emilie wasn't sure what to do. Should she leave, and hurry back to her house? Was she in danger? Should she tell him that she was from Germany, so he didn't assume she was the same as those his army had conquered? Or was that even more dangerous, exposing her to an angry populace? She glanced at the older man. He watched the enemy as the enemy watched him.

It was the waiter who broke the impasse. He motioned to an empty table, not far from Emilie, tucked in the shade with a commanding view of the boulevard. "Please, be seated, sir."

The officer nodded and walked to the table. He stopped and bowed slightly to Emilie. "Madame," he said, in accented French.

She didn't know how to respond, or what she was expected to say, so she simply nodded and smiled. She spoke German, but somehow a public café didn't seem the place to demonstrate it. It was safest to hide in the shadows, making no fuss, not calling attention to herself.

"It's a beautiful day, isn't it?" the German continued.

"Yes, it is a beautiful day," she replied. She wanted to seem friendly, but not overly so. Her heart was racing, fearing she might be whisked away into the staff car and taken to prison. But she had committed no crime.

"What brings you to the café?"

"I usually have a coffee before I open my store," she said. She pointed a block away. "All Things Napoleon."

He cocked his head. "All Things Napoleon?"

"It's military memorabilia. Books, weapons, toy soldiers, medals—anything related to Napoleon, his conquests, and his enemies."

"Interesting, I shall have to visit," the German said, looking at his watch. "But it's afternoon. When does your store open?"

"We closed today," she said, her voice quivering slightly. "I didn't know what to expect."

"I see," the officer said and then nodded respectfully. "I shall visit tomorrow."

Emilie smiled politely as he turned and walked away.

The officer glanced at the older man, nodding as their gazes met. The man responded but shifted his gaze to the newspaper. The officer stepped past him and sat, removing a pair of black leather gloves.

The waiter brought his coffee a moment later. The German took a sip, seemed to enjoy it, and observed the boulevard beyond, admiring the most beautiful city in the world.

Emilie had made her first contact with the Germans. But it wouldn't be her last.

CHAPTER 59

Ziegler and Bayer left the farmer and his daughter standing on their porch and went back to their car. The farmer eyed them curiously as they quickly departed, providing no explanation. He seemed to realize he had said something he shouldn't have.

"Let's see if the blonde is still with the doctor," Ziegler said as they got in the car. "I would guess she is not."

Bayer drove down the lane that led to the farmhouse and turned onto the dirt road that ran into France. Three or four minutes later, they reached Lucien Bouchard's farm. Bayer entered the dirt drive, guiding the staff car to the cottage.

"The truck is gone," Ziegler said as they came to a halt. "Let's see if anyone is here."

They got out of the car, scanned the property, and went to the entrance. Bayer knocked on the door while Ziegler paced back and forth. When no one answered, Bayer knocked again. Another moment quietly passed.

"Should I break it down, sir?" Bayer asked.

Ziegler pointed to the damaged molding on the door jamb. "Someone already has," he observed. He looked at Bayer and nodded.

Bayer kicked the door open. He withdrew his pistol from the holster and cautiously entered. "Is anyone here?" he asked in French.

The cottage was quiet. Bayer took another step, advancing cautiously, his pistol pointed at imaginary targets.

"It looks empty," Ziegler said. "But make sure."

Bayer went into each room while Ziegler waited at the entrance. A moment later he returned, shaking his head.

"Have they fled, or are they just in Tournai or the village?" Ziegler asked.

Bayer shrugged. "Nothing seems disturbed."

Ziegler went in the bedroom. He opened each bureau drawer and then went through the closet, shuffling the clothes. He stopped at the wall safe. "I wonder what was kept in here," he muttered. "I noticed it when we came earlier."

"The diamonds?" Bayer asked.

Ziegler shook his head. "Too small. But I did just make an interesting discovery, although not unexpected after talking to the farmer."

Bayer was confused. "What is that, sir?"

"No women's clothes," Ziegler replied. "Not anywhere."

Bayer shrugged. "Maybe the woman threatened the doctor to cooperate. She fled, but the doctor remains."

Ziegler went into the spare room. He glanced at the couch, walked to the closet, checked inside, and turned to leave. He paused, looking at the wall.

"What is it?" Bayer asked.

Ziegler pointed. "The nail in the wall. A photograph hung from it. But now it's gone."

"Something the doctor didn't want us to see?"

"Or something the doctor took with him," Ziegler said.

"Do you think they left for good?"

"Most likely," Ziegler said. "The blonde is smart. She knew we would question neighbors and find out they lied."

"Do you think he's an accomplice? Someone she knew before? Or did she come here when her car broke down?"

Ziegler shrugged. "We won't know until we find them. Let's look around back."

They went behind the cottage, checked the smaller outbuildings, but found nothing. They went to the barn.

"What's all this on the floor?" Bayer asked, looking at nuts and bolts and machine parts scattered in the dirt. "I don't remember seeing it when we last came."

Ziegler was quiet, glancing around the building. "Something was stored here, boxes or crates. I don't quite remember."

"They must have taken them."

Ziegler studied the mess and shrugged. "Why?" he asked. "It's nothing but junk."

"Maybe they delivered the boxes somewhere," Bayer offered. "They could be on their way back."

"I don't think so," Ziegler said. He thought for a moment—a house filled with men's clothes, a missing photograph. His face firmed. "She knows we're close. And she knows we'll find her. She just doesn't know when."

CHAPTER 60

"Where are you going?" Lucien asked as Camille drove away from the farm. She had turned toward France, and now they had crossed the border. "I thought we were going to Tournai?"

"We are."

"It's much quicker the other way."

"I'm not in a hurry to get there, I'm in a hurry to get away from the farm."

He looked at her quizzically. "Can you please tell me what's going on?"

"I saw the Gestapo at your neighbor's. They're probably at your farm right now."

"How do you know that?"

She turned and looked at him. "Because they're closing in on us."

` "Are we still going to Tournai?"

"Yes, I'll circle around and come in from the south," she said as she turned a corner, moving from one dirt road to the next. "I don't want them to see us."

He sat back and looked at Camille. "Who are you?"

"I'm Camille."

"Camille, a diamond thief who can open safes and speak multiple languages."

"You can't drink," she said, not replying. "Promise me. It's too dangerous. You have to stay clear-headed."

He held up his trembling hand. "Look at my hand. It's going to be much harder than you think. It's easy to say don't drink. It's much harder to do it."

"We have no choice, Lucien."

He put his trembling hand in his lap. She rarely called him by name. It was nice. He liked it. And as much as he appreciated her concern, and how important it was that he stay sober, he didn't think he could do it—or if he even wanted to. He would try, he had promised her he would, but he doubted he would succeed. He wasn't strong enough. He knew that, but she did not.

The kisses they shared were nice, he couldn't deny it. Even though he hadn't expected to be kissed. But she had exposed her feelings, which was rare. It took courage. But then, she never wanted for courage. She had more than her share. Maybe the kiss was a signal, a reassurance that they were together—through circumstances or divine intervention, it didn't matter. And if he needed a crutch, she would support him.

She continued down the back roads and entered Tournai from the south. She went down side streets, some no more than narrow lanes. There were few vehicles, some wagons drawn by horses. They passed a German staff car, a few motorcycles, but aroused no suspicion. Camille rounded a corner, paused to let a wagon loaded with furniture pass, and then steered the truck into a narrow alley and stopped.

"Come on," she said. She took a few blouses from her clothes satchel.

Lucien looked at her strangely but got out of the car. "What do you want me to do?"

"Get the crate that has the radio in it," she said. "I'll get one of the others."

He did as she said. She put the blouses on top of the parts, so it looked like they were filled with clothes, should anyone be watching. He followed her out of the alley and onto a side street that met a major boulevard a few doors down. She abruptly turned to a dressmaker's shop with lace and quilts displayed in the window. An older woman, her white hair in a bun, round spectacles perched on her nose, greeted them as they entered.

"The store is empty," she said. She looked at Lucien. "Is this another package?"

"Both of us, but not like the last delivery," Camille replied, referring to Henry Green, the English soldier.

"How long?"

"A few days at most," Camille said as she led Lucien to a set of stairs in the rear of the store. A rope was draped across them with a sign stating do not enter. She set the crate down and turned to Lucien. "Put it down and we'll get the rest."

Lucien did as he was told, still wondering what was going on. They hurried back to the truck.

"Get the crate with my other satchel," she said. "I'll get our clothes and the medical bag."

He did as he was told, and they hurried back to the store—first ensuring the street was empty. They carried everything inside and set it down by the stairs.

"Anything else?" asked Mme. Abadie, the old woman.

Camille shook her head.

Mme. Abadie went to the front of the store and locked the door. She hung a sign that read: be back in fifteen minutes. She then met them at the steps and moved the barrier aside.

"Come on," she said. She led them up a flight of stairs to a small landing, shelfs with canned goods in front of them, a closed door to the left, probably to her second-floor apartment.

Lucien stood there dumbly as the woman grabbed the left

rail of the shelf and tugged it forward. It opened, like a door, exposing a hidden stairway.

"Hurry," Camille said. "Get everything upstairs."

Lucien picked up the crate with the radio and started up the steps.

CHAPTER 61

Emilie and Jacques sat down for dinner shortly before seven p.m. She had prepared coq au vin, with bread, salad, and chardonnay. She was surprised Jacques was home. He had missed dinner the last few days.

"I hadn't expected to talk to Germans so soon," she said, relating her experience at the café. "His French wasn't bad, either. At least he made an effort."

"Was he rude?" Jacques asked.

"No, not at all," she replied. "He was stern but polite."

"The Germans can be ruthless. Don't think that this officer is typical. He is not."

She eyed him anxiously. "I feel like you know something that I don't. Can you share it with me?"

He shrugged. "I only know rumors from occupied countries. It won't be easy. And it'll get worse every day."

"Why can't you tell me more?" she asked, hoping he might reveal something she could share with Louie Bassett. "How do you know all of this?"

He shook his head. "You know I can't."

"But sometimes I feel like I know nothing about you," she protested. "And you're my husband."

"That's good," he said. "You should know nothing about me." Then he smiled. "Except that I love you."

She playfully smacked his arm. "But I worry. Why should you risk your life?"

"I do what I must, dangerous or not. All you need to know is that I work for the transportation department."

"Except that you don't work for the transportation department."

He frowned. "I'm trying to protect you."

She watched as he ate his dinner. She decided to focus on forged identity papers. It would give him another chance to admit they existed. "Shouldn't we just flee?" she asked. "Or at least make preparations?"

"I still think it's better to stay," he said. "I have my work; it can't be ignored. And you have your store."

"I'm still afraid of the future. I see stores closed all over the city. The terrified owners fled, trying to protect their families."

He hesitated, as if surprised she was so upset. "The Germans want the local economy to thrive. They need goods and services, too. Everything will be all right. Rough at first, but we'll get through it."

She suspected he spoke the truth. Germany would need businesses to operate. Someone had to earn money and pay taxes. Her store would do well—a new customer base with military backgrounds. Jacques was right. She had nothing to fear—for a variety of reasons, some unknown to him. But she had to pretend she did.

"I should see what German language books we have," she said. "I'll buy more if I can find them."

"You should," he suggested. "Increase your German and Austrian inventory—run adds to buy personal collections. I suspect you'll do well. You're a good businesswoman."

"Yes, you're right," she said. "It's a great opportunity."

"It is," he agreed. "Watch the other bookstores. You'll be shocked how quickly they carry German language volumes."

She nodded. "We'll adjust. We have to."

"The whole city will adjust," he said. "And if we're wrong, and we later decide to flee, I'll have documents prepared—identity papers, travel permission."

Emilie fought to stay silent. Jacques already had his papers. He could flee at a moment's notice. And he probably would. "If you think it's prudent," she said, feigning uncertainty. "You'll have papers made for both of us?"

"As a contingency," he clarified. "If it gets too dangerous. But for now, we do nothing different."

"Is it safe to open the store?" she asked. "I kept it closed today."

"Absolutely," he replied. "Germans buy books, too. You'll see."

"Will you still go to your government office?" she asked. "Or will the Germans suspect your real role?"

"I will do as ordered. But I will remain in Paris, no matter what happens."

Emilie looked down at her plate. Jacques already had his identity papers. And the second set were clearly for his lover. He had no intention of staying in Paris.

CHAPTER 62

Colonel Erik von Horn was commanding officer of the Gestapo's Tournai field office. A fanatical Nazi, intensely loyal to the Fuhrer, he truly believed war was the vehicle for Germany's destiny—world domination. Tall and thin, a career military officer, the Prussian was almost sixty, and determined to rule the region with no resistance from the residents.

Von Horn sat at his desk in Tournai, the largest office in the former Jewish law firm's building and examined dispatches from Berlin. After reviewing the first few documents, he saw a request more than an update, a demand that had to be met. He waved his aide into his office.

"Get Ziegler," he directed, face firm.

Five minutes later, Major Josef Ziegler tapped on the jamb of the opened office door. "You wanted to see me, sir."

"Sit," von Horn directed. "I'm reviewing the latest dispatches from Berlin."

Ziegler knew why he was in the room. But he pretended he didn't. "What may I do to assist, sir."

Von Horn cast an icy stare. "Where are the diamonds?"

Ziegler shifted in the chair. "I have yet to locate them, sir."

Von Horn's gaze was fixed on his underling. "Have you

made any progress? I know you found the woman's car, but that was a week ago."

Ziegler knew he had to be careful. He didn't want to incur von Horn's wrath. "We've twice come close to apprehending her. A pharmacist in the village saw her in a church steeple, with what appeared to be a radio. She had left an hour before we arrived."

"Are we monitoring radio communications?"

"Yes, sir, we are."

"Why haven't you found her?"

"We've come very close," Ziegler said. "While interrogating local farmers, we learned that she was hidden at a local farm owned by a man named Lucien Bouchard."

Von Horn eyed him sternly. "Has she been taken into custody?"

"Not yet, sir," Ziegler replied. "When Sergeant Bayer and I went to arrest them, they had already fled, minutes before we arrived."

"What does this man Bouchard have to do with it?"

"Perhaps little," Ziegler explained. "The woman may have sought shelter, someplace to hide until the fighting ended. His farm is close to where her car was abandoned."

Von Horn sighed. "Why did it take so long to find her?"

"It didn't, sir. We interrogated them, along with some other residents, but they pretended to be a married couple. Quite convincingly, I might add. The woman is very cunning, speaks French and German fluently. The neighboring farms were vacant, and it was only when we questioned a farmer some distance from Bouchard that we learned he had no wife."

Von Horn nodded, apparently understanding. "When you went to arrest them, they were gone?"

"Yes, sir."

"So, they only had a few hours head start?"

"At the most, sir."

"When was this?"

"About an hour ago."

"Did you search the property? Maybe she hid the diamonds and intends to return."

Ziegler hesitated. "We did search the property, but we didn't disturb anything."

Von Horn frowned. "I want every inch of the property searched. You will find those diamonds. Do I make myself clear?"

"Yes, sir," Ziegler said as he rose to leave. He paused, a thought occurring to him.

"What is it, Major?"

Ziegler reached in his pocket and withdrew the business card. "We did find this near the vault in Antwerp," he said, handing the card to von Horn.

"All Things Napoleon, Paris," von Horn muttered, and then turned it over. "What's this Antwerp address."

"It's a dock," Ziegler explained. "I suspect that's where the diamonds were supposed to be taken, but she never made it."

Von Horn studied the card. "Maybe this is her contact, this Jacques Dufort, and he's at this business."

"That's what we suspect, sir."

"We took control of Paris," von Horn said. "If the phone lines are operating, you may be able to get a call through."

"They weren't yesterday, sir, but I will try again now."

Von Horn eyed Ziegler skeptically, as if he didn't need the distraction. "You have three days to find the woman and the diamonds. If you don't, trains to Paris should be running by then. I expect you to be on one. You don't have much time."

CHAPTER 63

"Let me get everything up to the attic," Camille said to Mme. Abadie. "Then I have to get rid of the truck."

"Be careful," Mme. Abadie warned. "Germans are everywhere. And so are those who befriended them."

The steps to the attic were steep and narrow, not as finished and friendly as the stairs from the first to the second floor. Camille picked up a crate and started up the steps.

Lucien met her at the landing. "What should I do with everything?"

"Leave it at the top of the stairs for now," she said, handing him the crate with the diamonds.

The attic was cramped and dark, just a single room with a sloped ceiling. A narrow window at the far wall overlooked the rooftop of the building behind it. A cot sat against one wall, two straight-backed chairs against a brick chimney.

Lucien went down the stairs and retrieved another crate. Camille grabbed their clothing and the medical bag and followed him up. They put everything along the wall, beside the cot.

"I have to get rid of the truck," she said.

"What will you do with it?" he asked. "I need it for the farm."

She knew she couldn't tell him the truth, that he would likely never see his truck or the farm again. "I'll leave it in an alley, hidden well. It'll be there when it's safe for us to get it."

He gazed at her curiously, as if he wasn't sure he believed her. After a moment, he simply nodded.

She reached into her satchel and withdrew a beige kerchief. She wrapped it around her head, hiding as much of her hair as she could. "Wait here and don't make any noise. I'll be back soon."

"Do you need me to do anything?" he asked with a bewildered expression, as if he wasn't sure what was happening.

Camille smiled. "No, just wait for me. I won't be long."

She hurried down the steps and pushed the shelves back in place. She then went down to the store, put the barrier back across the steps and walked to the counter.

"Thank you," she whispered as she handed Mme. Abadie some money. "For our expenses—with a little extra. I have to get rid of the truck. I'll be back in thirty or forty minutes."

"Come in the store like any other customer," Mme. Abadie said as she followed her to the door and removed the closed sign. "We don't want anyone suspicious."

Camille nodded and stepped out. When she got to the pavement, she eyed an older couple walking down the street. They looked in shop windows. They weren't watching her. On the main boulevard, a German troop truck passed, but there wasn't much traffic. It seemed safe. She walked to the corner and turned abruptly into the alley. It was deserted. With a last glance to make sure no one watched, she got in the truck and drove to a connecting street.

She turned left, away from the city center. It was a narrow street, residential, with rows of townhouses and apartments. When she approached the outskirts of the city, she turned abruptly. She then drove across town, away from the dress shop. She would leave the truck on the other side of the city.

As she went down a cobblestone road, she looked in the rearview mirror. A German staff car passed the intersection behind her. It stopped and started to back up. She made a sharp right turn into an alley and punched the accelerator. When she reached the end of the lane, she looked in the mirror. The front bumper of the German car appeared at the foot of the alley, following her.

She made another right, turning before the German car fully appeared. She sped to the corner and made another right, traveling in a circle. When she reached the intersection where she had started, the German car sped down the alley she had left, pursuing her. But she had lost them. At least for now.

Camille went straight for three blocks. As she approached the next boulevard, she turned into a crowded alley to her right. It was cluttered with wagons, a parked sedan on wooden blocks at the end, one tire missing. Rubbish cans were scattered along the length. It didn't pass through to the next street as most alleys did. It ended at a brick building that fronted on the boulevard.

She idled to the very end and stopped when the front bumper touched the brick wall. She got out quickly, made sure no one watched, and moved some rubbish cans behind the truck to help hide it, making it seem like it had been there for a while. Then she hurried to the end of the ally and went out to the boulevard, walking briskly, her head down. Whenever soldiers or a German vehicle approached, she stopped and looked in the nearest shop window. Block by block, she got closer to Mme. Abadie's shop.

CHAPTER 64

Emilie knocked on Louie Bassett's door, glancing at the cemetery across the street while she waited for him to answer. The German occupation had progressed, more soldiers visible than on the day they arrived, and the takeover of government and industry had begun. The railroads had already been commandeered, facilitating troop movements around France.

The door opened and Louie peeked out, ensuring no one wandering down the street seemed interested in the woman arriving at his townhouse. "Come in," he said, ushering her into the parlor.

The room was dark, the drapes closed. Little sunlight filtered through, coming in from the foyer. Louie went to a window and parted the drapes to brighten the room.

"Any more information from Jacques?" he asked as he sat beside her on the sofa.

She shook her head. "No, nothing more. He's only been home for dinner once since the Germans came. He did say he's been going to his office every day. But he hasn't brought any more papers home—only those I photographed."

Louie frowned. "He's destroying them, so the Germans don't find them. Do you know what he pretends to be?"

She shrugged. "I don't know what you mean. He's in military intelligence."

"I realize that," he replied. "But he must have a fake position, a cover."

"He works in transportation, but I don't know details. Something with the railroads."

Louie paused, as if considering all to come. "His time is limited. The Germans will realize he has no function. Another reason why he's planning his escape."

Emilie sat back. "I've always felt guilty knowing I might be forced to betray him. But now I wonder if our roles have been reversed. Had he always intended to betray me? Or did it happen when he met his lover. Is anything in my life real—other than my store?"

Louie looked away, as if unable to face her. "I suspect you know the answer to that. As painful as it is."

She was quiet, the supposed spy who had been spied upon, the fake wife fooled by her fake husband. Maybe she really was nothing more than an insurance policy. What she thought was love and happiness was rehearsed and pretended, a part in a play—with the roles reversed.

Louie watched her closely as she reached conclusions. "Have you encountered any Germans?"

"Yes, I have," she said. "On the day they arrived. I went to the café. The outdoor tables were empty, just an older man with a newspaper and me. A German car stopped, and an officer stepped out. He nodded politely, chatted for a moment, and sat down. He ordered a coffee."

"Your impression?"

She shrugged. "Stern but polite. At least for now. I know it won't last."

"It'll get harder every day," he said. "Especially for those, like us, who have to fool the French and not openly defer to our German comrades. Never forget the role we play."

"When will we approach the Germans to tell them who we are?"

"Not yet," he replied. "I'll tell you when the time is right."

She nodded, leery of playing both sides of the conflict. She had her store to think about. "I value my customers above all else. My store is my life. I don't what to jeopardize that."

"Just be careful," he advised. "You can no longer trust your neighbors; you can no longer trust your friends. Self-preservation supersedes all else. That's what happens when fear rules."

She sighed, knowing what a dangerous game they played. "What do we do for now?"

"We act as we planned. You collect information and I route it to the right people."

Emilie would soon be risking her life, every minute of every day. She wanted some assurance. "Who is your contact?"

He looked at her, eyes wide. "Do you doubt I'm who I claim?"

She fixed her gaze on his. "I need to be sure. Each day brings dangers I never thought I would face."

"I understand," he said. "But I can't tell you my contacts or who I take orders from. You know that. It's too dangerous. For them and you."

"But your contacts will protect you," she said. "Not me. I am alone. At least until the phone lines are operating. Then I can contact my family."

"My network must be preserved above all else," he replied, not answering.

"But I feel exposed. I don't know what comes next."

"It's best not to think about it," he said. "Focus on our mission, live day by day, and do what we can to defeat the enemy."

She wasn't convinced. "I understand," she said, without much conviction.

He went to a table and poured two glasses of wine. He sat

beside her, handing her one. "I forwarded your photographs. They were very much appreciated. I wish you had more."

She shrugged. "I told you it's been quiet. I suspect that one day soon Jacques won't come home at all. He'll vanish with his lover."

"Sophie Silvain is her name," he said, almost apologetically. "They've worked together for months."

"I suppose it could be a professional relationship. But I doubt it. Especially after I saw the forged identity papers."

He nodded, respectful of her feelings "It started as a professional relationship."

"I wish I didn't know her name. Somehow it made it easier."

"Every day will get better," he assured her. "Just don't feel guilty about betraying him. Look what he's doing to you."

She sighed. "I have the store. I don't know what I would do without it."

"Has Guy Barbier come back?"

She shook her head. "No, I think he only comes when Jacques has papers for him."

Louie was quiet. "I need to know as soon as you learn anything about Guy Barbier or the diamonds. It's critical."

"I've heard nothing. But as soon as I do, I will tell you."

"You'll hear something soon. They're getting desperate."

CHAPTER 65

Sergeant Bayer turned into the lane that led to Lucien Bouchard's house, the outbuildings spread behind it. "The truck is still gone," he said. "It doesn't look like anyone is here."

"They probably fled together," Ziegler muttered, annoyed he had missed an opportunity. "We'll start by searching the cottage again."

They went to the entrance. Bayer knocked. They waited, but only for a moment. When no one replied he shoved the door. With the jamb already splintered, it swung open with little resistance. He drew his pistol and stepped inside. Ziegler followed.

"Is anyone here?" Bayer called in French. He walked through the house, room by room, while Ziegler waited at the entrance. "It's empty, sir."

They went through each room, again searching closets and going through kitchen cabinets. They looked under the bed, along the baseboard, behind any paintings that hung on the walls, and examined the opened safe in Lucien's closet. But they found nothing.

"Let's check outside," Ziegler said.

They went through the kitchen door and paused, surveying the property.

"If she dug a hole to hide the diamonds, we may never find them," Bayer observed. "It's over a hundred acres."

Ziegler looked at the planted crops. They were still close to the ground, early in the growing season. "Let's check the outbuildings again. If we don't find anything, we'll walk through the fields."

"I'll look at the chicken coop and the shed beside it," Bayer said, walking toward the stream.

"Feed the chickens," Ziegler said. "When we leave, we'll tell the farmer with the little girl to come and get them. I'll be in the barn."

The barn was undisturbed from their last visit. Ziegler strolled through, looking more closely than he had before. But he still didn't see anything unusual. It was the barn of a simple farmer, nothing more. Many of the tools and bits of machinery had probably been there for fifty years. And they might remain for fifty more.

Fifteen minutes later, Bayer came into the barn. "I didn't find anything."

Ziegler was on a ladder, looking up in the rafters. "There's nothing here, either. Just junk. This barn has probably never been cleaned."

"I suppose we can walk the fields," Bayer offered. "We may find evidence of a freshly dug hole, or dirt that's been disturbed."

"Let's start along the stream," Ziegler said as he climbed down. "She probably would have left her car and came right down the east bank."

They left the barn and walked past the chicken coop. When they reached the stream, they looked back at the property, gazing over the acreage. It was a small farm, but enough for a man to make a living. Remote, yet close to Tournai, it was serene, the stream slicing through it. The location was good, the soil fertile. It had likely been farmed for a hundred years—or more.

Ziegler stopped, transfixed, staring at the rusted French troop truck. A dozen different images ran through his mind.

"Is something wrong?" Bayer asked.

Ziegler turned slightly. "The truck," he said simply.

They shared a knowing glance, their gazes fixed on the relic from a war fought twenty years before.

"Let's check," Ziegler said, as they walked toward it.

They moved closer, studying a damaged vehicle that nature had claimed. "I wonder what the battle was like when this truck was bombed," Bayer said.

Ziegler scanned the surroundings. "I don't see any other remnants of war. Maybe it was hit by an errant shell or a plane."

"I suppose we'll never know," Bayer said as they reached it. He paused, eyeing the rusted frame. "We should be careful."

"Yes, we should," Ziegler agreed. "If she hid the diamonds here, she may have set some sort of trap to protect them."

"Like a small bomb," Bayer muttered.

Ziegler paused a few feet away. "The weeds are trampled by the door."

Bayer peeked inside. "The vines growing through the interior have been disturbed, some of the leaves are torn."

"Someone may have climbed in."

Bayer sighed. "I'll go in and take a look."

"Be careful," Ziegler warned. "Look for a trip mechanism."

"I don't see anything," Bayer mumbled, leaning in the window.

"I'll check the back," Ziegler said as he went around to the rear.

The back was open, the canvas cover rotted away. The bed was rusty, a hole near the wheel-well, a shrub poking through it, branches brushing the side. Rust spots dotted the bed, dirt and debris lying in places, all undisturbed.

"Nothing around back," Ziegler said when he returned.

"I found something," Bayer called from the cab. "Shoved under the seat. I'll toss it out."

Ziegler stepped back as Bayer threw out bloody bandages, boots, and a pile of clothes, neatly folded, stained with blood. He climbed out.

"The space beneath and in back of the seats has been freed of debris," Bayer said. "This stuff was under the seat, but much more could have been hidden there."

"Like diamonds," Ziegler said angrily. He gazed at the broken-down Minerva in the distance, abandoned along the highway.

Bayer climbed out of the truck and sorted through what was removed. "It's an English uniform. Lots of blood. Trousers are cut. Looks like a leg wound, left thigh."

"The neighbor said the farmer was a doctor. He must have treated a wounded soldier and helped him escape."

"Do you think he's still with them?" Bayer asked.

Ziegler paused. "It makes it easier to find them if he is. The doctor must have given him civilian clothes."

"Do you think he was here the first time we came, when the blonde spoke to us in German?"

Ziegler shrugged. "I don't know where he could have been hidden."

"Maybe he was here, in the truck."

Ziegler slowly shook his head, perplexed by this woman who always seemed to outsmart them. "There's much more to the pair than we guessed."

"Do you think he was an accomplice?"

Ziegler shrugged. "I don't know. I doubt her car broke down right where her accomplice lived."

"Then a chance meeting," Bayer suggested. "Or maybe they knew each other—just acquaintances."

Ziegler frowned and shook his head. "We were here. We had her and the diamonds in our grasp. But we let them get away."

"Don't worry, sir," Bayer assured him. "We'll find them. Especially if they have a wounded Englishman with them."

"I doubt that they do," Ziegler muttered. "The Englishman may be with the doctor. The blonde is likely alone."

"But with the diamonds," Bayer said. "No matter who she's with, we'll find her. It just may be a little harder."

CHAPTER 66

Camille patiently wormed through the streets of Tournai. She sometimes walked three blocks, retraced her steps for two, crossed boulevards that went in a different direction, and came back the other way. Throughout her journey, she studied every passing pedestrian and German soldier, making sure no one watched her as closely as she watched them. An hour after she had left, she reached the dress shop. She walked to the end of the block, turned, came back, and ducked into the store.

Mme. Abadie stood at the counter by the front door. She held a finger to her lips as Camille entered, nodding toward the back of the store. Two women wandered the last row, looking at some lace and chatting quietly. Camille pretended to browse the store as any customer would, cautiously watching the street outside. She went up and down the aisles, waiting for the women to leave, knowing she wasn't truly safe until she was hidden in the attic.

A few minutes later, the women made their selections and approached the counter. Camille moved to the back, near the entrance to the attic. She stayed behind the shelves, peeking out. But just as the women left, a German soldier walked in.

"May I help you?" Mme. Abadie asked.

The German nodded but didn't speak—he didn't seem to understand French. He entered the nearest aisle, looking at the merchandise housed on the shelves.

"I can help you if you like," Mme. Abadie repeated.

Camille wondered if she had been followed, even with the precautions she had taken. Had the German staff car she eluded found the truck or saw her strolling the city streets and tracked her to the store? She removed the kerchief from her head. It was one less item they could use to identify her. She folded it carefully and tucked it under some lace on a shelf. As the German made his way to the back of the store, slowly walking the aisle, she furtively moved to the front. But he could see her now, her blonde hair, not much else.

Camille took a doily from a shelf and went to the counter. The German still paced the store, looking up and down each aisle, occasionally glancing at her.

"Is that it, dearie?" Mme. Abadie asked, eyes wide.

"Yes, for now," Camille said quietly.

She paid for her purchase and left, hurrying to an adjacent radio shop. After ensuring no one watched, she went inside, staying near the front window. A male clerk glanced up from his newspaper, smiled at her, and returned to his reading. Camille hid behind a shelf, pretending to study small clocks and radios, but instead looked out the window.

A moment later, the German came out of Mme. Abadie's shop. He carried nothing; he had made no purchase. He stood on the pavement for a moment, as if undecided, and then turned, walking in the opposite direction.

Camille left the store, furtively hiding against the wall. The soldier entered a candy store two doors down. She darted into the dress shop, Mme. Abadie waiting.

"Hurry," Mme. Abadie said. She locked the door and put up her sign.

Camille ran to the back, scrambled up the steps, and opened the secret doorway. As soon as she stepped in, Mme. Abadie put the barrier back up on the steps as Camille pulled the secret door closed behind her.

Lucien was waiting at the top of the steps. "I was getting worried."

Camille held a finger to her lips. When she reached the attic, she whispered to him. "A German was in the store."

"What for?" he asked, eyes wide. "Do they know about the Englishman? Or was it the Gestapo?"

She shrugged. "It may have been innocent."

Lucien lightly shook his head. "A German soldier in a woman's dress shop?"

"He could have been shopping, but he's gone now. He went in a nearby candy store."

"Or he could have been looking for us. How did he find the store?"

Camille almost told him about the German car that had followed her. But the less he knew the better. "I don't think he was looking for us. Only a coincidence."

"I suppose," Lucien said, seeming to relax. "Maybe he's buying a gift."

"Yes, maybe," Camille mumbled. She grabbed the radio suitcase and took it over to the window. "I have to send a transmission. It can't wait. It's too important."

Lucien looked at her, eyes wide. "Isn't that dangerous, with a German nearby?"

She shook her head. "No, he won't hear me. He's halfway down the block."

Lucien wasn't convinced. "You're sure?"

Camille glanced at him and nodded. She opened the window slightly and hung the radio antenna outside. She inserted the crystal, put on the headphones, and started to transmit.

CHAPTER 67

Jacques Dufort walked down the boulevard, hunched over with his hands in his pockets. German staff cars passed, a troop truck, a black sedan typically used by the Gestapo, and an occasional bus or delivery truck. German soldiers mingled with pedestrians, stared in shop windows at French goods, and sat in outdoor cafes, enjoying the ambience of Paris.

He had almost reached Rue Serpente, on his way to Sophie Silvain's, when three German soldiers approached from the opposite direction.

"Halt," one of the soldiers said in German, his arm extended. His two comrades paused behind him, watching curiously. "Let me see your papers."

Jacques hesitated. He hadn't expected to be stopped. But he had nothing to hide, He fumbled in his pockets.

"You must always have your papers ready," the German directed.

Jacques smiled faintly, pretending not to understand. He wondered if the soldier knew he could break his windpipe with one quick thrust of his fist. He removed his papers from his pocket and handed them to the soldier.

The German scanned the documents, examining each

detail and description. After a moment, he returned them, eyeing Jacques harshly. He tried to speak French, badly mangling the question. "Why in army aren't you?"

"Critical work," Jacques said. He had been prepared for the question—and whatever else the German might ask. "I'm in government. Transportation. Railroads, mainly."

The soldier seemed to understand, at least some of the words. He eyed Jacques a moment more and nodded, turning away.

Jacques snickered softly and continued, not looking back. The new Paris, he thought, where a man can't even walk down the street without being challenged by the enemy. He wasn't afraid of the confrontation; it had merely been a show of superiority by a soldier who wasn't superior. And in the end, he would get all he was due.

Jacques reached Sophie's apartment. He tapped lightly on her door. She answered a moment later and led him in.

"Germans are everywhere," he said as they climbed the steps. "I was stopped while they checked my papers."

"Any problems?" Sophie asked, eyebrows arched.

Jacques shook his head. "They don't even know what they're looking at. They just know that they're supposed to check."

"I'll get some coffee," Sophie said as Jacques sat on the sofa. She returned a moment later with two mugs.

"Other than that, it's been quiet," Jacques muttered. "But it won't be for long. Never trust the Germans."

"I've barely gone out," she said. "Nor has anyone else."

"We'll have to be cautious. The Germans are easing in. But each day will get worse."

She glanced at the radio by the window. "I can't leave that out much longer. A day or two at most. I have nosy neighbors. Most fled but are starting to return."

"France will surrender any day now. Many more will return

after that. They need their livelihoods. Whatever jobs they had will still be here."

"I read in the newspaper that the first German arrived at 9:45 a.m., the cafés were open by noon, and the brothels were doing a brisque business by three."

Jacques laughed. "It didn't take long."

The radio started chattering, the methodical stamp of morse code. Sophie ran over and sat down, put on the earphones, and grabbed a notepad and pencil. "All that glitters," she said, mouthing the code as she translated.

"It's Camille," he said, hurrying beside her.

Sophie listened to dots and dashes, scribbling their meaning on her notepad. It lasted almost a minute, followed by silence. She handed the pad to Jacques and started to transmit.

Jacques read the message aloud: Diamonds safe. Trapped in Tournai. Please advise."

"I replied that her message was received and to standby," Sophie said.

"Tell her she has to get to Paris and deliver as instructed—as soon as possible."

"I'll offer some travel routes with contacts, too. If she needs them."

"We'll do anything we can to help her."

Sophie started tapping the message. She finished a moment later and paused, waiting for a response. After a moment of silence, the transmission began.

"What did she say?" Jacques asked.

Sophie read the message. "Understood. Will advise on help. Over and out."

Jacques sighed with relief. "No double cross. And she's not a thief. We can rule out worst-case scenarios. Although I don't know why we ever doubted her."

"We didn't," Sophie said. "We only identified all possibilities—including that she may have been captured."

"Now we know she wasn't. She wouldn't have used the code."

Sophie glanced at the message. "It's legitimate. We had a good exchange. She'll make her way to Paris and ask for help if she needs it."

Jacques nodded. "Camille is safe. The diamonds are safe. It won't be much longer."

"She still has to get here. Northern France is overrun with Germans. It won't be easy."

Jacques again reflected on his brief meeting with Camille. "If anyone can do it, she can."

CHAPTER 68

Sergeant Bayer drove down the lane that led from the farm of Lucien Bouchard and turned toward Tournai. "Should I stop to tell the farmer about the chickens?"

"Yes, of course," Ziegler said. "Have him go and get them. I can't let the poor animals starve."

Bayer rounded a bend on the dirt road and returned to the farmer who had provided information about the doctor. While Ziegler waited in the car, Bayer explained what had happened to the farmer, and asked him to get the chickens. A moment later, Bayer returned.

"What did he say?' Ziegler asked as Bayer got in and started the engine.

"He'll go get the chickens. He was surprised the doctor was mixed up in anything, claimed he kept to himself."

"He may not have had a choice," Ziegler surmised. "The woman could have appeared at his door, unknown and unannounced. She may have forced him to cooperate. At gunpoint if she had to."

"If we get close, he may cooperate with us," Bayer offered. "He might betray her."

"It's a possibility."

The dirt road became cobblestone, and they entered the outskirts of Tournai. "Should I go back to headquarters?" Bayer asked.

Ziegler hesitated. "Drive through some of the side streets."

"Are we looking for their truck?"

"Yes, even though it's unlikely we'll find it. But I suspect they may be in Tournai. It's the only place they can get help. I doubt that they're hiding on another farm."

"They could have gone into France."

Ziegler paused, pensive. "We'll check Tournai first. Then we'll consider other possibilities. They can't get petrol, so the truck has limited use."

Bayer drove into town. When he reached Rue Saint-Martin, he turned right and drove to the end of the road, moved up one block, turned around and came back. Then he repeated the process.

"If we had some clue that they were here, we wouldn't be wasting our time," Ziegler muttered.

"They'll be hard to find if they're parked in one of these alleys."

"I don't know what else to do," Ziegler said. "We know she's in the area. She can't be that hard to locate."

"I'll go up one street and down the next," Bayer said. "If you look in the alleys as we pass, maybe we'll see them."

It was a tedious process. They repeated the same pattern, searching streets and alleys, over and over. When thirty minutes had passed, and they had traversed an entire sector of the city, Bayer looked at Ziegler in the rearview mirror.

"What should I do next, sir?"

Ziegler hesitated. "Cross the boulevard and do the same on the other side. We've nothing better to do."

Bayer did as directed. He waited for a motorcycle to pass, then crossed the main road and started searching in another segment of the city.

"Hold it," Ziegler said. He leaned forward and looked out the side window.

"What is it, sir?"

"A dog digging through rubbish for food," Ziegler said. "His owner must have fled and left him here."

"I have half a baguette," Bayer offered, as if he really didn't want to part with it.

"Let me have it," Ziegler said, reaching over the seat.

Bayer gave him the sandwich and Ziegler climbed from the car. He started down the alley, the dog at first retreating. He knelt on one knee and held out the baguette. "Come on, boy," he said. "Come and eat."

The dog hesitated. He then slowly advanced to sniff the baguette. Ziegler tossed it on the ground and stood, watching the dog eat. He studied the alley—wagons, rubbish cans, a sedan up on blocks. Suddenly, his eyes widened. "Look, down at the end," he exclaimed. "Against the brick wall. Is that the truck?"

Bayer hurried out of the car to join Ziegler. "Let's go see, sir."

They walked down the alley, moving cautiously, leery of traps or an ambush. When they reached the end, they stopped.

"This is it," Bayer said. "See the crates in the back." He removed the top from one. "Nuts, bolts, machine parts. It matches the junk on the barn floor."

"It is the same," Ziegler mumbled. "But these crates are full."

"Maybe they had more crates?"

"Crates that carried the diamonds."

"It could be, sir."

Ziegler sighed. "Let's call headquarters for help. We can have a few soldiers randomly question residents. Maybe someone will know who owns the truck or saw them when they left it here. It'll be easy if the wounded Englishman is with them, much harder if the woman is alone. Although I suspect we'll find that the vehicle was abandoned, and the culprits are long gone."

"They could be hiding nearby, sir," Bayer said. "And if they're not, they can't be too far ahead of us."

CHAPTER 69

It was after dusk when Lucien heard the secret door open. He looked at Camille, eyebrows arched.

She held a finger to her lips. She reached in her satchel and removed the pistol she had taken from Lucien's safe. "Wait here," she hissed. She went to the top of the stairs, but then lowered the gun.

Mme. Abadie came up the steps, holding a tray. "Some baguettes and a bottle of wine."

Lucien went to the stairs and took the tray from her.

"I'll close the door," Mme. Abadie said.

She went down the steps, grabbed a wooden lever and pulled, closing the door. She then came back and joined Lucien and Camille, sitting on the wooden chairs next to the chimney.

"Thank you for the meal," Lucien said, biting into the ham and cheese baguette.

"It's all I could get on such short notice."

"We're grateful," Camille added. "For the food and everything else you're doing for us." She poured two glasses of wine and handed one to Lucien.

He hesitated, not sure whether to take it. He looked at the wine, afraid, his hand trembling. Most meals were consumed with wine. But wine was alcohol. What if he drank one glass, but couldn't stop?

"It's all right," Camille said softly, watching him. She knew the battle he fought, how hard he was trying. It was as if she admired him for his courage and would help him if he faltered.

He sighed and took the glass. He lifted it to his lips but only sipped it, resisting the urge to guzzle it down and refill the glass.

"How long will you be here?" Mme. Abadie asked, not noticing the battle that Lucien fought.

Camille sighed. "A few days at most. We have to get to Paris as quickly as possible."

Mme. Abadie hesitated, eyeing them uneasily. "Not an easy task."

"Is any transportation available?" Lucien asked. He was amazed such a kind old lady participated in a clandestine network. She had hidden Henry Green and helped get him back to England, or to a place where he was safe. Now she would help them.

Mme. Abadie thought for a moment, considering alternatives. "A vehicle is out of the question," she said. "No petrol."

"Can we move from one cell to the next?" Camille asked.

"What is a cell?" Lucien asked.

Mme. Abadie wasn't sure how much she should share. She glanced at Camille, who nodded subtly. "A cell is a compartment," she explained. "I am a cell, with a compartment on each side of me."

Lucien felt stupid. But he realized it was a world he knew nothing about. "I don't quite understand."

"I explained it before," Camille said. "The chain. Mme. Abadie is a link in a chain."

He nodded, a vague understanding crossing his face. "Does the chain reach Paris?"

Mme. Abadie eyed him cautiously. "Yes, the chain does

reach Paris. But it's difficult. The individual links are disrupted. Northern France is still home to much of the German army. Troops are only now moving, some southward along the coast, as France surrenders."

"So even though the chain exists, all of the links aren't functional," Lucien said.

"Exactly," Mme. Abadie replied. "It could be some time before they are."

Camille was quiet, as if plotting and planning. "Are the trains running?"

"Yes, they are," Mme. Abadie replied. "But the Germans commandeered the railroads. Trains run, but only to support troop movements. No civilians are permitted to travel. At least, not yet. You couldn't travel anyway, not without papers."

Camille was quiet, eating her sandwich and drinking her wine. Her gaze was fixed on Lucien's medical bag, sitting beside the satchels. Her eyes then widened, as if she thought of a potential solution. "Do you have anyone who can prepare German military documents?"

They were interrupted by a distant knock, loud and continually repeated.

"Someone is at my apartment door!" Mme. Abadie hissed.

CHAPTER 70

Emilie lay in bed, drifting off to sleep. It was late, just after midnight. Jacques was in his study, going through some documents. She had talked to him briefly, but he had seemed distracted. She left him alone, came to bed, and started reading. She assumed he would come to bed shortly. But he didn't, and she couldn't stay awake any longer.

She was almost asleep when she heard a knock on the front door. Her eyes opened and she sat up, listening. She could hear Jacques in his study. The chair squeaked as he got up, and then she heard his footsteps. She got out of bed and crept into the hall.

The front door opened. "Did you have any problems getting here?" Jacques asked.

"Yes, I'm violating curfew," Guy Barbier said. "I have to be careful. I can only stay for a few minutes."

"It's important," Jacques said. "I have an update from Camille."

Once they went into the study, Emilie could barely hear them. A few mumbled words, which she couldn't understand. It seemed like they were whispering, maybe trying not to wake her. She hesitated, not sure how much risk to take. What if she eavesdropped and got caught? But then she realized she might not get another chance. She had distinctly heard Jacques say he had an update from Camille. It was important. She had to find out what it was.

She tiptoed forward, still in her nightgown. She moved a few more feet and paused, barely into the hallway. All she could hear were hushed voices. She kept going, as quietly as she could, until she reached the parlor entrance.

"It is important," she heard Jacques say.

Guy Barbier replied, his voice carrying but the words not clear. Emilie took another step, easing forward. She stood at the edge of the parlor, against the back wall.

"She's bringing the diamonds to Paris," Jacques said. "She clearly understood she has to be here as soon as possible."

"But when is that?" Barbier asked. "I'm getting pressured to deliver them. They're critical, supposedly holding up radar upgrades in London. I don't think you realize the negative impact on the war effort."

"I do realize," Jacques insisted. "And so does Camille."

"Can't she get here any sooner? I thought Sophie gave her routes and contacts."

"She did," Jacques replied. "But Camille is still in Tournai, surrounded by Germans. Maybe she can't get out."

It was quiet, no one speaking. Or Emilie couldn't hear them. She took another step.

"Do we know how she's getting to Paris?" Barbier asked. "Maybe we can do something to help her get here quicker."

"All we know is what she transmitted," Jacques said. "She has Sophie's information, and she'll get here as fast as she can. I suppose a train would be best."

"Except the Germans are using them to move troops. No civilians are permitted to travel. At least not yet."

"Camille has her own contacts in Tournai," Jacques said.

"She was stationed there for two years. I'm sure they can help her. Maybe she has a vehicle."

"She can't drive," Guy said. "There's no petrol. She might get out of Tournai, but not much farther."

Emilie couldn't hear Jacques' reply. She took another step, but only heard mumbling. It was nothing she could understand. They must have lowered their voices. She had to get closer.

The conversation continued, still hushed. She dared to take another step. The floorboard creaked. She cringed, listening. It was quiet. No one spoke—not even whispering. She waited, afraid to even breathe. She leaned against the wall, hoping no one heard her.

"What are you doing?" Jacques demanded as he stepped into the parlor.

Emilie was startled, her eyes wide. She had to convince him she hadn't been spying. She held her hand to her heart. "Oh, it's you," she said, sighing with relief. "I was terrified. I heard noises and didn't know what it was."

He folded his arms across his chest. "Go back to bed."

"Is someone with you?" she asked, still feigning alarm. "I thought I heard voices. Unless it's out on the street."

"You did hear voices," he replied sternly. "I'm meeting with someone."

She looked at him strangely, eyes wide. She would transfer suspicion to him. "Who would you meet at this time of night?" she asked with disbelief. "It's after midnight. Isn't there a curfew?"

"Go back to bed," he said testily.

CHAPTER 71

Ziegler and Bayer spent the day randomly questioning Tournai residents. They met with limited success, a few vague recollections of a truck with a blonde woman driving, but nothing substantial. Colonel von Horn also lent them a half dozen soldiers to assist. They canvassed different parts of the city, asking shopkeepers and pedestrians if they had any useful information.

Late that afternoon, Ziegler and Bayer returned to Gestapo headquarters. Discouraged, they slumped in the chairs in Ziegler's office, not knowing what to do next.

"We wasted a day," Ziegler mumbled.

"Maybe von Horn's men will find something," Bayer offered. "They're still questioning people."

"I'm not so sure they will. Random questioning is rarely successful. It reeks of desperation."

"But we did find the truck, sir. She must be here somewhere."

Ziegler drummed his fingers on the desktop. "She could have abandoned the truck and taken another vehicle. Or left by boat."

They were interrupted by a sergeant who appeared at the door. "Major, I have a message for you, sir."

Ziegler frowned. He suspected it was from Berlin, passed through von Horn, demanding the diamonds. "Are you one of Colonel von Horn's men?"

Yes, sir, I am. Sergeant Frank from communications. We intercepted a radio message that I think you'll find interesting."

Ziegler glanced at Bayer, daring to raise his hopes. "What's the message?"

Frank read it aloud. "All that glitters. Diamonds safe. Trapped in Tournai. Please advise."

Ziegler sat up straight, eyes wide. "It's her. It has to be."

"I thought it might be the thief you're looking for," Frank said.

"Did you catch them?" Ziegler asked.

Frank frowned. "No, I'm afraid not, sir. Whoever sent it was very good. They knew just how much time they had before we closed in."

"Trapped in Tournai," Bayer said. "She's right here. We just have to find her."

"Were you able to limit their potential location?" Ziegler asked.

"Not by much," Frank said. "We ruled out the northern third of the city. But if they transmit again, we can find them much faster. We know the frequency, and we have a smaller search area."

"What does all that glitters mean?" Bayer asked.

Frank shrugged. "I suspect it's a reference, confirming the sender."

"Was there a reply?" Ziegler asked.

"Yes, sir, there was." He handed the paper containing all the communications to Ziegler.

"Make Paris delivery as soon as possible," Ziegler read aloud.

"As we suspected," Bayer said. "We might not know where they are, no matter how close, but we know where they're going."

"The question is, how will they get there," Ziegler mused. "Was anything said about transportation?"

Frank shook his head. "No, sir, not that we intercepted. Two additional communications were garbled. We were losing the signal."

Ziegler pursed his lips, studying the messages. "Thank you, Sergeant Frank. I suppose that's all for now."

"If we intercept anything else, I'll bring it to you immediately, sir," Frank promised. "You're close to apprehending them."

"Thank you, Sergeant. It's much appreciated," Ziegler replied.

They sat quietly after Frank left, contemplating their next move. "The business card is the destination," Bayer said. "It can't be a coincidence. Not now."

Ziegler removed the card from his shirt pocket and studied it for a moment. "We know what the Antwerp address is."

"The failed rendezvous, their escape point."

Ziegler nodded. "But after the radio message, this becomes much more than an old business card on which to scribble notes."

"It has to be the location for the Paris delivery," Bayer noted.

"All Things Napoleon," Ziegler muttered, staring at the card. "Emilie Dufort, proprietor."

"A phone number is listed."

"I wonder if calls are getting through yet," Ziegler said. He picked up the telephone on the desk and dialed the number. "I'll try again."

CHAPTER 72

Camille and Lucien went midway down the attic steps, just on the opposite side of the secret door to the landing that led to the apartment. She held the pistol cocked in her right hand as they listened closely.

"I'm sorry it took so long," Mme. Abadie was saying as she opened her apartment door. "I was downstairs in my shop."

Camille put her mouth to Lucien's ear. "Can you hear who is speaking?"

He shook his head.

Camille leaned against the wall, her ear against the plaster.

"No, I haven't," Mme. Abadie said. "But I wouldn't have noticed anyway. Many women in Tournai have blonde hair. Do you have a photograph? Maybe I can tell from that."

Her reply was met with silence—at least Camille couldn't hear what was being said. A few minutes passed, the content of the conversation a mystery.

"I stay in my shop during the day," Mme. Abadie said. "I have no employees. If I leave, or have to come into my apartment for something, I put a sign on the door that states when I'll return."

Camille heard a cough, murmured conversation, but nothing she could understand.

"I don't remember seeing a truck," Mme. Abadie said.

More murmured conversation.

"Many trucks come in the alley," Mme. Abadie said. "They deliver to different shops along the street."

Camile pieced enough of the conversation together to realize Germans were at the door. They were closer, each minute more dangerous than the last. Their questions showed they had learned from interrogating residents. They suspected she and Lucien were in the area. Maybe they had similar information from other parts of the city, where Camille had left the truck. But eventually they would narrow their search, with very unpleasant results.

"We have to leave soon," Camille whispered to Lucien. "Another day at most."

"How did they find us?"

"They haven't. But they suspect."

"What led them here?"

"They found the truck. And they're asking people around the city if they saw us or the vehicle. They probably got vague responses that a blonde woman was driving it."

"Then they don't know anything," he whispered.

"No, maybe not. But soon they will."

"Yes, of course you can come in," Mme. Abadie said. "I have nothing to hide."

Camille looked at Lucien, a finger to her lips. "Don't even breathe," she whispered in his ear.

"We're checking every room," a man's voice said in heavily accented French.

"It's just an apartment," Mme. Abadie said. "I only have a few rooms."

Camille and Lucien could hear two heavy sets of footsteps, boots on hardwood floors. They shuffled through the apartment, doors opening and closing. The sounds were distant, on the other side of the flat. Camille guessed it was two soldiers moving about the apartment, Mme. Abadie observing. After a few minutes, footsteps approached, much louder.

"It's only the kitchen," Mme. Abadie said. "But you can look through the cabinets if you like."

There was no response. It was quiet, eerily so. No one spoke. No one moved. After a moment, a set of footsteps moved slowly toward the landing. They stopped near the apartment door. Seconds ticked by, no movement, no sounds.

The door to the landing flung open. "What is this?" a German asked loudly. "Is this where you hide people?"

Mme. Abadie started laughing. "No, of course not," she said. "It's the stairs to the store, from my apartment."

The Germans stepped onto the landing, the stairs on one side, the secret door on the other. They paused, studying the shelves, the stairs, and whatever lay below.

Camille pointed the pistol where she suspected they were standing. She could imagine the Germans only inches away, eyeing the narrow shelves filled with spices and canned goods. She listened intently, judging their position by their footsteps.

"Show me," one of the Germans demanded.

CHAPTER 73

Emilie Dufort gazed at the customers wandering through All Things Napoleon. She was near the back of the store, unpacking boxes of recent purchases—books, toy soldiers, maps, and medals. She had even found German language books to buy. She was anxious to see how quickly they would sell. The store had already recovered its sales—it had emptied for a few days after the Germans first arrived. But people had gradually filtered back, a few the first day, more on the second. Now, in addition to her loyal clientele, she had German soldiers mixed among her regular customers.

The Germans had a thirst for all things French—as if their conquest had been a dream they feared would never be fulfilled. They strolled the broad boulevards in awe, admiring the architecture, cobblestone patios that rimmed the Seine and the beautiful bridges that spanned it. They bought French wine, pastries, lace, and cheese, treating all goods like delicacies that soon might disappear. But it would change. In a matter of weeks, they would no longer be tourists.

Residents slowly adapted to a world they never thought would exist. But when it did, and they were forced to confront it, they reverted to the most basic instinct all possess—survival.

They didn't welcome the enemy, most despised them. But they pretended to accept them—they had no choice—and kept their thoughts and fears private. For many, when the time to resist arrived, they would do what was needed to save France. But sadly, many would collaborate with the enemy.

When the telephone rang, Emilie put a box of newly purchased books aside and hurried to answer it. "All Things Napoleon, may I help you?"

"To whom am I speaking?"

Emilie paused. The caller spoke French, but with an accent she recognized—German. The connection wasn't good, the line crackling with an occasional hiss, but it was manageable. "Emilie Dufort, proprietor," she replied.

"Who is Jacques Dufort?"

She hesitated, suspicious. At first, she didn't reply, wondering why they expected to find Jacques at her store. She decided to avoid the question. "How can I help you?" she asked. "We have a large collection of books and memorabilia related to Napoleon and his enemies, like Wellington and Blücher."

"Who is Jacques Dufort?" the caller repeated.

Emilie didn't reply. The caller's voice, with the bad connection, was unnerving. She wanted to be careful and not say anything she might later regret. "Who is this?" Emilie asked quietly. "And why are you asking about Jacques? Is he all right?"

"This is Sergeant Ernst Bayer of the Gestapo. I want to know who Jacques Dufort is?"

Emilie cringed, suspecting the worst. "Is he in some sort of trouble?"

The line crackled and hissed. The German's reply was inaudible.

Emilie waited, listening, but the line was silent. "I'm sorry, Sergeant," she said. "I'm having a difficult time hearing you."

"The telephone lines have just been restored. They're still not working well."

"Why do you want Jacques?"

The line hissed, was quiet, and then crackled. The sergeant was speaking, his words inaudible. They then became clear. "...and I'm calling from Tournai."

Emilie stiffened, her heart racing. Camille, Jacques's contact, was from Tournai. And now the Gestapo called from Tournai. It had to be related. Camille must have been captured and gave Jacque's name to the Gestapo. Now they were closing in. "What do you want?" she asked, her voice quivering.

"I want to speak to Jacques Dufort."

"Jacques Dufort is my husband," Emilie explained. "This is my store—All Things Napoleon. Jacques does not work here. I don't know where he is right now."

It was quiet for a moment. "It's important that I reach him," Bayer said. "How do I do that?"

Emilie hesitated. She wasn't sure how much to reveal. But if she didn't cooperate, they would come for her—they knew where to find her. "He works for the government, in the transportation department. I will give you the telephone number of his office."

It was quiet for a moment. Emilie could faintly hear a discussion. The caller was talking to someone else. A moment later, after the line crackled again, he returned. "What is the number?"

Emilie gave him the information, even though Jacques was rarely there. "He's involved with the railroads," she said, telling the lie her husband had told her to tell.

"I will contact him," Sergeant Bayer said. "I have questions he needs to answer."

"You should be able to—"

The call was ended abruptly.

CHAPTER 74

"It seemed like she was hiding something," Sergeant Bayer said. "Or it could have been the bad connection. Maybe it was difficult for us to understand each other."

Ziegler sat back in the chair, his fingers arched together. "At least the line was working," he muttered. "I'm sure she was nervous, an unannounced call from the enemy. Why do you think she was hiding something?"

"She paused before answering my questions, as if she wanted to carefully craft her reply."

"She was intimidated," Ziegler reasoned. "No one expects a call from the Gestapo."

"Yes, perhaps. Her voice was trembling. But she avoided the questions. She didn't admit that Jacques Dufort was her husband until I asked her several times."

Ziegler paused, wondering who the woman on the other end of the line was—an innocent storekeeper or an accomplice in the theft of the most valuable diamonds in the world. "Let's assume for a moment that the wife has nothing to do with the diamonds," he offered.

"That could be," Bayer said. "It was her business card, but her husband's name was scribbled on the back. She mentioned her store, and the inventory she carries, several times."

"Was she confused you would contact her and ask for her husband?"

"Yes, I think so. Maybe that's why I thought she was hiding something."

"I think there's a reason why the husband's name was on the card, but with no contact information."

Bayer thought for a moment. "Maybe there is no connection between husband and wife—at least in regard to the diamonds. Maybe the thief happened to be in this woman's store and took a business card."

"And happened to scribble her husband's name on the back?" Ziegler asked.

Bayer shrugged. "I'm not sure there's any other explanation."

"But it's very clear to me."

Bayer chuckled. "I'm afraid I can't see it, Major. Can you please explain it?"

"Let's call the husband first," Ziegler suggested, pointing to the telephone number Bayer had written down.

Bayer picked up the phone and dialed, holding the receiver to his ear. Several seconds passed before he hung up. "No answer."

"I'm not surprised."

Bayer looked at him quizzically. "I don't understand."

"Did you really think the woman would give a stranger who claimed to be the Gestapo the best way to contact her husband?"

"Do you think she lied?"

Ziegler shrugged. "I'm not sure. But I'm beginning to think she was nervous for a reason."

"Either because she knows nothing—"

"Or she knows too much."

"What about the husband?" Bayer asked.

"I suspect there's no contact information on the business card because there doesn't have to be."

Bayer's eyes widened. "The radio messages."

Ziegler nodded. "I think the intercepted transmissions were between Jacques Dufort and the woman who has the diamonds."

"But we have no proof of that," Bayer said. "Only a business card with a name scribbled on it."

"That was accidentally dropped in a closet next to the vault where the diamonds were stolen."

Bayer shrugged. "I suppose they must be connected."

"It doesn't matter anyway," Ziegler said. "It's the only clue we have. And we're quickly running out of time."

CHAPTER 75

Camille leaned against the wall, pointing her pistol at the secret door. As soon as it cracked open, she would fire. She was confident she would hit the first German. The second would be too startled to react. She would shoot him, too. She only worried that Mme. Abadie may get caught in the crossfire.

"My store is right below," Mme. Abadie said to the soldiers. "I can take you downstairs to see it. You can go out that way."

Mme. Abadie's statement was met with silence, neither German speaking. Camille suspected they eyed her cautiously, gauging her sincerity. She tensed, her grip tightening on the pistol.

A few seconds later, a light pair of footsteps started down the stairs. "It's this way," Mme. Abadie said.

After a slight pause, the Germans followed, their boots pounding the steps. The noise grew fainter as seconds passed until it was no longer heard.

Camille relaxed, but still stood poised, weapon in hand. She leaned toward Lucien. "I think they've gone."

"Should we wait here?" he asked.

She nodded. "They could be back. We have to be ready."

Several minutes passed quietly. They heard footsteps on the

landing, which passed through into the kitchen, and then it was quiet again. Camille remained ready to fire, Lucien poised to fight. Perched on the edge of the stairs, they waited for the secret door to open.

"Camille," Mme. Abadie, whispered from the landing. "Are you there?"

"Yes, just on the other side of the door."

"They've gone. I'll wait a few hours, to make sure they don't return, and then I'll come up to the attic."

Camille lowered the pistol. "We'll be waiting."

Lucien and Camille went back upstairs, a dim light casting eerie shadows on the wall. "They know we're here," Lucien said.

"No, they don't," Camille assured him. "But we can't stay. They know we're in Tournai. And they won't stop looking until they find us."

It was almost midnight when the secret door opened, and Mme. Abadie came up the stairs.

"Are you sure it's safe?" Camille asked, still holding the pistol.

"For now," Mme. Abadie said. "I had quite a scare, though."

"What happened?" Lucien asked.

"They found your truck," Mme. Abadie replied. "They're asking residents if they saw a blonde woman driving it."

"What led them here?" Camille asked.

"The butcher across the street said he saw a truck in the alley, but he didn't see much else."

"Did you convince them?"

"I think so," Mme. Abadie said. "But they could come back, especially if they question others and someone says they saw you."

Camille looked at the old woman, risking her life on their behalf. "We have to go soon," she said. "A day at most. It's not worth the risk."

"Yes, you're right," Mme. Abadie agreed. "I'll have to behave for a while, until they are so busy chasing you that they forget an old woman who might have information."

"We need documents and clothing, maybe a disguise," Camille said. "I have a plan to escape."

"I have a wig you can use," Mme. Abadie said. "It's black, a Jane Eyre braided wig – with a large space in the back where you can tuck your hair. What type of disguise do you want?"

"A travel pass, from Tournai to Paris, for a German colonel and a nurse," Camille said. "With personal documentation. But the forgeries must be good."

"They will be," Mme. Abadie promised. "The printer is excellent—even has the rubber stamps the Germans use so frequently."

"We'll need uniforms, too," Camille said. "Can you do that?"

Mme. Abadie nodded. "I think so. Another contact has German uniforms, taken from dead soldiers. Whatever we don't have, I can sew."

Camille hugged her. "I don't know how to thank you."

"Don't thank me yet," Mme. Abadie said. "You haven't escaped."

CHAPTER 76

"Why would the Gestapo call me when they wanted you?" Emilie asked Jacques the following morning before she left to open the store.

Jacques shrugged and turned the page of his newspaper. "It was just a mistake."

"Why would they even want to talk to you?"

"It must have been about the railroads," he said. "I'm listed in the civil service directory as a railroad consultant. They're moving troops from northern France."

Emilie paused. It seemed a likely explanation. And he wasn't concerned. Maybe it was a mistake. "I gave them your office number."

"That's fine," he said. "I'll talk to them when they call. If they ever do. Maybe someone else answered their questions."

Emilie watched as he sipped his coffee and read the newspaper. He didn't seem to be lying. "I have to leave," she said finally, rising from the table. "We can talk more about this later. Will you be home for dinner?"

Jacques drank the rest of his coffee and stood. "Yes, I should be."

Emilie took his cup and put it in the sink. "Goodbye," she said, giving him a quick hug and a kiss.

He pulled her close. "Have a nice day at the store."

She went out the kitchen door while Jacques walked back toward his study. He certainly didn't seem worried about the Gestapo. But why call from Tournai when the Germans occupied Paris? Why not send someone to the store? But the call did prove that some of the phone lines had been restored. She decided to try and call Germany when she got home from the store. Maybe she could reach her family and verify all that Louie Bassett had told her.

Denis, her best employee, was unlocking the door to All Things Napoleon when she arrived. "Good morning, Emilie," he said, holding the door open for her.

"Good morning," she replied. "A man will drop off some packages shortly. I bought his entire toy soldier collection. It's extensive—the Russian campaign."

"That should sell quickly. We can use the inventory. Business has been good."

Emilie paused after she walked in. She couldn't stop thinking about the Gestapo. "Will you be all right for a half hour or so? I have an errand to run."

"Yes, of course," Denis replied. "No problem at all."

Emilie left, destined for Louie Bassett's townhouse. She had to tell him about the Gestapo. Jacques was in danger, even if he didn't believe it, and so was she. It was a quick stroll, and a few minutes later she was knocking on Bassett's door.

He was surprised to see her. "Come in," he said. "Information to share?"

Emilie nodded as she entered. "I have so much to tell you."

"Start at the beginning," he said as he led her to the parlor. They sat on the couch, and he leaned toward her, anxious to hear what she had to say.

She hesitated, thinking of all that had happened. "Jacques caught me eavesdropping on him and Guy Barbier."

His eyes widened. "What happened?"

"They were meeting in Jacque's study. It was late, just after midnight, and I was in bed. But I heard their voices and crept into the parlor. A floorboard creaked and Jacques came in and caught me."

"What did you say?"

"I heard a noise and came to investigate."

Louie frowned. "Not good at all," he said. "Did he believe you?"

She shrugged. "I'm not sure. It didn't seem like it at the time. He glared at me suspiciously, said he was meeting with someone, and told me to go back to bed. But he hasn't mentioned it since."

"Did you hear any of their conversation?"

She nodded. "I heard Jacques say that Camille is bringing the diamonds to Paris."

Louie's eyes widened. "He must have made radio contact."

"That's what I thought, too. And then yesterday, the Gestapo called the store, looking for Jacques. But they called from Tournai."

Louie paused, rubbing his chin. "Either the Germans are close to catching her, or they already have. Maybe she told them Jacques was her contact."

Emilie slowly shook her head. "No, I don't think so. The Germans wanted information. They didn't even know who Jacques was."

"But how did they get your phone number?"

"I don't know. Jacques had a vague explanation, that they were trying to reach him for railroad information."

"Do you believe anything he says?" Louie asked. "Especially given all you know."

She shrugged. "He didn't seem too concerned. I gave the Gestapo his office number."

Louie was quiet, lips pursed. "The Gestapo must know about Camille."

"But how did they get my information? Camille doesn't have it."

"Maybe her accomplice did, the man she met in Antwerp."

Emilie sighed and sat back in the chair. "They're closing in on Jacques, regardless of how they got his name and my number. And I think he knows it."

"I'm sure he's afraid something has gone wrong," Louie said. "Maybe that's what the fake identity papers are for—his escape."

"Or he's selling the diamonds once he gets them and taking off with his lover."

"I think it's all related—Tournai, diamonds, Gestapo, fake papers, Barbier."

Emilie frowned. "But it's collapsing. Or the Gestapo wouldn't have called."

"We can't let it collapse," Louie said firmly. "Not until we get the diamonds."

CHAPTER 77

Sergeant Bayer sat in a café near Gestapo headquarters, enjoying coffee and a croissant. He reached in his shirt and withdrew a photograph he always carried in his breast pocket—a picture of his family. His wife Greta and three daughters, now grown, standing outside their home in a village outside of Stuttgart. He wished above all else he could be there, teaching history in the secondary school, but the war was just beginning. France would fall, but England survived. And unless a negotiated peace was reached, he would be denied his family's company, except for a few precious days each year when granted leave.

He fingered the family photograph, smiling. Two of his daughters resembled his wife, tall and slender. The third was like him, short and stocky. He wondered if Major Ziegler thought about his family as often as he did, like when they were in the village. Ziegler had offered a rare glimpse into his private life, reminiscing about his two sons playing soccer and a small village where his father still managed a market. Sometimes it was difficult for Bayer to see the man behind the monster. But that's what war did. It destroyed everyone it touched, each in a different way.

He knew Ziegler was pressured by superiors to find the diamonds. But he didn't understand their value. What did diamonds have to do with radar, a modern technology that he knew little about? And how could some diamonds be so superior to others? He likely would never know the answers.

Sometimes he was relieved he was only a sergeant, serving a major who was somewhat of a riddle but good to him, nonetheless. Ziegler was not demanding or cruel, insisting he complete assigned tasks or face severe consequences. He treated Bayer more like a friend and spoke informally whenever they were alone. Bayer only had to follow orders.

He finished his breakfast and walked back to headquarters, stopping to watch a work crew remove debris from a bombed building. He wondered if it would be rebuilt; they seemed to be saving the brick. The city was coping, gradually adapting, trying to be what it once was. But he knew it couldn't, not with Germany strangling it. He watched the clean-up efforts a few minutes more and returned to headquarters.

When he entered the building, he went to the communications room and sought out Sergeant Frank. He had intercepted the radio message and overseen the random questioning of residents as they searched for a link to the vehicle he and Ziegler had found—the truck that came from the doctor's farm.

"Tell me, Sergeant Frank, what have you learned from yesterday's investigation?" Bayer asked.

"I split my men into five teams and we each took a different section of the city. We asked random residents questions."

"How did you select them?"

"We visited storekeepers or asked people on the street."

Bayer lit a cigarette. "A city of fifty thousand people. Maybe two-thirds here, the rest refugees. It doesn't seem the best way to get information."

Frank shrugged. "We have no photographs of this woman. We can't make posters or ask anyone if they've seen her. We can only ask about the truck and suggest that the driver was a blonde woman."

"Did you learn anything helpful?"

Frank shrugged. "About fifteen people thought they had seen the truck, and that a blonde woman was either in it or near it."

Bayer's eyes widened. "Were they all in the same location?"

Frank shook his head. "No, they were scattered around the city, which makes it less likely they saw anything useful."

"Did any location have more than one witness?"

Frank paused. "No, not really. We did focus additional efforts where people thought they may have seen the truck and the woman. We knocked on doors of houses, shops, and apartments. But we learned nothing additional."

"Were any more credible than others?"

Frank thought for a moment. "Yes, actually. Five or six seemed valid. They remembered details, like where the truck was actually parked or what the woman was wearing. It's just that no single description matched any of the others."

"I'll tell Major Ziegler," Bayer said. "I'm afraid his patience is exhausted. And so is that of his superiors."

Frank frowned. "He's been given a difficult task."

"Can you do anything else to help him?"

Frank was quiet for a moment. "I'll have my men revisit the witnesses who were most credible. Maybe they've remembered something more."

CHAPTER 78

"Do you want a glass of wine?" Camille asked as she and Lucien sat in the dark attic, wasting the hours away.

Lucien looked at the corked bottle, sitting on the planked wooden floor, two glasses beside it. He shook his head. "I can't."

She watched his response, the battle that consumed him. "I'll ask Mme. Abadie to bring up some water." She moved the bottle beside the chimney where he couldn't see it.

"One glass at dinner was hard enough. I was afraid if I started, I couldn't stop."

She felt such compassion, his life almost destroyed. "But you did stop."

"You don't know how difficult it was."

"You're doing well, Lucien. I'm proud of you."

He held out his right hand, unable to keep it steady. "I can't stop trembling."

She smiled grimly. "I know it isn't easy."

"But I am trying really hard."

She brushed the hair from his forehead. "Your survival depends on it," she said quietly. "I'm so sorry. The minute I stepped on your farm, your life changed forever. I had no right to do that."

His gaze met hers. "I haven't complained."

"You haven't had the chance," she teased.

He smiled weakly and was quiet for a moment. "When the Germans came, I was hoping they would kill me. I wanted to die."

She hesitated, waiting to see if he needed to continue, share the inner turmoil that had gradually whittled away his will to live. After a moment passed, she replied. "You couldn't forgive yourself for something you couldn't change."

He closed his eyes, as if hoping the pain would go away. "I wanted to save them so badly."

"I know you did," she said softly, gently caressing the back of his head with her fingers. "And so does everyone who knows you."

"Why couldn't it be me?" he asked. "Why did I live, not even injured, when they died?"

"Lucien, don't torture yourself. No one can answer that question."

He started to quietly sob. "It was all my fault. I was driving."

"It wasn't your fault, an inquiry proved that."

"Then who was at fault? Not them? The blame lies with me."

"No, that's not true," she said soothingly. "No one is to blame. It was an accident."

"I should have at least saved them."

"They couldn't be saved."

He was quiet for a moment, wiping tears from his eyes. "I don't want to live without them. My wife and daughter were part of me. Now there's a hole in my heart that can't be filled. I'll never be the same."

"No, you'll never be the same," she said, wrapping an arm around his shoulders. "But you need to look forward. Tomorrow still comes. Maybe not as bright, but still worth living. Just save a place in your heart for yesterday."

"That's so much harder than it seems. Especially when tomorrow can never be as good as yesterday."

"Tomorrow can be different," she said, gently correcting him. "You shouldn't compare."

"I just miss them so badly."

"I know you do," she whispered. She pulled him close, hugging him as he sobbed.

He leaned his head into her shoulder, the tears still coming.

She cradled him close, kissing the top of his head. And then her lips found his.

CHAPTER 79

Jacques Dufort followed Guy Barbier into the dimly lit warehouse. As he walked toward the office, he noticed empty space—some of the crates had been removed. The building had been crammed full on his last visit. Now some supplies had been distributed after only a few days of German occupation.

"We have a problem," Jacques said as they entered the office.

Barbier motioned for him to sit. He took a bottle of whiskey off the top of a filing cabinet and poured a little into two glasses. He handed one to Jacques and sat behind the desk.

"The diamonds?" Barbier asked.

Jacques nodded. "It's worse than I thought. The Gestapo is closing in."

Barbier's eyes narrowed. "They didn't catch Camille, did they?"

"No, it's not that bad. But they called Emilie at the store."

Guy cocked his head. "How did they get her number?"

"I have a theory, but not much more."

"Why call? They could have visited."

"No, not the Paris Gestapo. They called from Tournai."

Barbier's eyes widened. "Could they have gotten the number from Camille?"

Jacques shook his head. "No, definitely not. Emilie said they knew nothing. They were probing to see what they might find."

Guy frowned. "If not Camille, how did they get her number?"

"I think it came from Roger. He came to my apartment before leaving for Antwerp, a few days before I met Camille."

Barbier was confused. "How does that tie in to Emilie?"

"When he was in my study, I gave him the address of the dock in Antwerp where he was supposed to meet the fishing boat. I had a few of Emilie's business cards on my desk. He took one and wrote the address on the back."

"Along with your name as a contact."

Jacques nodded. "It's the only explanation."

"Why didn't he write down your phone number?"

"Because I didn't give it to him. He was supposed to contact me from the ship, by radio, when he left Antwerp."

Barbier frowned. "Except he never met the ship."

"No," Jacques said. "He never got out of the diamond exchange."

Barbier leaned back and thought for a moment. "Are you and Sophie prepared for all possibilities, like the Gestapo coming after you?"

"Yes, we are. We considered every scenario imaginable—even Camille betraying us."

Barbier was surprised. "Why would you ever doubt her?"

"It was just a theory," he offered. "We wondered if Camille killed Roger, stole the diamonds, and planted the business card on the body."

"She gets rid of Roger and, if the Germans take Paris, which they did, she gets rid of you."

"Yes, exactly."

Barbier thought for a moment. "I'm sorry, but no way," he

scoffed. "You can trust Camille with your life. She would never betray us."

"I realize that. Sophie and I just wanted to be prepared. I think Camille's last message proves her loyalty. She's trapped in Tournai, doing everything she can to get the diamonds to Paris."

Barbier pursed his lips. "I think a more likely scenario is the Germans killed Roger, Camille knows nothing about the business card, and she flees with the diamonds. The Germans find the business card and call Emilie."

Jacques nodded. "I'm sure that's what happened. We even wondered if she had been captured, but not after her last message."

"We know we can trust Camille," Barbier said. "And we know she's en route with the diamonds. But we have another problem."

"The Gestapo."

Barbier nodded. "Now they're after you," he said, and sighed. "I don't like it."

Jacques took a swig of whiskey. "Emilie said they knew nothing. And she knows nothing, either. She can't give them what they want."

"What reason did you give Emilie for the call?"

"I said that they wanted railroad information. But she didn't seem convinced. I know she'll have more questions."

"How are you going to explain that the Gestapo had your name but her phone number?"

"I'll say the operator made a mistake and got my name and hers mixed up."

Guy sat back in the chair. "She may believe you for now, but she'll have more questions."

Jacques shrugged. "I'll keep offering different explanations, none of which will be true—just to keep her confused."

Barbier paused. "It's about to get much worse," he warned.

"The Gestapo will call again. And they're one step closer to you. Did she give them your phone number?"

Jacques nodded. "At the office, but I'm not there anyway."

"They won't give up," Barbier said. "You know that as well as I do. They'll come in person or send local Gestapo to question you."

"If the Gestapo called from Tournai, they haven't involved local authorities. They haven't put the pieces together. We still have time."

Barbier nodded, his face taut. "If you do get caught, or they start closing in, you know what you have to do—as painful as it will be."

Jacques nodded. "I give up Emilie and flee with Sophie."

CHAPTER 80

Ziegler was sitting in his office, the map lying on his desk, when Bayer came in. "We may have more information about the truck, sir. A dozen witnesses claimed they saw it, but they're scattered around the city."

Ziegler frowned. "She probably drove through side streets before she hid it, hoping as many people as possible saw her. Just to confuse us should we question residents."

Bayer nodded and sat down in front of the desk. "That could be, sir. She is cunning."

"And always ahead of us, it seems," Ziegler said, frowning. "Does any of it tie together?"

"Not yet. But five or six witnesses seem credible, even though they're in different locations. Sergeant Frank's men will question them again."

Ziegler was quiet. Each step forward was another step back. "We are closing in. They're here in Tournai. We just have to find them."

"Let's hope Sergeant Frank's men find the right witness," Bayer said. "We'll keep monitoring radio communications, too."

"Unless they're already gone," Ziegler muttered. "They could have hidden the truck and fled."

"We don't know that they did," Bayer said. "Transportation is so limited."

Ziegler nodded, evaluating further efforts. "I think the man is with her. He can't risk returning to his farmhouse. He knows he'll be arrested."

"What about the wounded Englishman?"

"I suspect they took him somewhere safe, maybe another farm," Ziegler replied. "They can't travel with him. They would be apprehended immediately."

"We found their truck, so they can't flee by vehicle. Unless they steal one."

"Which she did before," Ziegler reminded him. "The green Minerva."

"But petrol is a problem."

"I had originally thought they planned to change vehicles, but they left all that petrol at the farm. It now seems unlikely."

"Unless they were forced to leave in a hurry," Bayer noted. "Maybe they saw us at the neighboring farm."

"Yes, perhaps," Ziegler mumbled, distracted. He imagined what he would do if their roles were reversed.

"They can travel by wagon, horseback, or bicycle."

"Or by boat into France, and then make other arrangements."

"Maybe the railroad?" Bayer offered with a shrug.

Ziegler slowly shook his head, still deciphering what few clues they had. "We'll wait another day or so," he decided. "If we don't find anything additional, we'll go to Paris. I just need Colonel von Horn to approve it."

"Do you think the message we intercepted is valid?"

"Yes, I do. I just don't know how they'll get out of Tournai and all the way to Paris."

"Trains would be easiest," Bayer said.

"But only military trains are running."

"Are they sophisticated enough to forge papers and create a disguise?"

Ziegler hesitated. "I don't know," he admitted. "We can have the station watched, especially trains to Paris."

"There is no direct route to Paris from Tournai," Bayer said. "The train leaves from Lille—just over the border."

"I thought troops from this area were being sent into France."

"They are, sir," Bayer said. "The train runs from here to Lille, which is only twenty kilometers, then to Paris."

"Does the train pass through or do passengers change trains?"

"I don't know," Bayer admitted. "But I can check."

"I suspect the train passes through Lille, depending how many cars are loaded with soldiers and supplies. I'm going to have the station watched."

"For a blonde woman in military dress?"

Ziegler nodded. "Any female soldiers sent to Paris to assist with the administration."

"Or medical personnel."

"Yes, perhaps," Ziegler muttered. "But I suspect this woman is clever."

"You don't think she'll take the train?"

"I wonder if she wants us to think she's taking the train, when maybe she is not."

CHAPTER 81

Mme. Abadie came up to the attic just before noon. She brought some cheese, bread, and water, and carried a bundle of clothes.

Camille took the tray and set it on the floor beside Lucien. "We don't know how to thank you, Mme. Abadie."

"No thanks are needed," Mme. Abadie said, smiling and peeking through her round spectacles. "Not much of a lunch, but I'll make a nice dinner. Do you have any wine left?"

Lucien held up the bottle, nearly full. "We only had two glasses at dinner."

Camille hid a smile. He was so proud that he hadn't drunk the wine. A small victory for most, a monumental achievement for him. She was proud of him, and he should be proud of himself.

"Try this on," Mme. Abadie said, handing the clothes to Camille. "It's a German nurse's uniform, exact in every detail. Even the undergarments."

Camille started removing her blouse. There was little room for privacy, but Lucien looked away while she changed. She took off her skirt and then picked up the uniform. The dress was blue and white striped, with a white collar. She put it on, followed by a long white apron with a matching cap. A white armband with a red cross fit snugly over her right bicep.

"Perfect," Mme. Abadie said, reaching forward to smooth the collar. "It fits nicely."

Lucien turned to look. "It's very good," he muttered. "Did you make that?"

Mme. Abadie nodded. "Yes, but I had a photograph as a guide. It's accurate."

"With the uniform and the black wig, I think my disguise will be perfect."

"Maybe a pair of eyeglasses, too," Mme. Abadie suggested, "to alter your appearance even more. And then some makeup to darken your light eyebrows so they match the black wig."

"What is my disguise?" Lucien asked.

"A man who helps me is coming later this afternoon," Mme. Abadie explained. "He'll have the nurse's shoes—they have to be authentic—along with a German uniform. He'll take your photographs, dressed in your disguises, to create your papers."

"When is the next train?" Camille asked.

"A military train leaves for Paris, through Lille, tomorrow at 7 a.m.," Mme. Abadie said. "Our contact at the terminal said some women—nurses and administrators—will be on the train, so it's a good time for you to make your escape."

"Any wounded?" Camille asked.

She shrugged. "I don't know."

"Why do we need wounded on the train?" Lucien asked.

"It's part of the disguise," Camille replied.

Lucien looked at Mme. Abadie. "I'm sure she'll tell us at some point."

"I will," Camille promised. "Now we have one more task to perform." She got the radio and poked the antenna wire out of the window. She inserted the crystal and laid her watch beside the radio.

"What's the watch for?" he asked.

"The Germans are tracing transmissions," Camille said. "We have limited time, or they will find us."

Lucien looked at her, eyes wide. "They can intercept the message and plot our location?"

She nodded as she put on the earphones. She started transmitting dots and dashes of Morse code. Watching the clock, she repeated the same message several times until she received a reply.

"What was your message?" Mme. Abadie asked.

She turned and smiled as she packed up the radio. "Leaving Tournai at dawn by boat."

CHAPTER 82

"Emilie is suspicious after the Gestapo called her," Jacques told Sophie as she sat on the couch, and he paced the floor. "I have to convince her the call was a mistake."

"I would be suspicious, too," Sophie said. "The Gestapo called from Tournai. How did they get her number?"

"They have a business card from the store. Roger scribbled some notes on it before he left for Antwerp."

"You had better be careful," Sophie warned. "Or Emilie will spoil everything."

"No, she won't. I won't let her."

"Do you trust her?"

He shrugged. "She is behaving differently. But the Germans occupy Paris. Everyone behaves differently."

Sophie eyed him as he paced. "Maybe there's more."

Jacques sighed. Maybe he couldn't see what everyone else did. "You're probably right. As always."

"I think you should watch her closely."

"Maybe I should," Jacques muttered, undecided. "I'll see what questions she asks. I know she's not done with the Gestapo call. I told her they wanted railroad information."

Sophie pursed her lips. "Why didn't the local Gestapo come

to visit her?"

Jacques sat beside her. "I don't know. But a visit is coming, I'm sure."

"Is she convinced you're not involved in anything?"

"She thinks it's beyond what I normally do, but I'm not sure why. I'll see if she mentions it again. It may not be as bad as we think."

Sophie was quiet, assessing the situation as she always did. "Emilie could be trapping you and you don't realize it. Aren't you suspicious? I certainly am."

Jacques sat back. "I did catch her eavesdropping while I was meeting with Barbier. It was after midnight. I thought she was sleeping. But she claimed she heard a noise and came to investigate."

"It might be true," Sophie said. "Or it might not be."

Jacques nodded. "I also found a document left on my desk. But I could have left it there."

"Where would you normally leave it?"

"In a large Napoleon book with the insides removed. I hide everything in there before I give it to you or Barbier. I had twenty pages of top-secret documents. But one was left out."

"Why would you think she left it there?"

"Because I woke in the middle of the night, and she wasn't in bed. I went in the parlor, and she was in the foyer. Said she couldn't sleep and was looking out the window."

"No," Sophie said, shaking her head. "I'm sorry, but it's too much of a coincidence. Did she eavesdrop on you and Camille?"

Jacques was quiet for a moment, reflecting on their only visit. "Camille did say she heard someone moving about the house."

Sophie rolled her eyes. "We should assume she knows everything. I think she's betraying you or preparing to. We just don't know why she turned."

Jacques hesitated. "I've behaved no differently. There's no reason why she should."

"But she is," Sophie insisted. "That's why she's asking so many questions. We just don't know who or what convinced her to do it. You once told me you didn't know a lot about her, only that she inherited the shop from her uncle."

Jacques was quiet for a moment, reflecting. "Our initial meeting was arranged, although I don't remember by who."

"Followed by a quick courtship and marriage."

Jacques shrugged. "Yes, but not that uncommon."

"No, it isn't. How many times have you met her family?"

"I met her family at the wedding—her brother and father. Her mother passed a few years ago. Emilie has some of her things—porcelain and paintings."

"Anything unusual about the father and brother?"

"They had thick accents," he replied. "I didn't think much of it at the time. They live right on the border, along the Rhine."

"Which side of the Rhine?" she asked. "You've never been there, have you?"

"No," he admitted. "We were supposed to go and visit, but the war started. No one traveled much after that."

Sophie was quiet, coldly calculating different scenarios. "We need contingency plans and the ability to leave Paris at a moment's notice. Especially if she knows more than we think she does."

"I need the diamonds first. I can't let Barbier down."

"I'm not so sure," she said. "Maybe we should get out of Paris while we still can."

He hesitated. "You might be right. The longer we wait, the harder it'll be. Especially with the Gestapo closing in."

"We can go south, into Spain, before the Nazis get a firm grip on the country. We would be close to your family in the south of France and not far from mine on the coast."

"Barbier is building a network into Spain."

"I know, I'm helping him. And we could leave before Emilie turns you in."

Jacques considered the contingency plan Barbier prompted him to prepare. "I can always betray her first," he said delicately.

Sophie studied him for a moment, an awareness creeping across her face. "Turn her into the Germans, claim she's a double agent."

"Exactly," Jacques said. "Barbier actually suggested it."

"We need to make her seem guilty."

"I'll start planting fake documents around the house."

"Where can you put them where she won't find them?" Sophie asked.

"She has a cuckoo clock from Germany, I'll hide some in there. And porcelain collectables from her mother. Some are large enough to fit folded papers inside. I can put others on the backs of paintings in the parlor."

"Good, I'll have the documents made," Sophie said. "I'll get some intercepted German radio transmission or stolen military documents. They'll be authentic."

"How quickly can you get them? She's already talked to the Gestapo. Now that we suspect her, I'm afraid of what she may have said."

"Only a day or two. I'll finalize our escape route, too. We'll leave as soon as we get the diamonds and give them to Barbier. If we have to leave sooner, we'll be prepared."

Their conversation was interrupted by Morse code coming from the radio—distinct dots and dashes. Sophie hurried to the unit, put on the earphones, and started scribbling the message. Then she sent a reply.

Jacques watched what she wrote: *Leaving Tournai at dawn by boat.*

CHAPTER 83

Major Josef Ziegler held a dispatch in his hand, having read it several times. The shades of his office were closed, only a sliver of light from a setting sun sneaking through the edge of the window jambs.

Sergeant Bayer came down the hallway and tapped on the partially open door. "May I come in, sir?"

"Yes, of course," Ziegler replied, his voice distant, his thoughts elsewhere.

Bayer looked at him curiously. He turned on the light. "Is everything all right, sir?"

"Sit, Sergeant," Ziegler said. He motioned to the chair.

Bayer sat down and eyed his superior. "Can I get you anything?"

Ziegler shook his head. "No, thank you, Sergeant." He tossed the dispatch onto the desk. "Orders from Berlin. Not what I expected."

Bayer shifted in his chair. "A transfer, sir?"

Ziegler nodded. "They're not pleased that the diamonds haven't been recovered. I have a few more days to get them. If not successful, I'm to report to Berlin."

"For what duties, sir?" Bayer asked softly.

Ziegler shrugged. "I'll learn when I arrive," he said. "But it won't be pleasant, I can assure you."

"I'm sorry to hear that, sir. You're a good man. And you deserve more."

"Thank you, Sergeant," he muttered, truly humbled. He fixed his gaze on Bayer, the closest he had to a friend. "I've been a good soldier. I've always done as ordered."

"Yes, you have sir," Bayer said, compassion etched on his face.

Ziegler sighed, slowly shaking his head. "I've even became what I'm not. I've held pistols to the head of men like Jacob Sternberg. I've killed when I had to, people who didn't deserve to die." He paused for a moment and then continued to ramble. "Even though it made me nauseous for days and I hid somewhere to vomit. I'm not the monster they made me become, Sergeant. I'm a simple man, with a family, who led a modest life before the war. But I did what I was ordered to do."

"Yes, sir," Bayer said quietly. "You have."

"And because I failed to find the diamonds, I will pay a heavy price. Those very tactics I used on others will now be employed on me."

"It may not be too late," Bayer said, trying to reassure him. "We still might find her."

Ziegler sighed. "She continues to elude us, Sergeant. Always a bit faster, a little smarter."

Bayer was quiet, giving his superior time to reflect. "Maybe not this time, sir."

Ziegler cocked his head. "What are you talking about?"

"A train leaves for Lille tomorrow at 7 a.m. It goes directly to Paris."

Ziegler's eyes widened. "All troops?"

"Administrative personnel, too."

"Are women included?"

Bayer nodded. "Clerks, telephone operators, a few medical

personnel. But primarily troops assigned to Paris."

Ziegler tapped his fingers on the desk, his resolve beginning to firm. "She'll be on that train. I'm sure of it."

"In disguise?"

Ziegler nodded. He leaned forward, newfound energy flowing through his veins. "It's the only way she can do it."

"What about her papers?"

"If she can get into a vault while German soldiers surround the building, and emerge unscathed with a satchel of diamonds, she can get the proper documentation."

"We've only seen her once," Bayer reminded him, "and only for a few minutes. We won't be able to recognize her—especially given all the women we've watched or questioned."

Ziegler paused, pensive. "You're right, Sergeant. We won't recognize her. We'll have to search the baggage of every woman who boards the train."

They were interrupted by a tap on the door. "Come in," Ziegler called.

Sergeant Frank entered. "I'm sorry to disturb you, sir," he said, nodding to Bayer. "But we've intercepted another radio message."

Ziegler glanced at Bayer. "Were you able to locate the transmitter?"

"No, sir. Not enough time. But the transmission was a simple statement, repeated several times, as if they wanted to make certain it was received."

"And it still wasn't enough time to track them?"

"No, sir," Frank said. "We only know that it came from the same part of Tournai as the last one. But when we honed in on the location, the transmission was terminated. The sender was timing it."

Ziegler frowned. "She probably was," he muttered. "What was the message?"

Frank read it aloud: "Leaving Tournai at dawn by boat."

CHAPTER 84

The door to the attic opened near 6 p.m. Mme. Abadie led a middle-aged man with thick glasses upstairs to meet Lucien and Camille. "This is Pierre," she said as they entered.

"Thanks for helping us, Pierre," Camille said.

"Anything to defeat the Nazis," Pierre replied, nodding to her and Lucien.

"What do you need us to do?" Lucien asked.

Pierre set a large case and a satchel on the floor. "I have to take your photographs for your documents."

Camille got her nurse's uniform and started removing her blouse.

"I have a German captain's uniform for you," Pierre said to Lucien. "Not a high enough rank to justify a private nurse, so your documentation will show you're a personal aide to General Hans Speidel, one of Paris's military commanders. I also have small duffle bags that a nurse and captain would use to carry their belongings, with some extra clothing to put in them."

Lucien glanced at Camille. "You thought of everything."

Pierre smiled faintly. "I have to," he replied. "The alternative is too horrible to consider."

"The documents have to be perfect," Camille said. "We expect to be questioned by the Gestapo."

"They will be," Pierre assured them. "I have several rubber stamps, typical of German documents, reflecting service in Poland, transfer to Belgium, and now to France. The military units use similar designs—an eagle over a swastika."

"Can you make the paper seem aged?" Camille asked. "Especially if we show a few years of service."

"Yes, of course," Pierre replied. "I've already prepared it. I baked it in an oven to create the patina, and then I frayed the corners."

Camille thought for a moment, identifying potential errors. "The documents have two signatures."

Pierre nodded. "My wife will provide the second signature."

Camille smiled. "Very thorough," she said. "I've seen forged documents where the signatures are the same handwriting. An alert German would notice."

Pierre smiled faintly. "We try to be authentic."

Camille paused, pensive. "But they can't be perfect. It's too suspicious. Can you add a small coffee stain to mine?"

"Yes, of course," Pierre said. "That should work nicely. No one will question it. Very realistic."

"Will my papers cause any issues?" Lucien asked. "A general's military aide will likely be asked questions."

"I don't think anyone will question you," Camille replied. "They'll be watching for women onboard. But we do need a good disguise."

"What if I have to speak?" Lucien asked.

"You won't," Camille said. "I'm going to bandage your throat to show a war wound. You're not able to talk. I'll speak for both of us."

Lucien smiled. "I'm impressed. In only a few hours, you've assembled disguises, arranged our departure, and almost have our papers prepared."

All That Glitters

"I just have to make sure we didn't forget anything," Camille said.

As they dressed, Pierre hung a large white sheet from the rafters and set a chair in front of it. He turned on a floor lamp, shifting the bulb to brighten the background.

Camille finished dressing and tucked her blonde hair into her black wig, fixing her nurse's cap on top of it. She then added makeup to her eyebrows to darken them.

"Add these," Mme. Abadie said, handing her a pair of black spectacles. "They'll change your look and make you seem older."

Camille put on the glasses and sat in the chair while Pierre took her picture.

When Lucien finished dressing, the process was repeated, although they added a homemade dye to his hair, graying the temples and a few random strands.

"The dye isn't very good," Mme. Abadie said. "It'll only last a few days."

"That should be more than we need," Lucien said. He glanced in a handheld mirror. "It ages me by a decade."

After Pierre had taken several pictures of each, and was satisfied with the process, he gathered his photography equipment. "I'll give the documentation to Mme. Abadie when it's finished, later this evening."

"It'll be ready in the morning when you leave," Mme. Abadie promised.

"Is there anything else?" Pierre asked.

"I do have a strange request," Camille said. "If we can manage it."

Pierre looked at her curiously. "Of course," he said. "What is it?"

"Can you arrange for a young couple, the woman with blonde hair like mine, to leave the city in a rowboat just after dawn, traveling south? They should have a picnic lunch with them, to prove their innocence if challenged."

"A decoy?" Pierre asked.

Camille nodded. "I set a trap for the Gestapo."

Pierre looked at her with admiration. "It's a brilliant idea. I'll take care of it."

"I'm trying to keep the Gestapo away from the train," she explained. "But I'm not sure if it'll work."

"It's worth a try," Mme. Abadie said. She turned to Pierre. "Do you have everything?"

Pierre nodded and prepared to depart. Mme. Abadie led him out of the attic, closing the secret door behind them.

"Are you sure this will work?" Lucien asked anxiously.

"It has to," Camille replied.

Mme. Abadie returned a moment later with a pelt of quilting material, thin but durable, a needle and thread. "I'll use this as an inner lining for your military duffel bags," she said. "I can secure your cargo in the material and sew it into your satchels. No one will cut the material. They'll only search what's inside."

"We just have to make sure it's secure," Camille said as she emptied the satchel with the diamonds. She took her clothes from her bag, folded them, and stacked them on the floor beside the extra military garments provided by Pierre.

Mme. Abadie measured the military bags and cut cloth from the bolt. Camille helped her space half of the diamonds in the material. She then folded the cloth over, covering the diamonds, and started sewing it together. When satisfied, she tucked it into the satchel, securing it with thread. She handed it to Camille to inspect.

"No thread visible on the outside of the bag," Camille said as she examined it. She put her hand inside. "Nothing moves. This is good. No one will be able to tell."

"You're an excellent seamstress," Lucien remarked as he watched. "Very fast, too."

Mme. Abadie smiled. "I've been doing it my whole life. I've hidden items in clothes and bags many times. Don't forget, this is my second war with the Germans."

"I was wondering how you formed a network so quickly, able to forge papers and find uniforms," Lucien said.

Mme. Abadie smiled. "We've done it before. Tournai was close to the front in the last war."

Camille watched for a moment, all parts of her plan coming together. "Mme. Abadie, the radio will stay, along with Lucien's pistol. And I'll leave the satchel with the drills and maps of the diamond exchange."

"Pierre can use the radio, gun, and the drills," Mme. Abadie said. "I'll destroy the papers."

Camille nodded. "Thank you so much for all your help. We'll take our duffel bags with the diamonds, and I'll have the medical bag."

Lucien cast her a look of admiration. "You've thought of everything."

Camille smiled weakly. "We had better hope that I did."

CHAPTER 85

Emilie eyed Jacques closely as they ate dinner. She had questioned him twice about the Gestapo phone call, getting vague explanations each time. She hadn't pressed him, hoping he would gradually reveal more. But he had said little, even avoiding her.

His face had paled when she said the call came from Tournai. But he had recovered quickly, claiming it was a mistake. He might have more information now—how close the Gestapo were, or if Camille had been captured. He was home so rarely that she wanted to take the opportunity to learn more.

"Did you ever find out why the Gestapo called?" she asked, trying to seem casual. "Were they able to contact you?"

"No, I never talked to them," he said and shrugged. "I don't know. It's strange, probably a mistake. Likely a railroad question someone else answered."

She pretended not to watch him as closely as she did. She knew when he was lying—she could tell by facial expressions, a twitch in his left eye. She wondered if he was aware of it. Not a good trait for someone in military intelligence.

"Maybe they want Napoleon books," he suggested. "Did you ever think of that?"

She cocked her head. "No, I didn't. It would be great if they did. But how did they get my telephone number?"

He shrugged. "Who knows? Maybe the Gestapo found your business card in one of their offices. Or a bookseller may have recommended you."

"What would my business card be doing in Tournai?"

Jacques looked at her curiously. "Emilie, you have customers all over Europe."

She had to admit he was right. She did have customers all over Europe, Tournai included. It made sense. "But why would they call me and ask for you?"

He sipped his wine. "I don't know. Maybe they asked a telephone operator, and they got the store and house numbers confused."

She hesitated. It was a good explanation, one she hadn't considered. "I suppose that's possible. But why would a customer call you? They did ask for you, as if they knew you."

"Just a mistake, I'm sure," he said, eating his dinner, unconcerned.

"Unless the Gestapo captured someone," she said, pressing. "And he gave them your name, and the operator mistakenly gave them my number."

He looked at her curiously, like he had underestimated her. "Anything is possible, I suppose. We'll never know unless they call again."

"Could this be an intelligence issue?"

"It could be," he said evasively. "But I still can't talk about it."

Emilie suspected she knew what had happened. She would pose it to Jacques and see if he confirmed it—willingly or not. "Maybe one of your contacts had your name scribbled on my business card, went to Belgium before the attack, and was captured by the Gestapo."

His eyes widened. His left eye twitched and he looked down

at his food, picking at his chicken with his fork. "I suppose it's possible. Unlikely, but possible."

She watched as he ate, distracted, shifting in his seat. "It really doesn't matter. We can expect the Gestapo soon, knocking on our door."

"They're only asking routine questions," he said. "I don't think it has anything to do with you or me."

"Is that what I tell them if they come to my store?"

"Just tell them the truth. You don't know what they're talking about."

"Should I send them to your office?" she asked.

"Sure, you can send them if you like. But my office is already overrun with German administrators."

Emilie stopped asking questions. She may not have learned the truth, but Jacques was clearly uncomfortable. She wondered how long he would stay in Paris. He had stacks of money and fake papers already prepared for himself and his mistress. Something strange was going on.

She just had to figure out what it was.

CHAPTER 86

The following morning, Major Ziegler borrowed two soldiers from Colonel von Horn. They left headquarters just after dawn, the staff car followed by a motorcycle with a sidecar, a machine gun poised and ready.

"I don't see anything yet," Ziegler said. He sat in the back seat with field glasses trained on the River Scheldt as it wound south.

Bayer drove along the banks. "You don't think they would go north, do you, sir?"

"Why go north if Paris is their destination?"

"They're not taking a boat the entire route," Bayer said. "They're only meeting someone to aid their escape."

"They could be anywhere then," Ziegler muttered. "Maybe they plan to hide at a farm along the river. Or meet an accomplice with a vehicle."

"If we don't find them going south, we can always check north."

They continued through Tournai, following the river. The sun crept higher in the heavens, only a few cottony clouds marring the summer sky. They reached the edge of the city, the buildings sparser, yielding to farms, and still saw no boat that seemed suspicious.

"Keep going," Ziegler ordered.

Two kilometers farther, a rowboat moved tranquilly through the water. A blonde woman faced them, sitting in the bow, a man in the stern handling the oars, driving the craft down the river past an occasional fishing boat.

"That's them!" Bayer exclaimed, pointing.

They parked the car fifty meters down the road and quickly got out, the motorcycle stopping behind them.

"Come here!" Bayer yelled in French. "Come here immediately!"

The two soldiers went down to the water's edge. They motioned for the couple to come to the bank. Ziegler and Bayer followed, and the four Gestapo waited as the frightened couple brought their boat to the shore.

"We did nothing wrong," the man shouted as they came closer.

"Please, we mean no harm," the woman pleaded.

When they reached land, the soldiers grabbed the boat and yanked it on the bank. The couple stared at them blankly, eyes wide. They raised their hands, surrendering.

"What did we do?" the man asked.

"Please, we'll never do it again," the woman promised.

Ziegler looked in the boat, a picnic basket wedged between them. He turned to Bayer. "Get the basket. It's holding the diamonds."

"Give me the basket," Bayer demanded in French.

The frightened man handed the basket to Bayer. He moved closer to the woman, wrapping his arm around her, pale and trembling.

Bayer took the basket and rifled through it.

"What's in it?" Ziegler asked.

"Two baguettes, some water, a bottle of wine, cheese, and two apples."

Ziegler frowned. "Ask them where they're going."

Bayer asked them in French.

"Just into the country for a picnic," the man replied.

Ziegler frowned. "Give the basket back and let them go."

Bayer handed them the basket. "You may go," he said. "We're looking for two fugitives. You resemble them."

"We haven't done anything wrong," the man assured them.

"No, we haven't," the woman echoed. "I swear."

"Go," Bayer said, waving them on. "Everything is all right."

The two soldiers shoved the boat from shore, and the man rowed away from the bank. They occasionally looked back at the Gestapo, afraid they might be followed.

Ziegler looked at Bayer with disgust. "We've been fooled," he said. "The radio transmission was intended for us. She must be on the train."

Bayer looked at his watch. "We have to hurry if we want to catch them."

The railroad station was on the northeast side of the city, past downtown, not quite five kilometers away. The soldiers on the motorcycle guided the staff car back to Tournai.

"Hurry," Ziegler said. "I think we'll make it."

The motorcycle raced ahead, clearing the path, the staff car twenty meters behind. They were approaching the city when they came upon a wagon parked in the road. The motorcycle swerved around it and stopped abruptly. Bayer braked.

"What is it?" Ziegler asked.

"Cows are crossing the road, sir."

"Cows!" Ziegler bellowed. He opened the door and stepped up on the running board.

A farmer stood in front of the wagon, guiding cows from a barge sitting on the riverbank to a fenced pasture across the road. Twenty head of cattle were halfway to the field, those in front passing through an opened gate.

"Get out of the way!" Ziegler yelled in German, motioning with his arm.

The farmer looked at him quizzically.

"He doesn't understand you, sir," Bayer said. He got out of the car and hollered in French. "Hurry, it's an emergency."

The farmer scrambled to the back of the herd and nudged the cows forward. They moved slowly, even with his prodding, mooing loudly at the inconvenience. A moment later, the gap at the edge of the road was large enough for the motorcycle to squeeze past.

"Hurry," Ziegler shouted as he climbed back in the car and closed the door.

They continued onward, racing down the boulevard. The streets had little traffic—an occasional wagon, a few German trucks. As the Gestapo approached, those in the motorcycle motioned for any vehicles to move over and let them pass.

"We're almost there, sir," Bayer said.

Ziegler glanced at his watch. "It's 7:15."

"We'll make it. The trains never run on time."

The Tournai railroad station was a large brick and stone building with a mansard roof that stretched for several blocks. Empty German troop trucks were parked before it, delivering soldiers for their journey to Paris.

Bayer sped toward the main entrance and screeched to a halt. He climbed out of the car, opened Ziegler's door, and they raced into the terminal. They ran across the building, out the exit, and onto the boarding platform.

The train was pulling away from the station, the last car fifty meters away.

CHAPTER 87

Lucien and Camille handed their papers to a German officer standing beside the conductor on the Tournai boarding platform. The forgeries were good, capturing even the minutest details German documents featured. To minimize any challenges, Lucien posed as an aide to General Speidel, one of the military commanders in Paris, and Camille as his personal nurse. They waited patiently while the officer examined their papers, cautiously eyeing the gathering crowd.

"Proceed," the officer said. He returned their papers, turning to those next in line.

"You're in the last row in the last car," the conductor informed them in French.

Camille pretended to vaguely understand. She pointed to the fifth car.

"Yes," the conductor nodded. "The last car."

She led Lucien down the platform. They boarded the last car of the five-car train and made their way to the back. Their tickets had been arranged by Mme. Abadie's contact at the terminal. Purposely placed in the last row of the last car, they were close to a rear exit should they have to escape, jumping from the train or hurrying off when it came to a stop. Lucien sat against the window, Camille beside him. A soldier was in the aisle seat, a young man who smiled politely as he sat down. The train quickly filled with soldiers, a few female personnel among them. Camille studied the entire car, marked the distance to the exit, noticed a fire extinguisher on the rear wall—a weapon if needed—and observed other passengers, ensuring no one gave them undue attention. She wanted to be prepared, should their journey not go as planned.

Their disguises were flawless. Lucien was dressed as a German captain, a bandage around his neck, slightly stained with blood. A second bandage covered his cheek, under his right eye. His hair showed streaks of gray. Camille wore her nurse's uniform with a black wig, makeup used to darken her light eyebrows, and black spectacles to further alter her appearance. She could feel Lucien beside her, trembling. The Germans terrified him, especially now that they sat in the midst of hundreds, confined in a train car for a few hours. But he fought two battles—the enemy and the bottle. And she knew how difficult it would be to defeat both.

"We made it," Camille whispered in Lucien's ear.

"The train is filled with Germans," he hissed, eyes wide.

"Try not to think about it. Look out the window at the passing scenery. In a few hours, it'll all be over."

As the train chugged away from the station, the first part of their journey was launched. They only had to get through Lille, the first station in France, twenty kilometers away. If successful, there was little chance they would be challenged again, and need only endure the ride to Paris—two hundred and fifty kilometers.

Their satchels were stuffed in an overhead bin, the diamonds spread between them, hidden in the lining. The medical bag was on the floor by Camille's feet. So far, none of the passengers had eyed them strangely.

"Three hours to safety," Camille whispered in Lucien's ear.

"If you see anything, or anyone that looks suspicious, tell me right away."

The soldier beside her glanced over, so she pretended to check Lucien's bandage. When she was finished, she met his gaze and smiled.

"Are you going to Paris?" the soldier asked.

"Yes, we are," she replied in flawless German. "And you?"

He nodded. "I'm excited. It's a just reward for all the fighting."

"Have you been in Belgium for the entire war?" she asked.

"No, I was in Denmark briefly, but I didn't see any fighting. Not like here."

"I think we'll all enjoy Paris," she said. "I'm told it's one of the most beautiful cities in the world. I'm very much looking forward to it."

The soldier chuckled. "I think everyone on the train is anxious to get there."

She smiled and looked away.

It was a short trip to Lille, barely fifteen minutes. The train pulled into the station and came to rest. Camille watched anxiously to see who would get on the train and who might get off. Four soldiers near the front, seated in the first two rows, stood and made their way to the exit. They had barely left when four came in from the terminal and took their place. Camille eyed them closely and determined they were no more of a threat than anyone else in the car. It seemed the rest of the passengers would remain for the trip to Paris. She sat back, started to relax, and looked from the window, past the edge of the station to the street beyond.

A Gestapo staff car raced up to the terminal, screeching to a halt.

CHAPTER 88

Jacques reached across the desk in his study and handed a paper to Guy Barbier. It was midmorning. Emilie had left to open her store and they were alone.

"Leaving Tournai at dawn by boat," Barbier read. "When did you get this?"

"Last night."

Barbier glanced at his watch. "They must be taking the boat across the border into France, as far south as they can get. Maybe they have a vehicle to get them the rest of the way."

Jacques studied Guy Barbier, his contact for several years. He was smart, intimidating, and very little got past him. Except for now. "That's what I thought at first," he said delicately.

"A train will be difficult," Barbier continued, "even if it is the best mode of transportation. The Germans control the railroads. Trains are filled with troops. I don't think that will change. They must have another way to travel."

"Read the message again."

"Leaving Tournai at dawn by boat," Barbier read. He paused, thinking. "They can spend a few days moving through northern France. The surrender will be formalized by then, less uncertainty. Then they can get a train."

Jacques watched him closely. "There's no password."

Barbier studied the note again and looked up.

"Camille's transmittals are supposed to start with all that glitters," Jacques said. "That's the password."

"The message is fake?"

Jacques nodded. "The question then becomes, why send it?"

Barbier pursed his lips. "Was it sent under duress?"

"One possibility."

Barbier shrugged. "It seems the most likely. The Gestapo made her send the message."

"For what purpose?" Jacques asked. "It doesn't provide any details, not if the Gestapo hoped to catch any of her accomplices."

"If there's no password, she was forced to send the message. There's no other explanation."

Jacques thought for a moment. "I met Camille, briefly, but memorably. Never underestimate her."

"Do you think she intentionally sent a fake message?"

Jacques nodded. "I think it has two purposes. She alerted me, to tell me she was on her way to Paris but included fake information to fool the Germans."

Barbier sat back in the chair, eyeing Jacques with a hint of doubt. "Why would she do that?"

"I suspect the Germans are close to catching her. And she knows it. She sent the message, knowing they would intercept it, so she could elude them."

Barbier studied him for a moment, considering alternatives. "Do you think she's using different transportation?"

Jacques nodded. "Or she isn't escaping at all. She might be moving to another location, waiting until it's safer to come to Paris."

"The message keeps the Germans focused on the river."

"Just a thought," Jacques said. "But without a password, all we really know is that it isn't true."

"The Germans control Paris. It's much different than when she left to steal the diamonds. Could she be trying to get to England? Maybe that's what she means when she says she's traveling by boat."

"I told her to bring the diamonds to me if Roger couldn't get them to London," Jacques said. "She also asked again when she sent her last message, I told her she has to come to Paris."

Barbier frowned. "We need to somehow decipher her message. She could be asking for help. We need to give her what she needs—no matter what it is."

CHAPTER 89

The German staff car screeched to a halt at the Lille terminal. "Hurry," Ziegler said as he flung open the door.

Bayer was right behind him, leaving the car door open. "The train hasn't left yet."

"Let's hope it's the right train," Ziegler called.

They raced to the terminal. Bayer opened the first door they reached. They ran inside and paused. The building was spacious, ticket windows spread throughout. German soldiers filled the terminal, waiting for trains, recently arriving, or crowding cafés and newsstands.

Ziegler and Bayer scanned the building, searching for the quickest way to get to the boarding platform. With so many soldiers milling about the station, it was difficult to see.

"This way, sir," Bayer said, pointing to an overhead sign at the corner of the building.

They crossed the terminal, fighting their way through crowds. A moment later they reached the exit.

"Hurry, "Ziegler said. "Before they leave."

Bayer pushed open the door. A train sat on the tracks, steam drifting from its engines. A railroad employee stood past the entrance, managing the crowd. Soldiers filled the boarding platform, a few civilians scattered among them. Most waited in pairs or small groups. Some prepared to board, others were not as anxious, perhaps waiting for a later train.

Ziegler and Bayer approached the railroad employee, an older man in a blue uniform.

"May I help you?" the man asked.

"Is this the train from Tournai?" Bayer asked in French,

"Yes, it is," the railroad employee replied. "En route to Paris."

"When does it leave?"

"In a few minutes." The attendant pointed farther down the platform, where a dozen soldiers stood in single file. "After they board."

Another string of soldiers exited the second car. As the last one left, the soldiers waiting to board moved toward the train.

"We don't have much time," Bayer said to Ziegler. "The train leaves as soon as these soldiers board."

Ziegler hesitated. "We can't delay an entire troop train so we can search for a thief who may not even be on board."

"We can get on, sir," Bayer suggested. "But we may have to go all the way to Paris."

The soldiers continued boarding, the line getting smaller. The attendant stopped them for a moment to speak to a sergeant who seemed to oversee them. The sergeant removed a document from his pocket and showed it to the attendant. A moment later, the line continued. The attendant moved away, watching the last of the men prepare to board.

"We have to get on that train," Ziegler said to the attendant.

The man shrugged and looked at Bayer. "I don't understand," he said in French.

Bayer repeated Ziegler's demand in French. The attendant nodded and replied.

"He said he has no empty seats," Bayer told Ziegler.

"Are there any stops before Paris?" Ziegler asked.

Bayer repeated the question and received a reply. "No, it goes straight through."

Ziegler hesitated. "We don't have permission to go to Paris. Only a threat from von Horn."

"We have to decide, sir. We only have a minute."

Ziegler knew he faced dire consequences if he didn't get the diamonds. Far worse than acting without orders. "It's a risk I have to take."

The train whistle sounded to signal departure, the engine belching steam. Bayer spoke to the attendant, who leaned toward him, listening. He then moved toward the train.

A second whistle blasted. The train began to inch away, the pistons chugging slowly. The attendant waved to the engineer, trying to get him to halt.

CHAPTER 90

"Look!" Camille hissed. She nudged Lucien and nodded toward the terminal.

Ziegler and Bayer had barged onto the platform. As Bayer spoke to a railroad attendant, Ziegler was more animated, pointing to the train. The attendant motioned to the engineer, as if he wanted the train delayed.

"We'll never get away," Lucien whispered, his voice quivering.

Camille watched Ziegler. "They won't be able to stop the train. Not with all of these troops on board."

"Can they get on?"

Camille was leery but prepared for the worst. "I doubt they have orders to go to Paris. But that doesn't mean they won't."

The train whistle signaled departure. The engine belched steam.

"They may not make it," Lucien said. "The train is leaving."

Another whistle sounded. The train began to inch away, each chug of its pistons stronger. As Camille and Lucien watched anxiously, the attendant led Bayer and Ziegler closer. He opened the car door and the Gestapo leaped onboard.

Lucien leaned toward Camille, eyes wide. "What are we going to do now?"

She could feel his body trembling. She had to calm him. "They'll go through each car and question the women, maybe search their baggage. They're looking for me and the diamonds. Don't talk if they ask you any questions. I'll tell them your wound prevents it."

An hour passed. They remained in the last row of the fifth car, anxiously watching the connecting door to the fourth. Bayer and Ziegler could burst through at any moment. But they hadn't yet.

The countryside sped past, farm fields, small villages, and the scarred battlefields of the First World War now stamped with combat scenes from the second. With France about to surrender, refugees walked the roads, not as many, their destination undefined. They seemed confused, wondering whether to return where they came from or push south. Remnants of war dotted the countryside—backpacks, troop trucks, damaged motorcycles, abandoned rifles. German soldiers patrolled major roads, moving from one location to the next, transitioning from battle to occupation. The French army had collapsed. For Camille, who had traveled this same route a few short weeks before, it seemed like she was in a different country—it wasn't the France she knew.

She glanced at Lucien as she prepared to address Ziegler and Bayer. He looked convincing in his captain's uniform, the bandages around his throat and on his cheek, gray strands in his hair. She was confident their disguises were good, their documents flawless. The Gestapo likely had little recollection of their brief encounter at the farm—especially given the number of people they had questioned before and after. They wouldn't recall details, even regarding their appearances—other than her blonde hair. Camille had to convince them of their innocence. While she waited, she visualized the encounter, planning what she would say.

"If they come to question us, I'll start talking, making conversation," she whispered to Lucien. "Try not to be nervous."

"What are you going to say?"

"I'll ask them questions, disrupt their thoughts. They expect everyone to fear them. But I intend to confuse them."

"I hope it works," he whispered, not sounding convinced.

"It will," she said, although she expressed more confidence than she felt. "If they even question us. They might wait until we leave the train."

She studied the soldier next to her. He was napping, not paying much attention to them—he had no reason to. No one did. She tried not to stare at the connecting door, even though she knew it could soon open.

Camille had a one-bedroom flat in Paris. They would be safe there. She could sort everything out, determine what was next. Paris was in turmoil—it may not be her final destination. Especially now that the Germans occupied the city. She didn't even know if Jacques Dufort was still there. But he was her only contact—other than her mentor, Nicolas Chastain. She would try to find Jacques, starting with his apartment. She would then get her next assignment. But at some point, she would have to tell Lucien that he couldn't return to his farm. Not now. She had destroyed any hope he might have of a simple life in the Belgian countryside.

Her thoughts were interrupted when the connecting door slid open.

CHAPTER 91

Emilie entered Louie Bassett's parlor. "I'm sorry to barge in on you," she said. "But Guy Barbier came to visit Jacques this morning. I think it was important."

He sat beside her, anxious for information. "What did they say?"

"I couldn't hear their entire conversation. Only a few scattered words. I had to be careful. Jacques caught me eavesdropping the last time Barbier came."

"No, you can't take any risks," Louie agreed. "Especially now that the Germans control the city. Jacques is too unpredictable. He's cornered."

"He avoids going to his office. He said the Germans are taking over administration."

"They are. I'm sure he finds it more difficult every day to pose as a civil servant."

"If that's what he's doing," she said. "He reveals nothing. I learn more about him from you."

Louie was quiet, as if wondering whether to share secrets—if he even knew them. "I could tell you much about your husband, Emilie. But it's information best saved for another day."

She realized he really didn't care about Jacques. He was focused on the diamonds. And she should too. "I had left to open the store," she explained. "When I got to the corner, I realized I had forgotten the name and phone number of a man who wanted to sell some memorabilia. I had left it on the kitchen table. I went in the back door to get it."

"And you heard Barbier talking?"

"Yes, he had just arrived. Jacques took him into his study. They were talking about Tournai."

"About Camille and the diamonds?"

Emilie nodded. "They discussed a message Jacques had received and whether it was fake."

"But you don't know what the message said?"

"I only heard a few words. I think it said something about a boat."

Louie stood and started pacing. "If Camille and the diamonds are in Tournai, she could leave by boat and come down the river into France. But only for one leg of her journey. She must have other transportation arranged."

"They weren't sure if her message was genuine," she continued. "I heard them say something about a password."

Louie rubbed his chin. "If she was told to use a password and didn't, something must be wrong."

"Could she have been captured?" Emilie asked. "Maybe that's why the Gestapo called from Tournai."

"Yes, she could be. Or the message might be a ruse, designed to trick either the enemy, Jacques, or both."

Emilie sighed, sometimes wondering if she would ever understand the intricate world of espionage. "How will we ever know?"

"We won't." Louie sighed and sat back down. "But we should prepare for the best scenario."

"I heard Jacques say that he thinks the message meant

Camille is on her way to Paris with the diamonds but may not be coming by boat."

"If Jacques and Barbier are convinced she's coming, no matter how she gets here, then we need to somehow get the diamonds when she arrives."

"I don't know how we will. Especially if she contacts Jacques directly."

Louie nodded, face firm. "She'll meet Jacques, deliver the diamonds, and he'll sell them to the highest bidder."

"And then Jacques and his lover disappear with their fake identity papers."

Louie pursed his lips. "I'm afraid that's likely true. We have to somehow divert Camille to you."

Emilie was quiet for a moment. "If she comes to the apartment, I may be able to convince her to work with us instead of Jacques. He's rarely home."

"Then that's what we must do. We have no alternative."

She mulled over what to say if Camille appeared at her door unannounced. She was starting to link the pieces together. "What about the Germans?" she asked. "Do we approach them and offer to assist? Or do we continue to use your contacts?"

"We need to get the diamonds first," Louie replied. "Then we'll approach the Germans. Not before. That's important."

"Why are the diamonds first?" she asked. "I'm in danger. I can't predict what Jacques will do."

"Just be patient," he advised sternly. "Diamonds first. Above all else."

CHAPTER 92

Major Ziegler and Sergeant Bayer had methodically moved through the train car, questioning all women, and examining their baggage. The first car was half-filled with nurses, and their investigation took almost an hour. Each succeeding car had fewer women, and they moved quicker, knowing some of those they questioned had little resemblance to the blonde they sought—either older or a different build. They didn't rule out hair color—hair dye and wigs could be used effectively.

The train was closer to Paris, much of its journey completed, when Sergeant Bayer opened the connecting door into the last car, and Major Ziegler stepped through. Bayer followed, sliding the door closed. They had gone through four cars, having found more female passengers than they expected, all enroute to Paris to assist with the occupation. A similar technique had been used to question each: Ziegler had meticulously examined their papers and found them valid, Bayer had searched their luggage. Nothing unusual had been found.

"Sergeant, we'll take the same approach," Ziegler said. "You search the baggage. I'll examine the documentation."

All That Glitters

"Yes, sir," Bayer replied. He glanced down the rows. "There's only a handful in this car. Fewer than the rest of the train."

Four rows from the connecting door, three women sat together in military uniform, two blondes, one with black hair. The two Gestapo stepped toward them, pausing in the aisle.

"Papers, please," Ziegler asked the woman in the aisle seat.

"Your baggage, also," Bayer requested.

The woman stood and removed a short gray duffel bag from the overhead rack and handed it to Bayer. She took her papers from her skirt pocket and gave them to Ziegler.

Bayer looked through the knapsack, finding nothing more than spare clothes and some personal effects. He didn't remove anything, only peeked inside, and felt through the clothing. It was a quick search, but an easy one. He returned the duffle bag a moment later.

Ziegler was more meticulous. He scanned the documents, checking the stamps, ensuring the signatures were different, feeling the texture of the paper. He then examined different line items, checking dates and accuracy. He handed them back to the woman and moved to the next, repeating the process, but adding questions.

"What is your Paris assignment?' Ziegler asked, eyeing the woman closely. She was blonde, a candidate for the diamond thief, but he couldn't remember what she looked like.

"Telephone and telegraph operator, sir," the woman replied.

Ziegler nodded and examined her documentation. The papers were rumpled, as if not cared for properly, but the line items were lengthy, her service extensive. He eyed the birthdate. She looked younger than her actual age. He tried to recall the woman in the farmhouse but couldn't. He had been so surprised by her command of the German language, so unexpected on a Belgian farm, that his thoughts had been disrupted—and that was likely her intention. He eyed the woman carefully, checking her eyes, her hair, her hands, but nothing was familiar. He returned her papers.

The third woman handed him her documentation. It was very similar. Everything was legitimate.

Bayer finished searching her belongings. "Nothing," he said.

Ziegler nodded, feeling defeated. "It seems we may have been tricked. Maybe she did leave by boat."

"I'm sure there's an afternoon train returning," Bayer said. "We can go back and do a more detailed search along the river."

"Yes, perhaps," Ziegler muttered. "But I'd rather spend a day or two in Paris. I want to explore the business card, the antique shop, before we return."

"Shall we go back to the first car?" Bayer asked. "We can check everyone again when they leave the train."

Ziegler saw the nurse in the last row, squeezed between two soldiers. "One more to question."

He walked to the rear of the car.

CHAPTER 93

Camille prodded Lucien with her elbow. "Here they come," she whispered. "You know what to do."

Ziegler walked toward them, Bayer behind him. His penetrating gaze was fixed on Camille, not wavering, staring sternly.

Her gaze briefly met his and she looked away, admiring the passing countryside. She acted as if the approaching Gestapo had nothing to do with her. She gave them little attention, all but ignoring them as they came closer.

"Papers, please," Ziegler said, his hand outstretched.

Camille smiled and fumbled through her pockets. She took her documents from her dress pocket, reaching beneath her nurse's frock. She glanced at them for a moment, ensuring it was what she wanted, and handed them to Ziegler. Even though her heart raced, she acted as casually as she could, pretending the major standing before her offered only another formality, nothing to be taken seriously.

She continued to faintly smile as he started to review her papers. "You served in Poland, sir?" she asked, in German. She pointed to a service medal on the front of Ziegler's coat.

He looked up, surprised she addressed him. "Yes, I did," he muttered, fingering the medal. "Mainly in Warsaw."

"I served in a hospital near Krakow, sir," she said, chatting as if they were old friends. "I was fortunate, I spent little time on the front."

Ziegler nodded, again examining her documents.

"I've been to Austria, too, sir," she said, pointing to another medal. "Such lovely countryside."

"Yes, it is," Ziegler mumbled, still reviewing her papers.

"May I see your bag, please?" Bayer asked.

"Of course," Camille said.

The soldier sitting along the aisle stood and stepped out of the way. Camille rose and got her satchel from the bin above the seats, the diamonds sewn into the lining. She handed it to Bayer.

"There's not much in there," she said. "I'll have to do some shopping in Paris."

Bayer chuckled. "I suspect we all will." He opened the drawstring and started to look inside. He blushed, finding her undergarments at the top of the pile.

"Personal nurse to Captain Hauptman?" Ziegler asked, handing Camille her papers. "Why would a captain have a personal nurse?"

Lucien growled, as if trying to speak. He handed his papers to Ziegler.

The major took them, looking surprised.

"He can't talk," Camille explained. "Not until his wounds heal."

"You are Captain Hauptman?" Ziegler asked.

Lucien nodded.

Ziegler gazed at his papers. "Personal aide to General Speidel, military governor of Paris," he mumbled. He checked the papers briefly, nowhere near the detailed examination he had given to Camille's and handed them back. "My apologies, Captain."

Lucien nodded and managed a guttural response that resembled no language ever spoken.

"Your bag," Bayer said, handing the satchel to Camille. "It's heavier than it looks."

"Soon to be filled with French trinkets," Camille joked. She smiled innocently and put her duffel bag back in the overhead bin.

"Captain," Ziegler said, nodding. He turned to Camille. "Fräulein"

Camille nodded as Ziegler turned and strutted away, her pulse not yet beginning to slow.

CHAPTER 94

Jacques Dufort tapped on the door, glancing up and down Rue Serpente to ensure no one watched. A moment later, Sophie Silvain ushered him into her apartment.

"Have you received any more messages?" Jacques asked as they climbed the stairs.

"Nothing," Sophie said. "But if any part of the last message was accurate, she's on her way to Paris."

Jacques sighed and sat on the couch. "I'm starting to have doubts," he said. "Do you think we could have missed something? Camille would never forget to use the passcode."

Sophie sat beside him. "If she was captured or compromised, she would have sent more messages. But she hasn't."

"I suppose you're right," he said. "The Germans would try to get information from us."

"And if she had been captured and they had the diamonds, why bother to send the message?"

"Unless they're setting a trap for us," Jacques reasoned.

"They could be. But I suspect only some of the message is fake. She sent it more than once, without the password, to ensure it was received. Maybe by us and the Germans. She is trapped in Tournai, close to capture."

"I'm sure she suspects the Germans are intercepting her transmissions. It's the best explanation."

"She fools the Germans and gets out of Tournai. Maybe she didn't leave by boat, or she left by boat but not on the day specified."

He pursed his lips. "I wish we knew for sure so we could help her. I have got to get those diamonds before the Germans do. And I'm in danger. I don't have much time."

"Don't worry," she said. "I think Camille is enroute, just not as described in the message."

A frown stuck on his face. "I still don't like the call from the Gestapo. I have no way of knowing what Emilie may have said to them—if they even called at all."

"We don't have much longer," she said. "If Camille escaped, and she has the diamonds, she'll deliver them in a day or two."

"We may not have another day or two."

Sophie went to a desk against the wall and removed some papers from the bottom drawer. She handed them to Jacques. "The German military documents you need to frame Emilie. Hide them in the apartment, somewhere the Gestapo will find them."

Jacques scanned through them. "These are good," he said. "Very authentic."

"I have some German currency, too, that you can stick with them. Large denominations, but counterfeit."

Jacques sighed. "I'm not sure I can do this. Her arrest will be horrible."

"It will be," Sophie said. "But it's better than your arrest. Don't you agree?"

Jacques nodded. He sometimes couldn't believe what Emilie might be doing. But he couldn't afford to ignore it.

"I've made all of our arrangements. The fake papers you had prepared are being modified, updated to reflect the latest German requirements."

"We need the diamonds first."

"Unless we can't wait," she said. "We don't know what Emilie is doing. I'll pick up our documents tomorrow. Everything will be ready."

"Where are we going?"

"Spain. Our contacts along the way are expecting us."

He nodded. Sophie was extremely efficient. He knew how much coordination an escape effort took. "It's good that you did all of this. My instinct tells me we don't have much time—maybe hours versus days. As soon as I get the diamonds, and give them to Barbier, we have to leave."

She hesitated, trying to make him see what he didn't want to see. "We can leave as soon as we get the documents if we really have to."

He looked at her, head cocked, trying to decipher what she said.

"Whether we get the diamonds or not," she clarified. "It depends on Emilie—not Camille."

CHAPTER 95

Ziegler and Bayer walked up the aisle of the fifth train car, casting a last glance at the three women communication workers sitting near the front.

"Should we return to the first car, sir?" Bayer asked, grasping the handle of the interconnecting door.

Ziegler held out his hand, signaling Bayer to pause. "It seems odd that the woman we're looking for doesn't seem to be on the train."

Bayer shrugged. "We may have been fooled, sir, like you said. Maybe she did leave by boat, but at a different time. Or they went north for a rendezvous, instead of south."

"Or she might be using a different mode of transportation."

"Even a bicycle—just to get out of Tournai. She had a bicycle at the village when she used the radio in the church steeple."

Ziegler considered different alternatives. "Yes, perhaps," he said. "Maybe we're wrong and she isn't on the train."

"We didn't find any diamonds, either, sir."

Ziegler turned to look at the nurse in the last row. She sat quietly, gazing out the window at the passing countryside, calm and relaxed.

"Is something wrong, sir?" Bayer asked.

Ziegler hesitated, but then shook his head. "No, I don't think so. Just something about the last woman. But I don't know what it is."

Bayer glanced back in the car. "The captain's nurse?"

Ziegler nodded. "She was very personable, not intimidated at all."

"Maybe she had no reason to be," Bayer suggested.

"She was impressive," Ziegler noted, stealing glances at her.

"She did seem more than a simple nurse," Bayer said. "Very intelligent. Knew your service medals, battle zones in Poland—the only woman on the train who does."

Ziegler shrugged, dismissing his doubts. "Yes, I suppose. Clearly comfortable in the military."

"Any issues with her papers, sir?"

Ziegler hesitated, thinking about her documents. He shook his head. "No, I have no doubt they were authentic. They even had coffee stains." He turned back toward the door. "It's easy to believe she was in Poland and Austria."

"It could be someone else," Bayer suggested. "One of the other women we overlooked. We can go through each car to see how they react."

"Maybe that's best," Ziegler conceded.

"But I would suggest spending the remainder of the journey in the first car," Bayer offered. "It was half-filled with nurses."

"I suppose if she is here, that's the most likely place."

Bayer opened the connecting door and they stepped into the fourth car. "Have you decided to stay in Paris once we arrive, sir?"

"Briefly," Ziegler replied. "First, I want to check in at Gestapo headquarters. I need to send a message to von Horn and explain why we're here."

"He did recommend a trip to Paris, sir."

Ziegler nodded. "Although I'm not sure he meant it. But if I phrase the message properly, and promise a quick return, I'm sure he'll approve."

"Do you plan to visit the antique shop?"

"Yes, as soon as we can secure a car," Ziegler replied. "The blonde may have eluded us for now. But we suspect we know her destination."

"We'll find her, sir. I'm sure of it."

Ziegler nodded. He knew his career, if not his life, depended on it.

CHAPTER 96

Lucien eyed Ziegler and Bayer nervously. They stood at the front of the car, whispering among themselves. Ziegler occasionally glanced to the rear.

"Ignore them," Camille whispered. She looked out the window, pointing to a farm as they passed. "Pretend you're looking at scenery."

Minutes passed, yet Ziegler and Bayer remained where they were. Bayer had his hand on the door, ready to slide it open and enter the next car, but then removed it.

"They're not leaving," Lucien hissed.

"They will," Camille assured him.

A moment later, Lucien subtly touched Camille's hand as Bayer opened the connecting door and he and Ziegler passed through. His hand was sweaty, his heart raced. He was trembling, trying not to think of how much he needed a swig of whiskey.

"You did good," she whispered, squeezing his hand tightly.

He leaned toward her, his head gently resting against hers. He was a simple man, a farmer who minded his own business, a loner who lived in the bottle—until he met Camille. He hadn't been sure he could fool the Germans—he actually doubted that he could. But he tried. Only to help Camille because she had helped him.

He glanced at the soldier beside her, his head in a newspaper. He held her hand; she squeezed it tighter. He took it as a signal. Both of what they'd accomplished and what they were about to do—deliver the finest industrial diamonds in the world to French intelligence. And maybe when it was all over, they would still be together.

"Don't ease up yet," she whispered in his ear. "We still have to get off the train and elude them."

"I'll do what you need me to," he said. "You were marvelous."

She smiled. "If you ask them questions before they ask you, it confuses them. They expect everyone to be intimidated."

"I certainly was," he admitted.

"I'm proud of you," she said. "You did fine."

Lucien glanced out the window at a passing village. Their journey shouldn't take much longer. "How do we avoid them when we get to Paris?"

"As soon as the train stops, we'll go out the rear exit," she whispered. "We can't take any chances. Ziegler may reconsider or grow suspicious. I suspect he'll stop each woman as she exits for more thorough questioning."

"Even though he questioned them once?"

She nodded. "He still suspects I'm on this train. He just doesn't know who I am."

"I suppose he wasn't fooled by the message about the boat—if he even intercepted it."

She shrugged. "He may have been. He could have gone to the river and then came after the train."

"He did miss the train in Tournai. Maybe he checked for the boat first."

"I suspect he has doubts, wondering if there was another

boat, or if it went in a different direction. That's good. We need to keep him confused."

Lucien turned and glanced at the rear exit. "Will he see us leave?"

"We'll move as quickly as we can," she said. "Once we're off the train, hold my hand, stay close, and follow me."

"Where are we going?"

"We have to get out of the terminal before Ziegler has time to reconsider. We'll take the metro."

He nodded, knowing they didn't have far to travel, maybe twenty minutes more. Soon they would be safe, away from the Germans who kept chasing them. But then he realized that the enemy occupied Paris.

There was no escaping.

CHAPTER 97

Emilie Dufort sat alone in her parlor, sipping a glass of wine. Jacques had left just after dinner, as he now did every night—if he came home for dinner at all. She suspected he visited Sophie Silvain, like he did on the evening she followed him. A supposed colleague, Emilie knew it was much more—it had to be. And if Jacques wasn't seeing her, he might be meeting Guy Barbier, a man Emilie had never liked. A feeling that was mutual.

She was getting anxious, suspecting she was more exposed to danger than she had originally thought. The Gestapo were after Jacques. There was no other explanation for the call from Tournai. And if Louie Bassett was correct, Jacques would soon sacrifice her to save himself. But she wasn't sure how. The Germans controlled Paris. Jacques couldn't do anything to her, not without her family intervening. But he didn't know that.

Louie Bassett hadn't given her much information, at least not about himself. She didn't know who he reported to, what his role was, or where he was from. His French was good, but the accent hard to define, maybe from the coast or a border region, just as she was. But she had many unanswered questions. What if he couldn't be trusted? What if he was only using her to get the diamonds? How did he know her family? He had provided a convincing argument, and valuable information that led to exposing her husband. But how did he get it?

Bassett made it clear that the diamonds were his primary objective. He claimed he did it for France, that Jacques had been led astray by Sophie Silvain and betrayed his country. Was Bassett from French intelligence, too? It seemed that he must be if he knew Jacques.

She sipped her wine and looked at the telephone sitting on the end table next to the sofa. The Gestapo had called from Tournai. It wasn't the best connection, but it was functional. She wondered if the lines to Germany had been restored. She could call her father, and if she got through, she could find out who Louie Bassett was, how they knew each other, and why Bassett had been used to deliver a family message. If her father was available, and not assigned somewhere in Germany to assist with the war effort.

She eyed the phone, undecided. It seemed safe to call him. Jacques wouldn't be home for hours. Not that it mattered. She had called home before the war, while Jacques was there. She had used a German operator, claiming they were so close to the border that she had to, and spoke in heavily accented German. He never seemed to suspect anything.

She reached for the telephone and dialed the operator. "Can you connect me to Germany?"

"Where in Germany?" the operator asked.

"Rheinau," Emilie replied.

Several seconds passed. Emilie could hear a crackling sound, hissing, and an occasional voice that sounded distant and dwarfed. She waited patiently as minutes passed. She was about to give up, when the connection cleared, and a woman started speaking in German.

"Hello, can you help me?" Emilie asked in German. "I'm trying to connect to Rheinau."

The operator replied, her voice breaking.

Emilie couldn't understand her. "Hello," she said. "I can't understand you."

The operator replied again, but the connection was so bad her voice cackled and broke.

"Please," Emilie said in German. "Can you connect me to Rheinau?"

A floorboard creaked, and Emilie turned.

Jacques stood in the parlor entrance. "What are you doing?"

CHAPTER 98

Twenty minutes later the train eased into Gare du Nord, the Paris railroad terminal. Ziegler and Bayer waited in the first car while the train came to rest. They rose before the others, moving toward the door, edging soldiers out of their way.

"I want to take another look at the female passengers as they exit the train," Ziegler said. "She still could be on board. We may have only missed her."

"It is the best way for her to get to Paris," Bayer replied. "But where did she hide the diamonds?"

Ziegler sighed, considering what he might have done. "They must be somewhere on the train—in a bathroom or under seats. A panel that the thief found and opened. We'll observe each of the women when they leave to ensure none carry more than they had when we interrogated them."

They stood at the main entrance and watched soldiers, nurses, and female military personnel step from the train and filter into the terminal. A smaller entrance near the rear of the train was used by a few, and Ziegler glanced at the other entrance, wondering if he could somehow observe both.

"Did you find any who were more suspicious than the others?" Bayer asked.

"A few," Ziegler mumbled. "But their papers were in order."

"You hesitated leaving the last car. Are you skeptical of those women—three communication workers and the nurse?"

Ziegler shook his head. "No, not really. But I keep thinking about the nurse in the last row."

"With the captain, aide to General Speidel?"

Ziegler nodded. "She seemed different. As you said, a bit beyond the usual nurse."

"She did have black hair," Bayer said. "But it could have been dyed or a wig."

"Yes, I suppose. It was just something about her, the confidence maybe."

"Why didn't you ask more questions?" Bayer asked.

"I saw no reason to," Ziegler said. "But she was certainly comfortable, chatting about Poland and Austria."

"As we left the last car, you told me her papers had a coffee stain on them. What does that mean? I don't understand the significance."

"It means they weren't forged," Ziegler said. "No one would be stupid enough to make a mistake like that."

"I suppose not," Bayer replied. "We also wouldn't want to harass them."

"No, we wouldn't," Ziegler agreed. "I don't need General Speidel counted as an enemy."

Bayer shrugged. "Maybe she did leave on a boat."

"And we just didn't find her," Ziegler mumbled, eyeing the passengers.

Bayer pointed toward the far door. The nurse and Captain Hauptman had exited from the rear of the train and were hurrying into the terminal. "I should have helped her."

"Yes, the captain was badly wounded," Ziegler said, eyeing

them cautiously. "And she has their satchels and the medical bag."

"I don't think she needs help with the captain," Bayer said. He held out his hand, stopping a nurse as she left the train so he could study her face. "He's mobile, only his throat and face were wounded. But her bag was heavy."

Ziegler paused, his mind racing. He turned to Bayer. "What do you mean that her bag was heavy?"

"She only had a few clothes in it, some undergarments, a spare nurse's uniform, and a few civilian clothes. But it was heavier than the other nurses' bags."

"It must be the diamonds!" Ziegler declared. "They're sewn into her satchel."

Bayer hesitated. "But the bag wasn't big enough. They emptied ten deposit boxes in Antwerp."

"Between the two of them they could carry it all," Ziegler said, excited. "Come on, hurry. They're getting away!"

They pushed through the crowd, primarily soldiers boarding or leaving their trains. The terminal overflowed with Germans, railroad attendants, and a few civilians. Cafés and shops lining the walls were filled with customers, a newspaper stand by the main entrance cluttered with patrons.

"I don't see them," Bayer said, craning his neck to scan the terminal.

Ziegler stepped up on a bench and surveyed the entire station. "There they are," he said. "Near the steps."

He climbed down and they raced across the terminal, pushing and shoving those that stood in their way. They were halfway across the station when Ziegler pointed to the steps. "They just saw us," he said. "Hurry! They're taking the metro."

They raced through the terminal, shouting at people to move. As they reached the steps, they had to elbow and push soldiers out of the way. They scrambled down the stairs as the last few people stepped onto the train and it inched away from the platform.

Ziegler's gaze met the nurse, standing at the train door, the captain beside her.

She nodded, smiling faintly.

CHAPTER 99

Lucien and Camille made their way to her apartment on Rue Chochin, close to the Sorbonne where she went to school. Located on the second floor, above an insurance company, it was a small flat on a quiet street, one that served her needs while in Paris. She led Lucien inside, the parlor overlooking the street, a bed and bath off to the side, the kitchen behind the parlor.

"We'll leave the diamonds sewn in the satchels for now," she said as she took him into the bedroom to a mahogany wardrobe. "But we'll hide the uniforms."

They changed into civilian clothes. She gathered their boots, folded their military clothes, and put them on the floor beside the duffle bags containing the diamonds. She pulled out the bottom drawer to the wardrobe, reached inside, all the way to the back, and undid a latch. She then wiggled a section of the floor, precut, from underneath the wardrobe. She put everything in the cavity between the joists—the satchels and the German uniforms—and replaced the floor section. Then she put the wardrobe drawer back.

"That's a fantastic hiding place," Lucien said. "No one would ever find it."

"Let's hope no one looks," she replied.

They left the apartment and stopped at a café for dinner—baguettes and cider. After they had eaten, they went to investigate Jacques Dufort.

"I'm getting overwhelmed," Lucien said as they walked down the boulevard. German soldiers paused to look in shop windows, mingling with Parisians slow to accept that the most beautiful city in the world was controlled by the enemy. "It's much different than the farm."

Camille smiled and slipped her hand in his. "Everything is different than the farm."

"Thank you," he whispered.

"Thank you for what?"

"Showing me how to live," he said. "I had forgotten."

She stopped and turned to face him, gazing in his eyes. She leaned up and kissed him lightly on the lips. "Tomorrow is always an adventure."

He laughed. "It is with you."

She smiled and led him to the side street where the first-floor flat of Jacques Dufort was located. She paused at the corner. "The fourth building on the right," she said. "That's where we're supposed to deliver the diamonds."

"Why don't we visit unannounced," Lucien said, "just to make sure it's safe."

Camille studied the door she had entered a few short weeks before, reflecting on all that had happened since she had. She didn't like risk. And if she went to the home of Jacques Dufort and he was no longer there, captured by the Germans or worse, she could put both Lucien and herself in danger. He wasn't ready to fight for his life—even if forced to. He was still learning to live without the murky mask of alcohol. A journey in progress, it came with challenges, taking time to complete. Small steps at first, but as each day passed, he grew stronger.

He was watching her, debating what actions to take,

wondering if she wanted to protect him. "It's all right," he said, as if he sensed her hesitation. "I can do it."

"What if he no longer lives there?" she asked.

"We just tell the current resident that we're trying to reach him."

Camille was quiet for a moment. "What if the Germans took him into custody?"

Lucien arched his eyebrows. "I didn't think of that. The new resident could contact the Gestapo."

She nodded, contemplating what to do. The longer she had the diamonds, the more dangerous it became. And the longer the Allies were deprived of their use. She had to get them to London. Jacques Dufort was the likely vehicle to get them there. But she had to be careful.

"Let's wait until tomorrow night," she said softly. "We'll come back tomorrow morning and watch the apartment, maybe check again in the afternoon. If it's quiet, tomorrow night we'll go to the door."

CHAPTER 100

Emilie went through four boxes of books she had just purchased, sliding them to the rear aisle of All Things Napoleon. When she had time, she would add them to the shelves. She yawned, tired from not having slept well. It had taken hours to convince Jacques she had only tried to reach her family on the telephone, making sure they were safe. Even though she had hung up as soon as she saw him, it was a reasonable explanation. He should have no reason to doubt it —except for her perfect command of the German language. As harmful as it could have been, she suspected he hadn't heard the entire conversation. Eventually he seemed to believe it was innocent, and that her linguistic abilities were common for someone who grew up on the border.

She was walking toward the front of the store when a German staff car pulled up along the curb. The driver got out and opened the rear door, and an officer stepped out. She looked over the store, a handful of customers walking the aisles, a few soldiers among them. She went behind the counter and waited.

The Germans entered, scanned the store, and approached

the counter. "I'm Sergeant Bayer and this is Major Ziegler, of the Gestapo," Bayer said in French.

Emilie's eyes widened. Bayer was the man who had called from Tournai. She suspected they were after the diamonds, just as she and Louie Bassett were. She decided to cultivate the relationship. It could prove worthwhile in upcoming days.

"We would like to ask you a few questions," Bayer continued in French.

"*Ich bin Emilie Dufort. Und Ich sprecke Deutsch,*" Emilie replied. "I am Emilie Dufort. And I speak German."

Their eyes widened. "Are you German?" Ziegler asked in his native tongue.

Emilie glanced cautiously at her customers. "Yes," she replied in German. "I was born in Rheinau, near the river."

"What are you doing in Paris?" Ziegler asked.

Emilie again eyed her customers. "Please, talk softly, Major," she said. "My customers think I am French."

"Which is it, Mme. Dufort?" Ziegler asked curtly. "German or French?"

She hesitated. She understood that this was a defining moment. "I live in Paris, but I will always be German."

"That's an excellent answer," Ziegler said. "This could be the beginning of a long friendship."

Emilie smiled faintly and nodded, looking furtively through the store. "But our secret, Major. As I'm sure you understand."

"Yes, of course," Ziegler replied. "I understand perfectly."

"Is this your store, Mme. Dufort?" Bayer asked.

Emilie nodded. "My uncle came to Paris many years ago. It was his store. I inherited it when he passed."

Ziegler looked at the aisles of books and memorabilia. "Interesting merchandise," he muttered. "I may become a customer."

"You're most welcome, I assure you."

Ziegler nodded. "We spoke on the phone, through Sergeant Bayer, when I was in Tournai."

"I remember."

"We haven't been able to reach your husband at his office. Are you sure he's there?"

She shrugged. "He meets with clients, usually in various locations, but rarely in the office."

"What does your husband do?" Bayer asked.

She hesitated. "He's some sort of civil servant. Railroads, I believe. He seldom talks about work."

"Where can we find him?" Ziegler asked.

She glanced at her watch. "He may be at his office now. Or he's at home in the evening. Around seven p.m. is best."

Bayer glanced at Ziegler. "Could you kindly provide both locations?"

"Yes, of course," Emilie said. She wrote her address on a piece of paper, knowing she had no choice, as well as the office building where Jacques sometimes reported.

Ziegler took the paper, looked at it briefly, and put it in his pocket. He withdrew a business card and handed it to her. "Do you know why a diamond thief in Antwerp would have your business card, with your husband's name written on the back?"

Emilie pretended to study the card, one of her questions answered. Did Camille have the card, accidently leaving it at the diamond exchange? She doubted it. She suspected there was more to the story. And she had to find out what it was. But she couldn't say too much. Louie Bassett had insisted she was not to work with the Germans until he had delivered the diamonds.

"No, I don't," she said simply. "Can you tell me more about how you found it?"

CHAPTER 101

Ziegler eyed Emilie Dufort. He suspected she knew more than she revealed. But he wondered why she wouldn't cooperate. If he really wanted to know, he could find out. He could haul her out of her store in front of her customers and take her to Gestapo headquarters. But he decided to take a different approach. He took back the business card. "The thief left it on the floor of the diamond exchange," he clarified.

Emilie paused, as if she wanted to be helpful but could not. "I'm sorry, Major," she said, slowly shaking her head. "But I don't know who that can be."

Ziegler moved closer, leaning on the counter. "What if I don't believe you?"

Her eyes widened. "I don't know why you wouldn't," she said, her voice quivering.

Ziegler watched her closely. "But there must be an explanation, Mme. Dufort. A customer or acquaintance? Someone you know from Antwerp or may have had plans to go there?"

Emilie hesitated, as if afraid to say too much. "I have customers all over Europe. Maybe the thief shopped at my store or purchased from one of my catalogues."

Ziegler gave her the card again. "Turn it over."

She studied the back. "My husband's name and an address I don't recognize."

"It's a dock in Antwerp," Ziegler said. "The thief's likely escape path."

"Did she escape?"

Ziegler eyed her curiously. "Yes, she did escape. But her partner did not. He was shot not far from the vault."

"Oh, my," Emilie said, moving her hand to her mouth. "I wouldn't know anything about any of that."

"Really?" Ziegler asked, arching his eyebrows. "No knowledge whatsoever?"

Emilie shook her head. "No, I'm afraid not."

"But how did you know that the thief was a woman?" Ziegler asked.

Emilie's eyes widened. "I didn't," she said. "I only assumed."

Ziegler cocked his head. "But why assume a woman? I never heard of a female jewel thief. Have you? Why make that assumption?"

Emilie shrugged. "I'm not sure. Only instinct, perhaps."

"Why is your husband's name on the card?" Ziegler asked.

"I don't know," she replied. "Maybe you can ask him when you go to his office."

"Maybe we can," Ziegler muttered. "We'll go there next."

"Late morning is usually best," she said. "But I'm not sure he'll be there."

Ziegler was beginning to lose his patience. "I suspect that, after we visit your husband, I will have more questions for you, Mme. Dufort."

"I have nothing to hide, Major."

Ziegler studied her closely, suspicious of the German woman who pretended to be French, owner of a store that sold Napoleon memorabilia. She seemed to know more than she was willing to admit. In time, she could be an ally, a valuable source of information. But first, he had to question her husband. And then he would have to question her, but under different circumstances.

Emilie looked about nervously, watching her customers. "I have to be careful, Major," she said as a man holding a leather book approached the counter.

"Of course, Mme. Dufort," Ziegler said. "We will talk another time."

Bayer nodded goodbye and went to the door, opening it for Ziegler.

They walked to the staff car. "What do you think of Mme. Dufort, Sergeant?" Ziegler asked.

"I don't think she's what she seems," Bayer replied as he opened the rear door.

Ziegler got in the car and waited until Bayer was in the driver's seat. "No, she isn't," he agreed. "But she's a source we need to cultivate, whether we remain here or not."

"I hadn't expected to find a German resident in the middle of Paris," Bayer said. "I wonder if she has family in Germany."

"We'll ask her at the first opportunity," Ziegler said. "And that could be this evening."

CHAPTER 102

Lucien and Camille decided to observe Jacque Dufort's apartment at different times during the day. In the morning, they saw an attractive woman leave, petite with dark hair, locking the door behind her.

"His wife?" Lucien asked as the woman walked toward Boulevard St. Germain.

Camille shrugged. "Someone was in the apartment when I first came. Maybe it was her."

They waited another thirty minutes, saw no activity, and left. They returned that afternoon, watched the apartment for an hour but saw no one.

"Maybe Jacques is no longer here," Lucien suggested. "Or he rarely leaves."

Camille eyed the flat. "Or any number of possibilities," she said. "Especially now with the Germans in control of the city."

"Not what you expected?"

She hesitated. "I'm not sure. No sign of Jacques, which makes me leery. Or anyone else, except for the woman."

Lucien glanced down the street, a quiet cobblestone lane that touched one of Paris's major boulevards a few blocks away. "Is it much different than when you first came?"

"No, not really. The street is the same, only a few neighbors venture out. The apartment is like any other quiet residence on a side street in Paris. No one would know that an intelligence network is operated from within—assuming it still is."

"What do we do next?"

"We return this evening," she said. "We'll knock on the door and see what we find. But first we'll circle the block, explore the alley behind the building, ensure we have escape paths if we need them."

It was almost seven p.m. when they returned. Camille eyed the street, searching for anything suspicious. Only a few people wandered the crooked lane, no evidence of any Germans. They went to the apartment, and she tapped on the entrance.

The door was opened a moment later by the woman they had seen earlier, black hair, slight. Her eyes widened in surprise when she saw them, and she stifled a gasp.

"We need to speak to Jacques," Camille said, noting her reaction. "It's important."

"He's not here right now." She nervously looked up and down the street.

Camille found her reaction curious. But at least Jacques still lived there. "When do you expect him home?" She eyed the woman cautiously, the slight hint of an accent. German, or maybe Alsace Lorraine. Suspicious, nevertheless. Not what she expected for the wife of a French intelligence officer.

"It's hard to predict. Since the…"

"Fall of France, the occupation of Paris," Camille said, still watching her closely.

The woman nodded. "Everything is different," she said. She hesitated, again looking up and down the street. "Would you like to wait?"

Camille sensed that something wasn't right. But she needed

to find out what it was. She looked at Lucien. He nodded subtly. "Only for a few minutes," she said. "If he doesn't arrive, we'll come back tomorrow."

"Please, come in." She led them into the foyer and then to the parlor on the right.

Camille glanced into the study, comparing it to her last visit, noting the umbrella stand by the door, the cane she could use as a weapon. She looked to the end of the foyer, a kitchen, a rear exit to the alley they had assessed earlier in the day.

They entered the parlor, nicely furnished, a broad window facing the street. A cuckoo clock hung near an exit to a back hallway. Shelves on a far wall contained fine porcelain, a beautiful bird, blue and white and perched on a tree stump, ivy crawling around it. It was complimented by several other pieces, wagons, tea kettles, more birds—all perfectly made with finely painted details.

"Can I get you anything?" the woman asked as Camille and Lucien sat on a sofa.

"No, thank you," Camille said, turning to Lucien. He shook his head and smiled at the woman.

She sat on a chair across from them, shifting nervously, continually looking toward the window.

"You must be Mme. Dufort," Camille said, her gaze wandering the room.

"Emilie," she responded, but didn't ask their names. "Is there anything I can help you with?"

Camille shook her head. "No, it's about a delivery I have for your husband."

Emilie's eyes widened, but she recovered quickly. "I would be happy to take the delivery for him," she said. "His schedule varies, especially now."

Camille glanced at Lucien, squirming in his seat, and looking at the paintings on the wall. He seemed an unwilling participant, someone fate had placed in her path. She lightly touched his thigh, reassuring him.

"I'm not sure when he'll be home," Emilie added.

"I have to give it to him," Camille said with a polite smile. "I'm sure you understand."

Emilie's gaze shifted from their eyes to their clothes, as if assessing pockets, places to carry something that would be given to her husband. She looked to the window.

A car pulled up outside, halting in front of her residence, the engine idling and then turned off. Camille tensed, turning to the window, the automobile not visible. The knock came a moment later.

"Who is that?" Camille hissed.

Emilie hesitated only a moment. "Camille, and yes, I know who you are. You are going to have to trust me. The Gestapo is at the door."

"It's a trap," Camille said, pulling Lucien toward the kitchen. "Come on."

"Wait, I'll help you," Emilie said. "Please, follow me. Hurry."

Camille eyed Emilie uneasily and then glanced at Lucien. After only a moment's hesitation, for they had no choice, they followed.

Emilie led them into the kitchen and out the back door. "Stay in the alleys," she said. She reached into her pocket, took out a business card, and handed it to them. "Come see me tomorrow at ten a.m. It's safe. I promise."

CHAPTER 103

Jacques Dufort had just turned the corner when he saw the Gestapo staff car parked in front of his apartment. He stopped abruptly, staying close to the wall. A German sat in the driver's seat, waiting for an unknown passenger. Jacques had to avoid his gaze. He eased back to the edge of the building, rounded the corner, and hurried down the street. He wasn't ready to confront the Gestapo—and he probably never would be.

He kept his head down, hands in his pocket, walking briskly to Sophie's apartment. He couldn't go back home, not now, maybe not ever. He had to get the diamonds. And then he might have to leave Paris, maybe even get out of France. His world was collapsing, and he wasn't sure what to do about it. But Sophie would know. She always did.

He wondered how much the Gestapo knew—or how much Emilie had told them. Did they plan to arrest him, or were they only asking questions? Until he knew the answers, he had to be cautious, avoid any contact. As he moved down one street and onto another, he turned away when approaching any Germans, hiding his face. Fifteen minutes later, he was at Sophie's door.

She answered, surprised to see him. "Is anything wrong?"

He waited until he was inside, the door closed, before replying. "The Gestapo are at my apartment."

She led him up the stairs. "That shouldn't surprise you," she said as they sat on the couch. "You know they're looking for you."

He frowned. "But it didn't seem urgent when they were calling from Tournai. It's different when they're sitting in your parlor."

Sophie rose and went to the window, peeking from behind the curtain. "No one is watching my apartment."

"I made sure I wasn't followed."

"You'll have to stay here," she said. "At least for now. It's too dangerous for you to go home."

He nodded. "Thanks. I appreciate that."

She returned to the couch, sitting beside him. "What are we going to do?"

Jacques hesitated. "We have to get the diamonds before we do anything. Have we received any messages from Camille?"

"No, nothing," she replied. "But I suspect she's on her way. Should I try to transmit?"

He shook his head. "No, it's too dangerous."

"We don't have much time," she said. "You can avoid the Gestapo, but not forever."

He frowned. "I'll have to talk to Barbier. Is our escape route ready?"

She nodded. "I have our documents and the route mapped to Spain. I formed a loose network, contacts along the way that can help if we need it. They know we're coming."

He sighed with relief. One worry was eliminated. He could always count on Sophie. "We just need to get the diamonds first."

"Jacques," she said, leaning closer to brush the hair from his forehead. "Maybe we need to forget the diamonds. Especially with the Gestapo closing in."

"I can't," he replied. "Not yet."

Sophie eyed him cautiously, as if hesitant to say what she might be thinking. "A day or two more, but that's it."

Jacques weighed the consequences. "If we're in danger, Barbier is, too. I don't know what Emilie told the Gestapo. But if she's pressed, she'll turn on him with no hesitation."

"Jacques, she'll turn on you, too. She probably already has."

He was skeptical. "I can't believe she would do that."

"I'm sorry, Jacques. I really am. But I don't think you can trust her."

Jacques hesitated, forced to realize he could be wrong. "Maybe you're right."

"Let's assume I am," she said, as if easing him into what had to be done. "We have to be prepared."

He smiled faintly. "You're always prepared. One of your many strengths."

"It's how we stay alive," she said simply.

"Yes, you're right. You always are."

"Did you plant the German documents I gave you?"

He nodded. "I put some in the cuckoo clock, others in different ornaments—all items she inherited from her mother."

"Then we really don't have to worry about Emilie, do we?"

"But the Gestapo were in my parlor," he said. "I can't take chances."

"Just tell me when you're ready. And I'll turn Emilie in to the Gestapo."

He realized it's what had to be done. Barbier had warned him. "What will you tell them?"

"That she's working for the French."

"I don't want her harmed," he mumbled. "I can't do that."

"She won't be. But it'll take a few days before she straightens it out."

Jacques paused, thinking. "We still need the diamonds. And I have things in the house I have to get—documents too important to leave for the Germans."

"Then you had better do it quickly—tomorrow if you can. And then, as soon as you're ready, I'll make the call."

CHAPTER 104

Major Ziegler stood at the front door to Emilie Dufort's apartment while Sergeant Bayer waited in the car. He wanted to speak to her alone. If he remained in Paris, he wanted to nurture their relationship. She could prove to be a valuable asset.

When no one answered, he glanced at his watch and knocked again, harder than the first time. He turned to Bayer and shrugged. But a moment later, the door opened, and he was greeted by Emilie Dufort.

"Good evening, Major," she said in German. "Please come in."

Ziegler eyed her curiously. She was flush, seemed anxious, but he didn't know why. "Is your husband home?" he asked as she led him through the foyer and into the parlor.

"No, not at the moment," she said. "He comes home at different times, depending on what he might be doing. Sometimes he doesn't come home at all."

Ziegler sat on the sofa, Emilie in a chair across from him. Was she offering hints about their relationship? Or was it innocent, an explanation for her husband's absence? He would have to tread carefully. "I can't imagine him spending more time away from you than what's absolutely necessary."

Emilie blushed. "Major, you're too kind. But I wonder if my husband would agree."

"I suspect he would," Ziegler said. He glanced around the room at the cuckoo clock and the collectables on the shelves. "Your home is lovely."

Her gaze followed his, to her porcelain ornaments. "Handed down through my family," she said. "My mother collected them. But she passed a few years ago."

"I'm sorry," he said, nodding with respect.

She smiled faintly, as if enjoying a memory. "Jacques usually comes home for dinner near six, unless he has pressing business. He must have been detained this evening."

Ziegler paused. He would question her instead. She could have valuable insight. He would focus on the diamonds—and what she might know about them. "You said at your store that you know very little about his work."

She shrugged. "He's sometimes secretive."

"But he works for the government?"

"Yes, he's some sort of civil servant—transportation, I believe. The railroads."

"Could he be in the military?" he asked, sensing she wasn't truthful.

She shrugged. "I don't think so. He has no uniform."

Ziegler wondered if she was lying, or if she really knew so little about her husband. "We went to his office today, but he wasn't there. When is the last time you visited his office?"

Emilie hesitated. "It's been more than a month. I don't go often."

Ziegler wanted to know more about Jacques Dufort. If he wasn't in the military, could he be a common thief who stumbled on a chance to steal the most valuable industrial diamonds in the world? "Does your husband have any money problems?"

She seemed surprised by the question, or the change in focus. "Not that I'm aware of. But I'm busy with my store. It's my life—I love everything about it."

Ziegler noticed she carefully measured each response. "Did he ever mention diamonds?"

She paused. "No, not really. He doesn't like jewelry." She held out her left hand. "No diamonds for me, only a simple wedding band."

Ziegler suspected a time would come when he could trust Emilie Dufort and she could trust him. But not yet. "Would you be surprised to learn that your husband works for the military, as an intelligence analyst?"

Her eyes widened. "Yes, I would," she said, shrugging meekly. "He claims to be a simple civil servant."

"His coworkers said he rarely visits his office. Only a few times in the last two months. And then only briefly, to get documents."

Emilie slowly shook her head. "I didn't know that. As I said, I'm occupied with my store. It's more work than you would think. I have stock to maintain, calls from people selling merchandise, evaluations and purchases, customers to tend to—even searching for specific items they may be interested in."

"I'm sure there's much to do," he mumbled, not very interested. He again glanced around the room, noticing the absence of family photographs. The apartment was cold, almost staged, as if it were a movie set. Maybe they did lead separate lives.

"Jacques is busy, too," she continued. "He sometimes meets clients here, in his study, or goes to their location. Maybe that's why he's rarely in the office."

"Perhaps," Ziegler replied. "But I suspect your husband works for someone in the military, doing specific tasks that require a certain expertise."

She shrugged again. "I'm sorry, Major. I really wouldn't know."

"Or maybe not then," he offered, suggesting an alternative. "Maybe he hires out his services, based on information he receives as a civil servant."

She eyed him closely, as if she hadn't considered his explanation. "I'm sorry," she said, shrugging. "It never occurred to me. He is secretive about his work. But he is a good provider."

Ziegler decided to probe the civil servant selling secrets. "Did you ever see evidence that your husband could be selling information? Large sums of money, or maybe he brings home documents and gives them to strangers, or whispered conversations late at night?"

"I would know nothing about that," Emilie said.

Ziegler nodded, eyeing her closely. She had replied quickly —a little too quickly. She knew something but was reluctant to reveal it. "I think I will have a lengthy discussion with your husband when I find him."

Emilie chuckled. "Maybe he's avoiding you," she said, glancing at her watch. "And that's why he hasn't come home."

"Yes, perhaps he is."

"But if what you say is true, maybe he has good reason to avoid you."

Ziegler fixed his gaze on hers. He could mold this woman into whatever he wanted, a good informant, a valuable source. He rose to leave. "You and I will be working very closely together. Mme. Dufort. I can promise you that."

CHAPTER 105

Camille led Lucien from Emilie Dufort's apartment, through the winding alley they had checked that afternoon. "We have to hurry," she hissed.

Lucien gasped. "We barely got away."

"I caught a glimpse of the Gestapo, standing on the stoop when we left."

"Ziegler?" Lucien guessed.

She nodded. "He's close, much closer than I thought."

"But he couldn't have known we were there."

Camille hesitated. "Maybe, or maybe not."

"I don't understand."

"He could have been there for us, he could have come for my contact, Jacques, or he could have been there for Emilie."

Lucien was confused. "Why would he be there for Emilie?"

"I'll tell you later. Let's get as far away as we can."

She avoided main boulevards, working her way through narrow lanes and cobblestone streets, staying in shadows. They paused, hiding behind rubbish cans to ensure no one followed, taking a torturous, twisting route.

"How do you know where you're going?" he asked, trying to keep up with her.

"I went to school at the Sorbonne, only blocks away," she said. "I know the neighborhood well."

"But German patrols are everywhere," he said, his voice anxious.

"No one knows who we are except Ziegler and Bayer. Come on, we're almost home."

She led him through the last alley, back to her apartment. They ducked into the doorway and went upstairs, collapsing on the sofa.

"We made it," Lucien said. "It's good that Emilie is on our side. They would have caught us if she wasn't."

Camille hesitated. "We don't know that she is."

He looked at her strangely. "She wouldn't have helped us if she wasn't."

"Yes, she did help us," Camille agreed. "But what does she want in return?"

Lucien shrugged. "I hadn't thought of that."

Camille was quiet, reliving the minutes in Emilie Dufort's parlor. "I think she's dangerous."

Lucien looked at her curiously. "I didn't get that impression."

She wasn't sure how much to reveal. She didn't want him any more anxious than he already was. "Did you notice her accent?"

Lucien shrugged. "Not really. Maybe very slight."

"German?"

He shook his head. "No, I don't think so," he said. "She's French, owns a store that features Napoleon memorabilia. But I suppose she could be from a border region."

Camille decided to tell him what she had observed, to see if he came to the same conclusions. "Did you see the family photographs?"

He hesitated. "I don't remember any family photographs."

"There were none."

Lucien shrugged. "That doesn't mean anything."

"The cuckoo clock," Camille continued. "It was made in Germany, an area close to the Swiss border, near Basel."

His eyes widened. "How do you know that?"

She smiled. "I know things most people would consider a waste of time."

"Maybe it was a gift," he countered.

"The porcelain collection is valuable," she continued. "It's Meissen, made near Dresden."

"I still don't see the connection. So, she likes German porcelain."

She paused. "Did you like the paintings? I saw you looking at them."

"Yes, beautiful landscapes, the Rhine River."

"German," she said.

"Or French," he offered.

Camille didn't reply. She looked at the business card. "All Things Napoleon. Emilie Dufort, Proprietor."

"Will we go tomorrow at ten a.m.?

Camille hesitated. "Only if we're careful. I don't trust Emilie Dufort. It may be a trap."

"She knew your name," he said. "Maybe she helps her husband. Do you trust him?"

"How does she know my name?" Camille asked. "I never met her. How did she recognize me?" She paused, pensive. "And I don't know if I trust her husband. I don't think we should trust anyone."

Lucien was quiet, not knowing the answer. After a moment, he replied. "Was she there the day you met Dufort? Maybe she saw you arrive or caught a glimpse as you left."

Camille reflected on her visit. "Someone was in the house. I could hear them."

"Maybe she eavesdropped."

"Maybe," Camille muttered. "Or maybe she helps the Germans but doesn't want us to think that she does."

"Why not turn us in to the Gestapo? She had the perfect opportunity."

"Because she wants something from us first—the diamonds."

"Or maybe she is working with her husband and that's why she saved us. We have to bring the diamonds to him. Do we have any other choice?"

Camille hesitated. "We can take the diamonds to London ourselves, through Spain or Switzerland."

"Won't it be difficult without a support network? Remember what Mme. Abadie told us? She's using a network built during the last war. How would we ever establish a new one?"

"We could do it," Camille said. "But it would be harder, far more dangerous."

"We never would have gotten to Paris without Mme. Abadie. How would we get to Switzerland? We wouldn't know where to start."

She scanned the business card. "Then I suppose we must visit Emilie Dufort."

CHAPTER 106

"I was afraid you wouldn't come," Emilie said as Camille and Lucien entered All Things Napoleon.

"We almost didn't," Camille said, eyeing the customers. "How do you know my name?"

"Not here," Emilie whispered. "Wait just a minute."

Emilie went to the back of the store where Denis, her loyal employee, was adding recently arrived books to a shelf. "Can you watch the counter for an hour or so?" she asked. "I won't be too long."

"Yes, of course," he replied, following her to the front.

Emilie approached Camille and Lucien, nodded subtly, and motioned for them to follow as she stepped out onto the pavement. "We're not going far," she said. "Just to meet a friend at a café around the corner."

"Why should we trust you?" Camille asked, stopping abruptly.

Emilie looked at her, trying to show sincerity, even though she suspected that, as soon as Louie got the diamonds, he would turn them into the Gestapo. "You have no choice. Ziegler is close, much closer than you think. Don't underestimate him. And don't trust my husband."

Camille glanced at Lucien and leaned close. "Be prepared for anything," she whispered.

Emilie pretended she hadn't overheard. "The café is safe," she said, trying to reassure them. "It's on the corner, anyone approaching can easily be seen."

"Tell me how you know my name," Camille said, more insistent.

"I was in the apartment when you came to see Jacques," Emilie explained. "I looked out the window when you arrived and saw you get out of the car. I was about to open the door when Jacques asked me to leave because he wanted privacy. He told me your name."

Camille didn't reply. She cast an uneasy glance at Lucien.

Emilie realized they would be difficult to convince. But between her and Louie, they would manage.

They walked a few more blocks and reached the café. A dozen tables were spread about the pavement, German soldiers at two of them. A few others were filled with civilians—couples and businessmen. Emilie led them to a large table with three empty chairs, the fourth occupied by a man of average height, brown hair and eyes, maybe early forties.

"I'm Louie Bassett," he said as he stood to greet them. "And you must be the elusive Camille. What an honor it is to finally meet you."

Camille nodded, studying Bassett closely. "My associate," she said, motioning to Lucien but not offering his name.

Louie shook his hand and motioned for them to sit. "I suppose we have some explaining to do."

"Yes, you do," Camille said. She eyed those in the café, the streets beyond, and Louie Bassett. She moved closer to Lucien.

"I'm part of a clandestine intelligence operation," Louie began. "It's managed from London—you may detect a faint accent. We've monitored Jacques Dufort and his lover Sophie

Silvain, for several months. They're traitors who sell their services to the highest bidder."

"I just learned about the lover," Emilie added. "A current colleague. The past few weeks have been difficult."

Camille nodded respectfully, as if it wasn't her place to know more. "How did Jacques enlist me for such an important mission, and coordinate everything at the diamond exchange—building plans, security information, key locations—if he isn't French Intelligence?"

"He is French Intelligence," Louie confirmed. "But he's a traitor. And so is his lover. Guy Barbier, a crook who commissioned Jacques to steal the diamonds, is a Parisian gangster with connections throughout the continent. I suspect he gathered the needed information."

Camille glanced at Lucien. "Where do you come in, M. Bassett?"

"I was assigned to find out what Jacques was doing. His communications were intercepted, exchanges which also exposed Sophie Silvain. But it was too late. You were already en route to Antwerp, an unknowing participant in his scheme."

"Who was Roger, my contact in Antwerp?" Camille asked. "I was supposed to take him to the port so he could get to London."

"He's one of Barbier's henchmen," Louie said. "Not French Intelligence, just a common thief. He was never taking the diamonds to London but back to Paris by ship. Jacques had already sold them to Barbier and was given a considerable down payment."

"Which I found hidden in his study," Emilie said. "But the next day, the money was gone."

"Then M. Barbier must be very angry with Jacques," Lucien said, speaking for the first time.

"Yes, I do suspect Jacques has more than the Gestapo to worry about," Louie agreed.

Camille turned to Emilie. "Why would you betray him? Because of his lover?"

"It's much more than that," Emilie said, smiling weakly and glancing at Louie. "I wasn't easy to convince. But it's more than revenge. I do it for my country, to preserve the life I live, the store I'm so fortunate to have."

"I approached Emilie, but she refused to believe me," Louie explained. "It was only after I shared some of her husband's secrets, Sophie Silvain among them, with other convincing evidence, that she decided to help me."

"I was shocked at first, but determined to do what I could," Emilie said. "I started eavesdropping on my husband and photographing documents he had hidden in his study."

"Documents he sold to Barbier, who then sold them to the Germans," Louie added.

Camille sat back, glanced at Lucien, and turned to Louie. "What now?"

"We're creating a network to resist the Germans," Louie said. "Spying, interfering, sabotage. Emilie plays a key role. Her store offers a good opportunity, especially with so many German customers."

"I've already befriended Ziegler," Emilie said. "As revolting as it was. But it's only the beginning."

"What do you want from us?" Camille asked.

"The diamonds," Louie replied. "As soon as possible. London needs them."

"Except I don't have them," Camille said. "But I can get them. They're in a safe location."

"I have a townhouse not far from Emilie's store," Louie said. "You can bring the diamonds there."

Camille glanced at Lucien. "We'll come to your townhouse, but not with the diamonds. First you have to prove that you are who you say you are. Provide information on me and my associate—Lucien Bouchard from Tournai. If you can manage that, and the information is correct, we'll give you the diamonds."

"Not what I had planned," Louie muttered.

"And if Jacques is the traitor you claim, I need to do something about it," Camille said. "I'll have to turn him in to intelligence authorities."

Emilie cringed. "I don't want him harmed. I did love him once."

"I thought of a better solution," Louie said. "We could give him fake diamonds. He can then flee with his lover, as he's already planned. Emilie found their forged identity papers."

Camille stood, signaling an end to the meeting. "We'll be at Emilie's store the day after tomorrow at 10 a.m. We'll then go directly to your townhouse. Have the fake diamonds ready."

Emilie looked at Louie and shrugged as Camille and Lucien walked away.

CHAPTER 107

The Gestapo had commandeered several buildings on Avenue Foch to establish their headquarters. The complex included a prison in which to hold and interrogate those engaged in suspicious activities, a wireless unit that transmitted bogus communications to the Allies from captured radio sets, and a division in development to monitor the Jewish population. During his stay in Paris, which was expected to be brief, Major Ziegler had been loaned a staff car and provided with a small office in a building down the street from headquarters.

Ziegler and Bayer discussed their meeting with Emilie Dufort the following morning, assessing the actions needed to recover the diamonds.

"I should have had you come into her apartment with me," Ziegler said. "I value your opinion and would have been interested in what you thought."

"I suspect she's involved in something, sir," Bayer offered. "And it may or may not be diamonds. Her business card was found at the vault, with her husband's name scribbled on the back."

"Yet she's German," Ziegler muttered. "An interesting piece to the puzzle."

"It could be a trick. She may only pretend to be German."

"She might," Ziegler agreed. "But the apartment had German influences—porcelain, paintings, clocks."

Bayer shrugged. "She could have lived along the border, but on the French side. She may be an operative, just as we suspect her husband is."

Ziegler nodded. "I had similar thoughts. But I found the absence of family photographs odd."

"In another room, perhaps?"

"I don't think so," Ziegler replied. He paused, thinking. "It reminded me of someone who doesn't want their identity known."

"Then why all the German trinkets in the parlor?"

Ziegler shrugged. "Easily explained as purchases, perhaps. Far different only a few short years ago."

"Do you intend to visit her again?"

"Absolutely," Ziegler said. "Emilie Dufort has information we want. But for some reason, she hides it. She offers to assist but is guarded."

"She may want something in return."

"But what is it? She's stalling. I just don't know why."

"Ask her to prove her loyalty. Don't tie it to the diamonds. See what she delivers."

Ziegler nodded. "I like that idea, Sergeant. We can use it as a bridge to a more fruitful relationship. She might prove valuable."

"Are we staying in Paris, sir?"

Ziegler sighed. "I hope so. I've requested a change in assignment and transfer of our responsibilities. I've informed my superiors that we're close to the diamonds."

They were interrupted by a staff soldier knocking on the

jamb of the opened door. "Excuse me, sir," he said. "I have a telegram from Berlin for you."

"Thank you," Ziegler said, taking the message. He turned to Bayer as the soldier left. "Our new orders."

Ziegler read the telegram and frowned.

"What is it, sir?" Bayer asked.

"My transfer has been denied," Ziegler said, a cloud crossing his face. "You will remain in Paris, Sergeant. But I'm to return to Berlin."

Bayer's eyes widened. "Immediately, sir?"

Ziegler shook his head. "In three days. For questioning and reassignment."

Bayer looked confused. "I don't understand, sir. Why would I not come with you?"

"I understand perfectly, Sergeant," Ziegler said. "It's not a reassignment. It's a court martial."

CHAPTER 108

Camille and Lucien left the café and started back toward her apartment. "I don't want to take a direct route," she said. "We'll circle a few blocks to ensure we're not being followed."

"I don't know how you do it," Lucien said, shaking his head with admiration.

"Do what?"

"Deal with the intrigue, the constant danger."

She shrugged and wrapped her arm in his. "I was trained. Just as you were."

He laughed. "Much different. I learned about the body and how to heal it. You learned how to break into safes."

"Not much different. Both skills. But you spent more time with your education than I did."

"I'm always amazed by the twists and turns. Now Jacques has been exposed as a traitor—by his own wife—and we give the diamonds to a complete stranger."

"What did you think of Louie Bassett?"

Lucien shrugged. "He seemed convincing."

Camille stopped abruptly, pretending to look in a shop

window. She turned, ensuring they weren't followed. "What if I told you Louie Bassett was an imposter?"

Lucien looked at her strangely. "I wouldn't believe you. He had an answer for every question asked."

"Did you notice his accent?"

"Yes, but he explained it. He usually works in London, but he's with French intelligence."

"Except for one minor detail."

Lucien stopped and turned to face her. "What might that be?"

"His accent isn't English. It's American."

He stared at her, eyes wide. "American? How would you know that?"

"Further evidenced by his shirt."

Lucien hesitated, as if recalling Bassett's clothing. "A blue shirt, not distinctive in any way."

"Except for the stitching."

Lucien chuckled and shook his head. "I don't know what you're talking about."

"The buttons," she explained. "The stitches on the buttons are lateral."

"And what does that mean?"

"Look at your shirt."

Lucien looked at the button on his shirt. "It's cross-stitched."

"American's use a lateral stitch for buttons. Europeans use cross-stitch."

"Are you sure?" Lucien asked.

She nodded. "His shirt was bought in America. His accent is American."

"Louie Bassett is American," Lucien conceded. "Then something is drastically wrong."

They reached Camille's apartment, and she unlocked the door. They entered, starting up the steps. "Louie Bassett is a fraud," she continued. "We just don't know what he's doing."

"What do we do now?" he asked as they walked into the living room, and he sat on the couch.

Camille sat beside him. "I'm going to meet my handler, my mentor. We have very little contact, he hasn't been active in intelligence lately, but this is an emergency."

"Are you sure he can meet?"

"Yes, he'll be able to answer some of the questions we have. Not all, but most."

Lucien paused. "Will he know what happens when this is all over?"

Camille hesitated. "I'll ask him for my next assignment. I don't think we can stay in Paris."

"I'm a simple man," Lucien said. "My farm is all I need. Especially now."

Camille realized it was time to tell him. It wasn't fair to let him have false hopes. "I ruined your chances of being a simple farmer the day I walked into your life. I'm so sorry."

He sighed, nodded slightly, understanding his life had changed. Whether he wanted it to or not. "What are our choices?"

She thought for a moment. "We have several. We can take the diamonds to London. Or we can stay in Paris and fight the Germans. Or we can turn the diamonds over and leave for Switzerland."

"Switzerland is nice," he said.

"It is," she agreed. "Beautiful lakes and mountains. What do you want to do?"

"I don't feel like I can run away," he said. "I did that for eighteen months, hiding in a bottle. You taught me to believe in myself and how to fight. And this fight has just begun."

"Two choices then," she said.

"We take the diamonds to London, and you get reassigned, or we hand the diamonds off and stay and fight."

She nodded. "But if we stay and fight, we have to somehow eliminate the threats posed by Emilie, Bassett, and Ziegler."

"We could turn Emilie and Bassett in to the Gestapo," he suggested.

Camille sighed. "I hesitate to do that. No one deserves the Gestapo. But I'll do as I'm told."

"What about Ziegler? And this man Barbier, who seems to be so powerful."

"If we take the diamonds to London, we need those answers first. We have to wrap up all those loose ends before we go."

"But how?" he asked.

Camille was quiet for a moment, assessing her plan. "I think I know how to trick them all. I just need to work out a few details." She turned, smiling, and kissed him lightly on the lips. "And I think I can give you what you want, too."

CHAPTER 109

Emilie turned when the door to All Things Napoleon opened. She wasn't surprised to see Jacques enter. She glanced through the store, ensuring no customers were nearby, as he approached the counter.

"The Gestapo are looking for you," she warned him.

"I know," he said. He furtively looked out the display window to the boulevard beyond. "I saw them at the apartment."

"Major Ziegler," she said, glaring at him. She couldn't help feeling angry and betrayed. But she wasn't sure why. Was it because he had betrayed her before she could betray him?

"Is he the one that called from Tournai?"

She nodded. "He came all the way to Paris to find you. He wants to talk to you badly."

He sighed, eyeing a black sedan as it passed on the street.

"He came here first," she continued. "I told him you would be home for dinner. But when you never arrived, I was forced to answer his questions for an hour while he waited for you."

"I can't risk talking to him," Jacques said. "Surely you understand that."

"He'll find you," she said, expressing no emotion. "Maybe not today or tomorrow. But soon. I hope you realize that."

Jacques sighed, glancing around the store. "I'll avoid him."

"Is that why you haven't come home?" she asked, her gaze fixed on his. "Or do you have a different reason?"

"Do you know what the Gestapo does to people?" he asked, not replying. "They'll do anything to find out what I know. And they won't stop until they get it."

Emilie was quiet. Jacques didn't suspect she was about to trap him, with Louie Bassett's help. But she wouldn't turn him into the Gestapo. She couldn't do that. She did love him once, regardless of her role in Paris. French intelligence would deal with him if Camille decided to report him. Or he could flee after he got the fake diamonds.

"How much did Ziegler know?" he asked anxiously.

Emilie shrugged. "He didn't share anything." She paused, about to lay the trap. "A blonde woman came to the house, too."

Jacques's eyes widened. "When did she come?"

"Just before the Gestapo did."

"The Gestapo didn't get her, did they?"

She looked at him strangely, pretending she didn't know why he was so interested. "Why would they care about a woman whose name I don't even know?"

He looked at her, face firm. "What did she say?" he asked, leaning across the counter. "It's important."

Emilie backed away. "You're acting like a crazy man."

He glared at her, mouthing his reply in measured monosyllables. "What did she say?"

"You're frightening me," she said, folding her arms across her chest.

"Emilie, please. This is very important."

She eyed him for a moment and then continued. "She asked when you would be home. I told her I didn't know when, or if, you were coming back."

"What did she say when you told her that?"

"She said to tell you she has a delivery for you."

His eyes widened. "When is she bringing it?"

Emilie shrugged. "She didn't say."

"Can you contact her? Ask her to bring it here, to the store?"

Emilie shook her head, enjoying how frantic he had become. "I have no way to contact her. And I wouldn't risk my store. It's all I have," she said, referring as much to their relationship as her business. "Especially now."

He didn't get the double meaning. "Is she coming back to the apartment?"

"She's contacting me tomorrow for instructions," she replied, not offering specifics.

Jacques sighed, brushing his hand through his hair. He grabbed a piece of paper on the counter and scribbled down an address, the apartment of Sophie Silvain. "Ask her to come to this address tomorrow at 8 p.m. with the delivery. Knock four times. And don't tell anyone else."

Emilie frowned and put the paper in her skirt pocket.

"Promise me," he demanded.

"Promise you what?" she asked, indignant.

"You won't tell anyone else."

"I won't," she said. "Do you think I'll tell the Gestapo? Don't be ridiculous."

He eyed her intently for a moment and seemed to relax. "Thank you," he said. "My life depends on it."

Emilie waited, wondering if he had more to say. When it didn't seem that he did, she asked the obvious question. "Are you coming to get your things?"

His gaze met hers, a hint of understanding, as if he realized she knew more than he thought she did. "What about the Gestapo?"

"They're not watching the apartment, at least not yet. But

they will be back. They told me they would. They're watching your office, too. I would suggest you avoid it."

"Can you bring some of my clothes here?"

"No, I can't. Go in the back door, through the alley. No one will see you. Get what you want—everything. And do it by tomorrow night, before your meeting with the blonde woman."

Jacques nodded. He seemed relieved, as if one of his problems had been solved. He turned and started for the door.

"Jacques," Emilie said sternly.

He looked at her, eyebrows arched.

"I never want to see you again."

CHAPTER 110

Major Ziegler and Sergeant Bayer walked into All Things Napoleon several hours after Jacques Dufort had left. Ziegler was desperate. He had to provide something to his superiors, preferably the diamonds, to avoid a forced return to Berlin. If he didn't, his career in the military would be over. Or it might be much worse.

"I will do most of the talking, Sergeant," he whispered to Bayer as they waited at the counter. "I need to take a different approach."

"Would you prefer to speak to her alone, sir?" Bayer asked. "I can wait in the car."

"No, I'll motion for you to intervene. I want Mme. Dufort to be frightened by us, anxious and uncertain."

"I'll assist in any way I can, sir."

"I know she's hiding something. We must get her to reveal it."

Emilie Dufort was in the toy soldier section when they entered. She glanced at her customers and hurried across the store.

"Good morning, Mme. Dufort," Ziegler said in German.

Emilie glanced at those wandering the aisles. "Please speak softly."

Ziegler glanced at her customers, none nearby. "I must be more considerate. Especially if we're going to work together."

Emilie nodded and smiled weakly.

"Has your husband been home?" Ziegler asked.

Emilie shook her head. "No, he hasn't. Not for several days now."

Ziegler cocked his head. "Is that unusual?"

She sighed, and leaned forward, as if sharing a secret. "I don't think he's coming home. Another woman, I suspect."

"I'm so sorry," Ziegler said. "I can't imagine why anyone would leave a woman as wonderful as you."

She smiled. "Thank you, Major. I appreciate that."

Ziegler eyed her curiously. Her sadness seemed genuine. Her explanation did not. It was time to change tactics. "Mme. Dufort, I'll be blunt. I suspect you have information that I need. Yet you're not willing to share it."

Her eyes widened. "I assure you, Major, that I am willing to cooperate."

Ziegler glanced subtly at Bayer.

"Do you know where your husband is?" Bayer asked.

Emilie shook her head. "No, I'm sorry."

Bayer continued. "We suspect he's involved with the theft of diamonds from Antwerp. Do you know anything about it?"

Emilie slowly shook her head. "No, I'm sorry."

Ziegler watched her closely. He knew when someone wasn't telling the truth. He sighed deeply. "Mme. Dufort, my patience is exhausted."

She looked confused. "I don't understand, sir."

"If you are going to assist, I need information now," Ziegler demanded. "If I don't get it, I can only assume you aid the enemy."

All That Glitters

"Major!" she exclaimed. "I assure you nothing could be further from the truth."

Ziegler glared at her, playing the role he detested but his position demanded. He reached across the counter and grabbed her wrist roughly. "If your husband doesn't have anything to do with the diamonds, tell me who does."

Emilie paled. "You're hurting me."

"It'll get much worse, Mme. Dufort, I promise you."

"Please, stop," she urged, glancing at her customers. "I'm German, just like you. I can help you."

"You had better prove it, Mme. Dufort," Ziegler insisted. "Because if you think having your wrist grabbed is painful, you have much to learn. And I can be a harsh teacher."

"No, please," she begged. "I will cooperate. What do you want?"

"Who has the diamonds," Ziegler demanded. "Give me a name."

Her gaze frantically wandered the store, as if searching for an answer she couldn't find. "Guy Barbier," she blurted. "The diamonds are in his warehouse."

CHAPTER 111

"I won't be long," Camille said to Lucien.

"Please be careful," he said with knitted eyebrows.

She smiled and kissed him lightly on the lips. "I will," she promised.

Camille left the apartment, destined for a clandestine meeting with her mysterious mentor, a man who many thought no longer walked in the world of espionage. He did—but only when absolutely needed. A source sought only in extreme emergencies, Camille had little choice but to contact him. She had to get the diamonds to the allies as quickly as possible. And she couldn't risk giving them to the wrong party.

She walked through the grounds of the Sorbonne. It was the college she had attended, its buildings, classrooms, and walkways so familiar. Students hurried past her, carrying textbooks as they went to lectures. Professors wandered by, always distracted, as if their next lesson was still being created. German soldiers passed, looking for something wrong, but not knowing what it was until they found it.

On a secluded path that led to a statue of General Joseph Joffre, the French commander during the First World War, two benches sat among shrubbery, rarely used and empty. Camille glanced at her watch, looked through trees and shrubs to search for anyone who might be nearby, and sat on the farthest bench.

He arrived a few minutes later. An older man who leaned on a cane, his white hair was matched by an immaculate goatee. His brown trousers were wrinkled, his jacket showing signs of wear. Nicolas Chastain, Camille's mentor, was a master spy, an invisible man who lived in darkness and rarely stepped into the light.

"Camille," he said, smiling fondly as he sat beside her. "My brightest pupil and most cunning operative."

"M. Chastain, it's so good to see you," she said. "You look well."

He nodded, smiling faintly. "Wrapped in a riddle you can't quite solve?"

She laughed lightly. "This play has a large cast of characters. Some are real, some are not. But I can't determine friend from foe. And I don't have the luxury of time."

"Are you hoping I may know the difference?"

She looked down the lane, ensuring they were alone. "Yes, I am. I have to make delivery to the right person."

"I see," he said, and sighed. "I was consulted on Antwerp. Of course, I recommended you. But you probably know that."

She smiled. "I suspected so."

He lightly grasped her hand. "Provide a name, and I'll see if I can help."

"Jacques Dufort."

"A good man. I don't know him personally, but I know he can be trusted."

Camille had suspected as much. Her intuition was good. "His lover."

He looked at her, head cocked.

"Sophie Silvain," she said.

He shrugged. "An expert on logistics and Jacque's colleague.

But I don't know if they're lovers." He chuckled and leaned toward her. "Not that I would know."

"How about Louie Bassett?"

Chastain frowned. "An American intelligence asset serving as liaison to the French. Much of his career has been spent in Paris."

Camille still had doubts. "What's your assessment?"

"He's more con man than intelligence operative. I suspect his taste for the finer things in life has made him seek income elsewhere. He was in Germany, the last I heard. Supposedly undercover on a special assignment."

"He's in Paris now, working with Emilie Dufort."

"Ah, that explains it. Issues to be resolved."

Camille digested what he had said. "Do you know much about Emilie?"

Chastain shook his head. "No, not really. Just what I've recently heard—whispers in the wind."

Camille smiled. "She's linked to the Gestapo, a major who followed me from Tournai."

He pursed his lips. "I'm not aware of any Gestapo connection. But she'll soon be removed from the equation. At least, long enough for you to finish what you started."

Camille considered the rest of the cast. "How about Guy Barbier?"

"Higher in the chain than Dufort. He can be trusted."

Camille paused, almost all of her questions answered. "The delivery will be made tomorrow."

"You should leave Paris afterwards," he said. "It's best."

She nodded. "I assumed I would."

"Any requests?"

Camille had discussed the future with Lucien. She wanted to blend both their worlds. "I assume networks will be formed, with safe houses to the coast, Spain, and Switzerland."

"I'm not directly involved, but your assumption is correct. Sophie Silvain has been assisting."

"The man who helped me in Belgium is with me now. He will stay with me."

"Camille," Chastain said, his eyes alive. "I didn't think you had time for love."

She smiled shyly. "I thought everyone did."

He laughed. "Yes, they do. I'm happy for you. Tell me about him."

"He's a doctor I met while stationed in Tournai." She lifted her blouse, exposing her scar. "He saved my life."

His eyes widened. "A good doctor is hard to find. And so is a good man. Keep him close."

Camille hesitated, wondering how to phrase what she wanted to say. "He prefers to be a farmer, maybe still help those who need medical care. But I think I might like that, too. Maybe a farm in a rural village, close to Switzerland but part of the network."

Chastain was quiet for a moment. He turned, his gaze meeting Camille's. "Consider it done."

CHAPTER 112

Jacques knew by Emilie's reaction that he was in serious jeopardy. And so was everyone around him. He had been suspicious for the last week or two, finding her behavior unusual. He had caught her eavesdropping, possibly rifling through secret papers, and making a call to Germany, even though she claimed she tried to contact her family and the call hadn't gone through. But her German had been good—much better than it ever had been before. She had explanations for everything, each of which served to ease his suspicions. But the aggregate offered a powerful portrait of betrayal.

As soon as he left All Things Napoleon, he hurried to Guy Barbier's warehouse, using the secret knock as a passcode.

A moment later, the door opened a crack and Guy Barbier peeked out. "Jacques, I didn't expect to see you, Come on in."

"We're in trouble, Guy," Jacques said. He glanced through the warehouse as they went to the office. More crates had been removed since his last visit, but most still remained.

"What's wrong?" Barbier asked, alarmed.

"I think Emilie turned."

Barbier's eyes widened. "What happened?"

"She's been acting strangely the last few weeks."

Barbier frowned. "Like eavesdropping on our conversation, even though she claimed she wasn't."

Jacques nodded. "But there's more."

Barbier sighed, rolling his eyes. "I never trusted her. Something about her. I just don't know what it is."

Jacques knew they had to hurry. "It's much worse. The Gestapo who called from Tournai came to Paris—Major Ziegler. Yesterday he went to the store and my office. Last night he was at my apartment."

Barbier gasped. "Were you there?"

Jacques shook his head. "No, I was walking down the street when I saw their car. I've been hiding at Sophie's ever since. But I don't know what Emilie told them."

Barbier looked out at the warehouse, half-filled with material to support French resistance to the German occupation. "We have to move everything."

"You have to get out, too," Jacques said. "I'm sorry. But you're really at risk. You need someplace to hide."

Barbier picked up the phone, dialing quickly. "We have an emergency," he said. "Clear the warehouse."

"How long will it take?" Jacques asked after Barbier hung up.

He shrugged. "Three hours, maybe less. We have a few trucks, but not much petrol. And a couple wagons. But we're prepared. We've been moving material out for a week now."

"We don't have much time," Jacques said. "This is the first place the Gestapo will raid."

Barbier rose and started toward the warehouse. "Anything else?"

"Yes, I actually have some great news," Jacques said as he followed him. "Camille is in Paris with the diamonds. She's bringing them to Sophie's apartment tomorrow night."

Barbier sighed with relief. "Finally, a victory. She made it."

"We don't have the diamonds yet," Jacques said. "But we're close."

Barbier pursed his lips. "Is there any risk using Sophie's apartment?"

"Yes, of course," Jacques said. "I just have to manage it, make sure we can escape if needed."

Barbier nodded, already plotting his next move. "As soon as you get the diamonds, you and Sophie take the escape route to Spain. From there, we'll get you to London."

"What do we do after that?"

"We'll have something for you, don't worry," Barbier said. "Probably south, near the Spanish border."

"That would be good for me," he said. "And Sophie, too. It's close to our families."

Someone knocked on the entrance door, the rhythmic code to announce it was safe.

Barbier went to answer it. "Come on, we have to get out of here. They're ready to clear the warehouse."

Jacques followed him to the entrance. "What do we do about Emilie?"

Barbier turned, face firm. "Tell Sophie to take care of her."

CHAPTER 113

Early the next morning, a German troop truck drove down a nondescript lane in the Left Bank of Paris followed by Major Ziegler's staff car. They turned into an alley, a rare coin dealer, open by appointment only, occupied the front of the corner building, an unnamed warehouse behind it. The troop truck parked in front of a garage door, blocking the exit, and a dozen men leaped from the back of the vehicle. Two soldiers ran to the rear of the building, which faced another street, standing guard over a second metal door that seemed little used.

Bayer parked the staff car twenty meters farther down the lane and opened the rear door for Ziegler.

"What a pleasant surprise we have for M. Barbier," Ziegler said, gloating as they walked toward the personnel door.

The soldiers spread out in front of the garage door, a mesh gate in front of it. Two went to the corner to ensure no one left through the coin dealer. They waited for Ziegler, poised and ready.

Ziegler went up to the personnel door and rapped loudly. "Open up," he called. "Gestapo."

Bayer leaned close, his ear to the door. "I don't hear anything inside."

"Maybe no one is here," Ziegler muttered. He looked at the narrow windows along the roofline, pigeons perched on the sills.

Bayer banged on the door, louder than Ziegler had. When a minute passed, and no one answered, he tried the doorknob. "It's locked."

"Knock one more time," Ziegler said.

Bayer hammered on the door repeatedly. "Open up," he hollered. "It's the Gestapo."

They waited a minute more. When no one answered. Ziegler motioned to a sergeant overseeing the soldiers who came in the troop truck. "Break it down."

The sergeant pointed at two of his men and they moved forward, each barreling into the door with their shoulders. When it didn't budge, they retrieved an iron bar from the rear of the truck, prying it between the jamb and the hinges.

"It's well secured, sir," Bayer said as they observed the men struggling.

"Try the garage door," Ziegler suggested.

Two additional soldiers moved forward. They broke the lock for the mesh gate with the butt of their rifles and swung each half open. Bending to grab the bottom lip of the roll-up door, they tried to force it up. The door creaked but didn't budge.

Ziegler frowned. He glanced up and down the deserted alley. He looked at the windows of neighboring buildings. Shadows peeked from parted curtains, furtively watching their first Gestapo raid. It wouldn't be their last.

The soldiers at the personnel door gradually pried the door from its hinges, the metal bending and groaning. A few moments later they shoved it inward, the steel stressing under the onslaught with a sickening screech. Soldiers barged in, machine guns ready. They fanned in different directions, searching the building.

Ziegler waited a moment and motioned to Bayer. "Let's go in."

They entered through the broken door. It was a spacious warehouse, empty. A smooth concrete floor was marked with tire tracks, some dirt and debris left behind. Tall steel pillars spaced evenly about the building propped up the roof. A tiny office sat to the right, nothing inside it except bare steel shelves attached to the wall.

"Nothing here, sir," Bayer said as they eyed the empty warehouse.

Ziegler's face was taut, his patience exhausted. He had hoped for a major arrest, or a warehouse full of weapons, or black-market merchandise. He had to convince those in Berlin he was needed in Paris, that he was making progress, close to finding the diamonds, and that his recall was premature. He was desperate to achieve even the slightest hint of success. But he had failed once again.

Bayer eyed his superior. "Maybe the culprits were warned we were coming. Or Mme. Dufort gave us bad information."

Ziegler walked into the warehouse, his boots echoing off the concrete floor. He stopped at a steel I-beam, something in French scribbled on it in chalk. "What does this say?" he asked.

Bayer read the writing and frowned. "It says: you're too late."

"They were warned," Ziegler growled.

"Do you think it was Mme. Dufort?"

Ziegler stared at the chalk graffiti, his face firm. "I don't know," he said. "But I do suspect she isn't who she claims."

Bayer shrugged. "She seemed sincere. Although she offered Barbier and the warehouse while under duress, frightened of what might happen if she didn't cooperate."

Ziegler sighed, nodding. "At least she gave us something. But I want more. Much more."

"Barbier must have emptied the warehouse and fled during the night, just ahead of our arrival."

Ziegler was quiet, faced with another failure. "Order the men to question nearby residents. See if they know anything about Barbier or what the warehouse held."

"Yes, sir," Bayer said, and turned to go.

"We should question Mme. Dufort again, too," Ziegler said. "Maybe an unannounced visit to her apartment. I can no longer afford to be nice to her. We're running out of time."

"Do you think we should arrest her, sir."

Ziegler hesitated. "Not yet. But soon."

CHAPTER 114

Lucien and Camille arrived at All Things Napoleon at 10 a.m. the following morning, per the arrangements they had made with Emilie Dufort and Louie Bassett. When they entered the store, Emilie was near the last row of bookshelves, talking to an older man who seemed to be an employee. When she saw them enter, she spoke to the man a moment more, and then came up to greet them.

"I've been expecting you," she said.

"Good morning," Lucien said, nodding politely.

Camille eyed her cautiously, armed with additional information from Nicolas Chastain. She had to convince Emilie and Louie Bassett that all was going according to plan. And as she stalled for time, she could deliver the real diamonds to Jacques Dufort and make her escape before they realized they had been tricked.

"Shall we go?" Emilie asked.

"Yes, of course," Camille replied, leading Lucien out the door and onto the pavement.

They walked four or five blocks and approached a townhouse near the cemetery. While Lucien and Emilie made idle conversation, Camille studied the landscape, ensured they weren't followed, and assessed any Germans encountered. As they reached their destination, Emilie knocked on the front door.

It was opened quickly. "Come in," Louie said, quickly glancing up and down the street.

Camille stepped into the foyer, followed by Lucien. She examined the house as they entered: hallways, exits, windows, potential weapons she could use—suspicious of a trap. She listened intently to ensure they were alone and heard no footsteps, creaking floorboards, or any signs that anyone else was in the townhouse. Knowing Bassett was a con man, and Emilie most likely an unwitting accomplice, she knew they would do nothing rash. They couldn't jeopardize receipt of the diamonds.

Louie led them into the parlor. Camille and Lucien sat on a sofa, Emilie and Louie on chairs across from them. It was an elegant room, fitting the tastes Bassett apparently enjoyed, and someone who sold secrets could afford.

"You have a beautiful home," Lucien said, eyeing plaster crown molding adorned with tiny cherubs.

"Thank you, I enjoy it," Louie said. He handed a satchel to Camille. "The fake diamonds for Jacques."

Camille took the satchel without examining its contents and set it beside her foot. "When do I deliver them?"

Emilie gave her a piece of paper with Sophie Silvain's address. "Tonight at eight p.m. He knows you're coming."

"And what is Jacques' fate?" Camille asked. "Do we let him escape with the fake diamonds or do we notify French intelligence?"

Louie turned to Emilie. "I can arrange his capture if you so desire."

Emilie hesitated, but then shook her head. "No, I can't do that. Let him go."

"As you wish," Camille said. She fixed her gaze on Louie Bassett. "Now, if you give me the information I requested, and can prove you're who you say you are, we'll bring the real diamonds tomorrow morning."

"First, tell me where the diamonds are hidden," Louie said. "Just so I know they're safe."

Camille was quiet for a moment, pretending to consider his request. "They're in a locker at the railway station," she lied, taking a key from her pocket, holding it up, and returning it.

"Isn't that risky?" Emilie asked, glancing at Louie.

Camille shook her head. "They're sewn into the lining of satchels similar to this one," she said, pointing at the bag containing the fake diamonds. "I'll get them tomorrow morning and bring them to you."

Louie seemed satisfied. "Then I'll proceed," he said. "I think you'll find the information I have quite interesting."

Camille smiled faintly. "I am curious."

"Your full name is Camille Bonnet, age twenty-five," Louie began. "You were recruited by Nicolas Chastain into French intelligence five years ago while attending the Sorbonne, here in Paris. You come from a wealthy family who live in Geneva, Switzerland."

Camille was surprised by what he had obtained. He did have connections with French intelligence, as Chastain had suggested. "All correct."

"You were assigned to Strasbourg, initially," Louie continued.

"Very close to where I was raised," Emilie added. "And where I occasionally travel to visit family. Perhaps our paths have crossed more than once."

"As war brewed, you were reassigned to Tournai," Louie said. "You remained there for two years, returning to Paris about six months ago."

Camille pretended she wasn't impressed. "Thank you for providing those details," she said. "But it's all available in my government personnel file."

"I agree," Louie said. "Although very few people have access to it."

Camille hesitated. "I suspect it could be purchased for the right price."

Louie shrugged. "Perhaps it could. But to convince you that I do have contacts, I'll reveal what I've learned about Lucien."

Camille hesitated, not sure if he wanted his past revealed, painful memories best left dormant.

Lucien saw her watching him and nodded subtly. "You can continue," he said to Louie.

"I also have contacts with Belgian authorities," Louie informed them. "Your full name is Dr. Lucien Rene Bouchard, age twenty-nine, born in the Belgian Congo to a government official and a pharmacist—your family still lives there. After attending the University of Brussels, you moved to Tournai to practice medicine. You were married to Marie Dupree and had a daughter named, Brigette, both of whom passed after an automobile accident eighteen months ago."

Lucien nodded, his eyes misty. "God needed two more angels," he said. "So, he took those I loved the most."

CHAPTER 115

"We leave for Spain tonight," Sophie said as Jacques brought two suitcases and a satchel into her apartment. "Right after we get the diamonds."

"I picked up some of my belongings while Emilie was at the store," Jacques said.

"What about documents?"

"I destroyed most of them, but some are hidden in the suitcase lining."

Sophie pointed to a suitcase and several satchels near the top of the stairs. "I'm ready, too. We're leaving by wagon, a farmer who is making a nearby delivery."

Jacques eyed her anxiously. "A wagon will take forever."

"We're only using it to get out of the city," she said. "Not the best transportation, but it won't arouse suspicion. We'll look like refugees."

Jacques shrugged. "I suppose it is safe. With petrol so scarce, wagons are used for everything."

"The farmer should be here by seven. He'll park in the alley around the corner. We can load our belongings and come back to wait for Camille."

Jacques looked at his watch. "It won't be long now."

"All the arrangements are completed," Sophie said. "Including a guide to bring us over the Pyrenees into Spain."

"Barbier told me that, once we're in Spain, our contact will make arrangements for us to take the diamonds to London."

Sophie nodded. "I talked to Barbier an hour ago."

"Is he safe?" Jacques asked.

"Yes, he finished emptying the warehouse yesterday, soon after you left. The Gestapo raided it this morning."

Jacques shook his head. "Emilie," he uttered with disgust. "I knew she would turn on Barbier. She's a traitor."

"But we're next," Sophie warned. "We have to be careful. If the Gestapo comes, we can leave by the fire escape or from the bedroom window."

He looked at her strangely. "But we're on the second floor."

"Come see," she said.

He followed her into the bedroom. The curtains were pulled back from the window, the bottom sash open. The adjacent building was less than a meter away.

"The man who lived in the adjacent flat fled Paris," she said. "I broke into his apartment earlier."

Jacques stood in the center of the room and looked out the window. "I only see a brick wall."

"Come closer."

He went up to the window and looked out. Across the slender alley, the window to the neighboring apartment was also open. The windows were offset, but not by much.

"We can climb into the other apartment and escape," she said.

He chuckled, shaking his head. "You never cease to amaze me."

She smiled. "Two escape paths, should we have to flee before we get the diamonds."

They went back into the parlor and sat on the sofa. "It won't be long now," Jacques said. "I just worry about Emilie. I don't know what else she may have done."

Sophie glanced at a clock on the wall. "I turned Emilie in to the Gestapo," she said softly. "They should raid her apartment any minute now."

Jacques' eyes widened. "They'll find the German documents I planted."

Sophie nodded. "She'll claim she was framed, but the Gestapo won't believe her. Not at first. But they'll let her go. She doesn't know anything."

"It'll still take a few days," Jacques said. "Enough time for us to escape. Do your contacts know we're coming?"

"Yes, everything is ready. We just need the diamonds."

CHAPTER 116

Major Ziegler frowned. He sat behind the desk in a cramped office, Sergeant Bayer in the chair across from him. "I have to prepare for departure. It seems my military career is coming to a close."

"Maybe not, sir," Bayer said. "You're making assumptions. Your next assignment may have nothing to do with not recovering the diamonds."

Ziegler sighed. "Perhaps not, but we'll soon see."

It was quiet for a moment, an awkward silence drenching the room. "Can I get you anything, sir?"

"No, thank you, Sergeant," Ziegler replied. "You've been a loyal driver and faithful companion for the last eighteen months, even a good friend and confidant. I've written a glowing recommendation for your file."

"Thank you, Major," Bayer said. "I'm very moved. I've always been honored to serve as your aide."

They were interrupted by a tap on the door jamb. A sergeant stood in the entrance. "An anonymous complaint, Major, referred to you."

Ziegler gave Bayer a curious glance and took the paper. He scanned the words, eyes wide, and read them aloud: "Mme.

All That Glitters

Emilie Dufort is a traitor to the Reich, stealing German secrets and selling them to the French."

Bayer's eyes widened. "You were right, sir. She was hiding something."

Ziegler scanned the message again. "If this is true. It could be a trick."

"After the failed raid on the warehouse, I'm inclined to believe it."

Ziegler rose. "Then I suppose it's time to arrest the beautiful Mme. Dufort. Find a few soldiers to assist us, Sergeant."

Minutes later, Ziegler sat in the back of his staff car on his way to Emilie Dufort's apartment. A motorcycle with a sidecar followed, two soldiers loaned to assist in the arrest.

"We'll search the apartment when we arrive," Ziegler said.

"I'm sure Mme. Dufort will protest vigorously," Bayer replied.

"As I would expect."

Ten minutes later, Bayer parked the car in front of Emilie's apartment and opened Ziegler's door. The major stepped out and they walked to the flat, the two soldiers behind them. Bayer knocked loudly.

A moment later, the door opened, and Emilie Dufort appeared. She looked at them curiously. "Hello, Major," she said. "My husband is not here."

"Step aside, Mme. Dufort," Ziegler said grandly. "I'm actually here to question you."

"Me?" she exclaimed as the Germans barged into her apartment. "What did I do?"

"We'll soon see," Ziegler said. He turned to the two soldiers. "Search the study."

"Major, what's the meaning of this!" Emilie exclaimed.

The two soldiers went into the study. One moved to the desk, rifling through drawers.

"My husband took all of his papers," Emilie said, her voice quivering. "Nothing is left. I checked."

After finding the desk empty, the soldiers started removing books from the shelves. They leafed through pages, looking for anything hidden.

"Please, be careful," Emilie pleaded. "Some of the volumes are very valuable."

"Sergeant, let's check the parlor," Ziegler directed.

Emilie followed them. "Major, there's nothing here, I assure you. Why are you doing this?"

Ziegler didn't reply. His attention was focused on the cuckoo clock. He took it from the wall and opened the back door. "What have we here?" he asked, removing some papers.

"I don't know what they are, Major," Emilie said. "I didn't put them there."

"Where did you get these?" Ziegler demanded. "German military documents, stamped top secret."

Emilie's fear turned to anger as she realized what had happened. "They are not mine, Major, I assure you. My husband did this to frame me. I assume you received an anonymous call?"

"Here's more," Bayer said, removing folded papers from a porcelain wagon. "German troop movements."

Ziegler turned to Emilie and looked at her sternly. "You're under arrest, Mme. Dufort."

"But my husband did this!" she exclaimed. "I'm innocent."

"We'll discuss it at Gestapo headquarters," Ziegler said.

Emilie eyed the clock. "Wait! The diamonds. I know where they are."

"The diamonds?" Ziegler asked. "You've claimed for days to know nothing about them."

"My husband will get the diamonds at 8 Rue Serpente at 8 p.m.," Emilie declared. "I swear to you."

Ziegler paused, eyeing her coldly. He suspected she lied to

save herself. But she could be telling the truth. He might find her husband, and the diamonds, at the specified address. Or he could find nothing—like Barbier's warehouse.

"I swear, Major," Emilie continued. "A blonde woman named Camille has the diamonds. She stole them in Antwerp."

Ziegler's eyes widened. Emilie knew details no one else would. Unless she knew a little and fabricated the rest. "Maybe you are telling the truth," he said, not quite sure.

"More papers," Bayer announced. "Taped behind a painting."

"We'll see if your husband has the diamonds at this address," Ziegler said. "For your sake, Mme. Dufort, you had better hope he does."

"The diamonds are there, Major, I promise you," Emilie said, relieved. "Thank you, I knew you would believe me."

"But I don't believe you, Mme. Dufort," Ziegler said smugly. "At least not yet. You're still under arrest."

Emilie's eyes flashed with anger. "You'll regret this, Major. My brother reports directly to the Führer. When he finds out what you did, he will destroy you."

"Yes, I'm sure he will," Ziegler scoffed, believing little of what she said.

"He'll have you court-martialed and shot."

CHAPTER 117

Camille arrived at 8 Rue Serpente with the duffle bags carrying the diamonds slung over her shoulder. She glanced down the street, where Lucien waited beside a plane tree. He held his medical bag, posing as a doctor to avoid suspicion, even though there was little activity on the slender side street. When satisfied no one was watching, she knocked on the door.

A moment later, a tall woman with brown hair opened the door. She stepped from the apartment and glanced up and down the street. "Come in, Camille," she said. "I'm Sophie. Jacques is upstairs."

Camille followed her up the stairs. A window was at the top of the landing, the adjacent building a meter away. The stairs opened onto a parlor, a kitchen beyond it. A back door led to a second exit or fire escape. A bedroom was to the right, a bath across from the kitchen.

Jacques Dufort waited in the parlor. He stood as she came in. "Camille, it's so good to see you. You made it."

Camille smiled weakly. "Yes, finally. Not quite as planned, I know."

"What happened in Antwerp?" Sophie asked.

"The Germans broke into the bank just as we opened the last deposit box. I used the building layout Jacques gave me to escape."

"Actually, Sophie got the layout," Jacques said.

"From one of the employees," Sophie explained. "She's my Antwerp contact."

"It was perfect," Camille complimented her. "The operation was flawless until the Germans came."

"What happened to Roger—Sophie's contact said he was killed," Jacques said.

"Yes, he was," Camille said. "We were leaving through a second-floor office, the secondary escape route Sophie provided, and had blocked the door closed. The Germans sprayed machine-gun fire into the room."

"Roger was shot to death?" Jacques asked.

Camille nodded. "I grabbed the bag, escaped, and went to the port, to the address Roger had given me. The Germans were already there."

Jacques glanced at Sophie. "Some of your radio communications were confusing."

"The Gestapo were in Tournai. They almost caught me several times. I suspected they were listening to my transmissions. I had to fool them."

Jacques sighed. "At least the diamonds are safe."

Camille handed the two bags to Jacque. "The diamonds are sewn in the linings."

"Brilliant," Sophie said. "I was wondering how you traveled with them."

"My contact in Tournai is a seamstress," Camille said. "She did all the sewing."

Jacques eyed the bags skeptically. "Should we remove them? The duffel bags are German military."

"Not now," Sophie said. "We have to get out of Paris as soon as we can."

"Will you take them to London?" Camille asked.

Jacques hesitated, glancing at Sophie. "Yes, a contingency plan."

"I have a route prepared, with contacts," Sophie said. "It wasn't our original intent, but the Germans arrived in Paris before you did."

Camille's face firmed. "No one could have predicted what happened."

"What will you do?" Jacques asked. "Stay in Paris?"

Camille shook her head. "No, I'm leaving tonight. But I'll still be part of the network."

"It's best," Sophie said, glancing at Jacques.

Jacques frowned. "Emilie betrayed us."

"I'm not surprised," Camille said, knowing it wasn't time to tell them what she knew. They had to hurry.

"We had best be going," Jacques said. "Our belongings are loaded in a wagon. We only waited for the diamonds."

They all rose, prepared to depart. "Good luck to you," Camille said.

Sophie smiled. "And you also."

"We'll meet again, I'm sure," Jacques added.

CHAPTER 118

Lucien gasped, eyes wide. A German staff car turned the corner, a motorcycle with sidecar followed. They raced down the tiny street, screeching to a halt in front of the apartment building. A soldier leaped off the motorcycle and darted down an alley, guarding the building's fire escape. The second climbed from the sidecar and hurried to the front door, joined by Ziegler and Bayer.

"Break the door down!" Ziegler commanded.

The soldier barreled into the door, splintering the jamb. Bayer and Ziegler rushed inside. The soldier remained at the entrance.

Lucien had to stop them, no matter what the danger. He owed it to Camille. She had saved him. He would save her. He ran to the building with his medical bag. As he approached the entrance, the German blocked his path.

"I'm a doctor," Lucien said in poor German, pointing to the bag. "It's an emergency."

The soldier hesitated, confused. He glanced up the steps, as if he wondered whether the raid and medical issue were related. When he saw Ziegler and Bayer cautiously advancing, he held his hand out to Lucien, ensuring he stayed where he was, and hurried up the stairs.

Lucien ignored him. He eased forward, slowly climbing one step at a time.

Ziegler and Bayer reached the top. They crouched, peeking into the apartment, weapons drawn. The soldier crept up behind them.

"Halt!" Ziegler shouted. A pistol shot followed. "No one move!"

Lucien thrust his hand in his bag. He grabbed a syringe and put it in his shirt pocket. He rummaged through the contents for a brown bottle and a cloth. He took them out, removed the cap, and soaked the cloth with liquid. He laid his bag on the steps and leaned against the wall, easing forward, a meter behind the last soldier.

"Stay where you are!" Ziegler ordered. A pistol fired. Another shot followed, but from a different weapon, the sound not the same.

Footsteps raced across floors. Another shot was fired. The bullet ricocheted around the room, finding the wall. Ziegler and Bayer dashed into the parlor.

Lucien crept up the stairs. The soldier in front of him peeked into the room, prepared to advance. Lucien rushed forward and grabbed him. He shoved the soaked cloth over the soldier's mouth and nose. In seconds, the man crumpled, sliding to the steps.

Ziegler and Bayer shouted commands. More shots were fired. Lucien peeked into the room. Ziegler and Bayer had ducked behind a couch, their backs to him. He could see the others in the kitchen, the table upended. They hid behind it, peeking out—Camille, a man, and another woman. They were trapped, a soldier at the rear exit, the Gestapo in the parlor.

Lucien eased forward, Bayer and Ziegler close. A floorboard creaked and Bayer turned. Lucien leaped toward him, forcing the cloth over his face. Bayer fought, pushing and punching. Each blow got weaker until he dropped to the floor.

Ziegler attacked Lucien, pushing him down, grabbing his hand. He wrestled with his pistol, trying to aim. "I'll enjoy killing you!" he sneered, his face contorted.

Lucien tried to break free, still holding the cloth. He struggled, but Ziegler was stronger—much stronger.

A shot rang from the kitchen, the bullet pinging past them. Ziegler ducked closer to Lucien, exposed to fire. He couldn't stay where he was. He turned, pointing his pistol, prepared to return fire. Another shot came from the kitchen, the bullet speeding in the opposite direction, toward the fire escape.

Lucien freed his hand. He grabbed the needle in his shirt pocket, fumbling with the syringe. Ziegler saw him and savagely swung an elbow. Lucien dropped the syringe and grabbed Ziegler's hand, fighting for the pistol.

Ziegler leaned forward, fighting. Lucien started to weaken. Ziegler slowly turned the pistol toward him. Another bullet came from the kitchen, whizzing past them, burrowing into the stairs.

Lucien released Ziegler's wrist and grabbed the syringe. He jammed it into Ziegler's neck and pushed the plunger. The contents flowed, a sedative once intended for Henry Green, the British soldier.

Ziegler screamed. He wrestled with Lucien as the sedative ran through his body. He pushed Lucien away. ripping the syringe from his neck. His eyes lit with rage. He pointed his pistol and fired.

Lucien flew back against the railing. His chest felt like it exploded, a piercing pain followed by numbness crawling through his body. He fought to breathe, tried to move but couldn't. He opened his mouth, gasping. The room was hazy, the lights quivering.

Another shot came from the kitchen. Ziegler's eyes

widened, blood spilling from his mouth. He fired again, an errant bullet hitting the wall, and dropped to the floor.

CHAPTER 119

Jacques peeked around the wall dividing the kitchen from the parlor, a pistol in his right hand. Camille and Sophie crouched low, behind the upturned table.

"No one's moving," Jacques said, lowering his pistol. "Not sure if they're dead or wounded."

The kitchen was sprayed with rapid shots from the fire escape. Four or five bullets whizzed past them, embedding in walls and cabinets.

Jacques ducked and dove to the ground. He emptied his pistol at the shattered window in the back door, shooting at shadows. Once his gun was empty, he started to reload.

Camille sprung from behind the table. She sprinted toward the door, flung it open and dove to the ground. When no one fired, she cautiously approached, stepping on to the fire escape.

"He's dead," she called a moment later. She came back into the kitchen.

Sophie and Jacques raced in the parlor, Camille just behind them.

"Lucien!" Camille exclaimed, sprinting to his side. "Are you all right?"

He lifted his head, face pale, eyelids fluttering. He fought to maintain consciousness, staring vacantly at three faces looking down.

Camille bent over him. She loosened his shirt and assessed the wound, blood dripping onto the floor below. She looked at Sophie. "He helped me escape from Tournai."

"Hurry," Lucien gasped. "You have to get out. There's a German on the fire escape."

"We got him," Jacques assured him. He leaned over Ziegler, putting his hand on his neck, feeling for a pulse. He stood a moment later. "He's dead."

Sophie checked Bayer and eyed the soldier lying by the stairs. "How long will these two stay unconscious?"

"Thirty minutes," Lucien muttered, grimacing.

Camille ran into the kitchen, grabbed some towels, and came back in the parlor to attend to Lucien. As she started to pack them around the wound in his chest, she found the empty whiskey flask in his pocket—his symbol of strength. The bullet had pierced the metal container and entered his chest.

"How is he?" Sophie asked, leaning over.

Camille slowly shook her head. "He needs a doctor badly."

"We have to get out of here first," Jacques said. "Quickly."

"Take Lucien to the German staff car," Sophie suggested. "We'll help carry him down. You can use their car to escape."

"We'll take the diamonds and leave as planned," Jacques said, starting to lift Lucien.

Camille helped Jacques prop up Lucien. ""We have to hurry. I'm sure the shots attracted more Germans. They'll be here any minute."

Sophie flung the duffle bags with the diamonds over her shoulders. She moved to Jacques's side, helping him and Camille as they eased Lucien down the stairs. His body was limp, he was barely conscious. They held him up, lifting him when needed. Taking one step at a time, moving as quickly as they could, it took only a few minutes to reach the pavement.

Glancing at a few pedestrians who pretended they saw nothing, they moved him to the staff car. Sophie opened the rear door. They helped him inside, struggling to get him into the seat.

Camille turned to face them. "Hurry, you have to go. I'll contact you in London through Chastain."

Jacques and Sophie raced around the corner. Their wagon was parked in a dark alley, their belongings loaded. The farmer they had paid to transport them waited on the bench seat. As they climbed aboard, he asked no questions.

"Go," Jacques said softly. "We have to get out of here."

The driver guided the horses into the streets of Paris, their hoofs clicking on the cobblestone. As they exited the alley and turned on to the boulevard, Camille sped by in the German staff car.

CHAPTER 120

Lucien shifted, his fingers tingling. He blinked, trying to open his eyes, but they fluttered closed. He tried again, fighting to lift his eyelids. Once his eyes were open, he saw a misty watercolor image that gradually began to focus.

"He's opening his eyes," he heard Camille say.

"Where am I?' he gasped, his lips parched.

"You're in my apartment," Camille said.

She placed a wet cloth on his forehead. "You were shot," she said. "A bandage is wrapped around your right chest and shoulder."

The images became sharper. He looked to the side of the bed. Camille stood over him, an older man beside her. "What happened?"

"You're a hero," she said, dabbing his face with the wet cloth. "Do you want some water?"

He nodded and tried to sit up, the pain excruciating. "A hero, how?"

She helped him rise, putting a glass to his lips. "The Germans raided Jacques's apartment while I was delivering the diamonds."

Lucien groaned as she eased him back down. "I remember. That's how I was shot."

"The wound isn't as bad as it seems," she said. "You're fortunate. Your empty whiskey flask saved you."

"I don't understand."

"The empty flask you kept in your pocket," she said. "The bullet hit the flask and was slowed considerably. It would have killed you otherwise."

He sighed, cringing from the pain. "I suppose it was more than just a symbol of strength."

"Much more."

He paused, the memories returning. "I didn't kill anyone, did I?" he asked. "Because I don't want to kill anyone."

"No," Camille said. "You used chloroform on two of the Germans and stuck a syringe with a sedative into Ziegler."

"What happened to him?"

Camille hesitated. "He was shot. He didn't survive."

Lucien was quiet for a moment. "Did Jacques and the woman escape with the diamonds?"

"Yes," the older man replied. "He and Sophie are halfway to Spain."

Lucien gazed at the man watching him, never having seen him before.

"Nicolas Chastain," Camille said. "My mentor and much more."

Lucien winced. "I wish we could have met under better circumstances."

"At least we met," Chastain said. "I suspect we'll see more of each other."

Lucien paused, his thoughts focusing. "How did I get here?"

"Jacques and Sophie helped me get you out to the street," Camille said. "I stole the German staff car, got you into the apartment, and ditched the car a few kilometers away."

"I had a doctor friend remove the bullet," Chastain added. "He comes by every day to check on you."

Lucien was groggy, his mouth still dry. But his thoughts were now clear. "How long have I been here?"

"Three days," Camille replied.

Lucien blinked, starting to tire. "What happens now?"

"I brought something for you and Camille," Chastain said. "For the next leg in your journey."

Lucien looked at him strangely. "I don't understand."

Camille lightly caressed his face. "It's the deed to our farm."

"Part of the network I'm forming," Chastain explained.

"The farm is in eastern France," Camille said, "close to the Swiss border."

Chastain scanned the deed and gave it to Camille. "Once you get there, a woman named Janelle will serve as your contact."

Camille kissed Lucien lightly. "It's as close as I could get to what you wanted."

Lucien smiled. "It's wonderful. Better than I had hoped."

Chastain handed Camille another envelope. "Money for you to get started and support the network. When you need more, Janelle will provide it."

"We play the role of peasant farmers?" Lucien asked.

Camille nodded. "And we help those fleeing the Nazis to get into Switzerland."

"A small village named Nantua is nearby," Chastain said. "You'll practice medicine there, too, but on a limited basis."

Lucien nodded, confident enough to face the future. His past remained a memory, held in the corner of his heart, always special, always there. "It'll be nice to start again," he said softly.

EPILOGUE
ONE YEAR LATER

The Gestapo released Emilie Dufort from jail minutes after her Nazi brother intervened. She agreed to work with the Germans, using Sergeant Bayer as an intermediary. No one guessed that All Things Napoleon, a thriving store of military memorabilia, was used by the Germans to spy on the citizens of Paris. Collecting information from her unsuspecting customers, Emile fed it to the Gestapo who used it to strengthen their hold on the city.

Jacques and Sophie delivered the diamonds to London and then went back into France, working Chastain's escape network to Spain. No one knew if they were colleagues, lovers, or both—a secret they chose not to share. They couldn't return to Paris, not with Emilie Dufort glued to the Germans.

Nantua, France was a lakeside village at the foot of the mountains, twenty kilometers from the Swiss border. Camille and Lucien Bouchard lived on a farm by the water, just outside of town, with their three-month-old son, Brice. To most in the tiny hamlet, they were honest people who lived simply, Lucien also acting as town doctor. But to a select few, they provided the last link in a chain that started in Paris, escorting downed

Allied airmen, Jews, and those most at risk from the Nazis to safety in Switzerland.

Camille often thought of Paris, her harrowing escape with the Antwerp diamonds, and those that played a part: Jacques and Sophie, Emilie and Louie, the Gestapo, Nicolas Chastain, and Guy Barbier.

She suspected their paths would cross again. But she couldn't say for sure.

ABOUT THE AUTHOR

John Anthony Miller writes all things historical—thrillers, mysteries, and romance. He sets his novels in exotic locations spanning all eras of space and time, with complex characters forced to face inner conflicts, fighting demons both real and imagined. Each of his novels is unique: a Medieval epic, four historical mysteries, two Cold-War thrillers, a 1970's cozy/romance, a Revolutionary War spy novel, and five WWII thrillers, including *All That Glitters*. He lives in southern New Jersey.

To learn more about John Anthony Miller and discover more Next Chapter authors, visit our website at www.nextchapter.pub.

ALSO BY JOHN ANTHONY MILLER

To Parts Unknown

In Satan's Shadow

All the King's Soldiers

When Darkness Comes

Honour the Dead

For Those Who Dare

Sinner, Saint or Serpent

Song of Gabrielle

The Widow's Walk

A Crime Through Time

The Minister's Wife

The Drop

Made in the USA
Coppell, TX
10 December 2023